PRAISE FOR *THE ENSE*

"In Ms. Gabel's terrifically entertaining debut, the frictions of long-term friendships are woven into the 'webbed, collaborative endeavor' of the quartet. Their music doesn't transcend the mess of living; it testifies to it." —*The Wall Street Journal*

"Pitch-perfect." —*People*

"Reminded me of Zadie Smith's *Swing Time* . . . The language that Gabel uses to describe both the pressures of prestige chamber orchestras and, simply, what it is to be a human in the world, is a work of art in and of itself. I found myself highlighting dozens of passages, marveling at just how impossibly relatable these people are. . . . It's the perfect form of escapism for me." —*Entertainment Weekly*

"This lilting, richly detailed story follows a group of friends—also a string quartet—as they grow and change together throughout adulthood. Told from alternative perspectives, it gives us a riveting look inside the world of classical musicians and an intimate study of friendships." —*Marie Claire*

"Phenomenal first novel . . . *The Ensemble* is really a love story. Love of music. Love of friends. Love of family. The genius here is that the reader becomes a part of the ensemble, too, so immersed in these people, that to call them characters seems a disservice. Like them, we feel the pull of time, the need for the music. In the brilliant coda, after we have become very aware of them as individuals, their lives are once again part of one single whole, and here, are collectively narrated, with the yearning of nostalgia." —*San Francisco Chronicle*

"Gabel's rich characters and melodic prose (fitting for a story about professional chamber musicians) make the novel a satisfying read. Comparisons to Meg Wolitzer's *The Interestings* are apt." —*Real Simple*

"[A]bsolutely sublime . . . Mark our words: you won't be able to put this exquisite book down." —*Refinery29*

"A page-turner of a debut." —*Nylon*

"A gorgeous debut novel." —PBS Books

"I fell so hard for the four friends in Aja Gabel's debut novel, which follows a young, ambitious string quartet as they try to sort out their complicated relationships to music and each other. The last time I wanted characters to be real this badly—or, you know, felt like they were—was when Lauren Groff's *Fate and Furies* came out. *The Ensemble* is about desire, disappointment and success, betrayal and loyalty, and the ways that our friendships shape the people we become. You won't be able to quit these characters." —*goop*

"Gabel examines the intricate complexities of their intense friendship, loyalties, and ambitions over a decade and a half in this book that itself reads quite like a lyrical composition. You'll come for the music and stay for Gabel's realistic portrait of modern friendship."

—*Buzzfeed*

"Stunningly resonant . . . With remarkable assurance, Gabel takes the four [characters] through their shaky early performances and expertly ties their individual and collective lives together with generous doses of empathy. . . . A virtuoso performance."

—*Booklist* (starred review)

"Gabel explores friendship and art with great warmth, humanity, and wisdom."

—*Library Journal* (starred review)

"Wonderful . . . The four characters are individually memorable, but as a quartet they're unforgettable."

—*Publishers Weekly* (starred review)

"Aja Gabel's ambitious debut novel is a beautiful study of just how apt a metaphor classical music is for relationships."

—*Vulture*

"Probably every group of musicians has a story to tell, some much more interesting. But the delight of this story is thanks to this young novelist's imagination and her near perfect sense of pitch. Aja Gabel's novel makes one want to know more about the making of music, but only if, as she does, it is told in such a sublime way."

—*New York Journal of Books*

"Aja Gabel's powerful debut offers a sensitive portrait of four young musicians forging their paths through life: sometimes at odds with each other, sometimes in harmony, but always inextricably linked by their shared pasts."

—Celeste Ng, *New York Times* bestselling author of *Everything I Never Told You* and *Little Fires Everywhere*

"With uncommon clarity and empathy, Aja Gabel brings us inside the passionate, complex, and sometimes cutthroat intimacy that exists among the four members of a string quartet. A wise and powerful novel about love, life, and music. I didn't want it to end."

—Maggie Shipstead, *New York Times* bestselling author of *Seating Arrangements* and *Astonish Me*

"Sweeping, romantic, elegiac, *The Ensemble* gives you the feeling of being inside the music of a quartet, a look into the relationships under the music, the love and heartbreak, set against their ruthless commitment to both their art and to each other. Aja Gabel is a phenomenon."

—Alexander Chee, author of *The Queen of the Night* and *How to Write an Autobiographical Novel*

"*The Ensemble* deserves a standing ovation. A gripping tale of four musicians' journeys through discord and harmony, life and love. Aja Gabel is a brilliant young writer with the rare gift of an old soul."

—Mat Johnson, author of *Pym* and *Loving Day*

THE ENSEMBLE

AJA GABEL

Riverhead Books
New York

RIVERHEAD BOOKS
An imprint of Penguin Random House LLC
penguinrandomhouse.com

The Library of Congress has catalogued the Riverhead hardcover edition as follows:

Names: Gabel, Aja, author.
Title: The ensemble : a novel / Aja Gabel.
Description: New York : Riverhead Books, 2018.
Identifiers: LCCN 2017004103 | ISBN 9780735214767 | ISBN 9780735214781 (e-book)
Subjects: LCSH: Musicians—Fiction. | Musical groups—Fiction. | Interpersonal relations—Fiction. | Man-woman relationships—Fiction. | Psychological fiction.
Classification: LCC PS3607.A2285 E57 2018 | DDC 813/.6—dc23
LC record available at https://lccn.loc.gov/2017004103
p. cm.

First Riverhead hardcover edition: May 2018
First Riverhead trade paperback edition: June 2019
Riverhead trade paperback ISBN: 9780735214774

Printed in the United States of America
1 3 5 7 9 10 8 6 4 2

Book design by Lauren Kolm

—For family—

The structure of landscape is infinitesimal,
Like the structure of music,
seamless, invisible.
Even the rain has larger sutures.
What holds the landscape together, and what holds music together,
Is faith, it appears—faith of the eye, faith of the ear.

—Charles Wright, "Body and Soul II"

THE ENSEMBLE

PART 1

String Quartet in D Major, op. 20, no. 4
—Joseph Haydn

"American" String Quartet in F Major, op. 96, no. 12
—Antonín Dvořák

"Serioso" String Quartet in F Minor, op. 95, no. 11
—Ludwig van Beethoven

May 1994

San Francisco

JANA

Violin I

It's a love story, the famous violinist had said, and even though Jana knew it was not, those were the words that knocked around her brain when she began to play on stage. The famous violinist, Fodorio, had coached the quartet earlier in the week, and it was what he'd said after they had finished a run-through of the Dvořák "American," which, according to Jana, was definitely not a love story. But here they were, the Van Ness String Quartet, performing in their final graduation recital at the conservatory, starting the shimmering notes of the first movement, and all she could think, as much as thinking was involved at all, was: maybe it was a love story.

It was a love letter to the country, as she understood it from her classes. Dvořák's European peasant take on American folk songs. But how could someone think this was a story of romantic love? It seemed to Jana to be more classic than that: a person falls for the dream of a place, for a life that could be lived there, for something they were not but might be. It was about the shimmering itself, that almost visible stuff that hovered just above the hot pavement of your life. Potential, aspiration, accomplishment. The famous violinist who had coached them—Fodorio, she could not bring herself to say his name—was sort of a hack, anyway, at least when it came to teaching. Jana would never tell him to his face, but she enjoyed the solemn interior pleasure of her disdain. What did he know? Here's what she knew: that the Dvořák "American" was about the simple opportunity of America, and that no one was more closely acquainted with identifying and consuming opportunity than she was. By the time Henry's viola solo entered three bars later she had decided again: no, it was not a love story.

It's a love story was not something Henry remembered from the coaching session, and certainly not what was running through his mind when he introduced the jaunty Americana melody in the third bar. Instead, what had glommed on to the inside of Henry was what Fodorio had said when he passed Henry his card as he was packing up his viola. *Call me if you decide this quartet business isn't for you,* he'd said. *I can set up a few recitals in front of the right people in New York. You could have a great solo career.* Henry had wordlessly taken the card, slid it into the velvet pocket inside his case, and had not moved it since. But the card throbbed there nonetheless. *If you decide this quartet business isn't for you*—as though Fodorio had already decided it was not for Henry, and was simply waiting for Henry to come to the same conclusion. But Henry hadn't decided anything at all. He never did, young as he was and blessed with the kind of talent that guided his life's decisions for him.

Whether or not it was a love story did not concern Daniel, as these days he didn't have room in his life for romance or enduring love, or any symptom or side effect of the two. Not when he had to practice twice as hard to keep up with the rest of the quartet and their maddeningly natural abilities, and especially Henry, whose obscene talent teetered on the edge of prodigy, who could play drunk, blind, in love or out of it. There was no space for love in Daniel's life when he had to work real jobs in addition to their schooling, moonlighting at a bar in the Castro, picking up wedding gigs when he could, and teaching beginning cello lessons to rich kids in Pacific Heights. *It's a love story*: sure, okay, but what else?

Of course it's a love story, thought Brit, though she thought everything was. This note here, and this one, this joyful countermelody, her second violin harmony, the collective intangible, the audible agreement. Her relationship with Daniel, which he'd rather coldly cut off a few days ago. Even the absence of love was a love story for her. Even this pain, this suffering. It was useful. Though she imagined one day no longer needing to know that, or she fantasized about rewinding her life and starting over so she was a person who did not have to know that, or she entertained the idea of a parallel Brit, living in a world in which there was no need to make sense of a man who up and left on the brink of love, of people who up and left, of a life strung together with all these little leavings, but she felt sad for this parallel Brit, an emptier sadness than she felt for herself now. They were all love stories.

And though no one would have explicitly admitted it, what it was about—love or something else—was entirely up to Jana: it depended on the way she took a quiet, sharp, and precisely timed breath in an upbeat before the first note, on the pressure of her attack on that first note, on the space she left between the first and second notes, on the degree and length and resonance of the vibrato she applied to the violin neck. It was up to her minute movements, certainly in the beginning of the piece, if not after. Even the way she closed her eyes, if she closed them at all, if there was a flutter to her eyelashes or a stern set of her brow, all of that determined everything that was to follow. Jana's job as first violinist was to lead, but these days her leadership had expanded beyond the physical. Her bodily and tonal decisions, one after another after another through an entire forty-minute program, now served as emotional leadership.

The power in this was both benevolent and wicked, and, to Jana, felt perfectly natural. She had always wanted to truly lead a group—and better still, to lead a group to greatness. It had to happen, it would happen, its future happening defined her. And where, in this narrative of greatness, was there room for a story of love? It wasn't any story she'd ever been told.

There was a reception in the large anteroom off the faculty lounge, and the quartet stood awkwardly along a wall at the back. Jana picked at the side seam of her dress, where she could feel her performance sweat drying stiff.

"We shouldn't stand together like this," Jana said. "We look like idiots."

"I think we should stand together so no one mistakes me for Daniel," Henry said, grinning.

"They're not going to mistake me for you," Daniel muttered. "For one, I'm six inches shorter, and for two . . ." But he didn't finish saying what the second reason was.

"Don't leave now," Brit said to Jana, gesturing across the room. "Here comes that guy. He gives me the creeps."

Fodorio strode toward them, buttoning his jacket and beaming. Jana stood up straighter. He was a prick, as she understood it, but a talented and successful one, and talent and success were two things she never turned her back on.

"Ferrari," Daniel said under his breath.

"Fodorio," Henry corrected him.

"Since when do you remember names?" Brit asked Henry, as Jana stuck out her hand to shake the famous violinist's famous hand.

"The Van Ness," he said in his thick accent. Where was it from? Somewhere in the Mediterranean? Jana had forgotten. He shoved past her outstretched arm and embraced her. Jana inhaled his scent: musk, tobacco, women. She smiled a gummy smile.

"I see our coaching session got you all far," Fodorio said, moving on to Henry, whose hand he took in both his hands.

"We were doing all right before that, though," Daniel said.

"He's joking," Jana said, shooting Daniel a desperate look. If he could not be an asshole now, that would be excellent timing.

"Am I?" Fodorio said, winking. Winking! He was now embracing a reluctant Brit, whose long blond hair fell around her shoulders like noodles. Angel-hair pasta when it spilled out of the box onto your kitchen floor. It annoyed Jana that she never put it up for performance. It was all anyone looked at on stage. It lent her a quality of accidental beauty, beautiful gold hair that just grew and grew as though she couldn't help it.

It was true, their recital had gone well. But Jana had fully expected it to go well. Everyone had been prepared, infused with the right amounts of fear and confidence. But this recital hadn't been the true test. While it was their graduation performance, and while all their teachers sat in the audience, grading them, and while a select number of talent agents and representatives from RCA and Deutsche Grammophon had also come to listen, it had really been a warm-up for the real deal: the Esterhazy quartet competition in the Canadian Rockies just one week away. If they won or placed there, it would be the beginning of the lifelong career Jana acutely wanted for herself, and for the ensemble.

They couldn't afford to screw up, and Jana never let that knowledge fade.

Fodorio—the famous violinist, the prick, the winker, the soloist on tour—also happened to be one of the judges for the Esterhazy competition this year, a fact Jana had tacitly but firmly noted early on in his weeklong residency at the conservatory.

She slid her arm around his elbow. "Would you get me a champagne?" she asked.

Fodorio smiled. "Surely."

"Oh, me too," Henry said.

Jana frowned. "You're not even old enough to drink, Henry."

"Also, get it yourself," Daniel said, peeling off to the makeshift bar. Brit followed seconds behind him, as though tethered.

Fodorio fetched two champagnes and leaned against a tall table with Jana. Henry had disappeared. Fodorio commented on Henry's absence, then asked Jana, "Where is your family, dear?"

"Oh." Jana shook her head, not wanting to explain. "In Los Angeles."

Had the absence been that gaping? Jana wondered. Was it obvious, the space in the audience where Jana's family was not? Then she remembered that neither Daniel's family (too poor to travel, "not plane people," Daniel had said) nor Brit's family (dead, as they were) had shown up, and this brought her a private comfort.

"Your own concert went spectacularly," she said, leaning closer. She'd gone to his performance with the San Francisco Symphony two nights before, though she usually didn't like going to any concerts when one of her own was so near. It muddled things, took up aural space. Attending Fodorio's had been a tactical decision. And she was only lying a bit now—she never used the word *spectacular*—but as she said, it had gone well. Fodorio was the kind of violinist who mistook his fame for rock stardom, and who played something like the Mendelssohn concerto as though he were Bon Jovi in tails. Jana didn't know where Fodorio got off. Peering at him from her seat in the middle of the mezzanine, she had not wanted to like the performance, but in the end, in the final movement, with his aggressive flourishes and demanding tempo, she had succumbed to his allure. Fodorio had his thing and he wore it well, a persona that radiated through the tender wood of his bow down to the strings and out the soundpost into the concert hall. A little calculated, Jana thought, but so expertly performed (and rabidly consumed), it was seductive.

"Thank you," he said. "I wasn't aware you were in the audience. You should have come backstage to see me. We could have had quite a . . . time."

Her champagne flute was empty. He was a magnet, two-sided, attractive and repulsive. Black curly hair strewn across his head in a way that seemed haphazard but was surely and entirely thought through. Cuff links, a salmon-pink dress shirt, a gray suit. He wasn't contractually required to come to their recital. He'd fulfilled his duty with the one coaching session—*it's a love story*—earlier in the week. Why was he here?

He reached a hand across the cocktail table to peel her fingers from her empty glass. His hand was strong and veined and covered with wiry dark hairs. Something about the brute strength of his grip won Jana over, an instantaneous reversal. What a player, with that hand.

"Really, though," Fodorio said. "You're excellent."

"I know," she said. "But not the way Henry is," she said, almost automatically. She always felt a need to acknowledge Henry's talent to anyone who complimented her, as if to say, I know what you might be comparing me to. I know my status.

"Well, no," Fodorio said, and his admission burned her a bit. She wanted more alcohol, something stronger than champagne. "But you'll have a great chamber career ahead of you. You could be much better, though."

Jana took her hands away from the table.

"No, no," he said. "I mean to say you *will* be better. With age."

Jana excused herself to get another drink, hoping there was liquor. What did he know? Well, a lot, she conceded. Enough to be selected as a judge at the most prestigious classical music competition in the world. Keep that in mind, she thought, carrying two gin and tonics back to the table where he waited. Her torso grew hot from bottom to top, seeing him. She would also keep that heat in mind.

There was a flurry of other conversations: the director of the conservatory congratulating her, questions about her plans for the summer (play and practice, what else?) and the future (Esterhazy, what else?), the group (Henry getting louder as he drank more; Daniel and Brit in heated, intimate conversation in various corners)—but Jana kept Fodorio in her sights all night, and she could tell that he kept her in his, too. Toward the end of the night, some embarrassing number of cocktails in—it was a celebration, after all—she escaped outside to smoke.

She walked a block away from the conservatory, up the hill. She pulled a cigarette from her purse and lit it, making sure no one was around to see her. She didn't know exactly why she hid her occasional smoking from everyone, but she did, and it felt good to have a secret from Brit and Daniel and Henry. Her mother had smoked, and the smell of it, of Pall Malls especially, calmed her when boredom led to an anxious jitter.

Sitting on a bench, Jana swung her legs around and turned back in the direction she'd come from, so the conservatory came into view, unassuming in its darkness. When Jana was a young girl, her mother—called Catherine, even by Jana—had often promised to take her to the symphony. She never did. LA Phil tickets were expensive, and Catherine said classical music was boring, anyway. Once, in high school, Jana took herself on a student rush price, lying to her mother about where she'd been. Jana told her she'd gone to a movie with friends, some blockbuster with Catherine's favorite actress. That was something Catherine could understand. Catherine sometimes worked and sometimes didn't. Jana could recall her waitressing and working at the jewelry counter at Mervyn's (and also being fired from Mervyn's), but more clearly she recalled the days she came home from school to find her mother still in her silk robe, smoking long, thin cigarettes on the back patio and practicing lines for a commercial audition she wouldn't get. Once, Catherine got a bit part playing a cashier on a soap opera, and she had recorded the clip. The VHS tape, marked "Reel 1" in her mother's thick cursive, sat in the center of the coffee table like a flower arrangement until it became sun-bleached and was no longer playable.

When Jana crushed the cigarette under her shoe and stood, a perfect shiver ran down her spine, and she wished she'd brought a coat. She picked up the butt and walked it to a trash can on the sidewalk.

"I see you."

Jana turned toward the voice. Fodorio leaned against a building, smoking his own cigarette. "But I won't tell," he said.

"I don't smoke," she said.

"I said I won't tell."

"You have the accent of a rich person," she said. "A person who went to boarding school."

"And now I've been found out," he said.

"See," Jana said. "I see you, too." She leaned on the wall next to him. The May chill raised goose bumps on her bare arms, and he draped his jacket around her.

"I hear your group will be competing at Esterhazy this year," Fodorio said.

"The rumors are true," she said.

Was this against the rules, an entrant in the Esterhazy fraternizing with a judge? Surely not. There were seven judges and three performance rounds, and besides, who could keep one drunk professional musician from smoking with another, even if one was drunker and not exactly a professional yet?

"I want tacos," he said.

"I know a place," she said. "But we'd have to walk."

They sneaked into the greenroom to grab her violin. Before she placed it in the case, he took the violin from her, their fingertips touching on the scroll, and examined it. "Nice axe," he said, adding, "for a poor girl."

As she covered her violin with the burgundy velvet protector and zipped up her case, his hand on her back was both a warning and a prediction. He did see her.

As they walked, Fodorio kept his arm around her waist, and she relaxed into it. It felt good to have a man touch her, though she would never admit that to anyone. He was such a man, though, older and larger and more forward than men in school with her at the conservatory, and for a moment an image of Catherine flashed through Jana's mind—her mother, poured into a sample-size designer cocktail dress, opening the door to her date, a large man who smelled funny and whose forehead shone like plastic under the porch light. Jana remembered sitting on the carpet, looking at the man in the open doorway, and her mother's own bare feet on the carpet, nervously squeezing the fibers between her toes. Catherine had let the man in.

Jana and Fodorio stumbled toward a taco truck Jana knew of, one permanently parked in a gas station parking lot, and they sat on the yellow curb and ate.

"Do you really think we're good?" she asked, adopting a false, girlish uncertainty that was unlike her. Jana thought the fastest and surest way to success was confidence. It had gotten her this far. That, and not wasting time with distractions like men or friends.

"I think you're young," he said.

"*We're* not young. Henry's young. I'm twenty-four."

"Well, your sound is young," he said between bites. "Which is good and bad. It means there's potential. But there's not really room for danger."

"We need more danger?" Jana laughed, her mouth full of taco. "Please."

"Well, it's true. A little too perfect, if you ask me. You did ask me."

"We have to win," she said. It was the first time she'd said that out loud, admitted it to herself, to anyone. "We have to."

"What would you do if you didn't win? What would you do if the quartet didn't work out?"

She sighed. The tacos were gone. There were only two more cigarettes in her pack, and she gave him one. "I don't know," she said. "Teach? Record a bit? Orchestra? Try to play solos when I can?" Saying it depressed her, took some of the wind out of her.

"You could have a decent solo career," he said.

"So I hear," she said.

"But you don't want to."

"Not if there's something better," she said.

"Is there?" Fodorio dangled the cigarette out of his mouth and spread his arms wide. "All this. Nothing better than all this. I'm smoking and eating tacos with a pretty violinist who happens to be fucking talented, she wants to tell me how to get back to the hotel, maybe come up, order room service because the symphony is paying for it. I'm going to fly to Sydney tomorrow, where it'll be yesterday, or today, or something like that. Now, what's better than that?"

"Are you staying at the Omni?" Jana asked. "That's right near here. You won't get lost."

"But I need you to show me the way," Fodorio said, blowing smoke into her smoke, his hand back on her knee.

She looked at the ground between her feet. Where was Catherine tonight? Why was Catherine on her mind? It was the dark conservatory, how the pretty but closed façade had reminded her of Catherine's face. Catherine, somewhere in Los Angeles, likely also drunk. It had been almost two years since Jana had spoken to her mother (a lazy abstention, no grudge in particular), but she felt sure she would know in some metaphysical way if Catherine were dead.

"All right," Jana said, standing.

Fodorio had a two-room suite with fuzzy bathrobes and a Jacuzzi tub up against a clear glass pane that looked out over the bedroom. He made love like he only called it "making love," when really, what she wanted was whatever the opposite of making love was—to fuck. His hair nearly vibrated off his head, his hands were coarse and perpetually moving. His lovely, expensive violin sat in its case, visible over his shoulder. She wanted it. She knew he knew she wanted it, wanted his sort of success. It wasn't that she was particularly pretty (tall for a woman, unobtrusively thin and flat, an angular, slightly forgettable face) or that he was particularly attractive (too hairy, some might say, shorter than he acted). They'd chosen each other for the reason most people chose each other: to get closer to some quality they didn't naturally possess. For Jana it was his accomplishment. For him, well, she supposed it was her hunger for his accomplishment. And here she was restless and tired and anxious and bored. While he roused himself on top of her, she thought: What was the thing the quartet was missing? How could they get it? How would she know when it was time to give up? Eventually Fodorio fell into a champagne nap, and Jana wrapped herself in a plush bathrobe and made herself a tourist of his hotel room, ambling and touching all his smooth things.

Here was his pristine Vuitton luggage, here were his damp European-sized swim trunks, here were the loafers he had worn without socks during the master class, lined up neatly in front of the mirror. And here she was in the mirror, an imposter, a poor girl from the cracked Los Angeles suburbs, a woman whose mother wouldn't have understood what Fodorio did or was, if she even cared to ask. And here on the dresser was Fodorio's wallet, textured black leather, falling open in her hands: $327 in cash, four credit cards, a New York State driver's license in which he appeared bloated and old, and a worn two-by-three-inch photo of a small girl with dark, blunt bangs, a school portrait, the neon teal background clashing with her fuzzy green sweater. She smiled big and toothy, and had fat dimples Jana recognized from Fodorio's face, a feature that made his smugness charming. She turned the picture over, and written on the back in cursive that seemed ancient, *Gisella, 6*. The writing a promise the girl's life would be so long and full of pictures that reminders of name and age would be necessary.

When Fodorio had coached the quartet earlier in the week, he'd criticized the tidiness with which they'd played Beethoven's "Serioso."

"Do you know what this is? This piece?" Fodorio asked, standing in front of them on stage. A few peers and teachers were scattered in the audience, waiting for one of his infamous eviscerations.

"Yes," Jana had said. "It's Beethoven's first push toward the more complicated composer he became later in life."

"Mmmm, not quite, my dear. It's this unconscious mess, like the tortured man he would become later in life. There's a difference. There's something tortured about it, and something that resists that darkness, no? Like here." He pointed to a passage in the middle of the movement, a run of difficult sixteenths that she shared with Brit. "You're playing these like they're unison sixteenths, but they're not."

"What are they, then?" Brit asked.

"They're *agitato,* a race against each other, almost angry at each other. They're competing. Here, let me show you," Fodorio said, putting his hand around the neck of Jana's violin.

His fingertips touched hers then, callus to callus. Startled, she let go of her instrument. He motioned for her to get up and when she did, Fodorio sat in her chair. He perched on the very edge of it, more off the seat than on, and peered at Brit from beneath large, trembling lids. With barely a breath, he started the passage, and Brit caught the downbeat expertly. Fodorio's notes landed a millisecond before Brit's, and his accents were irregular, poking at Brit's syncopations. Jana stood aside, awkwardly useless, the air emptied out of her. He was better than she was, yes, of course, but he was also better with Brit, with the group, *her* group.

Now he was on his stomach, naked still, lightly snoring, his arms curled uncomfortably, under him, a mere human. He looked unabashedly, embarrassingly, like a man, and when she tried to shimmy her arm out from under him, his heaviness confirmed it. Just a man, a body thick all the way through, unconscious on a bed. How disappointing, Jana thought, that someone capable of such intricate movements and sonic perfections could be just a pile of human hanging off a hotel mattress. That this collection of muscles and blood and instincts made up a father, one who likely had forgotten to call his faraway daughter.

Jana worked Fodorio's arm out from under him, and he snapped awake with a start, his fists curled up like a cartoon version of a boxer. Jana couldn't help laughing, but when he didn't think it was funny, something in her warmed. She took one of his hands and unrolled his fingers, one by one. They were slender, as they should be.

She held up Gisella.

"It's her birthday," he said. "She's six."

"She's seven," Jana said.

"Oh," he said, rubbing his eyes, sitting up. "Yes, seven. I meant seven. Oh, God, that makes me sound like a terrible father."

"I just know because . . ." she said, flipping over to the backside of the picture.

"I love her," he said, as though trying to convince Jana, and then angry that he had to convince anyone. "I don't live with her, but I provide for her in other ways. I can't see her that much because I have to travel to provide for her. And her mother wanted it that way—she was the one who gave me the ultimatum, she was the one who first brought up divorce. They could have traveled with me. But her mother made the decision, and what was I supposed to do?"

He went on, but Jana had stopped listening. It sounded like a speech he'd given himself in his head many times before, the slightly tinny, desperate tenor of his voice, the insistent diction, the rapid, uneven cadence, as though he was trying to get it all out before she could say anything. In any case, she didn't care whether he lived with his daughter or not, or whether he sent money, or whether he saw her only on holidays or two weekends a month. She cared, however, that this—this girl, this seven-year-old—could inflate and deflate him so. Moments before, he was a plain man on a bed, and here he was now, distracted entirely from the top of her breast peeking out of her robe, her messy hair, the smell of her damp skin. A child could do that to a person, a daughter to a father. She didn't know this firsthand, but here was evidence.

He continued to talk, and she tried to reach up through him to his center to flip some switch, to turn all his attention back to her, to be the object, the subject, the motif, to turn anything she wanted, to win.

To win.

He didn't seem to think they'd win at Esterhazy, but Jana saw he also made decisions like a musician, committed in each second to the possibility that everything could change, depending on the nearly invisible but distinctly audible movements of the violist's bow, or the edge of the cellist's tempo. Remain agile. Stay in the place where everything could fall apart—isn't that what he'd told them at the master class? That was where he lived, and though Jana did not (perhaps she was another breed of musician), she understood it. And could use it.

So while she was reaching up inside him in her imagination, she was also touching him on the bed, and her robe slipped off her shoulders, and her mouth swallowed his talking, and he melted easily into her, moving like a fish from one girl who would elude him to another.

But Jana pushed him down when he tried to roll her over, dug her short nails into his collarbone. "No," she said. She straddled him and his face blossomed beneath her. She rocked down close to his ear and said, "I want to win."

"Okay," he said, smiling. "You win."

"No," she said. "I want *us* to win. At Esterhazy."

He stopped smiling. His arch lifted her up. She held his gaze for as long as she could. She vacated her face, she inhabited only her primal self. She could have been anyone, she felt like anyone, but also felt most like herself. This is what she knew how to do—be the physical embodiment of a determined act of aspiration. This time she was a bundle of frenetic energy atop him, a woman held loosely in that place between triple *forte* and unbridled chaos. And in the final waves she let out a sob before collapsing onto him, she was small now, he was large again, their bodies were cold with sweat—just bodies that could, from time to time, do incredible things. She could have wept there into his metallic neck at the plainness of it all.

Her words came slowly because she was afraid, but the slowness lent them a sense of confidence. Tempo was always a strength of hers. She said: "If you don't help us, I will tell everyone that you said you'd help us win if I slept with you."

There was a pause, some counting of beats, a breath.

"Okay," he said, his hands on her back, patting her like she was a pet. "Okay. All right."

After he fell asleep again, this time noisily and deeply, she dressed silently and picked up the picture of Gisella from the carpet beneath the bed, where it had slipped, and tucked it into her purse before clicking the door shut behind her.

It was predawn in San Francisco, the hour when the city felt most like a small ocean town, morning sea birds swirling in the purple sky. But it was cold, and Jana walked briskly, regretting the choice not to wear tights. She found a lonely cab idling on the corner and hopped in.

At the door to Henry's building in the Haight, she leaned on his buzzer until he moaned into the speaker. She hummed back the exact pitch of the buzzer (D-flat) and he let her in.

Jana climbed the three floors two stairs at a time and nudged open the already ajar door. Henry's apartment, paid for by his rich parents in Napa—who were also kind, generous, witty people—was chilly. Beneath her feet crunched blank music sheets Henry had tossed to the floor, scribbled with phrases of a piece he was writing. Lined along the walls were crates and crates of classical music records, the only belongings besides his viola that he really carried around, city to city. He was attached to them in a way that made Jana feel tenderly toward him, like watching a child be protective of his toys. But at the same time his attachment also frustrated her. The records cluttered his life—he never unpacked or organized them, and he was forever searching for the right one when he needed it. It was just another way his life was needlessly wild.

She stepped out of her shoes and into Henry's bed, into the familiar comma made by his long body, and found the spot warmed, perfumed, raw. There'd been someone else here.

"Who?" she asked, elbowing him.

"Off-duty ballerina," he said into the pillow. "You?"

"No one," she said. "That stage guy and I went out to a gay club downtown."

He tightened his arm around her. "You spent a bunch of time with Ferrari tonight. How was that?"

"Just like you'd think it was."

"He give you his card, too?"

Jana lifted her head from the pillow and turned it toward him. "He gave *you* his card?'"

Henry didn't open his eyes but reached his arm across her to paw at the nightstand, where he produced a folded-up card with Fodorio's name on it. Jana sat up in the bed and unfolded it. On the back, Fodorio had scribbled: *For your John Lennon moment.*

"Your John Lennon moment?" Jana said.

"What?"

"What he wrote on the back. For when you want to leave the band."

"No one's leaving the band," Henry mumbled.

"Then why did he give this to you?"

Henry opened his eyes and propped himself up. "Because he's an egomaniac who wants to feel like he's helping me do something I don't even know I need yet?"

Jana rubbed the folds in the business card between her fingers. "Then why did you keep it?"

Henry looked at her like he felt sorry for her, but not in a pitying way. Tenderly, his face matching her meek timbre. At that, she would have let it go, dropped the card to the dirty floor and fallen asleep. But then he took the card from her hand and tore it into tiny squares. He popped the squares into his mouth, chewed quietly, and washed them down with a glass of water from the nightstand.

"Sleep now?" he said.

"Okay."

Together, they fell into a platonic slumber, as they'd done many nights before: a mess of tacos, sweat, rosin. They were friends, Henry like the brother Jana had always wanted. They were kindred in their prideful loneliness, the stubborn fermata held blankly in their centers that could just go on forever. They pushed their fermatas against each other, and were something close to satisfied. *Is there anything better?* Fodorio had asked her of his life, and she hadn't answered. She wasn't sure. She wasn't so far away from the failures and disappointments scattered on the floor of his life, but at least she had this, someone else's fermata. Jana dreamt of nothing. As for Henry, he slept with a dashed-off smile across his face, and she never could tell.

BRIT

Violin II

There was something nagging Brit, loping behind her more general sadness, and it was that she couldn't remember having actually chosen to want to be with Daniel. And this was what made her current situation more painful and aggravating—her life felt like an old, warped record, her pain circling back around and skipping on her lack of intention. She was sad, and she was angry with herself for being sad. She didn't like wanting what she hadn't intended to want as much as she didn't like being denied what she hadn't really wanted in the first place. She thought there was enough to be sad about without adding on the unfulfilled wishes at the edge of your life. For instance, a slightly wider left hand, a better violin. For instance, your parents to be alive again.

Brit couldn't deny she had been attracted to Daniel when they first met, and she knew he had also been drawn to her. Sitting on opposite sides of the table that first day in Counterpoint II, they'd noticed each other noticing each other. He hummed with nervous energy, quick to raise his hand to answer a question, possessing a spastic agility that betrayed his insecurity. A boyish face with large, nervous eyes and a nose not to be missed. And she caught him staring—at her face, her breasts, her mouth (her crooked eyetooth, even?)—when she offered answers to the professor's questions about the tonic pattern in *Don Giovanni*. She whispered to Jana, "I think that cellist is staring at me," and Jana rolled her eyes and said, "Not everyone is staring at you, Brit," but she tucked a strand of Brit's hair behind her ear when she said it so it wasn't entirely mean.

But he had been staring at her. Nearly two years later, after they'd formed the quartet and just before the difficult conversation in which they all decided the quartet would be what they'd pursue together, she asked him about it, in bed, in that postcoital moment where one feels free to say anything because nothing could be more embarrassing or intimate than what has just transpired.

"Yes," Daniel said. "I was watching you all the time then. I always thought you were pretty. You must know that you're pretty."

Brit hadn't known. Some girls grew up that way, knowing they were pretty, using it. Brit felt she hadn't been pretty until very recently, and the change made her uncomfortable; she was unused to men looking at her, seeing something she could barely see herself. In the mirror she looked how she'd always looked: pale skin, nearly blue-vein translucent; a puckered, downturned mouth (that tooth); oddly spaced features (nose too narrow, eyes large and far apart—like a cow, she'd once overheard a girl cruelly say); long hair, a dull shade of blond, boring, exasperated with itself.

"I don't know that," she said. What she meant was, *Tell me more about how I'm pretty.*

They were lying on their backs in bed, the sheets yanked up above their chests, staring at the ceiling, their fingertips touching down near their bare, damp thighs. Daniel had been exactly as she'd wanted him to be—kind but primal, and relentless in his pursuit of her satisfaction.

She'd been fine, she assumed. She'd been lost, in a good way. She was cold.

But he didn't tell her more about how she was pretty. Why didn't men do that? Was it because she wasn't really, except if they were having sex with her? Or was it because they truly believed she knew she was pretty and didn't need convincing? Or was it because they believed by virtue of their having sex with her, she would come to understand her physical beauty? What Daniel did instead was swing his thigh over hers and bring his rough hand to her belly, which he began to rub. He said, "This is fun."

"But we shouldn't rush things," she said, an answer to a question he hadn't asked.

"No, casual is best," he said as he worked his hand across her torso. Then he paused. "Do you think there's something wrong with me, that women don't want to date me?"

"Perhaps it's that you don't want to date them?" she said, smiling.

Daniel was an unlikely playboy. He was awkwardly large and small at the same time, shorter than average and a little stocky, disproportionate, with a curiously handsome face. There was something solid and undeniable about his body, everything tightly packed in there. Something glinting and playful about the way he carried himself, light and dangerous as a tumbleweed, apt to cut and suddenly whisk away. But he always had girls around, even if they never stayed long enough to matter, and Brit suspected his catch-and-release pattern would continue long after he let her go.

"Would we be good together?" she asked, and paused to consider the question, but she couldn't conjure up an image of the two of them, walking on a day-lit city street, holding hands, or trekking up a mountain somewhere, throwing backward glances at each other, teeth shining in the alpine air. She wanted to see it, to hear a soundtrack—maybe something like water running over a plate of glass, violins, sixteenths at the tip of the bow at the edge of the string near the bridge—but she couldn't. It wouldn't form, it wouldn't hold.

"No." He resumed his pawing. "We'd be . . . just awful together."

"You're right," she said, arching her back and winding a leg through his. "I agree with you completely."

Brit half believed they wouldn't work together. She'd often thought this, when he stubbornly scrutinized sheet music from behind the Coke-bottle glasses, or when he infuriatingly answered a question by analyzing in detail each side before settling on a studied waffle, or when he obsessed about the correct position on anything, everything—the history, value, and diversity of grace notes; the exact amount of wear an ebony frog could take before it needed to be replaced; the salty sting of the air in San Francisco, where they rehearsed, versus the air in (more affordable) Oakland, where he lived, and its effect on the wood of his cello. His compulsive precision made him an exceptional lover and a disastrous mate, an outstanding musician and an exhausting friend. Nothing unquantifiable could be perfect enough for him, and it was starting to become clear to Brit that unquantifiable things were the only things that had value to her.

That was why that moment in bed after they'd had sex for the first time, *I was watching you all the time then*, she knew she'd remember what he said for a long time. She had been right, after all. There had been a mutual recognition two years ago, of something mathematical but mysterious between them, seen simultaneously, something totally invisible and unexpected, but natural. Like the molecules of the air had been dyed and made bright, electric, tangible. It gave her faith in so many things—her beauty, her instincts, possibility itself. Most of all, the thrilling freedom of being truly unable to predict your life.

Which is how, she supposed, what happened happened. They continued to sleep together and told no one, especially not Jana or Henry. It was terrible fun. They played music, silly duets they hadn't played since their Suzuki days and contemporary duets they found in the sheet music warehouse. They got drunk and found videos of famous performers and criticized their technique, rewinding and fast-forwarding, frame by frame. They stayed up late, clawing at each other between periods of dozing, with the frenzy of the first blush of infatuation, a blatant desire to know every single part of the other's body, to exhaust that knowledge. They fell asleep on Daniel's cheap futon, head to foot, legs tangled in each other's arms, listening to Pablo Casals records, and woke only to the existential fuzz of a needle with nothing to play. They came to rehearsal sleepy, puffy with secrets.

At night, she found the divots in his breastbone made by the point on the back of his cello neck, and the light bruises that appeared and disappeared on the insides of his knees, depending on how long their rehearsals lasted. He ran his fingers through her hair, asked her never to change it. On nights after they rehearsed, he carefully avoided the rust-colored welt on the left hollow of her neck, even with his breath.

It could only go on so long.

Two days before their graduation recital, after a particularly rough rehearsal, they'd made up similar excuses of exhaustion, and Brit offered to drive Daniel home. There, she made him a late dinner—he couldn't cook, and he so rarely went out to eat, always just scraping by—and they ate at his bachelor-sized table with a Janos Starker record spinning in the background. She argued for Heifetz instead, and he responded by repositioning the needle at the beginning of the record, insisting she listen again, for what exactly he didn't say. She lit a candle she found in his dirty bathroom, and laid out cloth napkins, which were actually the soft towels she used to wipe rosin from her violin. When he wiped carbonara off his mouth, the napkin left a chalky white glint on his chin. She smiled and said nothing.

Unlike Jana and Henry, Daniel and Brit had both gone to academic colleges for their undergraduate degrees, and Brit felt an outsider kinship because of this. But Brit's connection to him went further, in that they both felt like they were missing families. He talked about his mother. Daniel was the second child from a generally loveless family in Houston, one whose struggles with money did nothing to bind them together, and whose peculiar, artistic younger son only furthered their cosmic expansion away from each other. His father worked on a construction crew that jumped from site to site, and his mother cleaned their small home in the affordable suburbs, occasionally cleaned other people's homes, and prayed. They quietly tolerated each other, made ends meet, cared that Daniel was successful, and cared much less that he was a musician. What he did, he did alone.

Brit was an actual orphan, though she didn't describe herself that way. Her father died of a regular kind of cancer when she was in college, and her mother just simply gave out—there was no other way to put it—a year into Brit's time in San Francisco. She had no siblings, either, no one to go home to. Brit was drawn to the story of Daniel's family, how he had one and was still a kind of orphan. He didn't seem sad about it, but matter-of-fact. They could share the same hurt, but in different ways. They bore the same wound, in different shapes. She learned to crave that dynamic between the two of them. She could be the fabric flapping in the wind; he could be the flagpole.

"My mother believes in destiny," Daniel said. "She thinks I was her destiny. And that mine is music."

"What, and you don't?" Brit asked. "That seems like a fine thing to believe in."

Daniel shrugged. “Sure, if you don’t want to have any responsibility for your life. Or control. Or ability to make things better.”

“Maybe that’s what your mother means, though, about you being her destiny. Don’t you think that’s why people have children?” Brit asked. “To make a better family than the one they grew up with?”

“No,” Daniel said, too quickly. “I guess that could be a reason, but it’s not the smart one. Especially when you don’t have money to pay for that family.”

Daniel was always talking about money, that was one thing. Money was never far from his mind, and he rarely paid for things, and he was always tired, working late at the bar he wouldn’t let any of them visit. He felt insecure about the quality of his cello and expressed this by always being the first to mention it.

“I don’t know,” Brit said. “We didn’t have much money, but we were happy.”

“Well,” Daniel said, “there’s a difference between your ‘not much money’ and my ‘not much money.’”

“Really?”

“‘Really?’ says the girl who got an inheritance to pay for this life here.”

Brit straightened her shoulders. He had a way of stinging that was quick and shallow. She would give all the money back from that small shack of a house if it meant having her parents around for just one more week, one more concert. She didn’t say that.

The effect of his nastiness registered across Daniel’s face. He leaned forward. “I just mean that we used food stamps and my brother and I slept in the living room in one of our places, and I had to ask for tuition remission for everything—everything—and this thing I’m doing, it’s like the least profitable thing ever, and none of you have to worry about that.”

"I worry about it," she said. She did, but not in such a way that it influenced any decision she felt was imperative. And she worried about him, about the way his worry had made him hard at the edges, all that determination and self-doubt wrapped up in his obsession with money. "I worry that you would let something like money keep you from something like . . . having a family."

"I'm not sure I want children regardless."

"Why not?" she asked.

"But why? Why would it be any better? Why add more people to the world unless you absolutely have to?"

Brit stirred the pasta around her plate, making delicate, unappetizing designs. She had never thought of herself as one of those women who absolutely had to have children, could not identify with the girls from high school who so swiftly wrote in to the alumni magazine about their babies—*The greatest Christmas gift I could ask for!* or *We are so in love with baby Isaac!* (already? does love happen so fast, ever?)—and yet, even though she was a modern woman, she could not picture wanting to have a child outside of wanting to have a family. Being a mother seemed an entirely different enterprise from being part of a family, a real one. And *that* was what she wanted, she realized suddenly, over the middling pasta. A family again.

"I always thought I'd meet someone who I'd love so much that that love had to spill out into another being. Lots of other beings. I want to have a child as an expression of love, I guess," Brit said. "I'm saying I *want* to absolutely have to."

She was surprised to find herself embarrassed at her speech. She sensed Daniel across the table, also ceasing to eat, his wineglass empty, both of them on the verge of the next thing—leaving or staying. He made no indication he wanted her to stay. She tried not to show that she wanted him to want it.

"I agree, I suppose," Daniel said. "That would be a nice feeling."

"Do you think you'll ever feel that?" Brit asked.

Daniel drummed his fingers on the table in time to Starker, who had just begun the prelude to the third Bach cello suite. "You know that part of the *Symposium*? Where Aristophanes talks about how humans were split in two by . . . by—"

"By Zeus," Brit offered. She already knew the story, but she let him tell it anyway.

"Right, by Zeus. And that desire is the pursuit of wholeness."

Brit remembered a bad translation from a college intro class, though she hadn't thought of it in some time. "I like that."

Daniel leaned forward. "But don't you think that's a little reductive? That someone can only be whole with someone else? What about everything that can make you whole without attaching yourself to something like a parasite? What about hard work and accomplishment and . . . like, inner harmony?"

"What's inner harmony?" Brit asked. Daniel laughed, but she continued, "No, really. How can you harmonize with yourself?"

Daniel stopped laughing abruptly. He folded his hands on the table. "Well, I don't know about you, but I contain many pitches. It's about moving from polyphony to harmony. People are so much music. People don't recognize that enough."

"So you're going to be alone forever because it's too offensive to your dignity to attach yourself to someone else?"

"You're not understanding," Daniel said. He leaned back, revealing to Brit small bits of sauce where the front of his shirt had touched the plate. "It's not someone else. It's the whole concept of fitting in someone else's . . . construction."

Brit didn't know how to say that it sounded nice to be contained in someone else's construction without sounding stupid, young, naive.

And anyway, even if she could have said it, he wouldn't have come around to see it from her side. He was too busy with his hammer and pick, chiseling away at a perfect likeness, freeing his ideal self from stone.

She could feel her face go slack, her chest hollow out. It was what she saw happen to Daniel's body when he sat down to play.

"Look," he said. "I suppose it all comes down to biology, anyway. Maybe there's a biological urge I'll feel for children. Maybe not. What I'm saying is it doesn't seem to have anything to do with love, not to me. And it definitely has to do with money, which, if you remember, I have none of."

His obdurate nature often presented itself in a refusal to really answer a question—he was more afraid of being wrong than of being nothing. He did this in rehearsal often, making Jana red in the face by not completely agreeing or completely disagreeing with her interpretation of a passage. It amused Henry, but Brit often stepped in to defuse the situation, which usually meant persuading Daniel to let Jana have her way. Daniel would play the passage the way that seemed best, anyway, which was always whichever way Jana articulated it on stage, and their instantaneous response in performance was a skill they had cultivated.

"I don't know," Daniel said. "That whole narrative of love and children, it all just seems a little too much magical thinking to me."

Starker was climbing up the fingerboard, heading toward the breakthrough arpeggio that required a difficult thumb position. The preludes to the suites always had these passages, ecstatic arpeggios that fully expressed the major chord, and then backed away into a modulated scale, before ending in dignified triple stops or broken chords. But before the ending, those ecstatic arpeggios threatened to dissolve into chaos. They were Brit's favorite parts.

And just behind her sadness, this thought pulsed: She wanted Daniel, not only in a way he didn't want her, but in a way he didn't want to want anyone. And she wanted him to be different, to want to have a kind of love that trembles over the lid of a shared life, to have a hierarchy of wants of which money was not an essential part. The arpeggios died away. Starker was back to the descending scales, working his way toward the end of the first movement.

"I like him for the Bach suites," Daniel said, switching topics. "Because he's no-nonsense. Starker. No frills. Not a romantic player, like Yo-Yo Ma. Not a messy one like Casals. Not a furious one like Du Pre—she always seems kind of angry. Starker is more simple. Good. Clear. I think that's what Bach intended. Not all this interpretive bullshit. What do you think?"

Daniel's cello stood in its hard plastic case against the wall by his bed. She knew he allowed his mother to believe playing the cello was the path God had chosen for him. She knew his father didn't care much for classical music. She knew his cello was cheap, and borrowed at that. She knew he would have to rent his tux for the performance, and that Jana and Henry would assume he owned it. She knew he would work a few more doubles at the bar this month to afford that rental. He grinned at her from his side of the table, no idea.

Go away, Brit said to her sadness. She knew how it could come.

"What do I think?" she repeated. "I think I prefer Du Pre."

"Ah," he said. "Of course you do."

Brit saw then that Daniel's articulation of their difference was his excuse not to fall in love. He was collecting evidence, always. She was ignoring it, always. She sighed. Really, she thought, they ought to have been able to predict this. She saw with sudden clarity the way he saw her. A pretty-enough girl across the table, the table in Counterpoint II or the fake dinner table here, now. A welcome distraction from the true goal of musical success—financial success. A girl who was not like him, not because her parents had died, but because of the money she had from their death.

"I should be going," Brit said when Starker completed the suite. "And I think—I wanted to say—we should stop this."

His face clouded for the briefest moment, then cleared. "Oh yeah?"

"Yes. It's too much, you know? With the competition coming up—"

"No, you're right. It's too risky to mess with that."

"Too dangerous."

"Right, right."

She stared at her dirty plate next to his, the napkins and knives on the table and the bits of pasta sauce everywhere. She knew he wouldn't properly clean up after this meal, and with their final rehearsal and then the concert, the dishes would crust in the sink for a week, at least. He was messy, this was a thing she knew about him—dust bunnies collected on her clothes when she was there, were carried back to her apartment—and as she stood up from the dinner's wreckage, she said goodbye to that knowledge.

There was no danger to Daniel's life, no risk. And none in hers, either, but his lack was because he cut his life carefully around it. It was better that way, she supposed. Perhaps they had to save all that danger up for the stage. Perhaps it was dangerous enough just to be a person, alone.

He put his hand on her back and took it away. "Okay," he said. "I'll walk you out."

There was an ease to letting go, she thought, especially if you never had anything to begin with. They walked down the close stairs of his shabby apartment building, smelling like their meal, the athletic fragrance of black pepper and pancetta, a smell that would for years bring reeling back a feeling of gut-sinking disappointment for Brit. The light was out in the lobby, as always. In the dark, before he pushed the heavy door open, she began to quietly cry. He didn't notice until they were standing in the plain light of the streetlamp.

"Hey, Brit," he said, but didn't reach out, his hands stuffed in his pants pockets.

"I'm fine," she said. Her chest was about to explode, her insides pounding like they were being impressed with a thousand tiny divots made by the back of a cello neck. She put her hand to her breastbone. There were no holes, no depressions: only herself.

They were useless together. She just had to leave, get in her car, drive home across the bridge—why did she always have to come to his place in Oakland, anyway, and he never to hers?—go to sleep, wake, rehearse, do it again and again, and play the concert of her life at Esterhazy. Just get through that. Everything could be the same, and then after, if they won the competition, if they played well, it might even be better.

She was being stupid, she thought. She shouldn't even be thinking about children. She could barely afford her apartment, and she was young and in a secret relationship—*not a relationship*—with the cellist in her quartet. And yet—disappointment, possibility snuffed out, never even lit. She pictured fingers snapping out a small flame over and over, and the hiccupping sound beat in her eardrums. It seemed like a microcosm of her entire life, the snapping, the snuffing, the resultant darkness.

She'd take a trip to New York this summer, Brit decided, see a friend who played with the Met. After the win at Esterhazy. Spend her money that Daniel so resented. Catch a few recitals at Carnegie Hall and lose herself in Patelson's music shop across the street for a few hours each afternoon, fill an extra roller bag with music, and come back to San Francisco like nothing had ever happened. She always liked visiting that musty music store after the storied concert hall; it reminded her that what she was participating in was an arc, bigger than she was, older than she'd ever be. Yes, she decided, on the short walk to her car, Daniel cautiously following behind her, I'll do that.

When she got in her car, there he was, still Daniel, standing half in the shadow of the streetlamp, hands buried in his puffy coat, shorter than he seemed close up. Brit saw the slightly hooked nose she noticed only in profile, the scruff on his chin like a mistake, his small dark eyes, the inscrutable mouth that twisted up when he was turned on, charmed, or being clever. But always most distinctive was his irregular wingspan, disproportionate to his height, which allowed him unlimited and unfair range down the neck of his cello: broad shoulders, arms that drooped out of his sleeves, almost in apology, never actually in apology.

Tonight his face looked like a flat beach, a blank cake, unfinished.

But Brit felt an old warmth at the sight of him. She had become the one looking now, always looking at him, watching for a sign, a smirk, a wink, a slight lean toward her when she felt sad, or waiting for a half-measure breath on her neck before he kissed her, some physical representation of the way he could give himself to her. But he never changed. *I was watching you watch me,* she should have said back. Would it have made a difference? *And now, still, watching you not see me.*

She drove away. She didn't remember the warmth in the morning exactly, just the feeling that something had slipped through her hands. The lurking voice: you don't want Daniel, you just want someone. The answer: no one wants you, not even Daniel. She woke up and practiced in the early gray morning until that feeling, too, slipped away.

JANA

Violin I

She feared they were already too old. That they'd wasted too much time getting here, to the start of their career, and that now it was too late. It had taken Jana a while to figure out, and to accept, that her path wasn't toward a solo career, but rather this webbed, collaborative endeavor. It had taken all of them a while, she supposed. And it almost hadn't happened.

Jana and Henry met at the Curtis Institute of Music in Philadelphia, where they'd both been excellent soloists. Jana was drawn to Henry's raw talent, and playing in a quartet with him was the closest she could get to the force of it. He'd been a bright, boundless light on campus, younger than everyone else, taller than everyone else, a better musician than everyone else, and eager to play anywhere and everywhere. He played with the confidence only prodigies had. She'd once witnessed him sight-read Stravinsky on violin while nearly blind drunk, and play it more flawlessly and beautifully than she ever could on a first go. The idea of failure had never gotten near him. He lived in a world without it. Jana loved that about him.

She'd met prodigies before, but she'd never met anyone like Henry. He always said yes. Did he want to play one more? Did he really like ensemble work? Did he want to go out after? Did he want to write music? Did he want to conduct? Did he want to try this new viola, this new restaurant, this new drink? Jana didn't know what it was that made someone so fearless. He was enthusiastically up for anything.

Once, after they'd finished a night of playing with two other first-year players (neither as good as them) and began packing up, Henry asked Jana about her life before. He assumed their lives in music had been similar.

"I used to be really jealous of my sister, Jackie," he said. "She didn't play anything, ever. She didn't even want to. The only thing I hated was all the stuff I missed out on because of practicing and lessons twice a week, like, I don't know, intramurals? I would have been good at soccer, I think. Jackie got to do all that. Who did you study with in California?"

Jana said the name of the Russian violinist who'd taken pity on her when Catherine had arrived drunk to pick her up from lessons. He'd given her a deep discount on lesson fees, and even still she did office filing for him after school to pay the rest. A few times she had to go down to only two lessons a month, when it was all they could afford.

"When I was really little," Henry said, "my mom wouldn't come to my recitals. Because it would make her so nervous she would sometimes throw up. For real."

Jana smiled and said nothing.

He went on. "But now she doesn't care that much. She's seen me play so many times. She doesn't come to my performances, but not because she's nervous. Because she already knows how I play."

Jana couldn't think of something similar to say. She struggled in the silence where she was supposed to respond. She finally said, "My mother's never seen me play."

Henry's face changed, lost some of its brightness.

"She doesn't really like classical music," Jana said. "But also, she kind of only likes herself. And vodka. And I don't know my father. So in a way, I guess it's good. I had no one to impress in the audience but strangers. And myself."

Henry put his viola case down. He studied her with a worried look. "Well, I heard you," he said. "Back in first year. You were good." And he hugged her, his long arms around her stiff body. One thing she knew for sure about Henry was that his talent was only matched by his tenderness. He hugged with his whole body, as though he wasn't afraid she wouldn't hug back. He hugged without needing someone to hug him back. She did hug him back, eventually.

So nothing bad had ever happened to him. That was it. That was what made someone unafraid.

Henry's peculiar absence of fear made him very popular with women, though Jana never thought of him sexually, romantically. She had no interest in being one of the girls (always older and less talented) he fell into bed with. What she wanted, instead, was for her playing to be associated with his playing, for his playing to scorch her and change her and better her. And while Henry's popularity at conservatory was far and wide, it hadn't translated into real friendship for him. There were the girls and there were the players, and no one offered themselves up to him in the middle ground. No one except Jana.

While they both let the conservatory push them toward solo or orchestral careers, they privately built a friendship upon hours of playing chamber music together. The other players who rotated in and out of their groups saw it as an extracurricular activity, and always abandoned them for more promising paths. But Jana and Henry stayed a consistent pair. She knew a solo career was what you were supposed to want and what Henry had been primed for his entire life, but she also knew that both of them had always been more engaged and more creatively determined—and simply had more fun—playing in string quartets.

One night during their last year, while they were playing late in a stuffy practice room, she brought it up. "What if we formed a quartet, like a real one?" she asked.

Henry needed some convincing. How could they find one person they liked, let alone two, and where would they find them? Why couldn't they just go on as they were, and keep playing together like this when they had time? Jana had prepared for these questions, and produced the application for the chamber music certificate at the San Francisco conservatory. It would be only two years, three at most, and they'd meet people there who wanted the same thing, she was sure of it.

"Otherwise it won't go on like this," she said. "I know what will happen. You'll be traveling or living abroad and you'll be famous and busy forever. And you'll forget about me."

That was when he'd decided. Jana saw it. She'd so rarely been vulnerable like that with him, with anyone. But it was the truth: she was afraid his career would eclipse their connection. And he hadn't ever had anyone outside of his family who valued his companionship over his potential career.

"Plus," she said, "you'll be lonely."

So they left behind the years they'd put in, and veered off in search of a quartet. They'd met Brit and Daniel almost immediately, both of whom had wasted their own time at regular colleges—Indiana University and Rice. So their start as a group was late. That was undeniable. For Henry, time wasn't such a big deal. He was young. But for Jana, the official commitment to the quartet was the beginning of the churning worry inside her that she would run out of time before she was ever successful, that she needed to ascend faster and more fiercely than normal, at Henry-like speeds.

That was what was on her mind the morning of their last rehearsal in San Francisco before the competition, instead of the sixteenths in Beethoven's "Serioso," which did need some attention, and suddenly she was anxious. She had the score in her lap and they were waiting for Henry to tune. He'd left his viola beneath a slightly open window in his apartment that morning, and the cold had contracted the strings and wood. He and Jana both had perfect pitch, so tuning could take forever to satisfy their testy ears. Daniel made no secret that he found this annoying and refused to sit for it, instead pacing the back of the stage. Jana knew he was just infuriated he didn't have perfect pitch.

They were due to fly to Canada that afternoon, with the first round of performances the next night. Four of the sixteen groups would be cut then, with three more rounds to go. *Just focus on round one,* Jana told herself. They would play the Beethoven, which had gone more than decently at the conservatory recital a week earlier, but in the time since had started to feel brittle.

Now they were testing the sound on stage, as if it was going to matter. They'd already played on this stage during their recital, and Esterhazy was going to be on a different stage, thousands of miles away. And besides all that, if Jana had learned anything from relentless performing, it was that chamber music was made up of a hundred minute responses to even more minute changes in both the environment and each other's bodies. Sometimes she was momentarily embarrassed at how well she knew Brit's thin left hand or the elfin knobs of Daniel's knees, perhaps better than she knew either of them.

In any case, Henry's scroll was propped on his knee, and his ear was turned close to the wood, and Jana was still worrying about their age.

She and Brit were both twenty-four. Henry was newly twenty (an ambitious, antsy prodigy), and Daniel somewhere near thirty—he didn't like to discuss his age. The groups winning the Esterhazy competition were getting younger each year, some still in conservatory. Nineteen-year-olds. And there they'd been, toiling away at a master's certificate in chamber music, as if it mattered to anyone but their teachers, whom they were too old to have any longer.

But she'd needed to study more, and they'd needed to find Brit and Daniel. Still, Jana often thought of how it would have been so much easier if they'd all found each other earlier, if they'd all gone to conservatory together the first time around. What Jana really wanted wasn't to have studied more, but to have grown more as a whole group. To grow faster, now. Or to somehow turn back time to five years ago and start growing together then. If they'd solidified their connection earlier, they might be more comfortable now with these big performances. This biggest performance.

"What's wrong with you?" Jana said.

Brit looked up, her eyes alarmingly wide. She'd been reticent all morning, making barely any noise but for her own private tuning. Her face was colorless except for a suddenly noticeable splash of freckles across her pale cheeks, her long hair tied back in a bun. Jana was annoyed. They couldn't afford to be lackluster.

Brit snapped back, "What's wrong with *you*?"

"Tuned!" Henry announced, running a hand through his long hair. He beckoned to Daniel. "Tuned! Sorry, guys, forgot it was going to be cold this morning. It's all good."

"Could you please get a haircut before the concert?" Jana said to Henry.

"Why don't you ask me five more times?" he said. "Call my mother and tell her to remind me?"

Daniel took his place again, stabbed his endpin into the rockstop. Jana cleared her throat. They agreed to run through only the openings of every movement of all three pieces. Jana had always been a firm believer that you have one good performance of any given piece in you a day, a superstition handed down by her first teacher, the Russian. Their conservatory coach had decried this idea, saying that if you don't have more than one good performance in you a day, you shouldn't be a professional. He'd have made them rehearse everything all the way through until their fingers were raw, then tell them to go zone out for three hours before coming back to the hall. But Jana liked the mysterious quality of keeping a full run-through of a piece until they were really on stage. It was like keeping a bride from her groom until she walked down the aisle—the groom knew what she looked like, but the deprivation made her appearance more sacred.

Not that any wedding was as important as the concerts they would play at Esterhazy.

Anyway, it was two days until their first appearance at the competition, but Jana felt that it was too close to risk a full rehearsal.

Her hunch about a lackluster attitude proved true in their run-through. She felt so stuffed with that idea that she tried not to speak at all while they were rehearsing. Brit was clearly in a mood, and Daniel was just an okay foundation, not his usual vocal self. Henry tried to smile at her across the stands, but she scowled back. They ran a couple of known rough spots, which were smoothed out, if devoid of the life they were capable of applying.

At the end, when there was nothing else to run through, Jana couldn't help it, the words came out of her mouth like a sneeze: "Bad rehearsal."

"Not really a rehearsal," Brit said.

"Well," Jana said. "We could use one."

"Bad rehearsal, good performance, isn't that what they say?" Henry said.

The four of them looked at each other in a swath of silence. What they'd just done in rehearsal hadn't made any sense, and no superstition was going to make Jana feel good about it.

The silence curled away like fog, and they dispersed from the chairs. As Jana put her violin in its velvet case, she heard Daniel clicking his case snaps shut and walking off stage, and Henry saying something quietly to Brit, trying to make her laugh a little. Jana didn't turn from her violin. There was nothing to say. The space had the unnamable yet pervasive feeling of a holiday spent alone.

As she slung her case over her shoulder, she felt Henry's presence behind her, and turned to find him smiling, joyful. "It's going to be fine," he said, holding out his arm. She slid hers through the crook and they walked into the wings, through the cold backstage, and out onto 19th Avenue. Outside, the fog had lifted, and a warm May afternoon alighted. The warmth was fleeting, though. It always was in San Francisco.

They walked north on 19th to Noriega, where Jana would tuck herself away in her apartment in the Sunset. Henry would continue walking, turn east along the park, to his apartment in the Haight. He liked walking. He had excruciating amounts of energy, and always seemed about to fly off the ground with it.

"So, what," Jana said, cupping her hand around a cigarette to light it, "you never have . . . doubts?"

"About what?" Henry smiled down at her. He was so tall and wide-shouldered and lanky, with floppy brown hair and an elastic face—pointy nose, wide smile, expressive eyes. Too much of everything in Henry: height, hair, skin, money, optimism, talent.

"I don't know. Don't make me say it." She exhaled.

"Say it."

"What if we're doing the wrong thing? What if we're wasting our time when we should be booking gigs at Alice Tully? Are we happy? Are we even moving toward happiness? I won't believe you if you say you don't think about it. I just won't. You're an android if you say it."

The street tilted dramatically up and they were slowed by a steep hill. Henry was unlike most people, she thought, totally unencumbered by pedestrian anxieties, never self-loathing and never too arrogant, exactly as confident as he needed to be, with an endless fount of warmth for music first, and musical people second. It was what she loved about him, and what made him so very different from her. She knew what he would say.

"I just don't think about it," he said. "I'm sorry. I can say what you want, if you'd like. If it'll make you feel better."

"It won't make me feel better. You're a bad liar."

"I wake up and I think, fuck, I get to do a whole day, you know? Write music, play music, listen to music. Eat, dance, drink—"

"—take a ballerina home."

"Take a ballerina home. Exactly. Though they're not much for eating and drinking."

"Right."

"What I'm saying is if I thought about all the ways I could be unhappy, I'd be . . . unhappy. Not to mention exhausted."

"So you just choose . . . not to think about it?"

"It doesn't feel like a choice. But yeah, I suppose it is. A choice I made so many times that I don't even have to make it anymore."

"Everything's going to be terrible." Jana thought of Henry and the ballerina he'd been with two nights earlier. How easy it was for him, everything. Sometimes she thought maybe she crawled into bed with him just to suck some of that optimism out of his pores.

Henry unthreaded his arm from hers and pulled her close. "No. Some things, maybe."

Like when you leave us, Jana thought, but did not say. *Or when we win the Esterhazy competition because I slept with one of the judges.* "Exactly," she said. "You can't tell the difference. So what's the point?"

"Of what?"

"I don't know. Life?"

"Are you seriously asking me that? Do we need to go to a hospital? Are you suicidal?"

"Henry. Come on. I'm serious."

"You're not. You can't be. You can't play the way you do and not understand the value of . . . pain."

"Who said it—Mozart or someone? 'With ease, or not at all.' What if *nothing's* easy?"

"Okay, one, I don't think he said that. Two, if he did say it, he's lying. And three, you misunderstand 'ease.' I think whoever said that means joy, not the quality of being easy. And difficult things can bring joy. And joy can bring ease."

They were nearing the corner where they'd split off, and Jana would walk the remaining two blocks to her apartment alone. With ease or not at all, she thought. Would there be joy at Esterhazy? Could there be joy with suffering? And who would do the suffering, anyway? And what would they be suffering from?

What she didn't confess, but so badly wanted to: *I blackmailed Fodorio into giving us a win, joy or no joy.* Henry wouldn't have understood. He didn't see it the way she did, and not because he chose not to think about how hard it all was, but because he didn't have to. He never had to. What she'd done was the opposite of ease. She would never tell anyone.

"We're going to be fine," Henry said.

"You always think that," she said. "It's easy for you to think that."

"I love you, Miss Jana," he said, kissing the top of her head. Henry was a different species from the rest of them, Jana thought. He would leave them because of it. Someday.

"Don't leave your viola by a window today, genius," Jana said. He let go of her and continued north, grinning back at her. "I love you, too," she said, waving a suddenly chilled hand.

It was too easy for Jana to describe her mother as an alcoholic. That there was a name for what her mother was made Jana furious, as though reasons (and excuses) for Catherine's behavior could be found in a medical textbook or a psychology course. Her mother was an alcoholic—and a pill popper and an occasional coke user and a pathological liar—but what she suffered from seemed to Jana to be more like self-delusion than any imbibed substance. And there was nothing easy about Catherine.

Before Jana was born, her mother had a spot on a heavily rotated detergent commercial, and she hadn't risen in the ranks much after that. When Jana was ten, her mother landed a role on a soap opera, but her character became possessed by demons and was killed off within a month of episodes, quickly forgotten in the myriad storylines. In between gigs, Catherine waited tables or walked dogs or sold makeup at department stores in the Valley. She was always auditioning, though, and because she was auditioning, there was always the possibility that she was going to get a part, and for Catherine, possibility was as good as potential, and she told Jana only the truly great had potential. Jana took up the violin as a child mostly so she wouldn't have to take the acting classes her mother pushed.

The other thing Catherine was always doing was letting men move in. Jana saw a montage of men carrying their boxes into the apartment, and then carrying them out, one after another, except sometimes their things were in trash bags and not boxes, and some of them were angry and slammed the door behind them when they left, and some of them left behind things like uncomfortable leather couches or a bandanna collection or gaming consoles. They weren't all so bad, though, and one of them stayed around awhile—Billy, who played Irish fiddle in a band every Tuesday at the Red Rose Pub, where her mother sometimes worked. Billy had a face full of stubble that always made him look dirty, and he picked up handyman gigs when he could get them. He tried to make Jana play Irish-style but she wouldn't play that loose, or couldn't, and by that time her Russian teacher had taken her on anyway, and he would have died if she'd told him she learned a jig by ear.

Jana remembered Billy liked war movies because he'd been in the war, and when *Platoon* came out, he dragged Jana to see it. She was sixteen and it was her first R-rated movie in a theater. Catherine refused to go, in one of her slumps after a string of bad auditions.

He elbowed Jana in the cold theater and whispered, "This guy's my favorite—Willem Dafoe."

Then Willem Dafoe's character died. All his men were watching him from a helicopter when he was shot in the back. He kept trying to get up and run but he kept getting shot. The music of Samuel Barber's *Adagio for Strings*, which Jana had played first violin on in chamber orchestra two years prior, swelled over the scene. Jana wondered what recording it was, was mildly bored by the violent visual that accompanied it. But when she looked over at Billy, the light from the screen flashing on his face, she saw that he was crying. Silent, masculine tears, but flat silver streaks down his cheeks for sure. He hadn't seen it coming, not even with the swelling music. What a fool, Jana thought, but in a kind way.

On the ride home, Billy said, "Oh boy, that was a movie, huh?"

It must have been some days later—Catherine was home and happy again, having received both a callback and a very large tip at the restaurant—when Billy knocked on her bedroom door. He poked his head in. Jana was cleaning her violin of rosin.

"Hey, can you play it? That soundtrack from *Platoon*?"

"The Barber?"

"Sure, that."

Jana nodded. "I could play it years ago."

Billy sat down on the floor by the door, just inside her room. "Play it for me now?"

Jana rummaged through her sheet music. "It will sound weird without all the other parts."

But she played it anyway. It required a pristine intonation, but with Jana's perfect pitch it wasn't so difficult. When there were rests in the music, she rested, and Billy didn't move in the quiet. Finally, she reached the climactic climb up the E string, the soaring scale that accompanied Willem Dafoe's death, and when she was done, she looked up and saw her mother standing next to Billy. She was holding two clear drinks, one in each hand.

"Baby, that was beautiful. Sad and beautiful," Catherine said, bending down to hand one drink to Billy.

"It was from the movie we saw together," Billy said.

Catherine frowned. "I don't remember you two seeing a movie together."

No one said anything because, yes, she didn't remember. Catherine kicked absently at the doorjamb with her high heel. "Well, anyway. Maybe Jana can play in the movies one day. You know that's where her name comes from, right? Jana Leigh? Like Janet Leigh. Janet Leigh is so pretty. Like Jana. Didn't I make a pretty baby?"

Catherine had shown Jana *Psycho* when she was eleven, too young. Her mother loved *Psycho*, always got scared and huddled under a blanket, sometimes called their creepy neighbor "Norman Bates" as a joke. "Baby, your namesake," Catherine would always say when they watched it. Jana didn't tell her mother she didn't like being named after a woman who was best known for being stabbed in the shower, or that she hated the screeching music that accompanied the murder scene. Couldn't she have been Tippi? Grace? Kelly? Or someone from something with a dignified soundtrack?

But Billy didn't answer, because he was still hearing the music. It seemed to Jana that around that time was when Billy stopped listening to his mother's blathering altogether, which is why she eventually kicked him out, and it wasn't like Billy was some saint—he didn't even say goodbye to Jana—but Jana thought about him when she thought about the moment she decided to really leave home, to go to conservatory and not look back. She thought about the parade of men who fell in love with Catherine and then fell out of love with her when they saw how myopic and medicated she was, or the men who didn't love her at all, the men who drank even more than Catherine did and broke lamps and frying pans and fences—and how she, Jana, didn't ever want to be around those men again, men who either needed too much or not enough. When she thought about Billy, she always remembered him clutching at the carpet in her bedroom, listening to her play while Catherine flitted around above him, how he'd seemed lost but aligned with Jana, not like a father (she never felt that from anyone) but like a brother, like he was saying, *Hey, we could be related because we both understand how special and exquisite this music is*. But Billy wouldn't have used that word—*exquisite*—and Jana wouldn't have, either, not until she left two years later, and then she didn't really think of Billy except for when she heard the Barber, which, now that she was a serious professional, wasn't that often. It was considered schlocky, especially since *Platoon*, and after that afternoon, Jana never played it again.

Back at her apartment, Jana made herself food and ate it standing by the stove. While she chewed, she wiped up the crumbs around the range with a new sponge. Nothing had ever seemed so lonely before, though she'd spent days exactly like this many times prior. Days like this were the atomic structure that made up her life. She didn't eat or drink with the voraciousness Henry had mentioned. She ate box pasta and pre-made salad mixes, and drank mineral water. She felt jittery and useless when she was not practicing or listening to music. So, in her non-music life, she learned to make her movements small and quiet, to lessen the guilt and assuage the nagging in her head. But why now, all of a sudden, was the pathetic deadness of her life revealed? Nothing had changed.

It wasn't Fodorio himself. She wasn't, like she thought Brit was, hungry for the attention of men. She was hungry to begin their professional life, and was it so terrible that she'd done something possibly against the rules for a leg up at Esterhazy? What was a small moral failing on the way to greatness? She could spend time convincing herself she had connected with Fodorio, seen in his wayward fatherhood a replica of the empty space inside her. She had let him talk, hadn't derided his life's choices, hadn't bothered him with hers. She had helped him be temporarily less lonely. She had forgiven him his mistakes. She had provided him a service, so why was it so bad if he provided her with something, too?

She wouldn't tell the group. Not ever, she decided. Brit didn't have the same sort of ambition she did, and wouldn't understand. Daniel would be angry with her, though really he'd be angry with himself, for not being good enough to win the competition flat-out. And Henry would think she was foolish, that they didn't need help winning, and he would be right, but only about him—*he* could win it alone. Together, she wasn't sure. And she needed to be sure.

This was the end of something, she thought, looking out the small square window above her sink at the top of Coit Tower in the distance. The end of their schooling, their student-hood, their tryout period. The period where they could fail. They'd fooled themselves into thinking it wasn't the same as conservatory because they were earning master's degrees, but it was simply an extension, a way to make it all right not to be good enough. But after this week, there would be no cushion, and the vertigo of that thought rushed through Jana's body.

And what would failure look like? A lack of: invitations to play, offers for management, post-conservatory residencies. An abundance of: years wasted, degrees earned, rehearsal hours clocked. Settling for: teaching private students who would, at best, be good in an extracurricular way (good for a future doctor), or clawing to a job leading a bad band at a junior high school, or (if she was a lucky failure) toiling away in the back of a violin section at a middling regional orchestra. In any scenario, there would be the slow shrug of dissolving a quartet whose union depended on other people wanting to be united.

Jana hadn't invited her mother to the recital or Esterhazy. She wouldn't have known where to send the invitation. Not really. The last time she'd seen her mother had been at a trailer park near Torrance, a nice one, with trees and children, but a trailer park still. Her mother had been drunk, thin, pretty in a sun-worn kind of way. A man was holding her up—Ray or something was his name. Catherine didn't do anything in particular that day, nothing unusually awful. They went to lunch, Ray stared at Jana's small breasts, Catherine drank four margaritas, and then they went back to the trailer to watch some television crime drama her mother liked. Catherine fell asleep during the show, and Ray said nothing until Jana stood up to leave. She thought her mother probably did not remember it very well.

It was easier not to contact her. She had Jana's number anyway, or could find her easily enough. But it was too taxing, those visits, pinging between her guilt for being a bad daughter and her hunger for a mother Catherine could never be.

Was that pain? Jana didn't know. It simply felt like the absence of something.

Here was Catherine's number, scrawled in the corner of an address book, under several other phone numbers that had been scratched out, numbers to her apartments over the years, those of men she'd lived with. Jana held the book in her hand, plastic-bound with yellowing pages.

If she called now, there would be no way Catherine could make it from Los Angeles, but Jana would at least have told her. Would not have to feel guilt about that.

She dialed the number the way she'd finished the food, robotically, without knowing where the muscle movement was originating from.

A man answered, of course.

"Ray?" Jana said.

"Who?"

"Who is this?"

"Who is *this*?"

"This is Jana. Is this Ray?"

"This is Carl. Are you calling for Ray?"

"For Catherine. Is she home?"

Jana heard a hand muffle the speaker, but he still yelled loud enough for Jana to pull the phone from her ear. "Katie! Janet's on the phone for you!"

Jana held her breath until her mother's voice came on the phone, a whole half-octave higher than she normally spoke.

"Janet?"

"It's Jana."

"Jana! Carl, it's Jana, not Janet. Oh, honey, so glad you called. I couldn't find your number, and Carl said he was going to look you up, but I didn't know if you lived in San Francisco or some other town, and maybe you aren't even listed, so we couldn't find you."

"That's okay. Hey, I'm just calling to say I'm competing in a big thing this week." Jana heard her own voice quaver. She closed her eyes. This was a bad idea.

"That's great, honey. Can I read about it? Will it be televised? Or on the radio?"

Her mother didn't understand how any of it worked. It was some kind of miracle that Jana had ended up a classical violinist: a chance meeting with Dmitri at the LA Phil on a school trip, hundreds of hours wearing a stupid paper hat at In-N-Out Burger to pay for the violin, and a nearly crazed desire to enmesh herself in something foreign to her mother.

"No. It's not that big a deal," Jana said.

"If it's no big deal, then why'd you call me? Sure it's a big deal. Did I tell you that I got a callback for this PacBell commercial? My agent thinks I'll get it."

Jana resisted the urge to say, *No, when would you have told me that, we haven't spoken in two years.* Instead, she said, "That's great. Who's Carl?"

"Carl lives with me now."

"What happened to Ray?"

"Ray?" Catherine laughed. "Oh, baby girl, that was ages ago. I can't believe you remember that."

Tears sprang meanly to Jana's eyes. She wasn't surprised at any of it, and her lack of surprise was what saddened her. She blinked.

"I'll send you a program. I have to go, Catherine."

"Yes, send me a program. I'll send you a copy of the commercial. If I get it."

"You'll get it," Jana said.

"Thanks. You too, honey."

She hung up without saying goodbye, and continued to stand at her sink, looking out the window for she didn't know how long. What did Catherine think Jana was going to get? She made a promise not to reach out to her again, and felt glad in her stubbornness.

She could have said, *I fucked a famous violinist so we'd win a major competition,* and her mother would have understood. With that thought, it wasn't shame or sadness that overcame Jana but anger that she had let herself be like her mother for a moment—let herself believe, foolishly, in the invisible, in the dreamy possibility of magic instead of the actual pursuit of greatness.

At some point, the sunlight in the square of window began to dip, and that was how Jana knew it was time to dress, pack, and rush to catch her—their—flight to Esterhazy.

BRIT

Violin II

After they ended their last rehearsal before leaving for Canada, Daniel walked off the cold stage without saying goodbye. Brit turned just in time to see his cello case on his back bouncing behind him as he disappeared into the unlighted hall. Henry, always aware of the subtle changes in other people's emotions and totally unable to talk explicitly about them, walked over to her and made a joke, something about the difference between Irish fiddlers and violists. Brit didn't exactly hear it, and laughed only to make him feel like he had indeed made her feel better. Being that attuned to each other's inner emotional lives was the sometimes unfortunate side effect of playing music together.

Brit blamed her parents. They'd been amateur musicians themselves, her mother a cellist and her father a trumpeter. They had other jobs, careers, even, but they always made time to play in the shitty community orchestra where Brit grew up in Washington. They hadn't been great players, but they were decent, and what's more, they loved it. When it became clear early on that Brit would be a good violinist at the very least, they encouraged her to pursue it, set her up with too-expensive lessons, shuttled her from orchestra rehearsal to orchestra rehearsal. After they both died, Brit thought maybe she'd quit. It wasn't too late to use her B.A. in English (she'd double-majored in music). She knew someone from college in New York hiring consultants—he wore heavy, fancy overcoats and said she'd be a "valuable advocate for the brand." But at her mother's funeral, a small affair with no one left to plan it but Brit, her mother's friends hugged her too tightly and said how proud her mother had been of her musical career. Brit couldn't tell them the truth, that without her parents pushing her along, she didn't know how far she'd make it.

But it wasn't just the music Brit blamed her parents for. It was this fairy-tale idea she had about love. After her father died, her mother was not with another man—never even mentioned another man—and some months before her quiet death it seemed to Brit that her mother had resigned herself to the idea that life without her father wasn't really a life after all. Brit's friends who were the children of divorce bemoaned their inability to commit, their fear of failure, but Brit couldn't conceive of love as anything but pure, lifelong, transformative, irrational, outside of any orderly system. And now, she supposed, ultimately disappointing. She had become melancholy without noticing, until one day she realized she couldn't remember the last time she'd been happy, the last time she'd been unworried about finding love or sinking into a despair that seemed like a churning storm always at bay.

Every man she'd loved—and there hadn't been that many—she'd loved blindly. Leif, in college, who whisked in and out of their relationship with such grace and speed she barely noticed it, who left her after her father's diagnosis, literally walking backward out of her dorm room, shrugging in apology. Julian, in her senior year, the year her father died, had been a snake, leather-jacketed and sulky, curling around her grief and then, when life demanded she come out of it, had slithered away. Jon, the line cook, who said he was philosophical evidence that it was possible to love two women at once (Brit, the second and lesser love; Brit, sad enough and worn-out enough by her sadness to settle for that silver tier). There had been men she'd loved who'd never even considered loving her, who never touched her, who listened intently as she talked about her dead father, before asking if she wanted cereal for dinner, if she knew how to iron (how did one *not* know how to iron?), and did she want to hear about their own tragic love lives.

And when her mother died, she resigned herself to occupying the two ends of a wild oscillation she'd inherited from her parents' lives and then their deaths: the raw, hungry desire to experience an inexplicable love, and the melancholic knowledge that she might never get to.

No wonder Daniel thought her brand of living and loving dangerous, risky. It was full of awful turns and gaping holes. Even Brit didn't want to say her history belonged to her. Daniel liked to say there was order to the suffering. He needed order because if there was order to the world, he could master it. He could ascend. He studied scores obsessively, with highlighters and different-colored pencils, marking patterns and changes in voice, looking for the logical order in the music. If he could have charted love onto a graph, he would have. Grief is evolutionarily determined, he would say. Falling in love is chemical, he would say. Staying in love is a choice, he would say. Love is expensive, he would say.

Their competing philosophies had seemed quaint until the other night, over the pasta, when it became clear to Brit that Daniel's wasn't a philosophy, but a survival tactic. He'd worked so hard his entire life, honed the obsessive studying and observing and concluding, because there was no one and no money to buoy him. How difficult for him to be next to Henry, Brit thought, rich and prodigious and shiny-haired Henry. But how difficult for Brit, too, to see Daniel's own richness—in his hard work, his intelligence, his desire—and to be held away from it.

So Brit felt the pain of Daniel's absence doubly, first as an experience of rejection, and second as loneliness inside that rejection. There was no one to share the pain with, not Jana and Henry, who didn't particularly deal in or ever dwell on romantic failures, and certainly not Daniel. She could not make sense of the fact that she could have feelings for someone—even *love* Daniel, had she said that aloud? Was it true?—and he could not feel the same way for her. Where was the order in that?

Back at her apartment after the rehearsal, she cleaned. She cleaned her violin, her rugs, her shower tiles. She wanted to go to the competition with a spotless apartment. She watched with satisfaction as the patchy mold disappeared and the coffee rings on the counter flaked off. She thought of Jana as she did this, feeling physically productive, tangibly accomplished. This was something Jana could relate to and Brit felt a sudden urge to call her, to get something to eat with her, to talk not about boys or the competition but just music, how Jana got to be so good, what had made her want to play in the first place. But Jana was closer to Henry, and closed off to Brit in general, to people in general. It made sense, Brit reasoned. People could disappoint you, fail you in lots of ways. She wished for the entire duration of cleaning the bathroom that she could be more like Jana, whose hopes rested safely in career aspirations that were ambitious but possible, and not at all emotionally risky. Then again, Jana seemed perpetually afraid the rest of them would disappoint her at any moment, and Daniel afraid he would disappoint himself.

She finished cleaning much earlier than anticipated, and sat on her lone couch in the living room that was also her bedroom, and felt—there was no other word for it—sorrow.

She remained in that state for another hour, like a minnow caught in a suddenly vicious eddy, until it was time to go to the airport.

Though it was becoming harder and harder to recall, Brit's childhood had been happy. She'd grown up on an island off the coast of northern Washington—to get there, you had to take a ferry from an Indian reservation outside Bellingham, the last real town before Canada—a nine-mile patch of land on the tip of the sound before it spilled into Vancouver, a place where evergreens lined the roads and the shore was audible from all the houses, breaking through the dense, wet forests that towered over them. There was an elementary school and a middle school on the island, where her parents taught, the classrooms mostly full of kids from the tribe that had originally inhabited the island, and most of those kids didn't make it over to the high school on the mainland with Brit.

Before high school, she hardly ever boarded the ferry except to attend her parents' concerts in Bellingham, or for an occasional trip to Seattle, instead preferring to follow or tear trails through the woods and up to the island's peaks. She would perch on a rock on the highest peak with lunch or a book and take in her private panorama: the silky water that seemed to effervesce with sunlight, the rest of the San Juan Islands peeking out like ancient mossy creatures surfacing, the long tip of her island petering off into rocks and beach and glinting fish. Summers, Brit saw orcas and dolphins chase each other in the far distance, squinted her way toward Canada, spied the richer residents' catamarans, the tourist dive boats, the whale-watching ferries. In the winter, when no tourists came, she and her father collected rain gear and made forts under tree cover, spending one night, maybe two if it wasn't so rainy, catching and releasing frogs, playing cards, tramping through familiar territory now sodden and sinking, like a whole new island. There were the gusts through the trees and the kissing of the water on docks and the always light rain on the roof and the bald eagles' long, zipping calls and even the slow slurps of the neon slugs in the early morning.

The whole island was encased in the quietude of its habitat.

That is why, Brit supposed, her parents chose that place to live, so their house could be filled with music instead. Brit's mother played the cello decently enough, though she never progressed past the sonatas of being a music minor at Reed. Brit had a violin in her hand before she had a name for it, and knew how to play it before she knew how to write, and her earliest memories were of playing duets with her mother, her mother's childlike delight at having a stringed partner once again. But Brit's father was a better trumpeter than her mother was a cellist, loud and bright, too good for the community orchestra. Every other year the conductor pulled him out to play or replay a trumpet concerto (there weren't that many), and the tacky smell of a brass mouthpiece always brought to Brit's mind her father at her bedside, lips on her forehead, pressing play on the *Mozart for Kids* cassette she liked to fall asleep to. Their old house, a small woodstove in the center responsible for heating it in the winter, brimmed with music. Though it was just the three of them, in their music the house contained the sounds of a much larger family, a philharmonic of children and holidays and schemes.

And then Brit's musical ability surpassed her mother's, and then her father's, and it wouldn't be entirely wrong to say that something tectonic shifted in her life when she started to board the ferry not just for high school but to go into Bellingham for lessons, and then Seattle to study with the symphony's concertmaster. Brit's parents were never anything less than happy that she'd shown remarkable talent and precision in the violin, gladly forking over their teachers' salaries for lessons and a better instrument and summer music camps, even when Brit no longer played with them. She didn't have the time. The last ferry to the island was at ten p.m. on weekdays, and sometimes she wouldn't make it back from the city in time and would instead crash with a friend and wearily take herself to school the next morning. When she did make it back to the house on the island, it was always dark: the dark of the trees velvety against the dark of the sky, the dark of the house around the smoldering remnants in the woodstove, something shivering up through her in the sudden immersion into the island's constant sonic ecosystem. In the mornings, when the ferry groaned into the dock at the mainland reservation, the sounds of cars and wheezing bus brakes and the nearby playgrounds filtered back into her as though filling empty spaces in her bloodstream.

Which is why, Brit supposed, she went as far away for college as she did. Indiana's music program was highly regarded, and she didn't want to miss out on a regular college experience by committing to a conservatory. And for a while, she was a regular girl with a singular talent, awkward and acting out in Bloomington. When she was there she missed the island and when she was home for the breaks she missed Indiana, and things felt balanced.

But then her father, never a smoker, got lung cancer, and it ate him up inside in the space of six months, and he was dead just before she graduated. She felt like a piece of her broke off then and drifted out to sea, though she wouldn't understand it that way for years, and she stagnated in Bloomington for a while, waiting tables and teaching little kids violin, and that was why she took the spot in the program in San Francisco, to be closer to her mother, who, in spirit at least, whittled away almost as fast as her father.

Now Brit would say that in those two years between her father's death and her mother's death she walked around lopsided, but she wouldn't truly feel it until her mother passed away in her sleep. The phone call delivering the news stole all the breath out of Brit like a cold wind, so that she actually dropped to the kitchen floor, gasping, the receiver clanking down with her. Ever since, Brit felt like she couldn't get that air back, not all of it anyway. And in a way, this new grief balanced out the other grief that had already broken off a part of her, and she became resigned to their muting implications. She was lesser. On the island, after her mother's funeral, she packed up the house and the instruments and made a fire in the woodstove and lay dimly on a cot on the floor, the primitive quiet of the place seeping into the emptiness where sleep should have come, the idyll of a gibbous moon (you noticed the phases of the moon only on islands) passing briefly through the window and just as quickly vacated.

Once back in San Francisco, she met Jana, who invited her to read quartet music one afternoon with her friends, Henry and Daniel. There was something stark in Jana that drew Brit magnetically, and made her say yes. Something tender in Henry. Something challenging in Daniel. Something wild to chase when they practiced. And what did they find in her? What was she to them? In the ensemble: proficient, subordinate, *pianississimo,* the smallest sound you could make, the only kind of sound that recalls its very absence.

On the plane to Canada, the seat between Brit and Daniel was occupied by the cello, his the only instrument requiring its own ticket. His black plastic case was beat up, and the remnants of a few torn-off stickers scratched Brit's arm when he leaned over to buckle his seatbelt. She was thankful for the object between them. They didn't look at each other the entire long flight to the mountain town, though she'd listened in as he joked with Jana at the newsstand in the airport. They'd riffed for a little bit on an inside joke Brit hadn't understood, and she nearly burst into tears standing behind them. It had been a rough week or so without Daniel's companionship, but that he'd maintained his connections with Jana and Henry stung.

It wasn't as though they didn't speak. They did. It was impossible not to. But they no longer ate dinners alone, or walked each other to the BART station, and she hadn't been to his place in Oakland since that night she'd walked away, though they'd seen each other every day at least once. Daniel could be friendly, sometimes overly so, and the friendlier he got, the more she withdrew. It reminded her too much of how they'd been, and also rattled false. When they rehearsed, however, he was irritated and distanced, and not just from her. He seemed frustrated, but she wasn't sure at what, exactly. She'd had to ignore it. She'd devoted her energy to preparing for the competition. Seemingly, they all had. Though Jana had mentioned a few times that Brit and Daniel seemed odd, she'd taken her questioning no further. Brit spent her free time trying to forget what it was like to have his attention on her only, and sent small prayers into the universe that she wouldn't have to see him give himself to anyone else, at least not too soon.

Which was why when, after the shuttle to the lodge, in the middle of unpacking her bags in a musty room, she was shocked to open her door and see Daniel standing there.

He looked like a small animal, hopeful and cheery but with a layer of desperation underneath. His hair stuck up at awkward angles. He didn't like to fly, and the flight had been stuffy and uncomfortable.

"Hey," he said. "Are you hungry? They're saying it might snow, maybe just flurries."

Brit was never going to say no to him. They wandered down the touristy main street in jackets ill-suited to a Canadian spring, especially one that carried the possibility of snow, and because it was dark or cold or very late, or because they tucked their chins into their chests and looked at the sidewalk, they ended up at the cheesiest, most touristy pub in the entire ski town, all wood and brass with rigid bench booths and overpriced, dull food. But neither of them suggested going anywhere else.

"Bangers and mash?" Daniel said, pointing at the plastic menu.

There was too much brimming at Brit's lips, things she wanted to say. She looked at Daniel dumbly perusing the menu and felt it wasn't the time or place, and also that the time and place were rapidly receding from her, that strange sense of vertigo you get when a wave you've let wash over your feet rushes back into the ocean.

He seemed to be in a good mood and ordered the bangers and mash. He made jokes at Henry's expense, jokes he and Brit had made privately, weeks ago, as if trying to conjure the same invisible, romantic mist that had hovered between them then. He looked her straight in the eye. Maybe it was the change of scenery, she thought, maybe it had changed something elemental inside him. This place, after all, was a little pricey, very unlike Daniel and his tight budget, and he'd gone along with that. Maybe it was the high stakes and the near possibility of winning that energized him. Maybe it was her. The place she'd worked to close off from him bloomed when he smiled at her.

"If we get food poisoning during the performance, I'm blaming you," she said, tucking the plastic menu between salt and pepper shakers shaped like moose.

"If that happens, we'll be dead by Jana's hand before we have time to blame anyone," he said.

"You know, we poke at Jana so much for wanting this so badly, but I think the rest of us do just as much, don't you? It's like one of those things you didn't even know you wanted until it's so close."

"Nah," Daniel said. "I wanted this. I just don't want it in such a bossy way."

"Ha," Brit said. "I might disagree with that, but all right."

"Do you?"

"Do I what?"

"Want it."

She paused. "Yes, of course I do."

They were so close to the thing they wanted—needed—for the next stage of their career, and if they got it, so many other things seemed possible. If they got it, what was to stop them from getting anything else?

"Not just the competition, I mean," he said.

"Then what? What else is there to want?" Brit asked.

"This. The quartet."

She stared at him. "Well, sure. That's—that's the whole point. Of all of this. That's the reason . . . the reason why—"

"—we're here. Yeah, I know, but I mean, sometimes you just get caught up in some idea."

Daniel was interrupted by the waiter, who carefully placed a huge plate in front of him and a moderately sized plate in front of her. Steam rose into his face. After the waiter left, Daniel whispered, "Wait, what are bangers again?"

"Sausage," Brit said. "What did you think it was?" Sometimes, the things Daniel didn't know—things that couldn't be learned by books or in school—astonished her. He seemed, on the one hand, so worldly, with a soft spot for Greek mythology and philosophy, an encyclopedic knowledge of music history and theory, but on the other, so inexperienced, so shut off from the rest of the world. From things like food. Eating, to Daniel, was probably just an act of survival.

He shrugged. "I guess I didn't think about what it was."

She laughed. "Okay. Well, try it."

They ate slowly, leisurely, as though they were old lovers on a date, enjoying the novelty of it again. Neither looked at a watch or a clock. This wasn't one of Daniel's moments of feigned fondness. This was the real thing. As he neared the end of his meal, Brit felt bolstered by the dark restaurant and his easy laugh, and she leaned over toward him.

"What I was saying before," Brit said. "About wanting it. I think you must know."

"Must know what?" he said, scraping his plate of potatoes.

"That I want this, at the expense of this—" She waved her hand in the space between them. "The quartet is more important. Otherwise . . ." She trailed off and placed her hand on his. "I do miss you."

He coughed and a little bit of potato spat out onto the table. He didn't see it, but she did. "Miss me? We spend all our time together."

She withdrew her hand from his, which had remained steely beneath her touch. He continued to chew, staring at her, and she felt herself go red, and wished she'd said nothing at all. She'd almost been there—over this—hours and days spent diminishing a thing that never even was, and here she'd walked backward. Of course he wasn't thinking about that. He wasn't ever thinking about anything other than how to be better.

And they should have left it there. He should have. Made nothing more of it, let it be an aberrant bubble in the otherwise seamless interpersonal weave of their strange little family. But, bound by stubbornness, by a drive to get it right, Brit assumed, he went on.

"I want you to know, if we weren't in the quartet—even if we weren't in the quartet"—he stuttered like a bird was caught in his throat—"I wouldn't be with you."

She felt a weight move through her, like a stone slowly sinking in her chest, stomach, hips, moving cruelly through the viscosity. She felt so heavy and full with this weight that it actually seemed like she might get stuck to the tacky floor of this nowhere pub and some official would have to peel her off, teach her to stand again, teach her about gravity, that nonsensical logic of bodies. It was the force of Daniel saying *that thing*—that thing one says that one cannot take back, after which nothing is the same. Here their story would take a sharp turn and change forever, she understood. He had swerved, and she had no choice but to swerve with him.

"I mean," he said. "I mean that you can't use the quartet as an excuse. We can't. That'll poison the whole thing. We just have to look at this, you know, objectively."

She nodded but she wasn't listening. How many times could she be made a fool of? This would be the last, she swore. She made a big deal of her meatloaf—she never knew she could make up so many things to say about meatloaf—and then said she was too full for dessert, but all the while, she felt the viscous parts of her being pushed out through her feet—she was leaving herself, she was all stone now. In the end, he did complain about the bill, and they split it precisely. She begged off to sleep, blaming jet lag. In the old rooms in the old hotel, everyone waited for a late snow that did not, in fact, arrive—though if it had, Brit doubted she would have felt it. She felt now completely outside herself, which is the most lonely you can feel, as it is impossible to name, impossible to point to, except that you can point to yourself, lying there on the bed, say: *Look at her, who is she?*

In this way, the concert happened without any of them being there at all, really. If the "Serioso" was also about love, Brit tried to remember the vast swath of her life when she didn't love Daniel, but while they were playing, it was impossible. His boyish face contorted uncontrollably, erotically. She wondered if he felt that way about her, too, watching her play, if anyone did. And she decided no, that wasn't quite the way she played. Brit liked nuance, liked to be the supporting voice, the harmonic line you didn't know you heard. But Daniel, as cellist, was a presence to be noticed. And like a grunting tennis pro, he couldn't manage his face when he was really inside of the music, he wore his effort there, and so it went practically unconscious, and he slipped into some liminal area where desire met work. He squirmed in his seat, propped his right foot on its ball, twisted his nose so that his glasses would stay up, and that mouth. She'd never loved someone's mouth before, hadn't even really thought about the mouths of men, but here was Daniel's, bow shaped or snarled by turns—how could it not be erotic? This was his submission, his participation in a disorderly beauty.

So this was the way she'd be close to him. It was as good as any, possibly better, Brit thought. What civilian, what regular other woman could have this intimacy with him, could know his body this way? She'd take it.

But another realization came over her, nearly in conjunction with the lovely one that preceded it: there would always be this distance. And here was the main theme of the "Serioso," bursting out of their instruments in unison, an incredible and brave composition, but Brit had never felt more far away from it. This was it, all she would have of him, of any of them, just this collection of mechanics, a finely timed—well, finely enough—working together. The physical truth of it was shattering, him over there and her over here, and no matter how hard she tried, Beethoven would not join them together.

Daniel was thinking of mechanics, too, though not in the same way. He was thinking that he'd chosen a career that should have been conquerable because the mechanics of it could be learned. And he'd learned so much, was so much older than the rest of them, and wanted it so bad, had nothing to fall back on—yet here he was, still sweating and struggling through the "Serioso." No one worked as hard as him. But he saw now that was because they didn't have to. Jana's high, clear playing was curated to perfection, Brit played evenly and subtly, and Henry hadn't made a single misstep, not even in rehearsal, in the entire time Daniel had known him. He became angry in such a way that—not for the first time in his life—he saw no way out of it.

During the third movement, Henry watched Daniel fully settling into his anger, an anger that seemed greater than their unison minuet. Henry saw everything, but he did not react. Perhaps that was the real mistake that night, Henry not trying to do something to show Daniel that it was okay, because that was the moment where everything began to unravel. But what was there to do to temper Daniel's anger? It ran as an undercurrent to the relentlessness and speed of this third movement, jumping note to note, cutting the edges more sharply, speeding up what was already a too-fast tempo set by Jana. But Henry didn't do anything to stop it. He didn't feel it was vital.

Jana would later take the blame for starting the fourth movement a tad too fast, but she would also blame Brit for failing to take her cue to slow down in the rubato, and Henry for taking the speed as a chance to make a wild, embarrassing show of his supporting voice, and Daniel, whose sixteenths simply couldn't keep up, whose fast sections came off messy, student-like. Why had she started it so terribly, though? The whole piece had been slowly building to this breakdown, in fact, and because she was leader, it was ultimately her fault.

She had been, of all things, nervous. She was never nervous. It wasn't part of her nature to be nervous. Confidence led her in all things, ever since she was a little girl, but she'd felt a sense she'd done something wrong hanging over her since before they took the stage. From the wings where she waited to go on, she caught sight of Fodorio in the third row, where the judges sat. He was dressed in all black, and his hair was in his eyes. She lifted her hand and held it up to catch his attention. When he looked at her, she began to smile, but his face did not change. Probably to an outsider it would have looked that way. It was that what registered in his face was recognizable only to her, and caused her shame. She wasn't ashamed to have slept with him—that she would have done anyway—or even to have threatened or blackmailed him, or whatever one called it. She was ashamed to have asked for help, to have admitted to being in the position of needing help. And the way he looked at her had acknowledged only that: *Oh, there you are, that person who needs help.*

When the quartet took the stage for the first round of performances—the round they would not make it past—all of them, each member, felt apart not just from one another, but from themselves.

Word that they would not progress to the next round of performances, during which they would have played the much kinder Haydn, wouldn't come until the morning, but no one needed a phone call to know it. They walked off stage to tepid applause and said nothing to each other. The only sounds in the greenroom were the clicking of the locks on their cases and the shuffling of music stuffed into pocket sleeves. The boys wordlessly took a car back to the lodge, but Jana and Brit walked. The night seemed cruelly cold now, much colder than May in San Francisco.

What they didn't say to each other: what next?

In the large hallways of the lodge, Brit followed Jana back to her room, and when Jana unlocked the door and turned to find Brit behind her, she said the first thing she'd said to anyone since the performance: "Why are you still here?"

"Let's just have one drink," Brit said. "Come on, you know you don't want to be alone."

"No, *you* don't," Jana said, but held the door open behind her anyway.

Brit thought for sure Jana would have a solution of some kind. That's who she was. Solution girl. She always had a plan, and the plan always had multiple steps. This kind of failure wasn't in the plan, but Jana was quick and determined. Brit wanted a drink, yes, and she also wanted to hear about Jana's plan for their future.

Brit opened the minibar and took out one of the tiny whiskeys. For Jana, she poured a small vodka over ice, a drink she'd seen her order at the bar they went to after rehearsals. When she handed it to Jana, Jana looked surprised that she knew her drink. But of course they all knew these small details. It was impossible not to after the hours of work and attention they'd extracted from each other. Brit sat on the floor, and Jana on her bed, legs crossed. No one opened the curtains or touched a remote or anything. They stared at the floor. Brit didn't know what to say. "I'm sorry" was either incorrect or not enough.

"Why are you looking at me like that?" Jana asked.

"I'm not," Brit said. "I mean, I'm looking at you, but not like anything."

"You guys always expect me to fix things."

"No we don't," Brit said. "Well, maybe Henry does."

"I tried to fix that tempo."

Brit wasn't going to touch this line of thinking. It was useless and unproductive to go over what exactly had gone wrong, at least so soon afterward. In any case, they had all been there. They all knew.

"At least our parents weren't here to see it," Brit said, and they both laughed. That was the sort of thing Jana would laugh at, something slightly morbid.

"Thank the Lord," Jana said, clasping her hands together in prayer.

"I want to get so drunk I forget it happened," Brit said.

"But then you'll have to remember all over again," Jana said. "It's the remembering that kills you, not the knowing."

"We came all the way out here. To do *that.*"

Jana leaned down and clinked her glass against Brit's whiskey bottle, which was empty. "Time for another."

They talked and worked through the minibar in the way Brit had imagined real college students did it, the kind of college kids who weren't practicing four to five hours a day, who weren't protecting their hands and fingers from minor injuries or cuts, who weren't banking on a clear head to get them through the next day's rehearsal, who weren't choosing friends based on their ability to play, and losing them for similar reasons. She liked to watch Jana unwind, as it usually seemed like all of her was closely rotating a center pole in her body. As she drank more, that pole became elastic, and so did her laughter, her speech. Her face, cold when she was concentrating, became beautifully angular when she was animated; her full lips and sharp jawline, like a painting of a person from a different time. Brit lay down on the floor and stared at the ceiling.

"Don't take a bath," Jana said, and they cracked up.

It was an inside joke. They'd been coached once by Jacob Liedel, the aging emeritus director of the conservatory, who sat with his saggy skin and liver spots in a chair inexplicably on the other side of the room, and shouted at them the whole time. He barely let them get through a phrase before waving his hands, interrupting them, correcting them. Brit admired his old-school edge, but she knew Jana found it upsetting, and the louder he yelled, the more strained her bow arm became, until Jacob finally yelled, "Don't take a bath!" and Jana stopped playing and said,

"What?" Jacob repeated: "Don't take a bath there. With that phrase." None of them asked him what he meant, but he said it two, three more times during the coaching session; afterward, at dinner, the four of them sitting in a tired silence, Henry said, "What's taking a bath mean?" and Jana and Brit laughed so hard they cried into their cheese fries and slid under the booth. Now and again they still said it to each other, with no consistency of context. To Daniel about his excessive foot tapping to count time: Don't take a bath. To Jana, when she was obsessing over the tuning of her E string: Don't take a bath.

"So, what's next is maybe a move," Brit said. "I think we have to move." She was answering a question no had asked out loud.

Jana lay down on her bed. "New York?"

Brit nodded. "No bathtubs there."

There was only one unsure element. Jana asked: "Do you think Henry will do that?"

"You'd know better than I would," Brit said. She knew Jana spent chaste nights with Henry, but she'd never asked her explicitly about it. Talking about boys wasn't really something they did together. Though they were as ingrained in each other's daily lives as significant others—even spilled over into that space—their conversations consisted of cues and crescendos and careers, not crushes. And Jana and Henry seemed more like siblings than anything else; Jana never moved or talked more freely than when she was around him, which is why this one-on-one Brit and Jana were having had been tinged with awkwardness before they started drinking. Brit realized they'd done something irritating, pairing off with Henry and Daniel as they had, girl to boy, girl to boy. Another reason to step away from Daniel, Brit thought. But toward what?

And toward what for the quartet? They were now a quartet without a country, no flag of the conservatory or the competition to stand under. A life of hustling, of trying to get signed, of starving in New York and trying to make it in the classical world, which didn't, at the moment, care that much for chamber musicians, at least not those who hadn't won competitions, or even placed.

"I think if we do it now," Jana said, "he might. But that asshole might poach him."

"What asshole?"

"Ferrari," Jana said, and she got up, opened up her violin case, and snatched something stuck into the velvet lining. She held it out to Brit. It was a small girl with black hair and a few missing teeth, one of those school photos against a neon background. She smiled wildly at the camera, the way you do when you're a kid.

"Who's this?" Brit asked.

Jana shrugged and took it back from her. "I don't know," she said, and walked into the bathroom, where Brit saw her drop the picture in the toilet. She did not flush it.

Jana came out to answer the knock on the door, which turned out to be Henry and Daniel, both of whom seemed fairly liquored up themselves. Henry was sweaty and Daniel swayed a bit. He was carrying something under a tin, as though from room service.

"What are you guys doing here?" Brit asked.

"We live here," Henry said.

"No you don't," Jana said.

Daniel walked toward Brit, who sat up. Immediately the room swerved and the walls started a slow spin. She put a hand to her head.

"I got you this," he said, and lifted up the tin to reveal a multilayer vanilla cake that had fallen over, its ribbons of icing smeared all over the plate. "Oh, oops," Daniel muttered, seeing the mess.

She felt several things at once: First, she felt outrage. As though cake could make up for it, the dessert they'd never have. He probably thought he was being some kind of poet, doing this, but what he'd said, what he'd essentially said to her, was, *I don't want you, no matter what.* The cake he spent his hard-earned money on was just for him, to make himself feel better, not for her to actually take anything from him, or for him to give anything of value. Second, she felt drunk. More drunk than she had planned on being, and certainly more drunk than she'd felt in a while. She felt like something was stuck in her lungs, and she was suddenly hot and nauseated, and wanted to both move urgently and never move again. And third, she felt touched, and a tenderness for Daniel, like a wound that had worked its way into the essential tissue in the center of her heart, one she couldn't dig out if she tried the rest of her life. He was a person trying to be a great talent, flawed and self-hating, living in this perpetual state of suspended tragedy, though there was no real tragedy, and she felt sad for him, and saw also that this cake, this was what he could do.

"Thank you," Brit said, taking the plate into her hands. The only way to make a life with him in the quartet was to accept that she could not make a life with him privately. She saw now that if one thing was to continue, the other had to end. At that thought, a pang went through her chest, piercing her wish for his love. She would live above the pain. She would eat the cake.

He smiled gratefully as she took it, and sat next to her as she ate, saying nothing. She wanted to know if he knew what she was doing, accepting his shortcomings, but not asking him was part of the deal. She put the fork and the plate down on the side table, and he inched closer to her. He smelled like rosin and beer. Their legs were touching, but the electricity of the connection was draining away. Here were his legs, and here were hers, simple parts of two bodies they'd come to know more intimately than anyone else's, in more than one way.

"I'm such a failure," Daniel said in a whisper.

It wasn't exactly an apology. And what she said back to him wasn't exactly the truth: "You could never be."

Some hours later, when they'd all drunk everything in both minibars and then some, when Brit leaned over the toilet and vomited onto the picture of the small girl, when whatever emotion had been lodged in her chest came up (along with vanilla cake), she finally cried. Jana knocked lightly on the door and pushed it open. She was holding a compress.

"Henry made this for you," Jana said, climbing into the empty bathtub next to Brit. They still wore their gowns, which were showing wear, Brit's bunched up around her thighs, Jana's wrinkly and sour with sweat. When Brit retched again, Jana reached over the rim of the tub and drew Brit's hair into a low ponytail. She held it there, and Brit liked her cool hand and the compress resting on the back of her neck, but she couldn't bring herself to say it. She just cried, and the tile edges around the toilet cut into her knees. Everything smelled like whiskey and rancid sugar.

"If only you'd put your hair up like I said . . ." Jana said, and Brit cried harder. "Oh, don't cry. Don't cry. You'll feel better soon."

Through the crack Jana left in the door, Brit saw Daniel and Henry open the curtains. They had found the classical music radio station and started blasting the Elgar cello concerto. Daniel was conducting at the window, playing Barenboim's part (Brit was sure it was the Jacqueline du Pré version—she managed to whisper, "It's du Pré," to Jana), waving his hands at the black window, over the imagined city, the city of their very first failure. He was trying to show Henry something with his conducting—*No, here is where the phrase begins, no, here.* Her stomach roiled. She was the kind of ill where you regretted everything, where you made imaginary deals with anyone, any god, to feel differently. Du Pré was climbing the E-minor scale to the climax, sixteenth notes all the way up to sixth position on the A string, playing *tenuto,* slower and louder the higher she went, perhaps the most dramatic notated cadenza Brit had ever heard, and she saw Daniel conducting *largamente,* like a man, with authority, passion, despite his ridiculous eyeglasses, even though no one was following him. This was what he cared about, and he cared about it deeply. "No, here, here," he said to Henry. "Just wait for it."

But they knew she was in the bathroom, sick, and Daniel dialed up the knob on the radio, looked at his reflection in the dark window, conducting the absent cellist. Henry tried to correct him—his downbeat was a little wonky—but Daniel went on, already too far into his own fake concerto. He was trying to be great, at the expense of anything else.

Brit looked at Jana, droopy in the bathtub, her dark hair coming out of its bun. Jana was hard but loving and almost weepy herself, Brit noticed.

"They're . . . sometimes disappointing," Jana said. "But who else?"

"Don't take a bath," Brit managed to say, croaking it, an ugly sound, and immediately after she said it—Jana laughing but noting the arch of Brit's back and anticipating her purge, changing her body just so to feel the strain of Brit's spine under her hand, and Daniel and Henry in their own separate concerts, one stone and one liquid, one earthly and one slipped through fingers, one breathless and one like breath, and du Pré hitting the highest E possible, gasping, there was no more string left, no more fingerboard—Brit leaned forward on her hands and knees and threw it all up, her primal sound like the beginning of something awful and essential, everything she had.

PART 2

"Prussian" String Quartet no. 21
in D Major, K. 575
—Wolfgang Amadeus Mozart

String Quartet in F Major
—Maurice Ravel

String Quartet no. 3
in F Major, op. 73
—Dmitri Shostakovich

August 1998
New York City

HENRY

Viola

When Kimiko told Henry she was pregnant, she did it loudly in a generic coffee shop in the Fifties they had never been to before and would never go to again, and followed the news with the information that she'd had two previous abortions, and what did he want to do about it?

Henry looked around the café, panicked. They were close enough to Juilliard that they could have seen colleagues, but Henry saw none. It was one thing to sleep with your student, and another entirely for her to be pregnant. He wasn't sure how his colleagues would classify the situation, her having confessed pregnancy and abortion to him in the same breath. It couldn't be good.

Kimiko fiddled with the straw in her iced coffee. Coffee? Henry thought. It seemed the decision had already been made. She looked calm, placid, but she always did, even when she was tasked with playing the infamously exhausting Britten Violin Concerto, which she'd just performed with the symphony. She never made anything look as difficult as it was. He liked that about her. Wait: Had she been pregnant when she performed it? How did these things work? When was that? He tried to spy her belly beneath her flowy dress, but he couldn't. The air-conditioning in the coffee shop suddenly produced goose bumps on his arm. His beard itched all over. Why did he have a beard in August? *I'm an idiot,* he thought.

"What do you want to do?" Henry finally asked. "How long have you known?"

Kimiko shrugged. "I was feeling sick during the Britten rehearsals, but I thought it was just, you know, nerves. I haven't been to the doctor yet. Maybe just a month?"

She didn't answer the first question. She flicked water drops from the straw onto the table, where they hovered like tears before popping. She was Henry's student, yes, but she wasn't so much younger than him, and she wasn't *really* his student. Part of the quartet's responsibilities as Juilliard's Quartet-in-Residence was to take on a few advanced undergraduates, and Kimiko was his best, the best he'd ever have, he thought. They mostly just spent lessons knocking around their favorite sonatas and concertos, and then after the lessons: dinner, bars, dancing, excellent sex. Not exactly against the rules, but certainly not encouraged.

"You've had—*two* abortions?" Henry said in a whisper.

She frowned at him. "Well, don't act like it's the worst thing in the world."

"I'm sorry. I just . . . I don't know what to say, Kim," he said. "What do you want me to say?"

She shrugged.

Henry made them leave the coffee shop and walk to Central Park. It was sticky hot outside, a Friday afternoon, and the city was emptied out. Crossing the street, he took her hand. Suddenly she had a fragile sheen, and he felt a quiver down to his core looking at her, like when he watched a doctor draw blood from his arm, the body's biological mechanisms laid suddenly, brazenly naked. No magic—just animal. He had to fight the urge to screw his eyes shut and breathe. His hand was clammy. Or maybe hers was.

"I'm twenty-two," she said when they walked north into the park. He hoped the trees would be a respite from the heat.

"I know," he said.

"Do you? Because don't forget you're already way into it, your career. I'm barely there."

"You just played the Britten with the symphony."

"You know what I mean. Not everyone's like you. Not everyone's a prodigy."

Henry hated that word, ever since the *San Francisco Chronicle* had done a lifestyle piece on him when he was fourteen, pimply and floppy-haired, premiering a commissioned work with the Napa Symphony. He'd been taken out of school, homeschooled by his mother—his mother, she'd probably be over the moon at this baby news—sent to Curtis years younger than everyone else, and never learned to drink, never had a girlfriend, not a proper one, really. He blamed, well, being a prodigy. Though could you, at twenty-four, still be called that? Was he now just a mal-socialized musician, a dysfunctional adult with rare faculties? Kimiko wasn't his girlfriend, even. They had sex and read music together (sometimes had sex in the soundproof practice rooms, but who didn't?), and that was about it. They ate, they fucked, they played, all whenever the need arose. They did none of the things Daniel and Lindsay did, like romantic trips and public fights, or Brit and her new boyfriend, like movies and museums and date nights in. Those things wouldn't have occurred to Henry. He became bored simply by conjuring the idea.

But did he love her? In the year they'd known each other, he'd never considered it. He loved her playing. He loved her thin, strong wrist and fluid bow arm, the striated muscles over her shoulder blades that pulsed when she performed in her strapless concert dress, how she played elegantly and brightly, a born soloist, but was, in person, fiercely opinionated, unsentimental, almost cold, yet in an endearing way. Now that he thought about it, she was very much like Jana. Henry could not imagine Jana and Kimiko hanging out together, though, just the two of them. He so rarely brought Kimiko around the quartet, and she so rarely wanted to come around. He and Kimiko had never, up until this point, formally discussed their relationship.

Henry swallowed. "How would it work?"

"Presumably I would gestate for nine months and then fucking push it out," Kimiko said, crossing her arms under her breasts.

They wandered under the shade of some trees, but it wasn't any cooler. It was so humid that Kimiko's long, loose dress was getting stuck to the inside of her thighs. Her family was in Japan. He'd never met them. She had been educated upstate, had no accent, flew quietly back to their Tokyo suburb once a year.

"It's just not like we have family around here who could help out," Henry said.

"Right."

"Or any money. Though I could get some money."

"Right."

"And after Esterhazy, we might move around a lot. A *lot*-lot."

"Right. I'm not an idiot. If you stay with the quartet, you'll be traveling."

"*If* I stay?"

"Everybody knows, Henry," she said. "Everybody knows you're out of their league."

Henry chose to ignore the comment. Kimiko needled him about his role in the quartet, but he chalked it up to her lack of chamber music experience. She'd been born a soloist, trained as a soloist, performed as a soloist. Chamber music was for her, like it was for many successful musicians, what she did in her spare time. It wasn't, according to her, what people with talent like Henry's did. "But I *do* do it," Henry would tell her. *Four rational people conversing,* Kimiko had derisively said to him, quoting Goethe's definition of a quartet: "four rational people conversing among themselves." Henry had found that offensive. He'd talked to Jana about it afterward. It made what they did sound so boring, as if there was anything rational about it, or conversational. Even Mozart, even Haydn wasn't teatime, parlor-room conversation. It was what he thought was most misunderstood about chamber music—that it was a kind of sense-making. For Henry, sense-making was perhaps the opposite of the point. He had fun in the chaos of four people; the chaos was what made it feel like art, like beauty.

Besides, his whole life, his talent had been leading the way, making the obvious, logical decisions for him. Choosing to stay in the quartet was not the obvious, logical decision. But for him, obvious and logical had nothing to do with real music-making.

"People move around with babies," he said. "Maybe we could trade lessons for nannying or something."

He hated the word *nanny* in his mouth, which was already parched. He talked it out some more, and minutes later he realized she had stopped responding. They were still walking, sweating. He understood her silence. No matter how much he talked it out, strategized, rationalized, there was no getting around it: they both could not have the careers they'd planned for and also have this baby. Someone would have to sacrifice the vision, settle for a lesser version of success. Ride out the other's version. It was pointless to negotiate. There was no use talking about it. He thought, fleetingly, of the card from that Fodorio character, the lurking promise of a solo career. He'd eaten the card for Jana, but the promise remained.

"When did you . . . terminate the other pregnancies?" he said, eventually.

She rolled her eyes. "You can say 'abortion,' Henry."

"When?"

"Once when I was sixteen, and once a couple years ago."

"Someone I know?"

"Why do you care? Let's talk about *this* time."

Henry couldn't think of a reason why it mattered, but he wanted to know. This bothered him. "I care."

"No one you know. A visiting cellist from Germany. He's married, has kids of his own. He wasn't even a very good player. Bad intonation. It was stupid."

"Oh, okay," he said. "This isn't stupid, right?"

She stopped walking and abruptly turned to him. Her voice was small: "It's not fair," she said. At first he thought the wetness pooled around her eyes was sweat—God, it was hot, fuck this city, he hated it—but then he saw it was coming out of her eyes, and kept coming. Her face was trembling, every part of it at once, messily, inelegantly. He'd never seen her cry before. It made him want to cry, too, and he never felt that way, and now he felt it rising in his chest and throat.

He cared. He cared about what had happened to her before he'd met her, about the babies she hadn't had. He cared what happened to her in this park, if she tripped, if she cried. He loved her, if that's what love was. They'd never been on an actual date. It was strange to sit in a coffee shop with her, to walk with her, without their instruments. But he loved her. Maybe because she was growing inside her a small pebble of a zygote half containing his DNA, maybe because she was the one for him, forever and ever. There was no telling. The choice to love her and to raise a child with her wasn't rational or sense-making, and in that way it was like the only other choice he'd ever made in his life. It was the beautiful, musical choice.

He put his arms around her, pulled her into him. She wasn't small. He wouldn't describe her that way, not now.

"No, this isn't stupid," she said, crying a country-sized stain into his T-shirt, and that was how he knew she loved him, too.

One way to say it was: when they moved to New York, Jana and Henry cut back on overnights because she lived on the East Side and he lived on the West Side, and she hated the crosstown buses and also walking across the park alone, especially with her violin, and there were so many people in their lives—so many people in New York City—that time alone became sacred and rare.

Another way to say it was: they were older, had grown up and out of it, no longer needed the physical rampancy and secret comfort of each other's bodies in bed after a blood-flushing concert or a brutal, prickly rehearsal.

Another way to say it was: the practice had marched right up to the edge of being inappropriate, and enough was enough. They'd never had sex, not even close. There'd been nothing sexually charged about their relationship. Nothing really romantic either, unless you counted that feeling of mutual recognition when someone wraps her body around yours and you both go unconscious.

And one more way to say it was: the context changed. They were no longer scrappy and trying to make it in San Francisco. Now they were "emerging," as the Juilliard intern who wrote their bios liked to put it, though Henry wondered how long you could be "emerging" until you were simply just standing in a doorway of an empty room, emerged, yet unnoticed. At Juilliard, they were treated as professionals, serious adults with serious endeavors, and their habit of co-sleeping suddenly seemed a childish leftover from a past and lesser life.

They had taken a little while to figure this out. The last time Jana had come over to Henry's, it was a night in early December, right as the season was beginning to slip into winter. The two of them, having grown up in the wet but generous winters of California, usually felt giddy and quaint huddled under layers of thin blankets. Still charming was the way the streetlamps flooded bronze light through the windows even with all the lights off, casting an anemic pallor on their cold cheeks. Still eccentric was the incessant honking and yelping, the churn of lives always in progress just outside the apartment walls. But that night they'd fought, a fight that, in their pajamas in the bed in the middle of the city, felt like a point from which they would not turn back.

That evening they'd gone, with Brit and Daniel, to a performance of the Guarneri Quartet at Carnegie Hall. They'd had to go, really—their dean regularly invited them to concerts so they could meet other groups and become familiar faces to programming officers at the various venues. Afterward, there was a party in a small, narrow cocktail bar across the street. Daniel and Jana had charged forward into the crowd, always the determined, well-spoken face of the quartet, neither from that tony world but both able to talk to moneyed patrons with a studied fluency. Henry often ran out of things to talk about with these people after they were done marveling at his youth. He noticed Brit spending an inordinately long time at the bar deciding what to drink, and when she finally had a glass of red wine in her hand, she remained staring at the rows of liquor bottles, her back to the crowd. Henry walked up beside her.

"Are you as bored—"

She jumped in her seat, tipping her glass and sending drops of red wine onto the front of his suit. "Oh, Henry," she said, dabbing at his jacket with a bar napkin. "I'm sorry. This looks expensive. Was it expensive?"

It was bespoke, but Henry hadn't paid for it. His mother had, a gift upon learning they had landed the Juilliard residency.

"It's nothing," Henry said.

Brit frowned. "It's sort of your fault, anyway."

Henry sat next to her and ordered a gin and tonic; the compact, buttoned-up bartender peered at him suspiciously but didn't card him. Brit had been in a mood lately. Really, she'd been in a mood for at least three years. Though neither Brit nor Daniel had ever explicitly spoken of it, Henry and Jana knew there'd been something early on, a romantic scuffle, a fast fizzle, and a subterranean burn as it faded away. The topic hadn't much come up during Henry and Jana's overnights, either. What was there to discuss? It had been years since whatever had once been between Daniel and Brit appeared to settle into a semi-comfortable stasis, a slightly charged status quo, with Daniel's rotation of forgettable girls (unremarkable two- or three-month relationships) and Brit's steady, low-grade longing for him (dignified in the shadows when she was waiting, and girlishly undulating when he turned his attention to her in the intermissions). Though lately something felt like it was shifting with Brit and Daniel, probably not unrelated to Brit's new boyfriend, Paul.

"I was going to say you seem quiet tonight, but not with a mouth like that," Henry said.

"Why do people always say that to me? 'You seem quiet.' What should I say back? 'Yes, that's because I don't want to talk'?"

"Okay, well," Henry said, standing.

"No, no." Brit put her hand on his arm. "Sit down. I'd rather talk to you than anyone else here."

"Oh, wow, thanks."

"I don't mean that. I just mean"—she gestured across the bar, toward where Jana and Daniel held captive a collection of miniature elderly ladies in chunky necklaces—"them."

Henry could tell, even from this distance, that Daniel's suit, the only one he had, fit even worse than the last time he'd worn it. The cuffs now revealed his wrists. Were Daniel's irregularly long arms growing longer? Was that possible? Henry saw the seams were gray from years of pulling. When was Daniel's birthday? Perhaps Henry could get him a custom suit of his own. No, he'd be resentful. Daniel kept taking off his glasses and putting them back on and taking them off. He hated wearing his glasses—he had once told Henry something about how they represented an evolutionary weakness—but he seemed to be squinting more and more these days, at things other than just sheet music. Jana, seen from afar, was all strange planes and angles. She was the sort of woman who was not exactly pretty but striking, not slender but skinny, someone who could look alarmingly different with the slight jut of a chin, a nose that could be pointed and regal in profile and unfortunately knobbed head-on, large eyes that were anime when tired but toothsome with the right smile. She was mutable even down to her dark hair, which could make her look boyish when it was tied back or halting when it lay across her shoulders. It was just like Jana to deny anyone a firm hold on her.

Brit, though, Brit always looked the same: freckles, plump skin, smile lines, pale and blond, sincere and kind, and Henry realized, sitting there, that he was grateful for her dispositional consistency.

"This is their natural habitat," Henry said. "They can be easily adored."

Once he said it, he saw it was mean, but Brit smiled a little. "Or they can *become* people who are easily adored. At these things I always feel like, when I'm talking to someone, I have to apologize for how . . . just . . . boring I am. I play the violin. What more can I say? Look, listen to Jana, you can hear her from here. That pitch is unnatural."

Jana threw her head back and laughed, a shrill laugh that Henry knew contained seething just beneath the surface. She could communicate with this crowd, but she didn't like it.

"It's not too bad," Henry said. "At least we have them to do it for us."

"They're not doing it for *us*," Brit said.

"Whoa, settle," Henry said. "Do you have something you want to tell Uncle Henry? What about this new Paul fellow?"

Brit softened and told him about Paul, how she could tell he cleaned his apartment before she came over, how she'd found a scribbled list of things from his day he wanted to make sure to tell her on his bedside table, how whenever she asked him a question he always asked her one back.

"Sounds like a good one," Henry said when she finished. "So why are you so angry right now?"

"I'm not angry," she said.

"Is it because you're angry at yourself for spending so much time pining for that guy? That guy in the bad suit over there?"

Brit went silent, though she leaned her head into his shoulder, drank her wine at the side of her mouth. From behind, from Jana's point of view, it must have looked like something else, at least fleetingly, because after the brief moments during which Henry felt tenderness for Brit's blond head beneath his but before he could say anything more, Jana was there, behind him, her hand in his hair. His hair!

"You both need haircuts," Jana said, and Brit withdrew.

Jana was scratching his scalp with her fingernails, sending white shivers down his neck, and the way the response was both automatic and charged irritated him. Now he linked the touch to Kimiko's touch: a different woman, a different context, a different impulse. The point where the wires crossed was buzzing electric, and it stayed lit inside him all night. Later that night, in bed, after Jana scooted toward him, cold under the quilt, he said, "Don't do that again, to my hair."

Jana paused. A siren wailed by. "I was just saying you need a haircut. I mean, seriously, you do. There's a public face we have to maintain."

"People could get the wrong idea," he said.

"What, with Brit nuzzling you in a bar? Sure."

They volleyed back and forth a few times, their barbs getting hollower as they got meaner. This kind of meanness was meant for people having sex, people who could later expunge the meanness in the half-tender, half-violent act of merging.

"Aren't you sleeping with anyone?" he said. "You know I'm sleeping with Kimiko, right?"

Of course she knew. Henry knew she knew. He also knew Jana had no intention of having a sexual relationship with him, and that his accusation was low and undermined years of tangled but necessary friendship—and that once he'd made it, the nights together were over. The dark room momentarily choked on itself. He actually coughed.

Jana rolled over, her back to him. "You're right. I don't think I should spend the night here anymore." And with that, she made it his idea and her decision.

She fell asleep fast and easy—when Jana made a decision, she did not unmake it—and Henry lay awake most of the night. It was the right thing to do, for both of them, so why did it feel bad? There was life, right out there, sirens and clanking bottles and the crazy bellowing man in the building across the way. It couldn't be more different from their life in San Francisco, all sky and studiousness and sea splash. Couldn't she also see things were changing—had, in fact, already changed?

The next morning, he awoke to Jana fully dressed (she'd smartly brought a change of clothes, black leggings and a black tunic, now cold and almost Slavic at this angle) and tiptoeing around his chilly room. What she looked like wasn't slippery at all, he saw now. Her face was serious, the aquiline nose and the whittled jawline, but really, it was the face of a girl trying out expressions and postures, its origin withheld from him now. He watched her gathering her things but also lightly grazing his things with her fingertips, his clothes and his dresser and his records stacked on the floor, feeling for what he couldn't say, feeling the varnish on his viola, the tips of the metal music stand in the corner, the molding around the doorway—Henry watched her know with her hands the stuff of his life, and then thought to himself, *This stuff isn't my life, my life's out there,* and he realized that his context had changed, but Jana's hadn't.

So it was very unexpected when on the evening after he and Kimiko had walked in the park for hours, and he'd watched her dry-heave by the closed-down ice rink and thought, stupidly, *My child is causing this,* Jana called him and said she was coming over. Before he could ask whether "coming over" meant "staying the night," she'd hung up.

Henry felt panicked. Jana knew he and Kimiko had been spending more time together. It wasn't a secret. But he'd have to tell her about the baby, and he'd have to tell her now. Fathers of unborn children didn't share beds with other women, even if they were just friends.

Jana arrived at his door, sweaty, just after sunset. She'd jogged to his place, though the heat index must have made it an unhealthy endeavor. Henry had never known her not to run. She was the type who couldn't sleep without it, who made sure their hotels had gyms and treadmills when they were on the road. She wore blue dolphin shorts and a tank top that was soaked through. He let her in, and she kicked her shoes off by the window unit and stood there, pulling the fabric from her stomach to let the cool air in.

"I have to stay the night" was the first thing she said. "I can't go back out in that."

Henry gestured to the window and 102nd Street below, heavy with heat and quiet but for a few sedans. "You're the fool that chose to run in this."

"Actually, the best time to run—when everyone's gone to the Hamptons," she said. Sweat trickled down the back of her leg. She looked up at him and grinned. "You're the one with the facial hair. What?"

"What, what?"

She shrugged. "I don't know, you're acting strange. Did you get a prize or something?"

Henry laughed. "No, I was just . . . standing here. Trying to think of what to eat."

"Good thing I'm an expert at eating."

Jana rifled through his fridge with a familiarity that bent Henry's heart a little. She was his sister. She found some lettuce and bacon and tortillas, and made them something close to a BLT. While she cooked the bacon, they both sat on the floor by the window unit to stay cool. They ate on the floor, too, with an old ottoman as their table. Jana's sweat had dried and she had started to smell like girl sweat, like two-day-old perfume.

"Doesn't the heat warp your records?" Jana asked, pointing toward the milk crates of records against the wall.

"Oh, I put all the nice ones in storage in Queens," he said. It was one of the first things he'd done when he moved to New York. He'd paid to ship his records out here, before he realized how insane it looked to have them lining all the walls of his small apartment. But he couldn't let go of them. He'd been collecting since he was a child: the rare recording of the Hoffmeister viola concerto, every major recording of the Bach suites, even obscure limited pressings of contemporary Chinese composers he'd once wanted to emulate. Getting rid of his records would be like saying all those years spent gathering them were over. And they weren't over—he was still in the midst of them.

"Well, that seems impractical," Jana said. "You should just sell them."

"I can't sell them. Why would I sell them?"

"Because if they're in storage, you're obviously not listening to them."

"But I could. If I wanted to. Jesus, Jana."

She raised an armpit, a bit of bacon hanging out of her mouth, and sniffed. "Are you offended?" She looked genuinely worried.

"No, no."

"What's wrong with you? Are you worried about Esterhazy?"

For a moment Henry didn't recognize the word. He hadn't thought about the upcoming competition all day. He'd thought about traveling, and leaving Kimiko, but he hadn't actually thought about what they were rehearsing for Esterhazy—a Shostakovich, a Mozart, and the Ravel they knew so well. It would be their second time at the competition, having made the smallest of splashes—like a hand slapping a pond, really—their first time, earning no prizes, but falling apart in the first round to the point of crashing the entire performance. It had taken them some months to recover from that, but by winter they'd gained management and the residency at Juilliard. This year was the year they were supposed to be in the Esterhazy game, for real. The board had changed the competition a bit—not only did they move it from May to

October, but they pre-scored and seeded competitors, so that any incidences of extreme stage fright or freak accidents wouldn't be weighted as heavily.

"Oh, I basically forgot about that," he said.

"Mm."

Behind Jana's head, if Henry squinted and focused, he could see a wedge of the Hudson.

"Are you seeing anyone?" he asked.

She pointed to her mouth and chewed. "Who has time?"

"Well, Brit and Daniel," he said.

"Yeah, but, they're more, you know, into that kind of thing than us," Jana said, and laughed. "I guess that guy from the St. Vincent asked me out, but . . . I don't know."

"The violist?"

A few weeks before, they'd played in a classical showcase and met the St. Vincent String Quartet. The two quartets shared a management company as well as career aspirations. The St. Vincents were from Montreal, all men, pretty and tall and sandy-haired, with varying shades of French accents. From far away, they looked more like attractive actors pretending to be in a quartet than actual musicians. Henry had found them difficult to tell apart. Of the eight groups they'd be competing against at Esterhazy, the St. Vincent was the best, though not better than them, at least by Jana's estimation.

"Yeah. Laurent."

"I can't believe that's actually his name."

"I know, I know."

"You should go out with him," Henry said.

Jana frowned. "What's wrong with you? You think I should date someone we're going to compete against in two months?"

"Who cares?"

She put her sandwich down on her paper plate. "You need to get ahold of yourself."

"Kimiko's pregnant."

He said it because he couldn't not say it. He'd spent the whole afternoon saying it in his head, making it feel real. And now that it was real, not letting Jana hear him say it felt like lying. Especially Jana, someone to whom he never lied.

Jana's sandwich sat on the plate on top of the ottoman like something from a different life, like an idea from a finished phase of their friendship they'd yet to mourn. The lettuce seemed to wilt immediately. Her mouth hung open, revealing a couple cavities filled with metal, and Henry could see her—see her in real time—scramble to think of a way out of this information.

"We're going to keep it," he continued, and Jana's grimace deepened. He regretted saying that part.

Her hair was falling out of her ponytail in the back, wisps here and there. He wanted to put his arms around her, and would have, in that other life, that sandwich life.

"Okay," she said. "All right. She's practically a child herself, but all right."

Henry didn't say anything.

Jana asked a series of questions and then answered them herself. She said: "I mean, if you want to be a father at twenty-four, go right ahead. When's she due? We'll have to make sure we're not traveling then. She's going to live here? Here? You should probably get a dinner table. You should probably get a different apartment, actually. One with, you know, walls. Dividing the space. Won't you need some more income? I guess it's not like your parents won't help you out. Also, you won't have time for video games. You don't have time now, as it is, but somehow you always make time."

He patiently listened to her list, the halfhearted insults tumbling out of her mouth. Henry didn't think Jana was a mean person; he thought she was a good person, with a meanness problem. And he thought, in general, she had good reason to be mean. She'd worked very hard. She'd had no help. She wasn't tolerant of failure. Of anyone's failure. But couldn't she see he wasn't failing her?

Jana stood and began to pace. The wicking fabric of her shorts rubbing together was the only sound in the apartment.

It occurred to him: he loved her, too.

In a different way from how he loved Kimiko. But love, nonetheless. They'd had no choice, if he thought about it. They'd been together so long, so intimately, that they had to love each other. Like family—which neither Jana nor Brit had. Nor Daniel, come to think of it. Henry was the one with a family. And now another one growing. He had an embarrassing abundance of family.

Henry did understand how they had become responsible for each other's well-being, each other's livelihood. When you were on your own, in whatever career, whatever you did affected only your own job. But with the quartet, they had to share a goal, distribute the dream between them, and trust that each of them had an appropriate sense of commitment. The commitment had a way of bleeding into their lives off stage, as well. There were so many ways to betray each other.

Jana stood with her hands on her hips in front of the window. The sun was all the way down now, but it still cast pale on the sky from below the horizon. Looking at her silhouette, Henry imagined how her upper body moved as one whole unit when she led the group. Like a baton, that firmness at her center the very source of energy for all of them.

Then she turned and faced an old program he'd tacked onto the wall next to the window. It wasn't framed or anything, but he'd felt weird throwing it away, so he put it there, where it curled up at the edges in the humidity. It was the program from their graduation recital, which he'd been handed just before they walked on stage. There was a photo of the four of them printed in black-and-white on the insert—they'd had it taken professionally, but until that graduation recital hadn't seen it out in the world. The photo, their first portrait as a group, had been taken on a cold day in February, and they'd been frustrated and restless. They were actually waiting for the light to change on Van Ness and McAllister so they could span the crosswalk, Beatles style, and Daniel was holding his cello by the curves, trying to shield it from other pedestrians. City Hall and the Ballet loomed in the background. In the photo, none of them was smiling, but they'd liked that shot the best. Something about the quiet waiting, the way they looked like they'd ended up crammed together on this sidewalk accidentally but were all of a piece, made them choose that picture over the posed one, where they were actually crossing the intersection, smiling awkwardly and looking at odds with their bodies. After the light changed, Daniel had rushed from the sidewalk, and when the rest of them failed to fall in line, he screamed "Fuck!" and a small child holding her mother's hand cowered. But before the light turned, they looked like they'd made a kind of peace with the restlessness, or had finally caught up with the anticipation.

The night of the graduation wasn't just the first time Henry had seen that picture in print, but the first time he'd seen them as a group presented so formally. It felt official. He had felt a part of something, which, though no one would feel sorry for him, hadn't come easily in his life. When you were a prodigy, the defining principle was that you were singular, standout, alone. Here, he was not alone.

He watched Jana study the program and the photo on his apartment wall, in which he—barely twenty then—towered over everyone else, his cheekbones sharp and his hair looking less messy than it was in black-and-white.

"I think you need to cut your hair and shave your beard," she said, finally.

He put his hand to his chin, felt the rough fuzz there. "Yeah, all right."

They walked to the bathroom, humorously small, and plugged in his clipper. The mirror was splattered with toothpaste, the sink a well for his beard trimmings. Jana reached down and splashed her face with water from the faucet.

"Okay," she said when she popped back up.

"Okay," he said.

She started with his hair, sliding pieces between two fingers and trimming a little at a time. She worked around the sides and then methodically across the top. She shaved his face meticulously, seriously, knitting her eyebrows when it came to his upper lip, tilting her head at an unnatural angle to get under his chin. It seemed to take forever, certainly longer than he'd ever taken to shave himself. He'd had a beard since they moved to New York. At first he'd grown it because it was cold, but then it got warm, and then he was afraid to shave it off, as though he'd have a blank space where his beard was. Which he would now, he guessed.

Jana took it all off. She didn't cut him once. He looked younger when it was all gone—he actually looked his age. There was his mouth. There were his lips. He couldn't stop staring at himself. Jana didn't look in the mirror once, but she looked at him directly, and over time, her gaze changed from jilted to kind, and then content, or something close.

She did stay the night one last time. They went to bed early, and she wore one of his big T-shirts from Curtis, identical to a shirt she also had, in her own apartment across town.

"It'll make you leave us," Jana said.

She didn't seem to require an answer. It wasn't a question. Who knew where this ended? Not him. What he heard in Jana's statement was not an accusation or a confrontation, but a confession: she saw this as the beginning of the quartet's falling apart.

She turned on her side, away from him, and put her hands neatly under her head. He mirrored her. The streets below were eerily city-quiet, a spatter of pedestrian laughter or old brakes floating up to his window every so often, the desperate shudder of the window unit turning off and on. They slept with only a sheet on top of them, and Henry felt the pillowcase against his shorn cheek for the first time in he didn't know how long. It felt like there was nothing between him and anything else. Jana suddenly seemed like a strange island in his bed, long-limbed and lanky and warm, emanating heat. How had he not seen her like this before? He curled himself around her anyway, and didn't move, not at all.

When she left the next morning, early and silently, he went back to bed to sleep for a few more hours. Just as he was about to fall asleep, however, the phone rang in the kitchen. On instinct he rolled over and reached for a pillow to cover his ears, but then he remembered he was now an expectant father, and that expectant fathers answered all phone calls out of fear. He tripped his way to the phone, but when he picked it up and said hello, it wasn't Kimiko calling, or even Jana, to tell him she'd made it home, or Daniel asking to borrow rosin again, or Brit seeing if he wanted to get lunch.

"You haven't called, and you've been in New York all this time!" said the man on the other end, his voice thick with a familiar accent.

"Hello?" Henry said again.

"I've been waiting. To make something of you. Let's meet. Tonight? Something's come up that you'd be perfect for."

"I'm sorry, who is this?"

"Don't be ridiculous. It's me," said the man, as though Henry was foolish to question his identity. "It's your old friend, Fodorio."

DANIEL

Cello

Daniel married Lindsay quickly and also on the condition that they would approach marriage nontraditionally. "Let's not be married like everyone else. Let's be married like us," Lindsay had said. She'd been naked when she said it, which made Daniel more amenable to the whole thing. They both came from families with parents whose marriages had failed in one way or another. Daniel's parents seemed to be resigned to a husk of a marriage, a sloppy financial partnership that resembled a marriage, their union undergoing decades of hardship, food stamps, tag sales, and public housing, leaving them two people stranded ashore, with only Daniel and his older brother as common threads. Lindsay's father was an enigma, a man living illegally in a knockoff Airstream in California with a woman younger than Lindsay, and her mother insisted on being more of a friend than a mother, making calculated life mistakes to repeatedly necessitate Lindsay's girlfriend-like advice and care. She often took the train from Boston to the city to sleep on Daniel and Lindsay's futon, "for a change of scenery," she said. It was because all their parents were such complete failures at the entire marital endeavor that Daniel and Lindsay got it in their heads to get married on a whim—partly in spite, and partly in the young hope that if they did it differently, maybe it would work. Mostly spite, Daniel thought now, remembering smugly how his mother had simply changed the subject—talked about adding chips to casseroles—when he'd told her they'd gotten married.

The other reason was that Daniel thought he could hitch his wagon to some of Lindsay's free-ness, not realizing that the quality of being free resisted the very idea of hitching, of attaching.

They'd taken an impromptu vacation to Costa Rica for Christmas a few months after they met, both bemoaning the idea of miserably going home to their families. The trip was paid for by a short series of catering gigs that Daniel kept secret from the rest of the group and his students, the money from which he was trying to save to have something to fall back on. But Lindsay said that money was for trips, and that they should fall back on the money now. Lindsay was petite, and tanned year-round, and had light brown hair that always had streaks of sun blond in it, as though she was perpetually blessed by good weather. She had an aggressively sunny spirit about her, too, that Daniel was at first exhausted by and then utterly addicted to. In Costa Rica, she wore the tiniest of rainbow-patterned string bikinis, purchased at a stand outside the airport—and sometimes only the bottom of the bikini at that. She didn't care about any sort of trouble long-term, not enough to be bothered in a permanent way, but she cared intensely about everything that was right in front of her. She'd seen a coati in the street outside their hotel and wept, chased it down, touched the dirty animal like it was holy. Daniel thought it too closely resembled a raccoon with a long rat's tail.

Lindsay was a social practice artist (for months Daniel didn't quite know what that meant) with a day job as an assistant fabricator for a woman who made mosaics in SoHo. Lindsay never made any money.

She'd played the oboe until college, which Daniel never told Brit or Jana or Henry because they'd never stop teasing him—all those reeds, the spit, the honking sound.

On their last morning in Costa Rica, two days into 1998, they'd woken from a stupor and immediately gotten high, Lindsay still not wearing anything, tossing herself around the small room like an early human, clothes unknown to her. She had an Orion's belt of moles beneath her right breast. Daniel was lying on the bed watching the ceiling fan whir, fighting the panic-turned-malaise that rushed in whenever he thought about going back to New York. He did not know yet that he was deeply unhappy there.

Then Lindsay brought up marriage, standing in front of the open window with its sheer curtains blowing in the humid breeze, a joint sizzling in her right hand, her left hand on her bare hip, one leg crossed over the other, partially hiding her illicit strip of pubic fuzz, her stance reminding Daniel of a magazine picture of Cindy Crawford, the first that had ever turned him on, the way she looked surprised to be caught half clothed, but also welcoming, as though she were saying, *Hey you, come join me in this crazy, pants-optional land.*

"We should get married when we get back. But let's not be married like everyone else. Let's be married like us."

Lindsay had a body like a photographer's subject—a torso the shape of a robust viola, down to the gentle s-curves around her abdomen, small, happy oranges for breasts—everything in its proper place, at once sexual and nonsexual in its naturalness. There was something untamed about her body, something mesmerizing about the way it switched from childlike to sirenlike and back again. She was the most unpredictable being he'd ever met.

"Everyone would think we were so careless," Daniel said, propping himself up on his elbows, but he was grinning wickedly when he said it, and so was she.

Why did Daniel marry Lindsay? Because she didn't ask anything of him. Because she didn't care that he was poor. Because she liked to position herself against whatever was supposed to be. Because her body wanted to be free. Because she wouldn't require anything of anything; her nature was to react, to take in, to tumble wildly back out.

On the way to his apartment from JFK, they stopped by the City Clerk's Office and applied for a marriage license. The next evening, they showed up again—this time with Henry as a witness—and married each other, suddenly mortally serious when they were fed the standard vows. Daniel wore his concert suit and she wore a white leather dress. She was the sort of girl who had one of those lying around.

Henry was a good sport about it, and brought Kimiko out to the Irish pub where Daniel and Lindsay celebrated afterward. It wasn't until rehearsal two days later that he had to face Brit and Jana about it. Jana eyed the ring he'd placed on his right hand, his bow-arm hand, and rolled her eyes. "Okay, congratulations or whatever," she'd said.

Brit was decidedly chillier. "Is there no waiting period for that?"

Lindsay and Brit had never actually had a conversation, not that Daniel had seen anyway. But Daniel and Lindsay hadn't been together that long, and he and Brit didn't have much occasion to hang out socially now. New York wasn't like San Francisco, where their quartet life segued into a social life. With Juilliard and the upcoming Esterhazy competition, the obligation was deeper and more serious, and somehow that had an inverse effect on their friendship, requiring it to be somewhat shallower. The city itself was also a part of the diffusion. With so much more to manage—their expensive apartments and their complicated transportation and the never-ending crowds—it was easier not to see each other. He saw it happening with Brit, when she began to bring Paul around, a hedge fund manager whom Daniel found insufferably boring but Brit seemed to love. She said it all the time—"Love to you"—before hanging up their studio office phone after practice. Paul was nice, Daniel supposed. And that was what Brit had always appeared to want: someone hungry for her to say she loved him.

And now, not one year into his marriage—he cringed at that word, so stodgy and foreign still—he and Lindsay had stopped saying "I love you" to each other almost entirely. Or at least they didn't say it when it wasn't an insult.

Daniel thought maybe it was the August heat and their lack of an air conditioner (Lindsay said it was bad for the environment; they couldn't afford one, anyway), but Lindsay seemed angrier than ever. The night before, she'd stood precariously on the couch in her underwear, tripping on the cushions, sloshing a glass of white wine in her hand, crying, angry at him for something he couldn't remember, repeating, "I *love* you. I *love* you and this is how you treat me." What did she love? Who was he? He wished she'd put some shorts on before fighting.

So now Daniel was taking her to dinner at a place they could not afford—Daniel could not afford—in Tribeca. Lindsay seemed pleased, and though Daniel wanted to remember what he had done to her to make her so mad, he mostly didn't want to bring it up. She slipped between emotions so easily, a pretty little eel. Sometimes he just watched it happen, bewildered.

"This place has zucchini foam," Lindsay said, pointing to the stiff menu in her hand. She laughed. "We should order that."

After they ordered, she leaned down over the table, her shirt falling off one shoulder. No bra. She barely ever wore underwear. When they'd first fooled around, she scooted out of her jeans and he was utterly shocked to find she wasn't wearing anything beneath them. He had a flash of the first time he and Brit had gone to bed together, how he'd made fun of the sweetness of her blue cotton underwear with worn-away white music notes on the rear, and she'd been completely unembarrassed. He liked that she wasn't embarrassed. It made *him* embarrassed, suddenly a witness to this whole private life someone had of choosing which underwear to buy, and when to wear it, and whether or not to take it off.

"I replied to a call for a muralist in this neighborhood," Lindsay said. "Inside a loft somewhere. They want their wife's name splashed across the original brick interior. Isn't that nice?"

"You do murals?" Daniel said.

She shrugged and her shirt fell further down her shoulder. "I can. I've done them before."

"Oh," he said. "Yeah, that's nice, I guess. It would be weird to have your own name on a wall in your apartment, though, don't you think? Like, it's *your* apartment already."

"Mmm . . . I don't know. It could be done right."

"Are you going to take the job?"

"I haven't been offered it yet. Were you listening?"

"Okay, well, if you're offered it, would you take it?"

"Duh. I need the money. We need the money."

There was a sweltering silence where neither said anything about the $28 price tag that came with the zucchini foam appetizer. He didn't say it seemed like they should pay less if they were just getting the foam of something. Lately she'd become more impatient about his inability to pay for a lifestyle upgrade, though he'd never been unclear about that. If Daniel didn't have the quartet, he had nothing, and even with the quartet, he had only a little. Their marriage wasn't doing his wallet any favors.

She went on about a project she was thinking of proposing, an idea for an installation in a corner park in the Village, a motorized swing that was lit up all night long and traced the pattern of constellations across a mirror buried in the dirt below. So people could ride it and look below their feet and see the disappearing patterns of stars. It would be expensive and she'd never make it, Daniel knew. But he liked to listen to her talk about it, to her ideas. Lindsay was, if nothing else (and there was a lot else, if he was being fair), endlessly sweet. Sweetly optimistic. Optimistically generous. Everything he wasn't.

And she was smart, too. Though lately that intelligence seemed submerged in her turbulent moods, intermittently visible like a dinghy in a stormy sea.

"What are you working on?" she asked. "How's the Shostakovich going? I love that piece."

The quartet was readying the Shostakovich Quartet no. 3 for the Esterhazy competition in a couple of months. They would also play the Ravel and a late Mozart Köchel, but the Shostakovich was the one they'd never performed before.

Their food came. Daniel had rehearsal in the morning. "Oh, it's better. It's good. It's depressing, you know, to work on that piece sometimes."

"Since when do you play anything not depressing?" Lindsay asked. She immediately had green foam on the corners of her mouth. He felt irritation bubbling in his throat.

"We play lots of things that aren't depressing," he said. "The act of making music is not depressing."

She rolled her eyes. "You don't have to be such a doctor about it."

"What do you mean?"

"Clinical. You're always so clinical. Like I'm asking you to look something up in the dictionary and tell me about it. I could do that."

"It's just what I think."

She slapped her fork down on the plate and it clattered loudly. "But what you think isn't fact, Daniel. Also, how about what you feel?"

"I feel like when I play music it's generally not depressing."

He knew he was goading her. All he had to do was yield just a little, admit the gray area, that something was unknown to him, and she would soften. But now she was swinging.

Lindsay said, "That's probably why you guys don't ever win at Esterhazy."

"Excuse me?"

"Art has to be sort of hopeless sometimes, I think, to be good. That's what I think."

"We've only competed once. And we knew we weren't going to win anything that time."

"So what, now you think you deserve it? You don't win by deserving it."

"The greatest players are the most joyful," he said, though as it was coming out of his mouth, he knew it wasn't true. He thought of Brit, kind and melancholy.

"Okay, Daniel, whatever."

"You know for that installation, people won't be able to see the traces of light in the mirror under the dirt. Not under the dirt. Even if it wears away from people's feet. Mirrors don't work that way."

Lindsay held up her left palm, where she had a blurry image of an eye tattooed across her life line. She'd told him she didn't remember getting it, that when she was nineteen she'd gone to a party with Jell-O shots and she loved Jell-O so much and when she woke up, her palm was bleeding, and a few days later she realized she could blink the eye by contracting her hand. She never ate Jell-O again. Lately she'd been holding her eye-palm up to him as a way of indicating she saw something he couldn't.

"That's kind of the point, dummy," she said.

"And also," he said, "the mirror would break after the first person jumped off. Bad luck."

They ate the rest of the meal in a protracted silence that seemed to deepen with each bite.

Finally, after the waiter cleared their plates, Lindsay said, "Oh, I forgot to say that your mother called today. She told me to tell you she's praying for us."

Daniel had been a late starter, ten years old when he first took a cello lesson, but he still couldn't remember why he'd started. His mother told the story that he'd seen an orchestra on a PBS show she and his father were watching and had said, as though struck by a divine idea, "I want to do that." This seemed unlikely to Daniel, not only because he'd never been inspired by an orchestra playing, but also because he didn't recall his parents ever watching TV together. Sure, separately: his mother watching daytime soaps once his father had gone to the construction site, his father watching Westerns at night until he fell into a liquored sleep in the recliner chair. Daniel's bedroom was between the living room and his parents' bedroom, and the mumbled, distorted sounds of the television joined up with muted noises of his mother turning and turning in bed, the closest his parents ever were at night.

It was around the same time, when he started playing cello, that his mother found Jesus. He knew this because he clearly remembered his mother telling him one night as she put him to bed that Jesus had come to her in a vision and that he'd let her know they wouldn't have to worry about money anymore, and that she hoped one day Daniel would also accept Jesus into his heart. He had gone to his cello lesson the next day and told his teacher, excitedly, that Jesus was waiting to be accepted by Daniel's heart.

"You could work on accepting these études into your heart," his teacher said, with a stern look and a slight frown.

Daniel felt embarrassed that he'd been so excited about Jesus, especially as his teacher's only scholarship student, already at a disadvantage. And now Jesus. It was the last time he let himself be excited by something he couldn't see or hear or touch.

After her vision, his mother was distinctly different. Everything good that happened seemed to be extra good for her, because it was evidence of God. She made Daniel attend church with her on Sundays until he joined an orchestra that rehearsed at the same time. His parents continued to fight about money, as his mother poured what Daniel's father called his "sweat-cured money" into the church collection plate. But Daniel's mother seemed less bothered by the fighting, calm in her conviction.

She said of Daniel's cello playing, "What a gift God has given you," and he thought it strange she didn't say what a gift *Daniel* was to her.

Once at dinner (hamburger meat mixed into box macaroni and cheese), he asked why Jesus hadn't come to help them pay his private lesson bill on time, and his mother reached over and held her hand out as if to slap him, but instead slapped her hand down on the plastic table, shuddering the glasses and sending the silverware skittering across the surface.

"That's an act of grace right there," his father had said.

Daniel didn't like thinking of his talent as being given to him. He worked hard and studiously, even when the other orchestra players found out that his tuition had been waived. His father begrudgingly worked off the lesson payments they couldn't make, with handiwork around his teacher's home. His father didn't like things that reminded him of his status in life, and trading his meager construction skills for his younger son's lessons in something sissy like the cello was doubly embarrassing.

Daniel's older brother, Peter, was out of the house by the time Jesus entered it, and Peter quickly surpassed their father, becoming a managing contractor in Dallas with his own rational, law-abiding, middle-class family. They were the normal kind of churchgoers, not rabid like his mother. At least when Peter came home, his father had someone to talk to.

As an adult, Daniel understood his mother's conversion to evangelical Christianity as simply the only thing big enough and mysterious enough to fill the vacuum left by the absolute failure of her marriage and life. But as a child, he'd been deeply unsettled by it, how his mother could go from being unexcitable one day to being thoroughly and eternally pleased by things, and pleased by her pleased-ness. She became more zealous in her faith as she aged. He supposed that as her children grew up, the hole got bigger, and her faith expanded to fill it. Undeterred by worry for her, Daniel moved out of their house when he went to Rice University, to a vermin-infested apartment near campus. Though his school was only a twenty-minute drive from his parents' house, it felt like a whole universe away. He'd chosen Rice so he could keep studying with his teacher, who was kind of famous in classical music circles. The school's music department was renowned, and he fit in, and his days were finally filled only with music.

When Daniel went home for Sunday dinners, his mother made the best pot roast and meatloaf and pasta salad. His father tended to his drinking, named it a hobby when Peter gave him a beer-brewing kit for

Christmas. He developed a back problem and a kidney problem and a prostate problem. He was yellowing and his mother was thriving.

What Daniel wouldn't admit was that he wanted to prove his mother wrong. He wanted to see her recognize a crack in her faith, that it wasn't a salve for life's problems. He wanted to show her that you could rise above your situation without the help of Jesus. He wanted to show her that it wasn't miracles that made people amazing, but hard work. He thought maybe he stayed in Houston so long after graduation, working in the music department and continuing to take lessons, because, in addition to being unable to abandon his parents as Peter had done, he was waiting for a way to prove his mother wrong. His mother held fast, and Daniel's life continued to be neither particularly blessed nor unblessed. He was a good player, his teacher repeatedly told him he had promise (promise, like a curse: *You're good but you could be great*), and the best years of his twenties slipped right through his fingers. He spent year after year filing music for the school during the day, taking lessons at night, playing gigs on weekends, and feeling increasingly insecure about his ascending age—until finally, in a fit that twisted one defiance into another, he decided to go somewhere else, try something else. He was too old to cut it as a solo artist, had spent too much time obsessively honing skill and not enough honing flair. But he could still try to make it as a chamber musician.

Before he left for San Francisco, he took his parents out to dinner at a sushi restaurant in Rice Village he knew they wouldn't like.

"Ma," he said, using a name for her he hadn't used since high school. "I don't think I'm ever going to become a Christian."

His father raised his eyebrows and stopped chewing, ordered a sake.

His mother, unfazed, used the diminutive: "Danny, I wish you would. You would be so much happier."

"I'm happy," he said. "And anyway, happy's not the whole point."

Her smile was placid. "All right, honey."

"What's the point, then?" his father asked, suddenly interested.

"*Free* is the point."

His parents stared at him blankly. "What do you want to be free from?" his mother asked.

Daniel couldn't say. He could say, actually: Free from you. Free from a belief system that says, paradoxically, that you can do anything you pray for and also have a predetermined destiny. Free from this sweltering non-city city and mid-level expectations and the dingy plywood walls built by their economic mistakes.

"*Success* is also the point," Daniel said. "You get one with the other."

He wasn't sure which came first, and no one asked.

"Perhaps you do," she said. "But you're not really experiencing life if you're doing that. You're not in the marrow of it."

He had never heard his mother say "marrow" before. Where had she learned to talk this way? Church, he guessed.

"Sure I am," he said.

But as they ate and talked of other things, he began to feel sick in the pit of his stomach. The eel, he thought, but later that night, lying in his dismantled bedroom among boxes of records and sheet music, he let the feeling that his mother was right sneak through a fissure in his defiant constitution. He thought of all the good things that had happened to him—his talent that he slowly perfected, his girlfriends whom he had learned to love to varying degrees, his decent looks and crystalline health record—but as he considered them, he cast himself simply as an excellent witness, a bemused journalist taking notes on his life, jotting everything down, trying to make it add up.

So when his mother said she prayed for him, which she did at the end of every phone conversation, he experienced a surge of anger. She thought she was freer than him, and so did he.

Daniel and Lindsay walked home from dinner, all the way uptown, holding hands and sweating in the dark heat (*At least we're saving cab money,* Daniel thought). Their hands were exactly the same amount of hot. It was like holding the inside of someone's hand, the blood and veins, where all the happiness and sorrow journeyed around. He was a little drunk, she a little more drunk. Tomorrow he'd sleep off his hangover and spend all day practicing, he decided.

They walked straight up Ninth Avenue for what seemed like forever. They were miles from home.

"Didn't you think New York would be different than it actually is?" he asked when they crossed into Midtown from Chelsea, the streets suddenly vacant and unlit.

"Hmm," Lindsay said. "I don't know. What do you mean? It's pretty great."

"I don't know, just maybe that it would be more . . . exciting. Or something. To live here. But you move here, and then you're just here. It's just where you live."

Lindsay squeezed his hand. "I think you're just in a slump," she said.

Lindsay was six years younger than him, unburdened yet by squandered time. If he was being honest, it had become clear to him that they wouldn't be together forever. Did she know that? He took it as a bad sign that he couldn't tell.

"What, I'm taking a bath?" Daniel said.

"Excuse me?" Lindsay said.

"Never mind."

"I think your slump is why we've been fighting. Why you said that thing last night," she said.

Now was his chance. "What? What thing did I say?"

"You know—about Brit."

"What did I say about Brit?"

"Are you on drugs?"

"I think you think that I think about Brit way more than I do."

"Well, you spend a good chunk of time with her."

"Well, I have to," he said, but he didn't like how it sounded. He did have to, but he also wanted to. On some molecular level, the group was just drawn to each other.

"Still. What you said, unnecessary."

"What was it? Lindsay?"

She let his hand go. Her youth was sometimes painful, not in a way where Daniel judged her for being young, but in a way that inspired a vital wish in him. To be as young to the core as Lindsay was. Her mercurial nature hummed with endless possibility. It was easy to mistake for confidence. She was nothing like him.

"You said that Brit never made you talk anything out, not like me. You used to like arguing things with me. You used to get off on that."

"No, I think I said that what I liked about the quartet nowadays is that we don't have to talk most things out. We kind of just play it out."

Lindsay shook her head, her light brown hair falling all over her bare shoulder. "No. You said Brit."

"I don't think so."

Lindsay sighed. He could tell she wasn't drunk enough to really fight, but was too drunk to let it go. He could envision her angrily hailing a cab with her eye hand, leaving him alone on the street, something smart and nasty coming out of her mouth before she slammed the car door and zipped off into the night. He hadn't said Brit, he was sure, but that's what she'd heard, so he might as well have. She'd never before been jealous of his past with Brit, but lately it had been coming up more and more.

"I like talking it out," she said. "That's what I do. You have an obligation now."

"I know," he said.

"I like to be really happy sometimes and really fucking sad sometimes and all the things in between. That's what I like. That's what I *require.*"

Daniel wasn't sure if there was all that much between really happy and really sad. He *should* know—he'd lived in that space his whole life. And beyond that, he was beginning to see that her free-spiritedness wasn't so free. He couldn't tell if he'd confused youth for freedom.

"Do you like what I like?" she asked.

How was he supposed to know? He could only remember her liking money and trips to Costa Rica. She seemed like a big blank page, unnotated staffs, no key signature. But he said, "I like you."

"Yeah, well, I *love* you," Lindsay said. "I *love* us."

What he didn't ask was: What is *us*? Were they married like *us*? Or did they just happen to find each other, two people who had built their lives entirely out of reacting to things they didn't like, all the while failing to define what it was, exactly, they were?

When they finally got back to their apartment on Amsterdam and Eighty-seventh two hours later, they were beyond exhausted, bone-tired and swollen from the heat. During their walk, New York had felt like it had before he'd moved here. Like the idea of the city, like promise, like something that could be filled up by all your experiences. When Lindsay opened the door, she didn't turn the lights on before grabbing him at the waist and pulling him onto her. He thought maybe she was crying a little, but when they began to have sex on the dust-bunnied floor—a cooler surface than the bed those days—it was difficult to tell in the darkness and humidity. They didn't even stop for water. Daniel didn't think about anything. Lindsay came like she resented it, crying out as if it was against her better judgment. Daniel's knees ached from the hard floor, like he was doing penance. After, they remained on the floor, Lindsay draped across his chest pocked with cello neck divots. His insides were the texture of Cool Whip, he thought, which was basically nothing.

"Hey, Danny? When your mother prays for us, what do you think she prays for?" Lindsay said. No one called him Danny anymore. He hated it.

Daniel stared at the popcorn ceiling, trying to find a pattern. Lindsay's voice was disembodied in the dark, but he felt her heedless warmth clinging to his, the eye on her palm boring into his skin.

"I think she prays we didn't make a mistake," he said.

Lindsay sighed and it was like he was sighing her sigh, as it blew straight through him. "I don't think so," she said. "I think she prays we did."

October 1998
Calgary, Canada

HENRY

Viola

On the descent into Calgary on their way to Esterhazy, the plane fought through the worst turbulence Henry had ever experienced. It rumbled and dropped, and Henry heard the small child behind him retch into a bag while kicking the back of his seat in time to the convulsions. Henry thought first of Jana, who sat in front of him next to Brit, unfazed and reading a magazine; and then of Kimiko, back in New York, newly pulled out of the morning sickness phase and into the part of pregnancy that made her glow from the inside as though she'd swallowed a lightbulb; and finally of his expensive, insured-but-irreplaceable viola in its case in the overhead compartment, jostling around. He felt troubled by the order of his thoughts, and the plane continued to rollick. He settled back on his viola above his head, and envied Daniel and the extra seat they'd purchased for the cello, which was strapped in between them. He should have taken his instrument out of the overhead and held it on his lap, despite what the too-tall flight attendant had told him about stowing his belongings for landing.

The rough descent didn't bode well for their trip to Canada. It was October, and this was their second and likely last chance at Esterhazy.

I'll call Kimiko from the hotel, he said to himself. *Tell her how much I love her. And the baby.* Kimiko was sure they were having a girl. She was busy learning the Mendelssohn for an engagement in Tokyo in February, when she'd be seven months pregnant. Between now and then she would record her first album with RCA. Her manager didn't know about the baby.

He poked Jana in the back of the head with his finger and she turned around, fixing her hair. "Hey," Jana said. "Stop it."

"Don't fucking screw this up," Kimiko had whispered in his ear when she saw them off at the airport. She pulled away from his ear and smiled. In New York, the fall sky was piercingly clear with a gust of erotic wind that lifted Kimiko's hair from her shoulders, and he hated to leave.

"Are we going to die?" he asked Jana.

"Eventually," she said, and turned back around to her magazine.

Brit shifted her head slightly to smile greenly at him. Kind Brit, he thought.

On the other side of the cello, Daniel looked tired and uninterested in Henry's anxiety. He'd been staying with Henry and Kimiko the last few weeks, sleeping on their new couch in their new apartment together, and though no one had used the word *divorce*—Daniel hadn't even really mentioned Lindsay—everyone knew there was something wrong. Daniel didn't wear his wedding ring anymore, which was notable but not as conspicuous for musicians as it was for non-musicians. Henry was growing frustrated with Daniel, not only for taking up space on his couch, but also for sulking around the apartment like it was Henry's fault he had to sleep there, and intruding on what was supposed to be a special time for him and Kimiko. Kimiko hated it, too. She thought Henry should leave behind the whole quartet endeavor, and had begun needling him with opportunities—to play with the Met, to pursue a couple of solo gigs of his own during her Tokyo trip, to try his hand at conducting, something he'd always been interested in. She thought their life would be more flexible if Henry wasn't also attached to three other people, and here was Daniel, physically attaching himself to their couch.

There was also the issue of Fodorio. In August, Fodorio had wanted him to fill in at a recital series at Carnegie, for a young Russian violist who'd developed arthritis in his bow arm. "Bad ulna," Fodorio had said. Henry had declined, as they had Esterhazy coming up, but Fodorio hadn't given up (anyway, Henry made it sound like Esterhazy was the only reason he was demurring). And he hadn't told anyone, not even Jana, not even Kimiko, that Fodorio was after him to make a recital debut. Fodorio would be here in Canada, no longer a judge, but an emeritus, and he wanted to have a meeting with Henry and introduce him to a few important international talent bookers. This made Henry nervous, not because he was afraid of the meeting, but because he was afraid of what Jana might say if she found out.

The quartet would give three concerts over the next five days. The circumstances weren't ideal.

His stomach jumped to his throat as the plane dropped one last time, and then the modest night lights of the city revealed themselves. Beyond the lights were the peaks of the Rockies that surrounded the city, into which they would soon be driving two hours. It was only late October, and the city already looked cold. He couldn't imagine how it felt down there, let alone up in the mountains. He wished he had brought a hat, or at least still had his beard.

The plane came in at an odd angle on the runway, or so it seemed to Henry, and it was only after the wheels smacked safely down and the engine roared in reverse that he let the tears spill down his cheeks. He'd been having a thing lately, crying jags that came out of nowhere—while he ate a greasy burger in Bryant Park, reading the paper, as the first fall leaves blew chilly onto his lap; when a middling undergraduate student made a breakthrough in a Beethoven sonata during a lesson (*Control your vibrato,* he'd said to the student a million times, and then all of a sudden she had); as he sat in a subway car parked somewhere in the bowels between Columbus Circle and Lincoln Center, the lights flickering on and off, unnoticed among all the bored commuters. Crying, always. Without warning, his throat would burn and contract, the muscles behind his eyes get syrupy, and he'd think of everything at once, everything sad and wonderful and potentially terrible, lost pleasures as well as felt pleasures. Just a glimmer of each, so that when he was crying, he wasn't really crying about anything, couldn't tell you if you asked him to—it was like trying to pinch a penny with Vaseline on your fingers. The quicksilver futility made him cry harder.

The crying annoyed Kimiko. She would swat at him when he got on a roll, angry that he was crying when she was the one who suffered through months of vomiting and now had a slightly puffy look like she'd let herself go. Henry experienced the crying as a thing that was happening to him, though, rather than a thing he was doing, and she insisted he was wrong.

The plane's interior lit up as they jolted to a stop. Daniel reached over and unbuckled his cello.

"Are you . . ." he said, looking at Henry like he was angry, like Henry had no right to cry because Daniel was the one whose life was falling apart.

Henry tried to roll his wet eyes. He shook his head. "It's just a thing that keeps happening," he said.

Daniel sighed and went back to cradling his cello in the seat like it was a baby.

A baby.

Henry was going to have a baby. Before the spring, due on the equinox, actually. They'd met with a doctor at Mount Sinai, a stern woman with cropped gray hair. Henry sat on the chair in the room, trying the whole time to hide his quivering legs. He sweat big rings in the armpits of his shirt. He was nervous, sure. Who wouldn't be? But it was more than that, like earth shifting inside him, something essential breaking apart, changing.

Then there was another issue, something the crying was a distraction from. Sometimes when he was practicing, his bow arm just gave up. His left hand could do all the fingerings, but his right hand and arm felt weak down to the bone. It was all he could do to pull the bow across the string, to make a sound, and an unbeautiful one at that. The pain felt like his body was in mourning—some fundamental grief, source unknown. He'd told no one. It was unsayable. If it turned out to be a real problem . . . He had a hard time even finishing the thought. If there was a real problem, an unfixable one, he felt as though he would have to rewind to the beginning, and not just the beginning of conservatory, but the beginning of everything. If it was a serious injury and not just a temporary malaise, it had the potential to be nuclear, and Henry thought if he didn't look at it right now, if he just powered through, it might morph and evolve into something he could live with.

It was just a phase, he told himself. A phase he'd probably pull out of, the way Kimiko had pulled out of morning sickness.

"Welcome to Calgary, or wherever your final destination may be," said the bored steward over the intercom. Henry drew a deep breath. Daniel rolled his eyes. Everyone was nervous and trying to hide it. How could they not be nervous, after their last trip here?

Jana and Brit were already holding their instruments, waiting to deplane. The cabin was getting stuffy, or perhaps Henry was getting hotter. He hated this part, waiting for the flight attendants to do whatever they did to connect the door of the plane to the Jetway. How hard could it be? Just open the door.

Once Daniel carefully cleared the way with his cello on his back, Henry stepped into the aisle and reached for his instrument in the overhead. He pulled down his viola case and slung it over his shoulder. The four of them walked through the airport single file, with big spaces between them, and some people stared, wondering if they were in a band or famous; and the whole time Henry felt like an imposter, like inside the case under his arm was not a viola but something dangerous: a gun he wasn't trained to use, an explosive he couldn't stop from detonating, a small, foreign animal—scared, volatile, and hungry.

Henry had been a happy child, one of those insufferably happy ones, his mother had told him. She said his happiness was the sort that when friends came to visit and didn't know what to say (*you know, baffled friends without babies themselves,* as his mother described them), a big look of relief came over their faces at such an obvious quality to remark on. Oh, what a happy baby. How did you make such a happy baby? Does he ever cry?

"You never cried," his mother said.

"In fact, you laughed a lot. Too much, maybe," his father said.

They were always going on about Henry's babyhood these days, ever since he had called to tell them the good news, after only a few phone calls in which his father mispronounced Kimiko's name and his mother demanded he send photos of her in the mail. His parents were good parents. He'd had an untroubled childhood, even as a prodigy, and had an untroubled relationship with his parents now. Life was too bright and too short to argue with family, he thought, especially when they were, on the whole, lovely people. His parents had never pushed him—in fact, they had rarely shown up to his concerts after a certain point, after he could drive himself, after there were too many, after they'd sat in the audience countless times before. At times he thought his parents were trying to make sure he didn't get too big a head. His teachers and conductors would fawn over him and his unlikely, grown-up sound, but his parents, never. "Good show, Henry," they'd say, and then ask him to tell them about the composer.

He had a sister, Jacqueline, and Jacqueline was talented, too, but in a looser way that always seemed to Henry more creative. She could choose what to do—make a film, paint a painting, learn the guitar. Her talent wasn't bestowed upon her. Now Jackie was a sous chef in Berkeley, with a wife and a dog and a backyard and neighbors who were professors with two babies and a chicken coop, an endless stream of eggs. When he told Jacqueline that Kimiko was pregnant, he thought he detected a hint of jealousy in her reaction, and he wouldn't have blamed her. Henry's life must have seemed glamorous and lucky to Jackie, the way Jackie's life seemed calm and confident to Henry.

Henry wondered now, for the first time, why he was such a happy child. Jackie always reasoned that he was happy because he knew there was one thing he couldn't fail at: music.

"The fear of failure accounts for the majority of anxiety and depression in this country," Jackie had said on the phone when he told her what their mom had said. Like she was some kind of scientist. Actually, her wife was a clinical psychologist.

"I thought the fear of failure drove people to be high achievers," Henry said, thinking of Jana, of Daniel.

Jackie huffed. "How would you know? When were you ever afraid of anything?"

He was afraid right now, Henry thought, as the quartet piled into a town car with an overly friendly driver outside the airport. He ran through a mental list: afraid of Daniel seeing him cry, afraid of crash-landing, afraid of Kimiko miscarrying, afraid of the pregnancy itself, afraid of telling Jana about Fodorio. But now, afraid of what? He wasn't afraid that he wouldn't play well, but that he wouldn't play well with the quartet anymore.

The car door closed in a thick silence, and Jana leaned her head against the window in the front seat, closing her eyes. Brit sat between him and Daniel in the back, and Henry could tell she was trying to fold herself tightly so as not to invade their personal space. It was silly how Brit was always so careful about crossing lines, he thought. He'd been more intimate with her than he had with most of the other women in his life, except for Kimiko and Jana. Henry thought he and Brit shared a profound surprise at the way people failed to simply and consistently be good. He recalled a drunken moment in a bar after a tepid recital in South Carolina, when Daniel and Lindsay had exited the bar after an ostentatious show of arguing and ogling and pawing, something cruel about Brit's neediness tossed off in the middle of the fight (Lindsay to Daniel: "Don't look at *her*"; Daniel to Brit: "And *you*, don't look at me that way"). The door swung wildly shut behind them, and Brit looked at Henry across the Lindsay-spilled Guinness that was dripping into her lap, and her eyes welled up, and she said, "Why can't he just be human?" and Henry said, maybe too lightly, "He wants to be more than human."

In the car, he tapped his hand on Brit's knee and she returned the gesture. She had no family to come to the concerts. His family would arrive the next afternoon, Jackie included. He *was* lucky.

"So what's the baby name this week?" Brit asked. "Ludwig?"

"Johannes?" Jana said from her slumped position up front, never missing an opportunity to poke fun at his forthcoming fatherhood.

Kimiko had thrown around the idea of naming their baby Wolfgang before she'd decided they were having a girl, and Henry had made the mistake of telling the group at a rehearsal. When Jana made a joke about it at a Juilliard dinner party within range of Kimiko, she made him pay for it at home. "Fuck you," she said, pouring a generous version of the glass of wine she allowed herself every couple of days. "Who is she to say that about our baby? It's not like I go around telling other people how Jana is flat-chested and bossy."

"Funny," Henry said now. "If we had decided, I wouldn't tell you clowns."

They had decided. Their daughter's name would be Clara Suyaki. Henry hadn't really had a say in the matter, Kimiko believing she gave him a win by allowing the baby's last name to be his (though hers was sneaked in there, too). If he told Jana, she'd think it was after Schumann's wife, and even though it was in part—Clara Schumann was a composer in her own right, Kimiko would say—he couldn't risk giving Jana any more sensitive information.

"Oh, don't cry about it," Daniel said.

In the car, they were crowded by their instruments. Jana's violin was up front with her, Brit's violin shoved down by their feet, and Henry's viola in the window behind their heads. Brit refused to touch anyone, Daniel's bad mood was palpable, and Jana pretended to sleep. There was nothing for Henry to do but wait for the hours to tick by as the car bypassed the city he'd seen from the plane and climbed higher into the mountains. He wanted desperately to open the window to let in some air, but he didn't, afraid of the altitude and the chill. He could hear his sister's voice in his head: *The altitude has already gotten to you, stupid.* He felt, in the breast pocket of his coat, a piece of paper so manhandled the edges had gone all raw, a scrap onto which he'd copied down Fodorio's number and the message from the business card Jana saw him eat, a scrap of paper he didn't know why he kept, but which he kept nonetheless, and took out only when he felt confused or lost, to read the simple and straightforward promise on it, the barely legible scrawl on the back: *Call me when you're ready to go solo.*

The hotel was reminiscent of a Swiss ski chalet, or what Henry thought Swiss ski chalets looked like: gabled with chocolate trim, a massive, crackling fire in the lobby, ballroom-height ceilings, bright-eyed attendants in patterned sweaters, guest rooms decorated with a mishmash of quaint quilts and throw pillows. The Esterhazy had switched hotels since their last appearance, and this one had more charm and character. Most guests in the hotel were there for the competition, whether to compete or to watch, and Henry kept an eye out for the St. Vincent quartet, those attractive, smarmy men from Montreal. The rivalry between the two groups existed only in Jana's head, he was pretty sure, but her theory wasn't helped by the fact that the four group members were tall, muscly men with French accents, who looked like they belonged on a rugby team and not in a quartet (they all probably had wonderful and appropriately thick Canadian sweaters). And they could win, maybe, which was really what bothered Jana.

With nothing on the schedule until the morning, when they would hold the rehearsal before their first concert later that evening, they retreated quietly to their adjacent rooms. Henry heard Daniel turn up the television in the room next to his. He walked to the opposite wall and leaned his ear against the cold surface: Jana made no sound. Probably asleep, he assumed. Brit was in a room on the other side of Jana. He sat on the bed to dial Kimiko.

The sound of her voice made him realize how wildly he missed her, how much he'd hated to leave her. He told her they made it fine, and Kimiko mumbled something he couldn't hear, distortion he blamed on distance.

"How are you feeling?" he asked.

"Juice," she said.

"You feel like juice?" he said, not sure if she had misheard or was simply being obstinate.

"What?"

"How are you *feeling*?"

"How are *you* feeling? Why do you always ask me that?"

Because you're growing our baby, he didn't say. "Because you sound weird."

"You sound weird. I was asleep. Did something happen?"

"There was turbulence."

"I was having a dream, too," she said.

He assumed the connection was bad.

"What was it?"

"We were—we were swimming," she said, summoning it up. "And singing at the same time. Swimming and trying to sing, but the water kept filling up our mouths, and I was choking. Or you were. I don't really remember."

"That sounds terrible."

"It was sort of funny, actually. God, I feel like a smoke, you know?"

"Well, don't."

"It tasted like . . . wine. Or a wine cooler, something like that."

"What? You smoked a cigarette?"

"No, the water we were swimming in. Maybe I wanted to choke because it tasted like wine."

"Okay, all right," Henry said. He felt his cheeks flush with the desire for a drink, and the satisfaction he felt at the idea that he could hang up and go down to the bar and get one.

"Okay, I'm going back to sleep," Kimiko said. "I love you."

"I love you, too," he said, and let the click of the phone punctuate her goodbye.

Daniel was always up for the bar, especially these days, and Henry collected him for a trip to the stately one on the first floor of the hotel. They might as well try to get past whatever tension was between them before the concert tomorrow. If you play together, Henry thought, you shouldn't also live together. The bar was lit like a funeral, orange and somber, and when Henry took out his wallet to pay, his right hand went jelly loose, like the tissue inside had just stopped working. He flexed a couple times, and pain shot up toward his elbow. He asked for a champagne bucket of ice on the side.

"You're having hand issues?" Daniel asked, in a voice that was tinged more with anger than concern.

When the bartender brought the bucket, Henry dunked his folded-up hand in it, picking up his Manhattan with his left hand. He took big sips. It was more than his hand, but Daniel didn't need to know that. "Don't tell Jana. It's not a big deal. I think it's the altitude."

"Yeah, not a big deal to you," Daniel said.

"You'd think it'd be the biggest deal to me, on account of it being my hand and all."

Daniel drank the cheapest beer on tap. He rolled his eyes. "When was the last time you screwed up in a concert? I bet never. You're *gifted* and *talented*."

Daniel was right. The last time Henry had messed up during a concert he'd been twelve, and he hadn't hit an out-of-tune note, just the wrong one, and no one had really noticed.

"It wasn't always so easy being . . ." Henry trailed off.

". . . a prodigy?" Daniel said. "Please. Tell me how hard it was to not even have to try to be good."

"Well, it's not easy now. I mean, just because you're good at something doesn't mean you necessarily want all of it, or even want to do it. Just because you have it."

Daniel raised his eyebrows. "You don't want to be in this group? That's seriously what you're saying right now?"

"No. I'm just saying that getting what you want isn't always fun."

Daniel sighed, his annoyance receding for a moment. "I guess."

Between them, immaterial, was the ghost of Lindsay, tiny and furious, always furious lately. Was Lindsay what Daniel wanted? Daniel's romantic desires had always seemed opaque to Henry. Henry briefly considered bringing up Lindsay, but thought better of it. What would he say to Daniel? Try harder? Be better to her? Be better to Brit? Go back in time and un-marry? Instead Henry said, "That's a skill one could devote some attention to, I guess. Wanting what you have."

Daniel looked up at him and his face reclaimed all of the dripping spite. "I don't need gratitude advice from you."

The drink wasn't going as Henry had expected. He drank more of his Manhattan and ordered another. He'd just wait until Daniel stopped resenting him for something he couldn't control. Hell, he resented himself, for potentially disappointing Jana, and for keeping his hand and arm issues from her. But he had to keep it from her. If she was worried about him on top of everything else, they'd have no chance tomorrow. Then they'd have no chance ever.

A girl punctured the silence between them.

"Get in a fight?"

The girl was so striking that he thought maybe he was the target of an escort scheme, or in the middle of some kind of prank. She was angular, with a chin that pointed straight down at the floor like she was making a judgment, doll eyes that took up most of her face, and a small, pert, smiling mouth. Her hair was long and dark and loose down her back. She wore a dress with a black lace panel over her chest, and she swirled a martini on the bar. He imagined she was the daughter of Eastern European immigrants, and he felt the Manhattan bloom in his stomach.

"Oh," he said, gesturing to his hand in the bucket of ice. "No, I just—it hurts."

"It's no big deal," Daniel said, not even looking at the girl.

"You must be musicians, then," she said, shifting in her stool. There were three seats between them, which Henry eyed warily.

"Yes. Are you?" Henry asked.

She laughed. She had the sort of forward, masculine presence that some kinds of men fell for. Was he one of them? He had no idea. "No," she said. "My family has a cabin up the mountain, and I forgot it was Esterhazy week."

"You wouldn't have come otherwise?"

She shook her head. "It's a bit insane. I'd rather stay in sleepy Edmonton than wade through the crowd. But I guess I'll get to hear a few good concerts."

Her name was Lucy, and she was a medical student, and when he said they were in a quartet whose first concert—first of three—was the following evening, she slid across two seats to plant herself next to him. Daniel quietly drank on his other side, though he made a point of looking at her. Henry's right hand was numb, which he felt was a good sign. Maybe when he thawed, the muscles might reset and forget all this business of hurting.

Lucy laughed easily, and asked questions naturally. She didn't stand for awkward pauses. She was thoroughly charming. He felt so relieved by her presence—what was she relieving him of?—that he relaxed into it.

"So what's wrong?" she asked.

He was nearly done with his second Manhattan.

"For one, I can't stop crying."

At that, Daniel looked up. "I'm Daniel," he said, holding his perfect, working hand out across Henry. Lucy shook it.

"I meant with your hand," Lucy said. "But okay."

"Oh," Henry said, wriggling his fingers in the ice. He'd truly forgotten the whole contraption was there. "I don't know. I think I'm tired."

"Your hand is in ice because you're tired?"

"I've been playing for twenty years. I can be tired."

"He was playing in utero," Daniel said, nudging Henry so hard he had to grab on to the bar to steady himself.

She shrugged. "Maybe he just needs physical therapy. I don't know about that crying thing, though. He might need therapy-therapy for that."

"That's what I've been saying," Daniel said, though he hadn't ever said that, not once.

Henry finished his drink and signaled for another. Three was too many on the night before a concert, he thought, but the thought quickly dissolved into the dim lights above him. "I only told you that because you're a stranger. And a doctor. A stranger doctor. Diagnose me."

"Well," she said.

She uncrossed her legs and crossed them the other way. It wasn't sexual attraction Henry felt the most then, though that was there. It was that she was so different from them. Lucy, someone who didn't know anything about his world.

"Since you're here," she said, "I think possibly pressure has something to do with it?"

"I think it's the altitude."

"Maybe that, too. But I was talking about, um, career pressure."

"This isn't very scientific."

"Are we talking about the weeping or the hand?"

"I didn't say weeping."

"Scientifically speaking," she said, playing with the lemon twist in the fingers of her right hand, "evolutionarily speaking, actually, tears are meant to signal to others that you're in danger. But it's something only your intimates would be able to detect."

"So it's a cry for help," Daniel said. "Pun intended."

"Indeed," she said, and as they smiled at each other across Henry, he suddenly felt like a guest on their date.

"Or there are some theories that say crying elicits compassion, so it's a way to save a relationship in distress. It's what endears babies to their mothers."

"Or fathers," Daniel said, looking pointedly at Henry.

"Sure, or fathers."

"I don't know what to do," Henry said like a hiccup. And then he felt actual hiccups coming.

She leaned in. She smelled musky and warm but when she spoke her breath was all lemon. "Are you staying here?"

Henry couldn't tell which one of them she was speaking to, and furthermore, it was coming: he was going to cry again. What version of Henry would have taken this opportunity? He tried to remember. He supposed he hadn't really cheated on anyone before because he hadn't really tied himself to anyone, not until Kimiko. But a version of himself, a younger version—a version more physically deft (ice clinking around his hand) and less subject to the gravity of choices (baby squirming in utero)—would have swept this Lucy up in his arms, taken her to his hotel room, and had quiet Canadian sex with her so Daniel wouldn't hear through the wall. He tried to summon that will now, but it wouldn't rise. What came instead was this goddamn crying. He blinked tears back furiously.

"I'm having a baby," he said, as if just realizing it. "We're naming her Clara. After Schumann."

Lucy frowned and sat back. She uncrossed her legs and hooked her heels on the barstool like she was going to stand. "Oh," she said. "Probably you're freaking out about that, then."

Daniel stood up to leave and Henry desperately wished he'd been the first to stand up. As Daniel walked away without him, he tossed back the rest of his drink. After a mumbled apology to Lucy, he left money under the bucket that was now full of ice water, and immediately the condensation started to bleed onto the bill.

"I'm sorry," he said again. "That's information you're supposed to give up front. I'm a creep. I'll get these drinks."

She stood. She opened her mouth as if to say something thoughtful or stern or cutting, but then closed it, pursed her lips, and shrugged. Henry saw her decide he wasn't worth whatever she was going to say. It made his head swim. He looked for Daniel, but he had gone.

He felt as though he was underwater. The halls were too wide, he decided, stumbling down a corridor the full length of the hotel before realizing his room was a floor up. It was like something had come loose inside his head and was actually floating around, knocking against his skull, a dumb fish. He tried to remember if there was a minibar in his room with snacks. What he needed was food. The halls were dark and old, and buried human noises pulsed through the closed doors.

His room did not, in fact, have a fridge, or even any crackers. And where had Daniel gone? He'd lost Daniel. Probably Daniel had lost him. Or that's how Daniel would likely explain it. When had they parted?

He sat on his bed and held his hand up in front of his face. It didn't hurt anymore. He couldn't feel it at all, actually. But that was the same as not hurting. He examined the thin bones and ropy meat on his fingers, his knuckles automatically cascading down as if holding a bow aloft. He held his hand there so long that it seemed to detach from the rest of his body and become an idea of a hand, like a painting of a hand or a sculpture of a hand, even as he moved it, front, back, front, back. This was Henry—his amazing hands, his incredible poise, his perfect pitch. Or it *was* Henry. But now, what was he now? Almost a father, an irritating boyfriend, an exiled friend, a deceitful quartet member.

And still, no food. Food would fix everything.

He didn't think of it as an excuse to knock on Jana's door. He really was starving, and he really had lost Daniel. He was hungry like he hadn't been in days. Since he could remember, maybe. An ability to measure time was slipping away from him. He knocked again, not knowing how long it had been since he last knocked. And then again, harder.

He heard a scuffle behind the door, and a bar of light streamed from underneath onto his feet. The door opened like a wave crashing over him, but in reverse, pulling and pushing him at the same time.

It was Laurent, as thick and well boned as he remembered him. Something snobbish about his look, even though his hair was a mess, his shirt wrinkled under his sweater. "Henry?" he said, infusing it with an accent so it came out "Hon-*ri*?"

The entryway was lit up, but the rest of the room was shrouded in semi-darkness, and at the border, where the light lost dimension, stood Jana. She was perfectly still.

"I was wondering if you had any cookies," Henry said.

"What's wrong with that?" Jana said, pointing to his right hand, lobster red from the ice.

He looked at it like it was new to him.

Jana pulled him inside and went into the bathroom, where she rummaged through the drawers for a bandage. Then, like someone Henry had dreamt into being, Daniel emerged. He'd been in this room the whole time? How long had it been since they'd left the bar? Henry gave up: there was no way to tell. And everyone here, without him.

"I didn't know where you'd gone," Daniel said, by way of explaining this strange collection of people in Jana's room.

But Henry knew they'd been talking about him. His hand, the girl, the crying. Or was it worse to entertain the idea that they *hadn't* been talking about him? That instead they'd been talking about something unknown to him? Perhaps Jana and Daniel had been bonding over what they shared, something Henry could never share, the hard work it'd taken to get there, the trying and the wanting and the failing. Henry had never had to try, had never thought to want or not want, and was unacquainted with failure.

Laurent leaned casually against the dresser. "Did you hurt it?"

Henry searched for words. "I don't remember," he said. "I think it's just acting up because of the weather. Or the longitude."

"The altitude," Laurent said.

"You don't have to be a jerk about it," Henry said.

Laurent smiled, a smile like a sliver cut through his face.

Jana was still wearing the same clothes she had been wearing on the plane, all black, but her face had the opened-up look of someone who'd just been kissing or laughing. She had an Ace bandage in her hand. Laurent hovered around Henry like he was a potentially dangerous creature. Daniel stayed back.

"Jesus," Jana said. "Our first concert is tomorrow, and you tell me about your hand now. No, you didn't even tell me."

"It feels temporary."

"Tomorrow, Henry. Are you going to be okay by tomorrow?"

"Hey, settle down. I just wanted some food," Henry said, looking to

Daniel for sympathy and finding none. "It's gonna be fine. It's easy. We'll play fine."

"We have to play more than fine," Jana said. "Don't you understand? I thought you understood. You're drunk and—and injured. This matters."

"You're the one with this oaf all night," Henry said, sweeping his good arm toward Laurent, catching a few fibers of Laurent's sweater on his fingertips. The light in the room seemed to dim. He could hear Daniel breathing.

Laurent stepped forward. His mouth had a knife-edged glint to it, the smile gone. "Maybe you should just go to sleep."

"Oh, great," Henry said. His voice was coming out hysterical, shrill. "Taking tips from this piece of work."

Laurent appeared to puff up, like a peacock Henry had seen once.

Jana put her hands on her hips, angry now.

"This guy's probably here for sabotage purposes," Henry said. "This guy's group needs it. Have you heard them play? This guy. Their Mozart is—"

"Henry, stop," Jana said, quiet and sad.

"—it's downright embarrassing, sounds like the 'Dissonance' quartet, but an accident."

"This is ridiculous." Jana put her head in her hands. "Just leave, Henry."

"Leave what? The room? The quartet?"

"Don't be an asshole," Daniel said. Finally, Daniel stepping up to the plate. A feeling like a warm water balloon being punctured spread in Henry's chest.

"You want to talk about being an asshole? You? King of assholes? Which evidence should we bring in first? Lindsay or Brit? Me? Kimiko?

Jana's the only one who's not mad at you and that's because maybe you two are peas in a blanket."

"In a pod," Jana said.

He turned back to her. "They can't play for real, Jana. They're a novelty, something to look at. Like French quadruplets. We don't have to be our best to beat them."

Looking at Laurent straight on was like trying to discern people in the streets from a low-flying plane. There were the cars moving about, funny yellow cabs and robotic headlights, but where were the people? Laurent's absurd attractiveness momentarily amused Henry, though he still felt like crying. There wasn't much difference between the two emotions. He smiled, his eyes grew wet.

"Go ahead," Henry said to Laurent. "Being a goon is the only thing you're really good at anyway."

Laurent just stood there, shiny like a prize. But Daniel stepped forward. "And what are you good at, exactly?"

"That's the problem," Henry said, smiling. "I'm good at everything."

Henry didn't even see Daniel's fist coming toward his cheekbone, but later he would understand the true measure of his own inebriation, and think of the events that occurred between his knocking on the door and Daniel's punching him as chalk drawings on a blackboard that someone had leaned against and smudged out. The force of the blow was enough to knock Henry back onto the mussed bedspread of one of the queen beds, arms akimbo, his face reeling long after he was down. The smile that had been there when Daniel punched him was skewed, in a different world now. As he lay there, when the only thing he could see was the expanse of the ceiling above him and the only thing he could hear was Jana's cursing, which was almost musical in its emotive content, Henry thought of three things in rapid succession. First, he thought of the coda that capped the first movement of the Shostakovich they'd play the following night—he used to love that piece—how it suddenly changed time signature and sped up, and everyone took a turn erratically sawing out the melody, and then they ended on this bizarre, optimistic ascending run—gentle plucked notes for him and Daniel, Jana and Brit on harmonics—like everything dissonant and off-kilter that had come before could be erased with three pastoral notes. They always nailed that ending, but it always felt strange, like it could go off the rails at any moment. That's the way it was written. Second, he thought of Daniel's hand, and how it would swell up if he didn't get ice immediately, and how Jana would blame him for that swelling. And third, he thought, with a bodily force that, had he tried to describe it, would sound synthetic or exaggerated, of how purely, ecstatically good it had felt, being punched, how it had felt like a choice, being punched—how it seemed to match with perfect equality the force that had been gnawing at him from the inside, how it sucked any pain he felt from his arm or his chest or his core or his imperfect heart and planted it in a welt on his cheekbone. He felt gratitude. He felt warmth all over his face, from blood or tears, he didn't know and didn't care. He was officially broken.

DANIEL

Cello

Daniel awoke from a dream like pulling himself out of a hot bath, the hotel alarm buzzing B-flat, his least favorite note (the second finger on the G string always wavering; the note never round, nearly accidental). What had he been dreaming? Something pleasant, he felt sure, something that had made him happy. But now the dream had escaped like smoke, disappeared into the atmospheric recesses of his subconscious, and he had no hope of recovering it. The unease he'd become accustomed to slid mercilessly back in, and he submitted to waking fully.

The hotel room had a static dry heat about it; a light snow had begun to fall. Before moving from the bed, Daniel glanced at his cello case in the corner, strategically placed close enough to and far enough away from the radiator heat, and made a note to move it to the bathroom while he showered, to let the humidity loosen the seams of the wood panels.

And then, of course, there was his hand. Sopping wet now, wrapped up in a makeshift ice-and-washcloth contraption that had melted through the bedspread. It was his right hand, his bow-arm hand, which, if there was going to be a fucked-up hand, was the one he preferred. That pain he could get through. If there had been pain in his left hand, the notes just wouldn't make. There would be no charging through that. He set about unwrapping to examine the damage.

Their dress rehearsal was in one hour, their concert in eight. Whatever subterranean feeling he'd had when he woke up, he was yanked out of it as though by a muscly tide.

Henry. Lindsay. Henry. Lindsay. Which person he'd injured should he think of first this morning?

Daniel pictured Lindsay in their apartment (was it now hers?), flipping through a design magazine at the small side table they used for eating, the window open, the sounds of an Upper West Side morning clanging through the room, sounds that, if heard discriminately or kindly, could resemble the leaf-crackling wholesomeness of an American autumn, but were really the unhinged dregs of a fleeting Manhattan October. No, she wouldn't be up yet. It was Saturday, and Lindsay would be sleeping late. She would make pancakes at noon and take a walk to Fairway, buy blueberries, eat blueberries in the park and then maybe nap there, if the sun was still high enough. The day would have absolutely no point, and she wouldn't care. She would think of one million things that day, and try to say as many of them aloud as she could, to whomever would listen. She would be as cheerful as the day was empty.

If it was possible to feel both contempt and nostalgia simultaneously for the same thing, that's what Daniel felt. Perhaps it was that feeling of being underwater—of being angrily helpless and helplessly drawn—that he associated with being with Lindsay. The amount of time they had been together could still be reasonably counted in months, and while it felt like an inevitable amputation, their parting, it also did feel like an amputation—missed and longed for in a second-degree kind of way, but gone for good.

Are you really happy? He could not stop the habit of talking to her in his head, even though it had been so long since they'd actually spoken.

He thought of Lindsay often, though not in the way he knew she wished he thought of her. He pictured her compact, pink body in their too-small, dirt-ringed bathtub, her legs draped over the side, laughing fitfully at some inane thing he'd said or done, some face he'd made, some way he'd been that was so easy—too easy—and had delighted her. He recalled the cold closed lid of the toilet where he'd been sitting, and the shape his hands made, curved like two parentheses holding the joke he'd constructed, and her face, freckled and sly and dotted with beads of steam and sweat. Of course that hadn't lasted, he thought, but how good it had felt to be tethered to someone's spotlight like that.

Answer: She had been happy. But that didn't mean she didn't also need things from him to cobble together more happiness.

Daniel unwrapped the last of the washcloth, and while his hand was red and wrinkly from the ice, it didn't appear to be swollen. There were two red cuts like winks on his knuckles, and those were sensitive. He clenched his hand and the winks opened like eyes. Like Lindsay's palm-eye.

It was perfect, really, his injured hand for hers. On their last night together, Lindsay had ecstatically and drunkenly tried to saber a champagne bottle at a friend's anniversary party (he'd reluctantly attended—in a resentful, perfunctory mood) and ended up with a jagged shard of a bottle of Veuve sticking straight through the webbed meat between her thumb and first finger, just left of the crooked eye tattoo on her palm. Her gin-loosened blood spurted briefly and then, when she held the hand above her heart as Daniel commanded, streamed down to her elbow and dripped onto her sandals and his slacks and the cab seat, all the way to Mount Sinai, where a pimply resident anesthetized her, extracted the shard, and stitched her up (four neat and dissolvable stitches, barely winks themselves) while she wordlessly looked on. It seemed not to hurt at all. Something about the way the halfhearted fluorescents lit their skin in the ER waiting room, or the way he'd crouched nervously next to the doctor, or the way she'd not cried once from pain or shock or the woozy speed of the cab ride home, or the way he'd held her by the waist like a stranger as they walked up the three flights of stairs to their apartment, or the way the apartment's bottled-up air had felt like a crush of gravity when they swung the door open, or the way he'd watched her unwrap the already bloody dressing over the kitchen sink and rewrap it with cheap paper towels, never removing his own jacket, his arms crossed, waiting for her to look at him, willing her to ask him for help, to hold out her frozen, broken hand for his healthy, seamless one, even though he didn't really want to help her, he just wanted her not to have done it in the first place—something about some part of it, or all of it, felt like one of those mosaics she was always tinkering with: cracked apart.

She didn't ask him for help. She kept her back to him like an indignant child, her shoulder blades poking through the straps of her dress. She didn't need saving.

Without turning around, she said, "You're glad it wasn't you, right?"

He didn't uncross his arms from his chest. "Sure," he said, and it was true.

"I saw you. You looked disgusted."

It was *disgusting,* he wanted to say. He had been horrified on an existential level. He'd thought of his own hand, and how he might never recover if something punctured it like that. How everything he'd worked for and wanted would be over. How fucked up it was that everything he'd wanted could be ruined by something so simple. He'd watched the thin arc of blood literally jump out of her impaled hand, like something trying to escape.

"I ran to you, Lindz. I tried to help."

At that, she turned around, half-moons of black makeup smeared beneath her eyes. The paper towels stuck out from the recycled medical tape at all angles. The makeshift bandage wouldn't last the night. "Exactly," she said. "But you should have tried to help me *before* it stabbed me."

It stabbed me, he thought, ha. You stabbed yourself. It was her own bubbling, free-spirited whatever that had made her stab herself. But even her free spirit wasn't free, at least not without injury.

They didn't even have enough left to fight it out. They undressed—though Daniel felt like she hadn't really undressed, not with her hand all taped up like that—and got into bed. He'd be lying if he said he didn't think of it, of turning her over, pressing himself against and into her, and proving how good and useful they were for each other by how their bodies could still want each other even when—in dire circumstances, in a hospital, in blood—they couldn't muster their dissipating love. They used to do it like their lives depended on it, like the lives of lovers everywhere depended on their sexual sustenance; they were participating in an important life force. Daniel hated to say that was what tied them together in the first place, but it was, and later he would come to realize that wasn't so bad. There were worse things than having a body's pull match your own, and there wasn't so much different when you tried to describe love in less physical terms.

But the possibility of sex passed out of his mind and through the open window, lowered now to a sliver in the changing seasons. They both lay like injured prey in the dark. He felt connected to his wife (a word that so quickly reclaimed its foreignness) that night only in that he knew she, too, was jerked in and out of sleep—whenever he woke, she replied with a bodily sigh, and while he stared aimlessly out the window, she coughed and winced herself awake, clutching her hot wet hand against her stomach. He watched the silhouette of his cello in its case lose its hard outline when the sun rose. Later, he found bits of blood-damp paper towel stuck to the backs of his knees and inside his elbows.

In the morning, she didn't move from the bed while he packed. He slung the bag and his cello on his shoulders and stood in the archway of their bedroom, backing out in miniature steps, while they tried to outlook each other, to find reasons in each other's faces to stay, to continue. What pained him most was that she looked at him from the mess of sheets not in any particularly unique way, but in an absolutely recognizable way. A way many women had looked at him before. The way Brit had looked at him from inside her dark car before she drove away from his apartment in San Francisco that night so many years ago (*Daniel, you want the wrong thing*). The way his mother had looked at him in Houston, full of God and pity, the friction of cicadas in the August night following as he'd driven out of town (*Danny, you could be better*). A look that was distraught because it was not entirely surprised. A look that said: *I always knew you'd do this.* And hadn't he known, too? In that bedroom in Costa Rica, when he'd been the one tangled in the sheets, looking at Lindsay alight all over the room, hadn't he told himself that he was marrying her because she would make him free and together they would be the freest married people ever, when really he was hoping freedom would mean he would have to give nothing? Hadn't he known that she would want something from him anyway? And if he really was being honest, hadn't he also known, in some seed-like way, that he wanted to give nothing because he had nothing to give, nothing but his music, or the dogged pursuit of it anyway, that he was as full up of music as he'd ever be of anything, and that he would eventually end up here—staring at his life with Lindsay like it had been wrongly stitched onto him and wanting to run frantically from it, a man made strange to himself, a man made alone?

Which is why he couldn't exactly say he regretted punching Henry. Who was Henry to have all the things one could want, that Daniel wanted—not one but two families, easy talent—and then go around crying about it? That attitude alone deserved a punch or two or three. But when his fist made contact and Henry's smile skewed itself off his face, and the two of them were just bone to bone, there was an unexpected communion, Daniel's rage meeting Henry's crisis, both men the most angry at their misplaced selves.

Daniel thought he wanted the right thing: to be better.

He examined his cello, which he'd left in an open case next to the tub while he showered. Steam had coated the outside, and he pushed his fingers against the seams to seal them. His cello was finicky with dry heat, and the millimeter expansion of the wood exacerbated a wolf on certain notes, making a single F-natural sound like it was two reedy notes, one a true F and one the product of a small rent in the cello where a seam was pulling apart. He decided to practice here in the hotel room a little before leaving for morning rehearsal, just to solidify the jammy sound.

In Henry and Kimiko's small apartment, they had to shove his cello next to the TV like a potted plant. Daniel had called his mother when he'd been staying at Henry's a week. He told her he was getting a divorce, though he and Lindsay hadn't actually spoken the word aloud. It was just easier to explain it to her this way.

"Oh, Daniel," his mother said, no hint of surprise in her voice. "I'm so sorry."

"Are you?"

"Of course I am," she said. "I don't want you to have to go through this."

"But you think I have to, don't you? You've always thought I had to."

She said, "I always thought she wasn't quite the girl you'd invented in your mind."

"Why can't people want each other in the exact same amount that other people want them?" he said, finally, in a small voice. He'd never spoken to his mother about these things.

She answered swiftly and calmly: "Because sometimes we need to suffer and break, and then be made whole again to be close to God."

Daniel hung up the phone.

His parents were not coming to Canada to hear him play. His mother sent a good-luck card to him and had written beneath an embossed illustration of flowers that his father's slipped disc was acting up again and she had to be around in case he fell. She enclosed a check for two hundred dollars. Daniel knew his father fell for reasons other than back pain, and he cashed the check without calling her to say thank you.

In the corner of his hotel room farthest from the radiator heat, Daniel took out his cello and arranged himself. He heard nothing from the wall he shared with Henry, not even the crank of the ancient shower. This would wake him up.

Daniel began with scales, as he always did, reliable and strong. When he was satisfied, he moved to the *pizzicato* portions of the Ravel, warming up his right hand, and then settled on the relentless triple stops in the Shostakovich. They were dissonant on purpose, but their dissonance had to be just so, or they would sound sloppy. Laziness in Shostakovich intonation was a classic mistake in these competitions—when you got tired, you thought you could hide in the noise. He started with the bottom notes and worked his way up, playing the three notes separately until they were the same exact pitch several times in a row, and then adding them up, perfecting the pivot of his bow.

In his mind he commenced a one-way imaginary conversation with Lindsay. Depressing Shostakovich? Ha. This had verve and spark and limitless energy. It was subversive and political and breathless. It was angry, not depressing, Lindsay. No one answered but his own cello.

He'd been playing the triple stops for ten minutes when Henry banged on the door for him to shut up, and when Daniel opened it, he recognized in Henry's purpled eye, swollen nose, and sorry stench his own wayward bruise. In that tacit way, they apologized to each other, and forgave themselves.

Brit looked at them like they were disfigured, and when she asked what happened, Jana said, "Nothing," at the same time Henry said, "I made Daniel hit me."

Brit turned to Daniel. Daniel said, "It's true."

"But why?"

"Sometimes you have to be broken down in order to be made whole again, at least in God's eyes," Daniel said.

Brit sighed. They set up quietly and started their run-throughs. What Daniel had told Lindsay was true—they no longer filled rehearsals throwing ideas around, debating and arguing over interpretations of phrases and *tenutos* and *sforzando* articulations. Instead, decisions were made with a series of subverbal cues: Brit's taking over the melody in the second movement and Jana's passing it to Henry in the fourth denoted who was in charge of that phrase; a slip of a bow tip could indicate ambivalence about the dynamic choice; and countless other movements were missives—a slight lean forward or back, a persistent attack at the frog, a certain brightness of tone, and when necessary, a furrowed brow, a frown, and a pause in playing.

Which isn't to say they didn't speak. They did, of course. But it was no longer the meat of what they did. At some point it simply became irrelevant, extra.

Brit's hair was still wet from her shower, and her hands were white with cold. She'd always looked so wide-open to Daniel, open in the face. She had a regular face, but it had a naked quality to it, a tendency to appear recently unmasked. Pale and clear and patrician, a surprise of dark, mannish eyebrows under her long light hair. Blue eyes, a direct nose, a small mouth, and an alto voice with little range that always came out calm and considerate, even when she was angry, even when she was sad. In the six years they'd known each other, she'd changed physically, become leaner in the jaw, creased around the mouth, more upright in her carriage, and less loose in the arms. But the exposed nature of her face remained the same—plump skin, a dash of freckles across her nose. She would still be beautiful when she was very old.

"You're swelling up," she said to Henry as they switched music from the Ravel to the Shostakovich.

He grimaced, and then grimaced at the pain of grimacing. "I'll ice it."

"Maybe makeup, too," Brit said.

"He's good at icing things," Jana said. "I think he should see a doctor about the hand."

"I don't need to see a doctor," Henry said. "It'll be fine. It's just stress."

Another group noisily entered the hall, clattering down the aisle. Their time was running out. They had a luncheon to attend, and then a short afternoon free before the concert. Maybe he would ask Brit to take a walk with him. They hadn't spent time alone in ages. Maybe years.

Henry and Jana seemed so caught up in something, playing through netting, that he wanted suddenly just to have Brit around.

They cut short the Shostakovich run-through, not even touching the final two movements. They usually felt a healthy dose of nerves before a concert, but this was different, perhaps having to do with Henry's purple eye or Daniel's cut-up knuckles or Jana's refusal to discuss it at all, and they were nervous in a new way. It passed between them like a cold current.

Jana stuck around to listen in on the other rehearsal, and Henry said he was going back to his room for more ice. Brit and Daniel walked out of the hall together and into the white morning. The dusting of snow had stopped, but the sky was still overcast. The vertiginous mountains towering behind the shops had the look of being both off in the distance and menacingly close, and something about their ghostly pallor and ragged outline, like a pencil drawing on the blank sky, added to Daniel's nerves.

"We should ski," Daniel said, because he couldn't think of anything else to say.

"I'll meet you at the top," Brit said. She'd tied her blond hair in a braid down the side of her neck.

"No, I don't ski."

"Eh, me neither."

"Too expensive," Daniel said.

Had they truly not been alone in so long? In New York, it was difficult to be alone. Everyone was always running somewhere, trying to catch the subway or a bus, meeting someone on the next corner, running into a coffee shop or a bookstore or a bodega for a quick this or that before the next thing. It seemed to Daniel that they'd all simply matched the pace of the city, in both their personal lives and their career. The clip was fast, and because the city always gave you something to do, it was easy to fall in line. Keeping up was easier than trying to make space.

But something about these mountains was slowing everything down. Even he and Brit walked more slowly than usual, ambling toward their hotel. The bottom of his cello thumped against the back of his thigh with every step, and he found it strangely pleasing. Brit was smiling, too, and she pulled a knit hat low over her head.

"So you're not going to tell me what happened?" Brit asked.

"I was being a prick and then he was being a prick, so it just seemed like the thing to do."

"Okay. Hopefully that's out of your system now. So we can play tonight."

"I hope so," Daniel said, though he was not at all sure. The problem didn't seem to be that something was in his system, but that something wasn't. "I hope his hand is okay."

"Yours, too," Brit said.

"Well, yeah."

"I don't remember it being so nice here," she said. "I think I was too terrified to see how nice it was."

"It's hard to imagine us then," he said. "When I think back on that group that competed—us—it's like . . . we were children."

"Well, we were something like children," Brit said. "Now we're having children."

"I was scared, too," he said.

"We weren't ready," Brit said.

"I know."

She cupped her hands over her mouth and breathed into them. She had poor circulation, always. Daniel remembered long ago waking in his bed at night because her chilly foot grazed his in sleep. On good nights, in better moods, he would clamp both his feet over hers until they warmed. Other nights, she was gone before morning.

All of that felt far away, though at the time it had felt very bad or good in an immediate and lasting manner. People just faded away, Daniel thought. Even Brit had, though he saw her nearly every day. You could learn someone's circulation, you could wake them in the middle of the night to make their blood flow, and then you could just stop.

"It's good we did it, though," Brit said as they turned the corner to their absurd hotel. "Competed when we weren't ready. You know?"

The walkway up to the lobby was long and steep. He stopped to take his cello off his back and roll it on its wheels the rest of the way. "Oh, you think? Why?"

"Because," she said. She was looking at the mountains. "It's like we paid our dues."

She sounded like his mother. Sayings people clung to in order to make themselves feel better, good luck attributed to purposeful graciousness. But looking at Brit blowing into her hands, and at the postcard mountains behind the hotel, he wanted to be the same as her. Believing in good luck and grace would not only be easier (and anyway, being easy wasn't such a bad thing), it would be freer, too. You could really make a mistake.

He rolled his cello behind him, and they started up the hill at an even slower pace.

"Do you want to go walk around after lunch? Maybe explore?" he asked.

"Oh, no, I don't think so," she said cheerily, as though he were asking her something totally pedestrian and unrelated to him, like *Do you like broccoli?* or *Are you a Virgo?* He experienced one of those moments of social clarity that cut so finely that Daniel knew that when he thought of it later, he'd say out loud to himself, *No, no,* as if trying to erase the memory. Here's who Daniel thought he was to Brit: someone with a shared history, someone interesting and comfortable with whom Brit might like to go on a walk. Here's who he really was to her: someone with whom a walk would be incidental and ultimately unenticing. There were two Daniels—at least two—and he nearly choked at how clearly he saw it.

When they reached the hotel entrance it occurred to him that for her, what he had asked was nothing—a friend, a cold walk, a casual question—while for him, it had been a gesture, an overture. An overture to what? He had no first movement in mind, no theme or motif. It seemed he should be able to go back, amend, erase. But there was no going back, only the electric pull of time yanking forward. He opened the heavy door to the hotel for her and she said, "Oh, thanks, Daniel," and walked on through, away from him.

The luncheon was boring—speeches from the committee, a bland fish patty no one could identify, handshakes with people whose names they wouldn't remember—and Henry didn't even show. Jana looked tired, shaken almost, and Daniel suggested in a general way that she get some sleep before the concert. She nodded and clutched his hand in a very un-Jana-like way before walking off with Laurent from the Montreal group.

Brit wandered away, too, and he busied himself with looking at tourist maps in the lobby, but he couldn't picture himself in any of the vistas. He couldn't picture himself anywhere, really, not even standing in this lobby.

He sat in a plush chair by the stand of brochures. He'd never been bothered by being alone. His brother had grown and married and left the house by the time Daniel was twelve, and the only person he'd ever lived with after leaving home was Lindsay. That he preferred to be alone had always been a problem between them. They didn't have enough rooms in the apartment. He wanted a space where he could go and not be bound by some invisible string to someone else in the vicinity. He couldn't be available for her every whim. She couldn't stand for him not to be. But how were you supposed to love someone if you didn't know what it was like to be away from her? Or what it was like to be just you?

After a while, he made his way back upstairs, and thought he should check in on Henry, to formally apologize or let Henry apologize, or perhaps both. He knocked on Henry's door, surprised at the quiet murmur of voices. Henry usually liked to practice in the afternoons, at least mess around a little with his own compositions. But the door pushed open at Daniel's knock, and Daniel stepped in.

"Henry?" he called, and the voices quieted.

"Daniel?"

But the voice that called his name was not Henry's. Instead, it was accented and laced with mousse and arrogance, and belonged to Fodorio, whom Daniel found sitting on the chair next to the desk, opposite Henry, who was standing, running a frantic hand through his hair. Fodorio: it took Daniel a moment to place him, how little he'd thought of the man in the past few years. He remembered him less as a former competition judge or a one-time coach of the quartet than he did as the guy who always appeared in the photo ads for symphonies, his Crest-whitened smile announcing a high-profile (and highly paid-for) guest appearance. But here he was, Fodorio, sitting in Henry's hotel room, on the day of one of their Esterhazy concerts.

"Fodorio's just visiting," Henry said.

"Well, yes," Daniel said. "I didn't think he was living here."

Henry smiled sheepishly under his bruise. He was so tall and lanky that his nervousness made him seem like a large bird from a different time, fluttering and trapped. "We were talking."

Fodorio did not stand, but offered his hand. "Daniel. I remember you. The troubled cellist, of course, of course."

Daniel took it. "I didn't think you were on the jury this year."

Fodorio waved his hand. "Oh, I'm not. But I still come, you know, just to get away and see what's what. More fun to watch if you're not jurying, if you ask me."

The lines in Fodorio's face were sun-deepened and definitely not present in the airbrushed photos he used for promotion. Gray stripes in the hair at his temples. Here, on this chilly afternoon, he wore a navy sport coat.

Daniel sat on the edge of the bed. "Well, what were you talking about?"

Fodorio leaned in, his elbows on his knees, his hands clasped. "If you must know, you. You and Jana and that willowy second violinist."

"Brit," Daniel said.

"Yes, Brit. A silly name, but a solid player. Anyway, we were talking about options. Possibilities. The future."

"For us?" Daniel asked.

Henry paced tiny steps next to the nightstand. "No, for me," he said.

Daniel said nothing. It was happening. Here it was, the moment Daniel first knew of Henry's intention to leave the group. It felt terrible, a panicky kind of terrible, the kind of terror you feel when something is happening to you and you cannot escape its happening. His brain scrambled for ways to get out of it, for ways to reverse it. He imagined walking backward, out the door, into the hallway, back through the lobby, and going on that walk, seeing that lake, taking in that vista, alone. This would not have happened had he chosen to be alone.

"Are you going to be sick? Do you need to lie down?" Fodorio asked.

"No," Daniel snapped. "I'm just—I'm taking in this information. That you're trying to take . . . our violist . . . away."

"I'm not trying to take anything," Fodorio said. "What do I have to gain? I'm advising him of his options is all. A talent like that shouldn't waste away—well, not that the quartet is wasting away. But, you see, quartet playing for your entire lifetime, even for a short while, can warp your technique. You forget how to play solo, the careful nuance, the clarity, the bravado. You are never asked to use it. So it withers a little. A lot. I've seen it. And someone like your friend Henry here, his sound shouldn't mute itself like that. And it *will* happen, sooner rather than later. One day, he'll wake up, pick up his viola, and the sound will be three-quarters of what it was, no matter what bow arm he uses. Then, a year later, half as bright. Then a quarter. Then he's disappeared. Not that there's much of a market for viola soloists, but there's something."

Fodorio sat back, his point made, and recrossed his legs. His loafers were freshly shined and caught the mountain light peeking through the blinds.

"We're only talking," Henry said.

Daniel couldn't remember the last time he'd played like a soloist. Fodorio was right, and that was what was really making Daniel feel sick, the way he agreed with Fodorio. Solo playing was different. It involved hardly any listening, no matter what teachers or professionals said, it just didn't. The musical sensitivity was to yourself, mostly. Were you being your best Brahms? Was this your most *glissando*-y Gershwin? But quartet playing was almost all listening, sensitivity to three other people. You could not play alone, at your own tempo, or with your own idea—you couldn't even breathe alone. So, no, he had not played with bravura in some time. The realization pinned him square in the gut, as though a sign had been tacked on: *Nothing to see here.*

"We're conversing," Fodorio said.

"Okay," Daniel said. He wasn't going to beg Henry to stay. There were so many things he wanted to say to him, about how they hadn't really even made it yet, and he should wait for that, to see what that feels like, how he owed it to them to stay—for what, he wasn't sure, exactly, but it seemed that if Henry left he'd be breaking off a corner of the group and leaving them lopsided and limping, and when had they ever left him lopsided?

But perhaps Henry was leaving anyway, growing his own family. He was the only one of them with family here at the festival, after all. Henry had always been an outlier that way.

Daniel stood. Fodorio held up a hand and said, "Aren't you going to ask me?"

"Ask you what?"

"Why I didn't talk to you about this kind of career?"

Daniel swallowed. "No, I wasn't going to ask you that."

"So you know, it's not to do really with talent. It's the way you play. You and the other two, the women, you all play the way you're supposed to, like chemicals mixing together—no, no, it's good. It wasn't so good four years ago, let me tell you, it was a bit chaotic, but you must go there, to the place of chaos, if you're to find the balance. And back then, it wasn't awful, either. You didn't lose because you were awful. You lost because there was almost too much energy, energy you all didn't know how to *use* yet. Anyhow, you three, you're like that, but Henry here, he's got a different type of spark."

"I didn't ask you," Daniel said.

Henry took a step toward him. "Don't tell anyone else, okay?"

"I won't. I also won't tell Fodorio about the tendonitis in your arm or your hand or whatever. He wouldn't want to hear something like that."

Daniel left the room, trying with effort to slam the door, but it would not slam. He charged down the hall looking at his feet and ran roughly into Jacqueline, Henry's sister, at the end of the hall. She was the opposite of Henry, short and dark and serious. The stark difference between them always surprised Daniel, no matter how many times he'd been around her.

"Oh!" she said. "God, are you all right? Don't tell me . . ."

He touched Jacqueline's arm. "I'm sorry. No, everything's fine. Your brother's in his room planning some kind of escape, but whatever."

Jacqueline laughed. "He always is. He's the kid that goes into a room and looks for all the exits. He can't feel comfortable unless there's a way out. You know that."

Do I? Daniel wondered. How much did he know intuitively about his quartet members without consciously stating it? He knew Henry was a flake about being on time and also goofy and warm and brilliant. But did he know what Henry needed? Were they giving it to him? Could they?

"Don't worry so much," Jacqueline said. "If there's one thing I learned being related to Henry—hell, being related to anyone—it's that you have to trust that they're going to be there. That's the only thing that motivates people like Henry. That's where the binding-someone-to-you part comes in. Your faith that they'll show up. Worrying doesn't do shit."

"What about punching him in the face? Have you tried that?"

She rolled her eyes and began walking past him. "Don't worry," she said again, like someone who was truly related to Henry.

In his room, Daniel worked his way through the Shostakovich by reading the score. Technically, the Ravel was the more difficult piece, but they'd performed that before, many times. It had been the first really difficult piece they'd mastered. But the Shostakovich was less organized, or less obviously logical. It took an exhausting amount of concentration to pull the phrases together, to make the fragments and jumps compose a whole. You could not miss a millisecond in the piece. It was helpful to look at the score, which Daniel always had at his feet during rehearsal. It was helpful to see it all laid out like that. Sometimes he read scores like people read books, before bed, over coffee, for a good story. But reading the Shostakovich quartet scores was, for Daniel, much like reading a Russian novel: when you finally understood one desperate line, you then had to be able to see it twofold—first, as part of the larger tragedy, and second, as stand-alone grace.

Once he'd played the whole piece in his head, all the parts, he closed the score and placed it on the desk. What did he know about staying or leaving? There were divorce papers to file, the paperwork a cruel punishment for having failed a government-aided promise. It all sounded like such a failure—divorce—and he'd never so frequently disappointed people as in these past several months. He was thirty-three, and so far, the most he'd ever felt about anything was about the absence of Lindsay, and what he felt was a light shining on the absence of himself. He felt more emotions about her departure than he ever did when he'd actually been with her, and that depressed him further. He could fall into passionate love with an outline of Lindsay, a Lindsay-shaped loss, more easily than he could with her.

And even now, slowly getting ready for this important concert, he was trying to methodically run through his loss, to balance the emotional budget. Trying to work it out with a pencil and paper, talking to Lindsay in his head, trying to make sense of things. Trying to put these little pieces of their relationship into a mathematical equation, even if the result was always zero. *This* because *this*.

But his decision to marry Lindsay had been in part because *this* hadn't equaled *this*. They were so unlike each other that it was constantly kinetic, sparking. His relationship with the quartet was similar in principle, but different in practice. It was also kinetic, but in the process of making music, the friction was quieted. Of course, they could never match perfectly on a personal level. And of course Henry was thinking about leaving. Someone always would be.

Daniel ran into Henry and his family in the lobby. Henry looked less purple and swollen than before, and said nothing of Fodorio. Henry's mother hugged Daniel hard, and he felt glad that someone's family was here, at least. It made everything seem less high stakes, all that unmitigated love. Daniel saw that it wasn't just an absence of money that kept him from having a fallback like the rest of them, but also an absence of family.

The girls had gone ahead, so they walked with Henry's family to the hall, their instruments on their backs. Henry's mother asked all sorts of questions, though not the ones she shouldn't have (about Lindsay), and Henry's father made good-natured jokes about Canadians and Henry's eye. How had Henry ended up such a man-boy with a family like this? Daniel wondered. But then again, Henry, six years younger, was actually still a boy.

"Are you crying?" Henry asked as they broke off from his family.

"Shut up," Daniel said.

"Well, I'm not. Hurts enough, though."

"Don't tell Jana that. She'll think it was the reason if we don't win."

"Nah, I think it's good," Henry said. "It'll fuel the fire, you know?"

Daniel didn't know.

They had their own private dressing rooms, and Daniel practiced the tough spots in the Shostakovich, running through them seven, maybe eight times until they were perfect, until his fingers had memorized the positions once again, and playing it felt easy. He felt confident about the performance, at least the part in his hands.

But he was still sore from Brit's refusal to go on a walk with him earlier in the day. He couldn't let it go, and it hummed annoyingly in his mind as he rehearsed. Was she punishing him for choosing Lindsay? Did he regret choosing Lindsay?

He knew he didn't regret losing Brit—they'd spent not even six months together, and all that time they hadn't been together, not really—nor was he in love with her now. There were all sorts of reasons they weren't right for each other, and she was no angel. She loved people too easily, for one. Daniel had always felt that when she touched him back then, he had to peel her hand off him, to remove himself from her gaze, if he wanted to get away. And she had a way of asking him too many penetrating questions—what had it been like growing up in Texas, why didn't he believe in God, what time of night was he born—but not enough of herself: as in, she would never ask herself why she loved someone, or why she couldn't simply decide not to feel bad if someone didn't love her back. She didn't think about things in ways that allowed her to make choices. She was always the victim. She also looked sort of bored when she wasn't smiling, which was whenever she was playing or thinking, and you could tell she didn't think about or practice what she said before it came out of her mouth, so sometimes it was difficult to understand her. And she over-pursed her lips when she made words with an *oh* sound, so as to hide the snaggletooth on her left side. That was annoying.

They were also very alike, and back then Daniel thought their kindred nature would have a canceling effect, that one would X out the other. They were easily excited by each other's thoughts. Those few months they spent together, they often sat on the couch tangled in each other, the conversation between them like a car accelerating, gaining speed, shifting up and up, cruising. Daniel had never before been so excited simply to talk with someone. Sure, her long pale legs poked out of her dress and tucked under his, and they both knew they would end up in bed after the conversation burned out, but first there would be animated arguing about Heitor Villa-Lobos and South American folk music and the state of contemporary composers, especially the pretentious contemporary composers they knew, or whether Henry was ever going to grow up or compose something or conduct something, or if Jana really liked any of them—and how did Jana get that bright sound anyway, was it the action on her strings, was it her old-school Russian teachers, was it just the way she'd always played? Conversation had never been more thrilling or exhausting, and he'd never felt more exposed. As if he were talking to an original version of himself, a version who could see the layers of fakery and armor he put on to get through the day, the week, the part of life where he was trying to be something. Brit had been substance; she had been solid. She had been too much.

The point was that the old Brit and the old Daniel would have jumped at the opportunity to waste an afternoon taking a walk together in a ski village. He supposed those people were gone now, and he couldn't afford to regret it.

He played over the solo he had in the fourth movement, a haunting melody that spanned all four strings, required perfect intonation, little vibrato, and precise agility. Everybody was exposed in the Shostakovich, and he wanted to get this right. He had the music in front of him, but he closed his eyes while he played and pictured the score. Rests on all the parts but his, the long slurs across the staff, simple black notes, spaced a civilized distance from each other, and then Henry joining in, harmonics, and Jana taking over the melody. To see it was to play it.

But when he reached for the F on his D-string, the wolf bowled out instead, and the shock of it set his hand off, and the next four notes were painfully out of tune. He opened his eyes. He stopped playing. He'd sounded terrible. He'd made a mistake.

Once they were sitting under the warm lights of the stage, the welcome applause fizzling out, Daniel had completely forgotten how they'd gotten up there. He couldn't *remember* it. What he could remember—even as they began to play the first few phrases of the Mozart—was arriving in the wings early and finding only Jana there, waiting in her narrow dress, looking at the dark stage, their four empty chairs arranged just so. In the shadows, he saw that Jana's face had changed in the past couple of years. She looked grown now, the planes on her face purposeful and womanly, her brown eyes slim and focused. He was sure his own face looked older.

"Did you ever think we'd be here?" Daniel asked, palming the neck of his cello in his suddenly sweaty hand.

Jana looked at him. "We were here four years ago."

"No, I mean. You know, *here* here. Like about to do this."

"We haven't done it yet. And after that rehearsal today, I'm not sure we're going to." Jana crossed her arms and looked at the floor, marked with white tape that meant nothing to either of them, yet she didn't turn away. "But to answer your question, yeah. I did think I'd be here."

Daniel smiled. "Me too."

For a moment, they both looked out at the auditorium, mostly filled. Neither was looking for family.

"I guess your parents aren't here?" Jana asked.

Daniel laughed a small laugh. "No."

"I sometimes forget about your family," Jana said.

Daniel said nothing, but he thought, *Me too.* Where would they be about now? His mother in the bedroom, reading the Bible among many cheap decorative pillows, his father parked in front of the television, unshowered, vodka in hand.

"It's not fair," Jana said. Her voice was small, unusual. "That we had to escape those . . . the past, our families."

"No, it's not fair," Daniel said. "At least Brit's past escaped her. She always acts like the victim of her situation, but in a way, she's kind of lucky."

The houselights dimmed and he swung around to call for Brit and Henry, but there they already were, not five feet behind him, Brit's white face like a ghost in the dark, stricken. He hadn't known she was so close, that she could overhear him. He moved toward her as if to say something, but nothing came. *I didn't mean, I don't think, I can't say, I'm sorry, I love you.* Though those sentiments were true, they would have sounded like lies, because here was a despicable, rigid, naked, malformed version of Daniel they could finally both see. But before he could say anything, the lights brightened, the applause started, and they were ushered on stage.

The Mozart began, unkind to matters of human strife.

The three others started the piece, Daniel *tacet* for the first few phrases, and it was comfortable, classic Mozart, if richer and fuller than his early quartets: Henry's playful eighths under Jana's high melody, and the familiar hints of "Eine Kleine Nachtmusik" sneaking in every now and then. It was a perfect piece to start a performance. *Oh,* the audience seemed to say, *this is something we understand.* It was joyful, though Daniel's heart churned under it all. He could not bring himself to look at Brit, not even when they shared the same inside line, broken and dissonant.

Someone had once told him that playing Mozart and Haydn quartets was like all your organs coming together in your middle—your solar plexus turning up into a smile. There was no smile at the center of the piece right now.

In the space between the Mozart and the Ravel, where they shuffled their music and let their arms go slack (take this time to rest your muscles, he always told his students, breaks don't come very often), he looked over at Henry, whose swollen eye made it look like he was winking, and maybe he was winking. He looked at Jana, whose stony face belied an undercurrent of worry. The Mozart had not gone off seamlessly enough to ensure the rest of the performance. In fact, it had felt like something apart from them, like seeing a long-departed ex-lover, how you recognized the great big swath of love you once felt, though you were no longer compelled by that love.

They began to play the Ravel, the opening of the first movement requiring a light, liquid touch, the phrase starting as if joining in on an already-begun elemental melody. Here, they were ramping it up. The piece was beautiful but also tragic, building to angry, aggressive moments and then backing down again to the Monet-like theme. Even in the second movement, when everyone was *pizzicato,* it was a symphony, each attacking their instrument, but in time and in song.

But did they play it that way? Daniel had no way of knowing; his brain was still back in the wings, frantically searching for a way to erase that look from Brit's face.

The final movement of the Ravel, *Vif et agité*, short and exciting, ended on an optimistic F-major chord, but it was a different kind of F major from what they'd need to begin the Shostakovich. They waited a respectful amount of time to let the air clear between pieces. Daniel could see Jana sweating, the sheen around her hairline. He was sweating, too. He tried to catch her eye, but she was staring at the first page of the Shostakovich, and he knew she was trying to hear it in her head before she led the opening. He needed to catch her eye. If they didn't connect—if someone didn't connect—this whole thing would fall apart.

And then she looked up, but not at him. Instead, through him. He looked at Henry, who was staring back, and Daniel remembered with a start that he was the one who began the piece, with a lone version of the somber melody. He began, and Henry entered midway through his phrase, his version a smidge quicker. And when Brit entered, and then Jana, completing the round, each tempo was subsequently different, an attempt to correct that only amounted to disjointed time. But everyone kept playing. There was no other choice. Daniel heard it: they were each playing as though playing alone, together. They hadn't played like this in years.

Panic swelled in Daniel's chest, his hands growing damp, and when he heard the sounds—a primal moan followed by a woman's scream—he thought it was simply the aural manifestation of his insides.

But it wasn't. A few other high-pitched shouts sounded from the audience, and Jana abruptly stopped playing. The rest of them wound down like a toy turning off. Jana shielded her eyes from the stage lights and peered out over the audience. The stage manager stepped out of the wings and held up a hand to Daniel, pressing a finger to his earpiece. "Wait," he said. "We're figuring out what's happening." And on his cue, the houselights brightened. Daniel saw, in the very back left side of the theater, a group of people standing up, bending over something, someone.

Jana sat back down. "Are we supposed to just sit here?" she whispered.

"No one's looking at us," Brit said.

"Well," Jana said. "I guess we get to start that over, but not play it like a piece of shit this time."

She stared at Daniel, and Daniel looked down at his feet, his scuffed black shoes that used to be shiny, felt his tux jacket pull on his back as he slouched. It had been his fault that they'd started the Shostakovich badly (slowly, lazily), but it wasn't entirely his fault that they hadn't found a way to fix it. None of their whole selves had been there. They'd all left parts of themselves somewhere off stage tending to preoccupations, worries, betrayals. The brazen Shostakovich revealed what the Mozart and the Ravel had kindly hidden: they'd been not at all the cohesive group they'd found so easily these past years.

That realization was frightening for everyone in the group. For everyone but Henry. Henry felt it with a wave of relief so thorough he had a moment of nausea. He was free.

The stage manager came back on, crouched in between Brit and Daniel, one hand on each of their arms, and delivered the news. There'd been a heart attack, he'd heard, or something like it, and all involved parties had exited the theater and gone on to the hospital. No, they didn't know if the victim (was he a victim if he wasn't dead? what did one call someone who merely suffered from a heart attack but lived?) was okay. And yes, they should begin the Shostakovich over, and the part of the piece they'd played before the incident would not be judged as part of the competition.

Henry considered saying, "But I don't want to." But he didn't say it, because though he might not have wanted to play or continue playing, he *could* play, and he could do it quite well, swollen eye and all. He felt his brain inside his skull like a body of water in which deep sediment had come loose, and this thought—*I don't want to*—breaking the liquid surface with a satisfying if mostly soundless pop.

Daniel's thoughts were more frightening. Someone could be dying, he thought. Someone was probably dying. Everyone was just organs and blood pumping along, and no one was free of that. No one was free. His panic morphed once more, this time into the idea that he had, indeed, walked through life disappointing people.

Before they began again—and how grateful they were to be given the second chance, and how terrible the reason—Daniel forced himself to look at Brit, straight in the eyes. Perhaps that was why they'd all been so sloppy. The inside voices couldn't even look at each other.

She looked back at him, tilted her head, and as the houselights dimmed and the stage lights blinded, she mouthed something. He couldn't quite see it, but Jana cleared her throat, and he began, and six and a half bars in—he would always remember this, six and a half bars—he realized what she had been mouthing: *Love you*. Not as a confession. Not as an insult. Not as a proclamation. But as a fact: I love you, even when you are your worst self, even if it's you who takes this competition win away from us. I love you because we all love each other because we have to. It's in some contract somewhere that no one ever saw or signed. A lived contract. I love you because if I don't, there's nothing, empty chairs, a dead man, fluttering paper music.

Henry hadn't remembered signing on to a contract, though. When had he made the choice? He could recall the choice to have the baby, to commit to Kimiko; standing in Central Park in August—sweating down his back, the way nothing moved the tree leaves, the heavy heat just sitting on top of them, suspending everything in resigned, observant stillness—he'd felt the switch flip, if he hadn't already switched it himself: *I choose this*.

But now the Shostakovich was already under way, Daniel having begun it with all of them this time. Henry played because that's what they did. They played. They did it because they were good at it. Henry was especially good at it. But what if he was especially good at other things, too, things like being a partner to Kimiko, or a soloist, as she'd been prodding him to be, or a father? What if he was better at being a father than he was at playing the viola, or what if he was just as good? What if he was worse?

Here were these people, one of whom had punched him squarely in the face the night before. How were these terrible, beautiful people worth excluding entire sectors of living? Why were they—once unchosen, regular people, colliding in regular ways with other regular people—now linked to each other inextricably, tied by old binds, each breath wound around the breath of three others, like a monster, like a miracle?

Jana knew it was worth it. She played the Shostakovich knowing for sure it was worth it. But she'd been shaken this trip, not just by Henry's strange behavior and Daniel's emotional malaise, but by the handsome player from the St. Vincent, Laurent. He'd shown an interest, Henry was right, and if Henry was going to blow up his life with love, why couldn't she? Being with Laurent could be willed, the way she'd willed this quartet into being, the way she'd willed them to Esterhazy a second time. It worried her, though, in a small way. She had never let in the external world before, not in the way Henry was doing, and she didn't know if there was room in her career for it. During the Shostakovich, this time around, at least, there was absolutely no room for anyone else.

Brit was also letting go of people. It was what they had to do to play. With her look, she'd released Daniel, but she had really meant to release herself. It had been years—*years*—that she told herself she was over him, and she was over him in all the ways it was possible to be over this man who sat next to her every day and played music. There was, she realized in that first Shostakovich movement, a piece of him that had grown into her, and likely the other way around, and that was how she knew they were doing well, professionally. It was how she knew he'd been hurt earlier in the afternoon, when she declined the walk, and how she knew exactly the moment he understood the words she'd been mouthing and that he was grateful, and sorry, and also unchanged. It was an admission—*love you*—she was done denying, and also done indulging.

With Brit's look, Daniel was released from who he had momentarily been, which, as the first movement (which Shostakovich had retitled from "Allegretto" to "Blithe ignorance of the future cataclysm" to avoid accusations of formalism) unfurled, made him consider who he had been, but he couldn't access it anymore, and that was because who he had been was dark and closed and hard. He should be open—a familiar feeling, as music had always made him feel that way, bigger and fuller. It was because there was a story—one Daniel found so comforting—in the scores, where he was able to see it all at once, to see what he heard. Stories always filled you up.

This was the story of the Shostakovich quartet, as Daniel saw it in the black conversation on the score in his mind: The first movement, Jana trying to convince the audience of a placid pastoral theme, and the supporting notes martial, marching always forward, and as the martial themes start to overtake the pastoral melody, Jana fights back, and at the end, in an accelerating coda, Jana wins, two soft notes plucked in time to two harmonic eighths. But then, in the second movement ("Rumblings of unrest and anticipation," definitely not "Moderato con moto"), Henry's plodding three notes repeat, relentless—Henry looking a little relentless himself, his face strained, his work showing for once, but his sound clear and exacting—and Jana's extended solo, different now, not lining up with Henry's three-note cycle, the notes manipulated so as to appear in a different time signature completely, and the melody not pastoral at all, but wild. Angry. Daniel saw the competing time signatures on the page. Shostakovich was a beast whose work was difficult for many listeners because his quartets could not be fit into a mold. They, too, wanted to be free.

Daniel lost sight of the score, which coincided with a realization of what Brit had always been trying to convince him of—that it wasn't just music that made you bigger. People did. People gave you stories. People made you expand.

And at the start of the fourth movement, Henry found his reason, too. Because these were the groaning sounds of one kind of family, the whoosh of blood, the gulp of muscles, the hiccup of veins. What else was there to do but make them?

Daniel had no score, but a story. Here were those triple stops, played together but apart, and Daniel's haunting solo, the solo a lament, the fourth movement mourning into the fifth movement, and the fifth—which Shostakovich retitled "Why? And for what?"—furious for a time until the very end, where that same pastoral theme that had begun it all was played once more, this time greatly diminished, barely audible, slower, uncomplicated—all that desperation giving way to, well, giving up. What was the original title, the Italian one? Daniel could not remember. The movement wound down and down until Brit guided Daniel and Henry to a series of slurred whole notes, one after another, so many and so long and so low that it was as if they were merely tapping into a seismic chord that made the earth vibrate at an otherwise unheard frequency, and at last Jana plucked her final two notes—*Okay, I'm giving up hope, you can, too*—and the notes didn't end, but died.

The result was unquantifiable. There was the way they felt during—lost, unreal, having dreamt the same dream in front of hundreds of people—and the way they felt after—depleted, used, but by each other—and the way everyone else felt after—elated, celebratory, brimming. It was hard to tell where their feelings ended and others' began, not after the hour or so they'd spent on stage, tapping into each other, deliberately eliminating the boundaries between their bodies and their brains, making porous their expressions.

That performance exhaustion was why, as soon as they stepped off stage and the stage manager walked up to Henry with a fragile urgency and stood so close to him their noses practically touched—and told Henry it was his sister who had collapsed in the audience, who had been taken to the hospital, who had halted the performance, and it was her wife who had cried out, and that his sister was now in the hospital down the mountain, in some kind of condition no one knew, but his whole family was there (had missed the performance), and there was a car waiting for him, and his presence was requested immediately—Henry's reaction was flat, unreadable. There was no expression left.

The group stood around Henry, shoulder to shoulder, breathing the same hot breath for a few seconds before anyone said anything.

"I'll go with him," Daniel said, and proceeded to give out instructions. Brit would call Kimiko and Jana would call their manager to talk about next steps. Jana took Henry's viola out of his hands and packed it up for him, and it was only as Daniel and Henry walked out the back way, down an empty delivery hall to a town car waiting outside, that Henry said, "Wait. What? What happened to Jackie?"

Daniel didn't know, but he said, "Something with her heart."

The car was the same kind that had driven them there from the airport, and what had felt cramped then now felt too big and empty, the air steel-cold. Henry's face fell into an impatient frown.

"It'll be okay," Daniel said, reaching his hand out to the space around Henry's knee, though not quite touching it.

"I didn't even know," Henry said. "Someone should have told me. We should have stopped playing."

"I don't know," Daniel said. "Maybe. We did stop, I mean. But then we started again."

Daniel's words, pointing out the obvious, hung in the air long enough that he thought perhaps Henry was going to lash out at him for saying, once again, nothing. For having nothing to say. For committing to nothing. But he saw, in the flash of streetlights as they approached the bigger town at the bottom of the mountain, that Henry's face barely registered him. Henry's face, and his mind and body, were in another place entirely, one Daniel couldn't have gone to if he tried his hardest.

At the hospital, Daniel waited outside the room where Jacqueline was while Henry went in. The blinds in the window to the room were partially open, though, and he glanced through. Henry's parents and Jacqueline's wife stood around the bed, and he saw Jacqueline, with a gray pallor to her skin but her eyes open, and she smiled when Henry broke the circle. He saw the side of Jacqueline's wife's face—what was her name again?—puffy and tear-streaked. Her name was Anne.

Daniel sat on a bench next to a vending machine that buzzed with a bored but terrified hum. His dress pants were wrinkled, and his sweat-stained undershirt was starting to smell. He should call Brit or Jana, but he wanted to have something to tell them first. His fingers tingled with post-performance rawness. This was a strange way to come down. Usually after a performance, people handed them drinks and small plates of food and complimented them—and Daniel usually drank one drink more than the amount he should, and ended up strewn across the foot of a made hotel bed, drooling on the comforter until early morning. Here, there was no one, an empty hotel room waiting for him, a private family moment happening on the other side of a wall. He was on the verge of divorce, and had accidentally hurt Brit before the performance, and how was the performance, anyway? It was hard to tell out of context. He counted the flickers of the fluorescents, but found no regularity to them.

He should call someone, he thought again, but he didn't. And here's why: He was, in some small corner of his tired, crooked body, satisfied that something terrible had befallen Henry. Henry, to whom nothing terrible had happened in his entire life, who was given—without asking—talent, love, family, purpose, ease. And Daniel understood, ultimately, that this would not alter Henry's life—that he would continue to receive blessings from whatever Henry reservoir of Henry goodness existed—but here, now, he was in pain, a real kind of pain, not a pain Daniel knew (Daniel, whose family hadn't suffered from physical illness, but from a kind of illness that came with communicating across separate planets), but it was a tangible pain nonetheless. He would be temporarily broken, and when Daniel thought about it, he imagined that he and Henry might recognize each other in a new way.

After some time, Henry's father, gray-haired, his face pocked with smile lines, came out of the room, put his arm around Daniel, and explained that Jacqueline had fainted, possibly due to undiagnosed cardiomyopathy, they weren't sure yet, symptoms brought on by the altitude and drink. It was an issue with her heart muscles, a long-latent disease now affecting the way those muscles constricted. She should be fine with medication and a slight lifestyle change.

"No more heavy foods for her," he said, chuckling a little, actually chuckling. "Gonna be hard as a chef."

"I'm so glad," Daniel said. "I'm glad she's going to be all right."

"Me too, son," Henry's father said. "You should go now. We'll be fine. Go celebrate. That was one hell of a concert."

"Was it? It's hard to tell."

"Oh, no, I think you know," his father said, and winked. A world where fathers winked. Henry's father hadn't even heard the whole concert, and he was saying this. Daniel felt a crushing in his own chest, like two icebergs meeting. He wanted to hug Henry's father.

Before Daniel could make a decision about the hug, Henry and Anne came out into the hallway, animated, and Henry's father walked back into the hospital room.

"She's okay," Anne said, and repeated all the information Henry's father had just reported. Anne, whom Daniel had met only once before, hugged him. She was small, built like a child, and her whole wiry frame clutched on to him. When she let go, she said, "Thank you for coming with Henry. He can be kind of unreliable in getting places, as you probably know."

Anne left to go grab coffee from the cafeteria, and through the window to the hospital room, Daniel saw Henry's parents embrace over Jacqueline's bed.

"Go back and tell the girls, and I'll be at rehearsal tomorrow morning," Henry said. Daniel had never heard Henry speak with such calm conviction before. "I'm going to . . . stay."

He'd tripped over that word: *stay*. Daniel looked at him, trying to decipher this new version of Henry.

Henry went on. "Listen, Fodorio made an offer, and it was really good. Like really good. But I . . . turned it down. For now. I've gotta deal with"—he gestured to his right elbow. "I think it's tendonitis, which should be fine, right?"

"Should be fine," Daniel said, having no idea. It depended on how much scar tissue there was, how long he'd been ignoring it, how badly he wanted what Fodorio had to offer.

"But I'm gonna stay here tonight. You go."

"Are you sure?"

"Yes," Henry said, touching his eye. "If you don't leave, I'm going to punch you in the face."

The icebergs were melting into each other. Daniel's whole body felt cold, then hot. He knew that if he spoke, he would cry. Something was changing.

Once back at the hotel, Daniel found the post-concert reception winding down, and he found Jana at the bar, chatting with a festival organizer. He told her about Jacqueline's condition, how Henry was staying the night there, and that everyone was all right. Jana seemed tired, but relaxed for the first time in a very long time. Daniel asked if it was the wine. No, it was the performance, she said.

"We played really, really well," she said, touching his arm. How rarely they touched, the two of them. And then, because she knew why he was there, she said, without him asking, "Brit went up to her room, but she wanted you to come find her once you were back."

Daniel stood outside Brit's door for a full minute before knocking, imagining that he was trying to think of what to say, though he wasn't. Nothing was coming. The space in his head where he would have been planning out his words wasn't exactly empty, but wasn't full of anything he could name, either. He knocked.

Brit opened the door looking sleepy and invited him in. She was still wearing her concert blacks, and she had a half-empty glass of wine on the nightstand. Her room was a mirror image of his, the bathroom on the opposite side, and she had a king-sized bed instead of his two queens. She poured Daniel a glass and he told her about the hospital, and Henry, and Jacqueline.

"Cardiomyopathy, something where your heart muscle is too small to pump blood," he said, settling in on the reading chair opposite her bed.

"Actually, it's where your heart muscle is too big," she said absently. "Still, same difference."

He was regularly surprised by the things she knew. He supposed it was because she read so much. "Why would your heart muscle being too big make it not work?" he asked.

She shrugged. "I don't know. I just remember the doctor trying to explain something to me about it when my mom died. Basically, the blood that isn't pumped backs up into your whole system, your lungs and stuff. You drown in it. That isn't what happened to my mom. Well, not exactly. But similar."

"Oh, I'm sorry," Daniel said, feeling useless, like a stuffed animal on the chair.

"It's okay," she said.

"No," he said. "I'm sorry. About before."

"It's fine, you know," Brit said. "I know what you meant."

"I don't even think I mean that."

"Whichever. It's fine. I should have told you that before we started playing."

Daniel said, "I almost punched someone else today."

"Oh yeah? Who?"

"Fodorio," he said. He drank some more, closed his eyes hard, screwed them shut.

"Are you okay?" Brit asked. "Is it Lindsay?"

"No, Fodorio, I said."

"No, I mean, maybe this thing with Lindsay's got you overtired or something."

He sighed. "There's nothing with Lindsay."

She drank the last of her wine. She tapped her fingers idly on her wet, empty wineglass and he wanted to flee. He fought the urge.

"That's what I mean," Brit said. "It's all right to feel bad about it, even if you wanted it."

"Wanted what?"

"You tell me," Brit said. She sprung upright. "Actually, I have to call Paul before it's too late. Do you mind? Real quick. Don't go."

She perched on the far end of her bed and dialed Paul. Daniel listened to her end of the conversation without pretending he wasn't. She said nothing of note, nothing he would remember later, nothing that made his heart skip a beat, nothing that made him think of Lindsay or try not to think of Lindsay. Except at the end of the call, Paul must have said goodbye without saying "I love you," and Brit said it quickly: "I love you," with a miniature question mark at the end, a half-step higher in pitch that communicated something that made Daniel want to go sit next to her, hold her like he'd hold a cello, smell the rosin in her hair.

He stayed where he was, though.

He couldn't hear if Paul had hung up before he heard her say it, or if he'd said it back and then hung up, but in any case Daniel waited a beat after Brit put the phone down to clear his throat. She looked at him as though she'd forgotten he was there.

"Dating you," she said, setting her jaw and mouth in hard, mathematical lines. "Dating you was like being in a desert, being really thirsty, like about-to-die thirsty, and seeing this oasis, a big, wide lake, and running toward it at top speed, and then when you get there, there's just nothing. Nothing there. It's just a mirage."

He leaned forward on his chair and clasped his hands together. "Oh," he said. And then, "I'm sorry."

"Yeah, you said that," she said.

"So."

"All I'm saying is that Lindsay seems a little like that, too. Like, not all the way there. So maybe it's just hard to have a relationship—a marriage—when both people are so similar like that."

Daniel knew she was wrong, at least about Lindsay. Lindsay had been there. Oppressively there. There in every moment, sucking it dry, asking each one to be the most important moment of all the moments. Daniel had been the one not there, unsure of where *there* was, undesirous of the longitude of moments that made up *there*. He'd thought her there-ness would make him exist. Maybe it had, but maybe too late.

"Or maybe it's hard to have a marriage when you're also married to three other people," Daniel said.

"Or maybe she's just tired of running toward you. Or you to her."

Brit moved around the room, taking her earrings off and placing them in a bowl on the credenza, removing her heels while standing, one leg bent behind her at a time, pulling her blond hair up into a high ponytail. He watched her, and she didn't look at him once. She was a flamingo, a strange animal, partially see-through, partially solid, a new creature, uncategorized. She went into the bathroom, and she came out in sweats and a large Indiana University T-shirt, her face scrubbed clean of makeup. Her face was at once familiar and entirely out of his reach. The same freckles and open eyes, a vision from a part of his life that was quickly receding, or had already gone.

"Well," Daniel said, standing. "I guess you're going to bed. I should, too."

"No, stay," she said, and something inside Daniel leapt at her use of that word, again tonight, here as though she wasn't saying, *Daniel, stay,* but the euphoric impossible: *Stay, this feeling.* "Tell me about Fodorio," she said, clearly believing him to be making a joke.

She lay on the bed on top of the covers, two big pillows behind her. He sat back down on his chair.

"Well," he said. "He looked older and so shiny at the same time. Like an old shark. Well, actually, I've never seen a shark in person. Is that weird? Anyway, he was doing some wooing, trying to convince Henry that it would be best for him to leave the group. But Henry wasn't falling for it. I don't think."

"You don't think? You don't know for sure?"

"It's not important. What's important is that he said we played alike."

"Who?"

"You and me. And Jana. Us. That we play . . . together."

"Well, of course we play together."

"No, that we're of the same—that we come from the same source. Or something. That we . . ."

But he couldn't finish. The words wouldn't do it. He would continue to talk around it. In any case, he knew she knew what he meant.

"He said it wasn't that we were terrible last time," Daniel said. "It was just that we hadn't reigned it in yet. I guess we were too young."

"Do you think Henry's going to leave when the baby's born?" she asked.

He shifted in his chair. "I think . . . I hope he'll have a hard time leaving if we win this thing."

"I hope he doesn't leave."

"Me too."

"Do you like Paul?"

Daniel shrugged. "He's all right, I suppose. I don't really know him."

"You do," she said. "You know him. That's him, what you know."

"Do you like Paul?"

"I love Paul."

"Oh," Daniel said.

"Come here," Brit said, and then made a face. "Not like that or anything, but lie on the bed with me. This bed is so big."

Daniel took his jacket off and threw it over the chair, and loosened his tie. His armpits were still damp through his undershirt.

He lay on the bed, but there may as well have been an entire bed between them, it was so big. His movements didn't jostle her at all. They talked without looking at each other.

"Would it help if you told me all the terrible things about Lindsay?" she asked.

"No," he said.

"I didn't think so. What about all the wonderful things?"

"No, not that, either. That's sort of not the point."

"What is the point?"

"I'm glad Jackie's okay," Daniel said.

"Yeah," she said. "Me too."

"I'm glad she's alive."

Brit's eyes were closed. "You know, just because my parents died doesn't mean that anything escaped me. Or that I escaped anything."

Daniel was starting to think that nothing escaped anything. He didn't say it, but she knew. They lay there for a while, silent in the heater hum of the room.

Daniel said, "So Lindsay has this tattoo of an eye on her palm."

"I know," Brit said, her voice wandering.

"With eyelashes and everything. But then she stabbed her hand with a piece of glass—on accident—and now it's healing, and I think the eye is going to be all fucked up. Elongated." He held up his own hand to show her where Lindsay's stitches were, and where the eye was. Brit nodded wearily. "Or it'll look closed or something. About that, she doesn't even care, though."

"Hm." Brit hummed. She was falling asleep.

"She just doesn't care," Daniel said again.

Brit said nothing, her breath steadied.

"It's both things. Wonderful and terrible," Daniel said. "Both things at once."

Daniel didn't move from the bed, though he didn't fall asleep. Inch by inch he scooted closer to Brit until there was a cello-sized distance between them. She slept with her lips slightly parted and her clean hands folded over her stomach. He resisted the impulse to lift one of her hands and match it with his. He turned on his side and clasped his hands under his cheek, pulled his knees up. Then he did something he hadn't done but to music, perhaps ever: he surrendered. Even though she never saw him do it, he gave in, completely, to her presence. In half an hour, he could feel the heat radiating off her skin, like an ecosystem unto itself. After an hour, he felt sure if he touched her, she would give him first-degree burns. Her body was churning out heat, even from her faraway feet. He didn't touch her; she no longer needed him to warm her. He lay there trying to catch some of what she gave off. He figured she must have moved out of a REM cycle when she rolled onto her side, toward him, crushing the invisible cello between them in the interim of her private dreams. She closed and opened her mouth a little wider—there was her one crooked tooth on the left side, he could feel it with his tongue just by looking—and she rubbed her feet together. He stayed there, waiting for her eyes to flutter open, and when they didn't, when they refused in their tireless unconscious satisfaction, he got up and turned the heavy knob and walked out of the room, clicking the door shut behind him, leaving the imprint of his heavy body on the bedspread next to her. Though later this would be the night that was remembered for having pivoted their careers, for the performance that would begin every bio from here on out—"Winner of the 1998 Esterhazy String Quartet Competition"—a night remembered not for anybody's black eye, or scuffed-up knees, or thermal skin, or punctured hand, or wounded pride, or even ragged heart, but rather for their raw, ringing renditions of Mozart, Ravel, and Shostakovich, it seemed one and the same to Daniel—the cycle through the classic, the romantic, and the tragic, or the movement from joy to hope to despair—which is why when he thought of this night, he always thought of Brit's sleeping body next to his awake one, always went back there, felt her heat, and wished with each recall that he'd chosen not to leave but to stay, to remain in that moment, to honor it as it constellated all their shared moments that came before it: that he'd waited, that he'd believed that from that single moment something remarkable could happen.

PART 3

Adagio for Strings from
String Quartet in B Minor, op. 11
—Samuel Barber

String Quartet in C# Minor, op. 131, no. 14
—Ludwig van Beethoven

String Quartet in D Major, op. 11, no. 1
—Pyotr Ilyich Tchaikovsky

March 2003
Los Angeles

JANA

Violin I

Jana found it annoying that Carl had chosen to have her mother's funeral on the day after the invasion of Iraq. Of all the days. Not only did it represent a complete lack of a sophisticated understanding of the world and its goings-on—and it wasn't that hard, just turn on a TV, for God's sake—but it also meant getting around the city would be impossible. She was tasked with picking up the flowers in the morning (by Carl, *Carl,* she could not believe she was being ordered around by a man she'd never met before the previous night—a man who, for a time, thought her name was actually Janet), and it took an hour to get to the shop because of street closures. She felt guilty, complicit in something, as she drove past the angry young white people with signs that read *Honk for Peace,* and she didn't honk, because it all seemed so self-important, so self-righteous, and she didn't believe in it. Sure, let's not invade Iraq. But no, my honking won't stop it. And anyway, what was peace? And anyway, no one had ever made Jana feel part of something in this town, and she wasn't about to help anyone else feel the benefits of community, not on this morning, on the morning of Catherine's funeral.

Jana had a secret, though. She was going to adopt a baby, a girl from Ethiopia, a girl who had been born two months ago, on January 1, but whose destiny had been in the making for two agonizing years. After the home visit and the endless amounts of paperwork here and over there, and then a waiting period in which it seemed like the only kind of motherhood she'd experience would be the tenderness she felt for that paperwork she'd spent so much time with, Jana had finally been sent a referral, two pictures stapled to a dossier that listed stats Jana couldn't have cared less about—height, weight, gassiness—but the pictures, the pictures Jana kept in a cardstock envelope in her purse.

In one photo, the baby girl was laid against a background of clouds made from cotton balls, wearing a full bear suit that was entirely too big for her, and Jana could only make out her small face, which was clearly on the edge of a crying fit: release me from this cage of a bear suit! *Oh baby,* she'd thought, *I know how you feel.* And in the second, the baby in normal baby clothes, belly down on a blanket, smiling, plump and with an optimistic tuft of black hair. She'd felt, as all the parents on the forums wrote, as though she knew the baby, this baby that did not come from her but was going to belong to her for eighteen years. Begrudgingly, she admitted it wasn't possible, she didn't know the baby, she just wanted to know her. But secretly, she thought her sense of kinship was special, unique: *This baby and I are going to be found soon.*

It was a secret from everyone, even the quartet, even Henry. Not that Henry would have had time to help her with it. Clara had just turned four and Kimiko had recently given birth to a boy they named Jack, and Kimiko was trying to play and record semiconsistently, leaving Henry to run around like a maniac, arriving at rehearsals with child spit-up on his shirts and sour bottles in his pockets and sometimes—many times—

babies in strollers. The quartet had just accepted a position in residence at a fancy university an hour north of San Francisco, where they would teach and play and run a chamber music series. It was a posh position in a lucky location, and Henry's need for a yard and more bedrooms for his offspring, as well as his much-voiced desire to move closer to his sister, had been a large part of the group decision. There was also the matter of the way New York had changed in the last two years: now every city event was charged, every trip in and out of the city harried, the guilt that tinged the pleasure Jana felt when she left the city, and the way staying was a political statement. Even the concerts in the city were laden with intention and meaning that Jana thought obscured the real, pure underbelly of music-making. It was time for the quartet to move on, for more than a few reasons.

So everyone was busy in the process of buying property or renting a place in California, of moving their things from New York back to the Bay Area, and in the middle of it, of course, Catherine died. There were conflicting reports about exactly how it'd happened. Catherine had been sickly for a few years now—no one who drank that much wouldn't be—but she was still relatively young. She'd gone out drinking with friends one night and then left alone to try to find the LA River (the LA River? Jana had never purposely gone there and she'd grown up there). Catherine's body had been found washed up under an overpass between Los Feliz and Atwater. It was an unseemly way to die, but not entirely surprising to Jana, or to Carl, apparently, who insisted on flowers and a late-morning funeral in a church Jana had never known her mother to attend.

So, the flowers. Carl had ordered enormous tacky explosions of arrangements that Jana had to carry back to the car one at a time, wires and basket twine poking her all the way. Their fragrance made her roll down the window on the drive back, which meant she not only had to pretend not to see the protesters once again but also pretend not to hear them: "Don't attack Iraq! The world says no to war!"

The protesters peered into her window at the stoplight, and she tried to stare straight ahead. How foolish she must look, she thought, these flowers celebrating in her backseat as bombs dropped in the dusk on the other side of the world. The morning was bright and clear and calm, Los Angeles in March, like Los Angeles in most other months. The protesters wore linen shorts and didn't sweat.

"Honk for peace!" one shouted into Jana's window.

Slowly, she turned her head to look at the protester, a woman with gray hair tucked behind her ears, eclectic tortoiseshell glasses perched on her nose. When Jana looked at her, the woman grinned—grinned like a girl, one side of her smile yanked up higher than the other.

"Fuck this," Jana said evenly.

The woman didn't falter. "Exactly," she said.

Catherine hadn't been all bad, but she had been bad at knowing anyone other than herself. Jana did contact her again after that call before the first Esterhazy concert, a few times, and even saw her once, when the quartet swung through LA on their first western tour circuit. Jana had felt so exhilarated then. They'd given master classes in Salt Lake and befriended students afterward, really excellent students; they'd been the centerpiece of a festival in Portland, playing outdoors to a quiet crowd in a ridiculously verdant summer; and they'd made a triumphant return to San Francisco, their old teachers hosting reading parties late into the night. And in LA, they'd played Royce Hall, and Catherine and Carl had stumbled in halfway through—Jana saw them out of the corner of her eye during a rest in the Beethoven opus 133—and afterward Jana had let them take her out to dinner.

But Catherine spoke only of herself, and asked Jana only one question: did she have a man in her life?

Daniel and Henry, Jana wanted to say, but didn't. She and Laurent had just broken up and it had been altogether uneventful, though they'd stayed together for two even years. He delivered the news to her in a letter sent from Montreal, where he'd accepted a teaching job at McGill, his own quartet dismantled after they failed to place at the Esterhazy where the Van Ness had triumphed.

Dear Jana, he'd written, the formal salutation like he'd never spoken to her before. *Montreal is: as I remembered it, steep and full of beautiful people and fresh mussels and a seediness that refuses the gentrification your Brooklyn seems to value. I find I've found myself here. And also, though not as an afterthought, it occurs to me in this cold northern autumn to tell you that I've met a woman, a Québécoise who doesn't play music but teaches philosophy, which seems to me somehow related and yet excitingly apart. We are a more useful match, and you must know something like this anyway. It hasn't become physically intimate between Michelle and me, and I hope you'll send my extra violin via courier.*

I find I've found myself here. Jana had rolled her eyes when she read that. So like Laurent, to put together a sentence that could make a gesture toward meaning and end up meaning absolutely nothing. Of course you were there. That's where you were. And the way he strung those last two clauses together in one sentence, as if the fact he hadn't physically cheated somehow earned him the favor of her sending his second violin via courier.

Laurent could never really stand that Jana was more successful than he was, and she could never really hide that she knew it. The imbalance didn't bother her, but it was a fact, and it affected decisions, and she wasn't going to apologize for it. They'd sealed the beginning of their relationship with the crack of Daniel's punch to Henry's face in that hotel room, but they couldn't ever really reach that pitch again. When they broke up, Jana felt something like relief, at not having to constantly nurse an undercurrent of disappointment anymore.

So it was particularly annoying when, at the diner (Catherine couldn't spring for something that didn't have mirrors along the booths, that didn't have booths, whose menus weren't coated in plastic?), Catherine and Carl sat across from Jana, expectantly. Did she have a man?

"No," she said. "No boyfriend. I'm so busy."

Catherine's face fell. Well, it had already fallen. She was sallow by then, she wasn't getting any parts, not even for mothers. She didn't look good. "Oh, dear. You're just like . . ." Who was Jana like?

"You're just like yourself, I guess," Carl offered, digging into his breakfast-for-dinner waffles.

"You were always like yourself," Catherine said. "Just doing your own thing. I like to think I made that environment for you, so you could be so independent."

Everything Catherine said, even when it purported to be about Jana, was about herself. Jana wondered now if Catherine had ever had that moment that mothers describe, that flood of selflessness that comes in the seconds after you give birth. When your very self rushes out of you and love for this stranger being comes in to fill it, like water, every crevice. But then, so what if she had? For Catherine, even that feeling would've been a kind of self-love: look at what I created. And with that thought, her own self would come rushing back in.

It made Jana angry, as though she had been swindled into loving a person who only craved her love. She could not now un-love her mother. Even after the diner, where Catherine drank too many tiny airplane bottles of red wine, when they stood outside by the cars, and Carl wandered off to buy an already out-of-date *USA Today*, Jana had said, with traffic zooming down Ventura Boulevard, "I love you, Mom."

"Oh, Carl loves me, too," Catherine said dreamily, her fuzzy hair around her face, the lit-up street seeming to electrify her silhouette.

She grabbed Jana's hand and held it for a brief second, like she was squeezing a rosary, and then let it drop. It happened so quickly Jana didn't have time to respond. Her mother composed herself and tossed her keys to Carl, who was buried deep in a story about the new millennium, and instead the keys landed on the windshield with a smack that cut through the traffic noise and startled Jana out of the moment. Later that night, Catherine would call Jana, crying hysterically, to tell her the windshield was breaking, had slowly grown spider cracks, veins against the dark sky, the whole way home. She was afraid if she got in the car again to take it to the shop, the glass would come shattering down on her. She was crying so hard it was difficult to tell the difference between words and moans. Jana could hear Carl banging around in the background. Her mother howled.

"You don't have to go in the car. You don't have to go back in," Jana said. "It's okay. You can stay outside. You can."

This fucking church, Jana thought.

It was ostentatious, like the flowers, and even if Catherine had been a good friend to people, even if she had been the most famous drunk in the Valley, the pews wouldn't have been filled. And so it felt pathetic to have Jana and Carl on display in the first row, a smattering of people awkwardly seated behind them. She didn't know how to look like she was appropriately grieving. She'd worn black, the same concert blacks she used to wear in the pit or in chamber orchestra. Black dress pants and a black blouse, her hair tied neatly back, off her neck, makeup caked on her violin hickey.

There was one more request from Carl, whose belly poured over his belt like he did not care at all, who pushed it ahead of him wherever he went. A favor besides the flowers.

"Would you play some songs?" he'd asked. "Your mother would have loved that. She told everyone about her famous violinist daughter."

Jana could count on one hand the number of times Catherine had come to see her play or even asked about her music. But funerals weren't for the dead. They were for the living, and Carl was inhabiting this widower role as though at the end of it was some kind of prize. He spoke softly, in cadences that lilted toward sadness and then tumbled back toward gratitude. He held everyone's hands in both of his hands. He sighed audibly and often. What was in it for him? Jana wondered. Certainly Catherine had no money. They weren't even married. The house was a step up from the trailer, and the car, the one with the replaced windshield, was still cracked in other, less visible places. And now Carl would have to drink alone.

She decided it wouldn't hurt anyone or anything to play part of a Bach partita. A Bach partita never hurt anyone.

Jana turned to survey the crowd and saw Brit in the back row, easy to spot with her blond hair pulled over one shoulder of her black dress. Brit had flown in that morning and driven straight to the church, and would have to fly back on the red-eye after the reception, because she had a slew of students to teach, before closing out her studio for the move. Brit took on more students than any of them, certainly more than Jana, who had one or two Juilliard students at any given time, students who didn't really need her. It'd been nice of her to come, Jana thought. Surely Brit would cry before Jana did. Brit would cry so Jana wouldn't have to. She waved her thin hand at Jana, and Jana waved back.

Carl spoke first, his voice wavering at exactly the right moments, sliding up the scale just enough for him to catch his cry in a handkerchief. Jana sighed.

"Catherine," Carl said, as though calling out to her, looking up—actually looking up—at heaven, and then came a litany of lies, or what Jana considered to be lies. Catherine as a generous partner. Catherine as an endlessly curious woman. Catherine as an adventurer. Catherine as someone who took a chance on Carl, who welcomed him into her life, who took care of him. The woman Carl described was like a ghost, an outline of a person Jana thought she would like, a blank space that shot straight through her. She glanced around. Who were these people? What had her mother been to anyone else?

Then came a few women Jana didn't know, some of them present the night she drowned. Jana felt her palms dampen as Carl took the podium again to introduce her performance.

"And now we'll hear from Catherine's only daughter, Jana, playing one of Catherine's favorite pieces, Barber's *Adagio for Strings*."

Jana couldn't help the grimace on her face. They had agreed on the Bach. Had Carl misunderstood? Did he not know the difference? Had Catherine actually told him about the Barber? Had she remembered? She stood and looked around, as though someone might rise from the pews to defend her. When she approached Carl, who had his smug hands folded across his belly, she whispered, "You mean the Bach?"

He smiled and shrugged. "I put it on the program," he said, gesturing to the printer paper crumpled in his hand.

Jana sighed and took her violin out of its case, aware of dozens of eyes watching her, suddenly panicked at not looking distraught enough. But she couldn't—she couldn't be distraught while she played. She tapped the strings to make sure they were in tune and, with her chin clamped down on the chin rest, glanced at the audience. Were they an audience? Was that what you called attendees at a funeral?

She found herself looking for Billy, but he was nowhere, missing. She was now older than he'd been when she last saw him. He would be unrecognizable. He could have been any one of those men.

So she would play the *Adagio for Strings*. She couldn't think of a good reason not to.

She thought of a good reason not to the moment she began: it was an ensemble piece, an intimate arrangement. It made no sense without the other parts. Alone, the chords weren't thickened and textured, and though the first violins led the charge for most of the melody, the piece didn't quite have the richness of tragedy that it did when the seconds came in, when the violas were purposefully dissonant, when the celli climbed up to thumb position. When she was younger, when she'd played it for Billy in her bedroom, what he'd done was that thing you did with children. You filled in the empty spaces they couldn't. You did a little magical thinking with them. You taught them about it, about how to do it—how to see and hear things that weren't there. That's why she had felt completely normal playing this piece for Billy solo, when it really wasn't a solo piece. She had been just a child.

Now Jana thought maybe everyone could hear it, the missing parts. Surely Brit could. She felt like an idiot, ashamed, holding the long whole notes, hearing the absence of the other parts.

She finished, and her cheeks were wet. She didn't know why she was crying, or she couldn't say.

Jana dutifully dragged all the flowers from the church to the afternoon reception, where she tucked herself into a corner of the coral-colored kitchen next to a bucket of white wine bottles, with Brit.

No one knew what to say, so they said that: "I don't know what to say." Which meant Jana had to reassure them, which was a perverse way for this whole thing to work, she thought.

Brit stepped in to save her sometimes, pretending to know Catherine, using the bits of information Jana remembered telling her over the years. *She was a delightful actress, a woman who loved to laugh, a woman who loved love.* Jana couldn't see through Brit's narrative, though she stared hard at her lips when she talked. Was Brit lying? Or just stringing together what good parts she did know? That was, after all, the way Brit seemed to see the world, as a bunch of good parts connected by gaps where the really bad parts were.

"I was supposed to play a partita," Jana said as Brit refilled her Sauvignon Blanc.

"Which one?"

"Three."

Brit frowned. "Hm. Not the most funeral-appropriate music."

"Yeah, but it would have at least sounded normal as a solo piece. What the hell was that, springing the Barber on me?"

Brit filled her own glass now. "You didn't have to play it. No one would have known the difference."

"Oh, but Catherine in heaven would have known the difference," Jana said, pointing a finger up at the ceiling. Maybe she was a little drunk already.

Brit didn't smile, took a drink.

"Well, no. Probably she wouldn't have known the difference, either," Jana said. "I would have known the difference."

"Sorry I was kind of late," Brit said.

"Oh, God, thank you for coming," Jana said, a little too loudly. "I'm sorry—yes, thank you. You're here. Jesus, if you weren't here, what would I be doing right now?"

"I was just held up because of the protests by the freeway. I would have been more on time if not for that."

"You should have seen me trying to get these flowers." Jana gestured toward the arrangement crowding her hair. "I practically had to sign petitions to get through stoplights in Glendale."

"It was a beautiful rendition," Brit said. "Of the Barber."

"Even without the rest of the music?" Jana asked.

"Nah," Brit said. "I heard it."

Jana shook her head to disagree with Brit, and the vase of flowers by her head began to fall in slow motion. First petals brushing her forehead, and then the weight of the vase against her hair, and then the briefest brush of thorns against her lips, and then a clump of dirt and pollen on her shoulders. Brit's hands reached out to try to catch the vase, but too late, it had already crashed onto the coral kitchen tile, breaking into six or seven large, pretty shards at their feet.

Jana brushed the hair out of her face and with it came a few stems and a single orchid bud, hard and unopened. She held the bud up to the light, and she and Brit looked at it for a while before starting to giggle. They were soon laughing so hard that they had to bend over, their faces over the vase shards, spilling a little wine on their shoes and the floor. Time slogged on into early evening, past the time when finger foods were appropriate, and then they were the only ones left besides Carl, and they were still giggling in the corner, darker and drunker now than when they'd begun.

Jana was barely sad when Laurent didn't return, and she did send his violin via courier to Montreal with a note: *I'm glad Montreal is: as you'd remembered it. Good luck with yourself.*

She'd been alone since. Her aloneness felt like both a result of her stubborn persistence (something she was doing to herself) and a burden to bear (something everyone else was doing to her). After a certain amount of time, it began to seem like no one could understand her as well as she understood herself, and the longer that was true, the more deeply it was true. Though the longing was there—sure, it would be nice to have someone else cook her breakfast every once in a while, or kill the cockroach, or help carry the groceries up the stairs, or occupy the sometimes frustrating and useless expanse of sheets—the aloneness had carved a canyon so deep and wide, it swallowed and dissipated any romantic possibility. At a certain point, it became easier to go to bed early with a book or a movie and a potent sleeping pill, maybe a glass of wine if she had gone running that night, and sleep in the mild unhappiness that would one day just feel so regular it could be confused for happiness.

The quartet filled her life, anyway: the traveling and recording sessions and negotiated engagements, the EPs and the teaching, the way New York zigzagged your life around so it was possible to become distracted from the general emptiness of it, especially after 9/11.

And then there was the physical pain to deal with. A knot in the base of her spine had been tended to by doctors and spinal specialists and acupuncturists and chiropractors and massage therapists. She used a ridiculous buffer pad behind her when she rehearsed and sweat through the pain during performances. She'd had all kinds of MRIs and scans, and no, there was nothing tumorous there (and for a brief moment she'd been disappointed—the path would have at least been clearer, choices made for her), just a nagging disc out of place. The doctor said she'd been sitting upright and twisting her core around for thousands of hours more than the average person, and that this was bound to happen.

They all had some version of their bodies bearing the weight of their work. Brit's violin hickey was continuously infected, and she slathered lotions and creams on it to quell the burn. Daniel had recurrent shoulder problems and his own personal massage therapist, Erica, whom Jana suspected he'd slept with. And Henry had tendonitis in his right elbow and wrist, to a degree he hadn't explicitly said, but the ravages of which Jana had begun to notice in the bow pressure of his *fortes*, which were a little louder and stiffer these days.

Jana's lower-back problem felt like a little patch of suffering come to colonize her tissue and fuse with her bones. She knew she wouldn't die from it. But it felt like death, giving in to the pain. Which is when she began to look into adopting. Which she wouldn't say was the opposite of death, but all the doctors and the meds got her thinking about the pills her own mother took—and also just about her mother, and what it was like to be a mother, and how could you do that in so much pain, or on so many pills.

Jana couldn't imagine it.

Especially not with her back twisted up and a relentless travel schedule and a tiny apartment in Brooklyn. But a calm had come over her professional life, or a tamped-down anxiety, now that the quartet had reached a point where they no longer had to hustle for gigs, and they had a manager and a publicist who reviewed paperwork and provided arrangements, a rehearsal space they never worried about paying for, priceless instruments on loan, wealthy patrons, the stamps of Juilliard and Esterhazy, years of experience that had slowly matured into confidence.

Though there may not have been a clear reason to have a child—no husband, no family to speak of—there was no longer any reason not to.

Henry made it work. Why couldn't she? As she spent weeks and months sifting through information and scrolling through potential adoptees and reading adoption narratives, a new version of herself began to emerge: a Jana who went to bed tired not from a pill but from exhaustion at having carried a child all over the city, who bought small clothes for the small human, who decided what the child would wear until the child began to decide for herself, who marveled at that child's transition into sentience, who grew a little thicker around the middle (not that she couldn't use it) eating cupcakes with the child (or maybe the child would like salt, she didn't know yet), who met other adults who did not play music but held jobs in offices, but who knew Jana the way you know someone who has suffered like you have—even a Jana who grew angry with the child, maybe most days became angry, at least at first, but then at least the anger was directed at someone else, someone *of* her but not *her*, not her lithe, spackled, alone self.

She kept her plan a secret because it felt natural to keep it a secret. She told no one in case it failed. If she tended to it privately, it would remain sacred. This was, she imagined, what it might be like to actually be pregnant.

Jana considered writing Laurent: *I find I've found myself a mother.* She didn't, of course. But it was true. She'd found a mother: herself.

Brit was the one who suggested a drive, before she had to get to Burbank for the red-eye, and Jana tossed her the car keys. The rental was a blindingly white Dodge Neon, the interior smelling of fresh Crayolas, and Jana rolled down the window and leaned her head out in the wind once they were on the 101. No one touched the radio. The wind was noise enough.

"Where should I go?" Brit asked.

Jana shrugged.

"Take me somewhere cool," Brit said. "Some part of LA that doesn't seem like LA."

Jana remembered a dusty hike up Griffith Park with one of Catherine's more outdoorsy boyfriends. She'd been small and she'd fallen, scraping her knees, and Catherine had picked her up and carried her, roughly at first, and then gently. She pointed out the Hollywood sign in the distance, through haze and smog even back then.

Jana directed Brit east and Brit wordlessly drove. The road wound around the park and then through it. Technically, you weren't allowed on the trails after sunset, but Jana didn't think they'd be caught. Everything felt safe and new tonight. They parked at the base of the trail and got out of the car. Brit grabbed Jana's wrist when they saw a coyote eye them through the trees.

"Late for coyotes," Jana said, and started up the steep incline.

They followed the trail around a grassless mountain that had no view until it did, suddenly, opening up, revealing the whole canyon below.

"What's at the top?" Brit asked.

Jana said, "Um, the sky?"

The hike was tiring, and by the time they made it to the fenced landing—which required them to practically claw at the ground with their hands—they were both breathing hard and sweating, and a layer of dust coated their funeral clothes. They were limp with fatigue. Maybe they'd gone too fast.

They stood at the top and looked out. For a good while they couldn't see anything.

"I can't see anything," Brit said.

Jana knew what she was looking for, though, and said, "Wait."

The lights of the many clusters of office buildings burned below them. Which crop of lights was downtown? Jana had no idea. One looked like the other. A gray haze settled just above the buildings, and above that a few stars were visible. Otherwise, nothing.

"Carl's eulogy was stupid," Jana said. "Delusional."

"Yeah?" Brit said.

"Yeah. Will we be delusional when we're old?"

Brit scoffed. "We're kind of old already."

"Older, then."

Brit sat down in the dirt and Jana followed. "That's one way of looking at it. But maybe also there's a way of looking at it like, that's the gift your mom gave Carl."

"What, a descent into narcissism?"

"Self-love, let's call it. Maybe he felt important because he got to take care of her. Everyone needs someone who allows them a way to love themselves."

"Oh yeah? Is that what Paul allows you to do?"

"We're breaking up."

Jana laughed, but Brit didn't. Brit rubbed her knees with her hands like she was shaping them. "Oh? For real?"

"I think so," Brit said. "The fat lady sang. The conductor put his baton down. The fermata over the rest faded out. Epic rest."

Jana considered Paul, a blond man with wide shoulders, a man in a suit, a man not quick to laugh, but quick to smile—a man whom, despite the years they'd all orbited Brit, she couldn't say she really knew. He looked like he was related to Brit. He receded into the background.

"I want to show you something," Jana said, and got up, dusted off her legs. She led Brit back down the mountain, and at the halfway point, turned down a small, nearly invisible trail through bramble and scrub grass. In the dark, it was impossible not to get your legs scratched up. Brit put her hands on Jana's shoulders at one point, and Jana felt with her foot for the next hold so as not to bring them both down. The bottom of this trail opened up into a field circled by a concrete walkway, and Jana paused so their eyes could adjust to the new dark.

"What is *this*?" Brit asked. "We might get murdered here."

"It's the old LA Zoo," Jana said. "It closed in the sixties."

"God, it looks like everyone just ran away from it one afternoon," Brit said.

They spoke quietly, though there were no animals to wake. In a circle around the field were stone pens, weather-buffed former habitats for animals—ghosts of monkeys, tigers, emus—small enclosures whose bars had been removed so you could walk back into the shadowy recesses. They entered one, and the icy cold coming off stone hit their skin immediately. Brit grabbed Jana's hand and held it as they walked farther, turning a corner into a cave, the place where the trainers must have entered the enclosure, curving steps leading back to a barred-off doorway. The stone walls were covered in graffiti, and beer cans crunched under their feet.

"It's the place that feels the oldest to me in LA," Jana said, her voice tinny and sharp in the habitat. "Nothing really feels that old here, and yeah, you're right. There's something about this that feels preserved, like everyone just up and fled all of a sudden."

"What do you think happened?"

"The animals died? Don't know. Someplace better came along, probably."

Jana liked the old zoo because no one came here. No one talked about it as a place to visit, no tourists mobbed it. It was too far east for most people to care, and tucked inside this huge park with lots of other hiking trails. But it was a living ruin of the place where she was from, its grounds a little bit decrepit, always dirtied from high school students or vagrants passing through. It was a ghost of itself, one whose walls hadn't yet crumbled.

She led Brit farther up the path, to the line of cages, ten or so, which curved around the hill. The cages were human-sized, and the bars were made of thick iron. Jana opened one cage and walked in. Brit stayed outside.

"Monkeys," Brit said, threading her fingers through the bars. "No, birds. No, I don't know."

The ground beneath Jana's feet was thick in leaves and dirt. There was a back exit to the cage, but that lock was sealed shut. She traced her fingers over it anyway.

"So," Brit said. "I really didn't think the *Adagio* was so bad."

"Please. It was like a sixth-grade recital up there." Jana turned back to Brit, slung her arms through the bars next to her.

"It was like the missing parts were—"

"Missing," Jana said.

"Right."

"I'm going to tell you something now," Jana said.

"Okay," Brit said, taking her hands out of the bars and coming around to step inside the cage with Jana. "It's weird there's nowhere to sit in here."

"I'm having a baby," Jana said, and then held her breath, waiting for a response. She'd never said that sentence before, not even to the social workers and agency staff she'd met with.

"Oh," Brit said, touching her own stomach. She was still whispering. She was looking at a spot in between the two of them, as though Jana had conjured something. "Oh."

"I'm getting one, I mean. I'm adopting. A girl from Ethiopia," Jana said.

"What's her name?" Brit asked.

"I don't know yet."

"Not Catherine?"

"God, no." Jana laughed. "That would have made Catherine feel so old."

She laughed again just thinking of it, the mixture of horror and confusion Catherine would have expressed upon hearing this news, and in the middle of her laugh, Brit lunged at her, arms open, and embraced her. Brit hugged her partly as though she was the one who needed the hug, with that kind of super-conscious physical force. Brit's face was buried in Jana's neck, her arms wrapped tightly around Jana's back. It was a raw force of warmth, this embrace. Brit had a slight floral scent and her hair was soft and in Jana's hands no matter where she placed them. Jana could feel Brit's chest expanding and contracting against her own as she breathed. It occurred to Jana perhaps for the first time why men loved Brit—why *people* loved Brit: she was able, in a way that most people weren't, to give and receive goodwill. In Jana's whole life, she could not recall ever having been hugged like this. This one was all-encompassing compassion. Brit was an equal planet to Jana, and the two of them were temporarily merging, gravities combining. Jana accepted the kindness.

"I'm so happy for you," Brit said into Jana's hair.

When the cage latch creaked in the wind, Brit's grip loosened, and they pulled away from each other. They looked around for animals, ghost or real.

Jana could tell Brit really did feel happy for her. The baby wasn't even with Jana yet, and Brit already felt the happiness of the thing that was to come, the very idea of it. She believed in invisible things, in possibility. In that way, she was like Catherine.

It was strange in the dark to feel so seen. Jana could barely see Brit, but she could feel her there, breathing hot into the space in the cage, her own body still warm from the embrace. In that absence of actual vision, Jana allowed herself to accept something most people spend their days running from. She stood in the knowledge that there were people who saw the parts of her that she did not want to see herself—the anxiety buffering the nastiness, the desperate quality to her ambition, the tarnished sheen of her past—and that one of those people was standing right in front of her, seeing her be seen. It felt awful, like her skin had been peeled away and whatever was beneath was burning against the cold air. But it also felt like family.

Jana reached through the dark to take Brit's jaw gently in her right hand. She tilted it a soft twenty degrees and brought Brit's lips to meet her own. Whoever said women's lips were pillowy was wrong, thought Jana. Here they were two parts of a hot, slick organ, an open cage for a sound that took seconds to form, build, and travel through the body, cousin to the tongue, translating something that was untranslatable and lawless.

What happened wasn't sexual, but Jana knew it would be impossible to tell anyone else about the experience without misrepresenting it that way, and so she vowed right after to never say anything. It was, however, about intimacy. She'd wanted to be as close as possible to the person who saw her—in the moment when this feral, empty part of her past met this specific, warm part of her present. She'd wanted to merge. But what she discovered was both disappointing and comforting: the kiss was nothing as intimate as the years they'd already spent together, the furious making and unmaking of music, the knowledge of each other's nonverbal, preverbal, extraverbal selves. She should have known better than to connect their lips; their callused hands were closer to the truth.

When Jana pulled away—it wasn't exactly pulling away as much as coming to the end—Brit's lips were shiny in the dark. Neither of them apologized.

They left the cage together and walked back up the hill, back toward where they'd come from. They walked silently, though Jana was sure Brit had more questions about the adoption, and the reasons for its secrecy. But she didn't ask, and Jana was grateful.

"I see it!" Jana said, stopping, pointing, finally not whispering. "Do you see it?"

Brit stood on her tiptoes, and the tilt of the earth almost sent her flying. Jana held her hand until she righted herself. Jana pointed through the muck and the smog that had cleared for a minute, and across the canyon, up at the edge of the horizon, was the blurred-out Hollywood sign.

"Oooh," Brit said. "There's the other LA."

"If we had our violins, we could play that song at the beginning of the Paramount Pictures—"

"—with the clouds and the stars—"

"—and the mountain."

"We'd need a drum kit."

"And some other things."

"I think we could do it. We should learn it back home. Henry's kids would like it."

"Let's go to it. The sign."

Jana smiled in the dark. "Sure."

But no one moved.

There was another kind of pain, too, one more difficult to name.

Laurent's letter had arrived in late August of 2001, as the quartet was preparing for the start of the concert season in which they would tour nationally, a tour that would start with their debut at Carnegie Hall and take them around the perimeter of the country, hitting all the major classical music cities. Their debut at Carnegie was scheduled for a Thursday in late September. Jana took Laurent's final departure as a sign that things were clearing out for the start of the new phase of the quartet's career. She was truly free now to focus on their tour program, the centerpiece of which was ambitious. The musically complex, physically exhausting, emotionally wrought, somewhat inaccessible, and absolutely relentless Beethoven opus 131. Perhaps the most well-known of the late Beethoven quartets—those written when his deafness had begun to close in on him and drive him mad—the 131 was infamously difficult. Seven movements played straight through *attacca,* with no break, it was nearly forty minutes long, demanding of both the players and the audience. But if they were going to debut at Carnegie Hall, they'd reasoned, they might as well do it in a big way.

She'd been mired in the score that morning—Daniel had purchased one for each of them so he wouldn't be burdened with being the only one to have a score this time—the morning of September 11, having gotten in the habit of waking early and, before doing anything like showering or eating or even changing, listening to the most recent recording of her private practice or the quartet's rehearsal while reading along with the music. She was sitting at her desk with her headphones in (thanks to the complaints of her neighbors, another terrible thing about being a musician in New York), reading through the last few pages, trying to figure out how they could move from the frenzied sawing of the final minor burst to the understated C-sharp major of the ending in a way that sounded less like an accidental arrival at a major key and more like purposeful consternation. She'd been sitting there in her pajamas, thinking this through, backtracking and listening, marking up the score with better fingerings for the transitions, when the sounds of Daniel's pounding on the door broke through.

They'd all moved to Brooklyn for more space and cheaper rents in the past year (except for Brit, who stayed with Paul in Manhattan), but Daniel actually lived in Jana's neighborhood, two blocks south. He couldn't get through on the phone to anyone, and he'd run over to her apartment. She didn't have a TV, so he took her by the arm, so tightly he left a pale yellow bruise, up to her rooftop, where they watched the plumes of black smoke across the water and the towers fall, one by one. Jana couldn't remember them saying anything to each other. For a while afterward, she tried to construct a narrative out of it, what she thought and when she thought it, and when the thoughts changed. But eventually she gave up, and the memory of watching it happen was like a wide gray space in her brain. Then she thought of it as something akin to attending a massive funeral of someone you didn't really know: at a certain point, it was all just faceless pain, making your own experience of it unimportant.

Rehearsals after that ceased for a few days, as they couldn't even get to their rehearsal space, let alone focus on the music. For Jana—and she would never tell anyone this—she would always connect the Beethoven 131 with that helpless feeling of watching the towers burn and smoke and collapse, the inability to make sense of the transition from the minor to the major, the way the story resisted her in the chaos. She grew to hate the way the 131 ended in a major motif that felt suddenly out of place, outdated, a pathetic imitation of optimism, now rendered truly stupid after all that had come before.

It was Brit who suggested a dry run of the 131 in public a week before the Carnegie debut. She'd heard about a vigil at a cathedral in Brooklyn Heights that would welcome a performance from them. Jana thought they might spoil whatever magic they'd have at Carnegie with a free concert for a bunch of people in mourning, but she couldn't figure out a way to say that without sounding cold and heartless. It was arranged. They would play the entire piece as people walked up to a makeshift shrine and lit candles or placed prayer cards.

"But this isn't exactly a meditative piece," Jana said, leaning over to Brit before they were about to begin playing.

"It's just music," Brit said. "They just want music so it's not quiet when people are crying."

Which seemed to Jana like the worst reason in the world to play music. But as they played, with no one really listening, or not *just* listening but listening and paying tribute, or listening and weeping, or listening and praying, or listening and thinking, or listening and trying not to think, Jana saw that yes, it was just music, and that was perhaps its best attribute. It was art as part of the landscape, movable, livable art, and what these people needed was that, an apparatus of art to hold them up for a while.

And for the quartet as well. It took some of the pressure off, with no one really focusing on their performance but simply experiencing it. So they experienced it, too. And Jana couldn't say the 131 made any more sense than it had before, had any more of a cohesive narrative, but their playing of it lost some of its clunky self-awareness, some of its awkward loneliness, and in that strange way a total national disaster became part of their musical story. When they finished playing, no one applauded, which was the only time in their entire career that had ever happened; since then, to Jana, applause after the 131 felt obscene.

She had no partner with whom to lie in bed that month and the months after and discuss the pink chaos of the city, but if she had, if some man had lain next to her and asked what she felt and when she felt it and how it had changed and why, she would have said that in the beginning she was afraid to feel anything, because she didn't want to co-opt anyone else's authentic pain—she and Daniel on her roof under the clear sky, privately tamping down their doubled, tripled, quadrupled mourning (the inadequacy of human mourning was part of the horror)—and that after the vigil concert she felt useful (music solved the inadequacy with extra-human expression, if only temporarily), and so she let herself feel sad, which was in itself useful for her as a performer, and then after all of that, after the Carnegie debut and the tour and the way their lives became busy and full of concerts and engagements and teaching and interviews at the same time her life emptied out, like she was hanging upside down, lint drifting from her turned-out pockets, the city settled into an agitated, anxious resilience, and she didn't want to be filled up with that, not now, especially not now, and she felt bad for that, for her desire to flee from unease, to switch randomly from a diseased understanding of the world to a major chord, but weren't they old enough for that, to turn away, to move away, to have children, to have unadulterated successes, to be angry at the deafness of the world and then go deaf to it by hoping something good could happen, by making something good happen in all the shit and at least you are here, strange, faceless man in my bed, at least you are here to shrug with me, run your hand along my shoulder, call me by a name only you use, and say, well, at least in all these disasters big and small we have each other.

Brit drove them to the airport and Jana switched over to the driver's seat. Brit slung her bag over her shoulder and leaned in through the window to give Jana a kiss on the cheek, her hair whispering Jana's face.

"You were good," Brit said.

Jana tried to make her face as wide-open as Brit's. "So are you. Thank you for being here."

Back at the house, Carl was still up, and Jana poured the two of them drinks under the low ceiling at the lit-up kitchen counter, the rest of the house dark and silent and holding the energy of everyone who'd once filled it, giving the space the confessional feeling of a bar after closing. Carl talked and Jana refilled the drinks, and replaced the ice when it melted, and Carl told stories about her mother that Jana wasn't sure were entirely true, at least not true to the person Jana had known, but sure seemed true to Carl, who even teared up once or twice, now coated in the emptiness of his life post-funeral. There was a trip to Ojai, camping in Joshua Tree, a lost weekend in Tijuana (food poisoning, a likely story). He softened into himself. No, Jana softened to him. There was a lot of liquor to finish. There was the way he described Catherine describing Jana—ambitious and quick-tempered though given to brief sentimental crevasses—which was a Jana Catherine had once known, and Jana smiled at that version of herself, waved, called hello across the divide. Whatever Carl was mourning, he was also mourning himself, that much was clear. He had to tell himself a new story, but before he could do that, he had to tell all the stories from before.

Some days later, on the way to the airport, Jana was surprised to find a diminished but dedicated group of protesters on the same corner she'd previously encountered them. The worldwide protests were over, weren't they? But here they were, fervent in their small numbers. While stopped at the light—now in traffic, many others ignored their chants—Jana rolled down her window. One man cried, "Wooo!" as though at a rock concert. They bobbed their signs up and down. Maybe it wasn't so self-important after all. Maybe if they gathered enough times, for long enough, loudly enough, the war would end. No, probably it wouldn't. But it was nice to think so. Thinking so was all they were asking, Jana supposed.

Jana leaned on her horn with one arm and hung the other out the window, her hand balled into a fist. She didn't know what to say, what one said in these situations. She thought only of clichés—*Fight the man! Power to the people!*—sayings like that.

A few of the protesters heard her honk and screeched, looking for the source. She waved her fist around until they saw her. The day was bright and clear, the same as it had always been. When they spotted her, their faces changed, rose up, like she'd given them a gift, and their cries were louder, their signs bobbed heartily. Jana smiled but shook her head. Nothing would change, but wasn't it something, she thought, the things we could convince ourselves of, the things we told ourselves not until they were true, but until they were real.

July 2007
Northern California

BRIT

Violin II

Brit couldn't read and listen to music at the same time. She didn't know how anyone could, really. And Paul liked listening to jazz, and he liked to read the newspaper on Sundays at the counter in their condo, and he liked to do both at the same time. This seemed to Brit like the worst version of each activity. She knew she was supposed to like jazz—her father, the trumpet, "My Funny Valentine," Byrd—but she didn't. It seemed to spring out of a different place from the music she'd internalized, and the looseness, the modulation of keys and blurry edges of intonation, all that, when she listened to it, made her aggressively distracted. She was always trying to put jazz music back together in her head. And Paul, proud of his seven-days-a-week subscription to *The New York Times*, always read the paper section by section the same way each Sunday, whereas she only picked up the Arts & Leisure section, after it was puffed out and picked through by him. She always turned the music off when she read it. It seemed to Brit the newspaper only gave you party talking points, hollow horror, and she wilted a little each time they were at a gathering and Paul pulled out a headline he'd stored away for conversation: "The way we've lost Fallujah, despite bolstering the Iraqi police force." *Bolstering*?

The newspaper and jazz were why they were late to the Allbrights'. "Tradition," Paul said, snapping the paper in front of his face and leaning back into the stool.

"Habit," Brit said, tying her bathing suit straps behind her neck.

"Whatever you want to call it," Paul said. "It's the Fourth of July. I can do what I want. No one'll notice if we're late to a pool party."

"It's not a pool party," Brit said.

"Then why are you wearing a bathing suit?"

"It's not a pool party for *us*," Brit said, pointing to her violin case by the door. The Allbrights were major donors to the music program at the university, and though they had an annual pool party in their enormous Sonoma home for faculty and staff, they always set up music stands and chairs and had their piano tuned and a stack of fresh scores under the cabana by the outdoor bar. Maisie Allbright usually wanted the quartet to play something slow and sad, and by the end of the evening, she'd stand right in front of them and cry and sip her daiquiri while her husband, Richard, disappeared into the house, into another bottle of Scotch, into bed. They were expected to perform, but then they were expected to watch the Allbrights' performance, too. It was exhausting.

Brit waited for Paul to finish his paper. She stood in the kitchen the entire time, watching him, listening to the music. He didn't look up once, and she didn't disturb him once. This was how they fought: by not fighting. Outright arguments weren't Paul's style, or Brit's either, though over the years it had become hard to tell who'd led the charge. They grew into or around each other's flaws, like knotty, ancient trees. He was easy, which is why it was so good with him for those early years. *I've finally gotten what I deserve,* Brit remembered thinking when he'd been the one to say he loved her first, when he'd been the one to chase her out the door when she was angry, when he'd been the one to say let's move in, let's merge bank accounts, let's never vacation apart. She'd never been with someone who seemed so grateful for her, more grateful than she was for him, and she thought that was the way it had to be, someone always carrying more of the gratitude. But then five years went by, and the quartet decided to take the job in California, and she'd waited for him at their Hell's Kitchen apartment one Wednesday, prepared to say she was going, prepared to break up with him, like she'd told Jana in LA—that she'd understand if he didn't want to go, since New York was his home, but it was the next logical step for the quartet, and she had to go for her career, and that she'd loved him anyhow. But the word *California* had barely escaped her mouth and he was already alit in the computer's glare, looking up openings in finance in the Bay Area, real estate prices, weather probabilities. She never even had the chance to say that she was okay with their breaking up, and so it was like a scream that she never got to scream but couldn't swallow, caught perpetually in her throat.

How could you say no to a man who followed you like that? That kind of following was only familiar to Brit through the quartet.

And then it was ten years. Ten years since they'd begun dating, and here they were, in their carpeted condo in the part of the small city that was better than the part the students lived in, but not as nice as the parts the dot-com guys lived in, the burnt summer filtering through plastic blinds and the air conditioner kicking in and jazz on the CD player, like some imitation of a life.

It wasn't that she didn't love him, or that he wasn't kind. She did, of course, and he was, absolutely, but after a while it got to seem like they'd reached a moment where it was really pleasant, like the highest form of pleasant it could be, and then they'd stayed there. And stayed. And now she was nearly forty, and it was about time she admitted that the life she was living was actually her life, not some precursor to her life, and that the reason she wasn't living another, perhaps better, life was that she'd met someone decent with whom she'd had something very important in common: a desire to be in love.

He looked up brightly when he finished the last section, like he was happy to have a news digest fresh in his mind. "Thanks for waiting, lovely," he said, and walked over to her, kissed her on the forehead, and untied the tie behind her neck.

He walked away into their bedroom, laughing, asking for five more minutes, he had to find his swim trunks. He said that phrase she hated, *swim trunks*. She retied her bathing suit.

The drive to the Allbrights' was all windy roads through the country. The day was hot, and she cranked up the A/C but he rolled down a window, and then they had a standoff. Finally, she said, "Think of my violin, Paul," and he silently closed his window and turned the radio up.

The Allbrights' home showed its wealth with its total lack of coherence. The front of the house was all circular gravel driveway, molded shrubs, Italian pillars, and the back was sixties mod—a lap pool, a vintage cabana, a croquet course in new grass. And the inside, marble and parquet, heavy sliding doors and glass room dividers. They were so rich they could decorate however they wanted, whenever they wanted, change themes on a whim and never mind informing the rest of the house.

Maisie took Brit's hand and kissed her on the cheek, smelling like baby powder and vodka. Maisie had a truly painted-on face and gray-and-white hair swept up into a bun that had to be half fake, and wore a designer caftan and kitten heels.

"You're finally here, dear," she said, leading her through the cold house and back into the hot day to the pool area.

"She just wouldn't stop listening to Chet Baker this morning," Paul said, though Maisie didn't appear to be listening.

Outside was a shock of children. Brit was always alarmed the way they seemed to throw themselves all over the place when they were near a pool or any body of water, like they just believed the water would magically buoy them.

Henry's daughter, Clara, ran up to Brit, dragging a pool noodle behind her in a damp path on the concrete, her long dark hair wet down her back.

"Do you know how to cannonball?" she asked, and then fell into a fit of giggles, like the joke didn't depend on Brit's answer at all, and ran away.

Kimiko and Henry waved from the outdoor bar, and Jana and her daughter, Daphne, were in the pool, in the middle of a lesson on floating. It was still strange to see Jana with Daphne, Jana as a mother, which was something Jana always seemed to be embarrassed about. Her transition into motherhood had not been as seamless as everyone hoped it would be, though it was as private a struggle as everyone expected. Daniel was playing croquet with some of their better graduate students (mathematics and engineering PhDs, always the best violinists, though arts majors were better cellists) in shorts and no shirt. Now that he'd reached what might be the early part of the middle of his life, he'd grown into his hooked nose and his long arms—Brit saw that nothing looked like a mistake on him anymore. His face had transitioned from boyish to sly, even down to his small mouth, which more frequently broke into a smile these days. She spotted patches of gray on his chest hair and when he looked up, she looked away.

This was the kind of California that was sometimes so unbelievable that it was nearly unbearable, and there was nothing for Brit to do but relax into it. She sat on the edge of the pool with her legs in the water, tossing children toys and quietly cringing when they called her "auntie," and accepted plastic cups of wine from Maisie, who wanted to know when she and Paul were going to get married, and to tell her about how she'd once sung with the San Francisco Opera, and what was her favorite opera. She heard Paul say to Henry, "And that's one good thing to come out of all of this, the Iraqi police force."

"Do you have a favorite of these children?" Maisie asked, leaning into Brit. She was already a little drunk.

"I like whoever's not crying," Brit said.

Paul was over with little Jack, who really was too little for his age. He went to doctors and got shots of hormones—while his smallness was worrisome, it meant he could stay adorable. It was like he was refusing to grow up. He'd be the smallest in his kindergarten class. Could she say he was her favorite?

"I had a favorite child," Maisie said. "It was the middle one, Jordan. She was so quiet. You must have been a middle child."

"I was an only child," Brit said.

"Ah, same thing," Maisie said.

"Is Jordan still your favorite?"

"Oh, Jordan's long passed."

Brit wanted to ask of what causes, but the answer would only deepen the mystery, surely. When children died, it was always an unsolvable mystery.

"What about you, dear? Where are your parents?"

"Oh, they're dead, too," Brit said. She never liked to say *passed*. It was a silly word for what happened to people.

"Yes," Maisie said, and the two of them looked out over the indulgent pool glinting sunlight and the children who sloshed around in it, rising and falling with the subtle waves. That anyone stayed alive at all was a mystery not worth talking about.

Brit found Daniel around the side of the house, going long for a football. She waved him over and said they might have to play soon if they were going to beat the fireworks and the drunkenness—"my own," she said—and he agreed, dropping the football on the spot.

"You should probably put a shirt on," she said.

"I think Maisie would prefer I didn't," he said.

"I demand Tchaikovsky!" Maisie said when they'd set up, Daniel with a borrowed shirt (of course he couldn't find his own) and Brit having to untie her bathing suit under her tank top so that her violin could fit squarely in its spot on her neck. The children screamed in the background. Paul lay on the grass near them, but had a ladies' straw hat over his entire face. For all Brit knew, he could have been sleeping.

"Daphne, I swear to God," Jana said, hovering above her seat and angling her bow at her daughter, who had just bopped another child on the head with a croquet stick. Brit already felt drunk.

"E-flat minor?" Daniel said, more to them than to Maisie, but Maisie leaned in.

"Oh, no," she said. "You must do the *Andante cantabile*. It will break my heart."

"You sure you want your heart broken?" Daniel said, smiling. He was flirting.

"By you, always," Maisie said, floating backward, settling into a lawn chair.

"Well," Henry said. "The lady wants what the lady wants."

"The lady wants Daniel," Jana muttered, and Brit coughed and handed out the music.

The parts she provided were fresh and unmarked, nothing like their own tattered copies, whose markings were dated by the fade. The older Brit got, the less she wrote on the page, the less she even looked at the page. It was there mostly for show; they could play the piece, most pieces, with no music, no stands, nothing between them. But to do that here would be to show off, and so they unfolded the new music and clipped it to the stands with clothespins so it wouldn't fly away in the breeze.

This was useless, Brit thought as the cabana walls flapped like the snap of Paul's newspaper in the morning and the children cried indiscriminately and Maisie Allbright held her hand to her heart. What was the point? Their sound would go nowhere outdoors, especially a piece as soft and tender as this. Brit's bathing suit slipped a centimeter down her back.

No one asked if anyone else was ready and they started the piece like they were joining a song that had already begun.

Brit couldn't help blushing. Paul, her new boyfriend, had said *fuck* in the hush of Patelson's, and though they were on the upper level in the mostly empty choral section, she thought she could see the conductor of the Met at the counter below, preparing to buy a stack of scores, and he looked up sharply at the accusation. It was like cursing in church.

"I wouldn't say I *fucked* him," Brit whispered.

Paul shrugged. He'd used that word, though he didn't seem at all angry, just curious. Brit had a fleeting wish for him to be angry when he said it, at the thought of her having sex with Daniel. But Paul was smiling, amused at the thought of her salacious history.

It was June of 1997, the early evening still burning sunlight, and they were in the early stages of dating. She was showing him one of her favorite places in the city, this relic of a music shop in what was once a carriage house, an institution full of mothballs and creaky floors and rows of sheet music organized by sometimes bizarre logic in every crevice. When you exited out the back of Carnegie Hall, you were practically compelled into the store across the way, though no one who wasn't a musician would have taken a second look passing by.

Paul had bouncy hair for a man, strawberry blond, springing out of his scalp and lying in a smooth swoop across his head. He had clear skin and a quick laugh, and a face so evenly proportioned that it was sometimes forgettable. She'd had to meet him several times to register his face in her memory. He dressed well (that day, a thick navy polo shirt and well-cut slacks), had good table manners, worked in money but wasn't governed by it. He adored her.

"It was only a few months. Maybe six," she said, flipping through some Handel.

"Do you sing?"

"Who, me?"

He laughed and put his arms around her.

"What about you?" she said.

"Sing? Only scat."

"No, I mean who was your last girlfriend?"

He let her go and ran his hands through his hair. It sprung back into shape perfectly. "A real one? The last real one would have been Sarah. About three years ago. For three years."

He went on about Sarah—she'd really loved volleyball and lacrosse and had been an athlete at a small college in New England and then an accounts girl in advertising, and she'd had lovely shoulders and yes, he'd loved her, but she'd been angling to get married from the get-go, and why get married if nothing was wrong, he wondered—but all Brit thought about was that he must have broken up with Sarah around the same time she and Daniel had stopped doing whatever it was they'd been doing, and how Paul had been nursing his wounded heart at the same time she'd been nursing hers all the way over in San Francisco, and she liked to think it was cosmic, that simultaneous heartbreak.

Years later, she would tell him this, long after they'd moved in together and she assumed she wouldn't have to feel foolish for having thought that they were linked by destiny and loss, but he'd made her feel foolish anyway. He said, "But I broke up with Sarah over Christmas, so there goes that fantasy."

"Show me more," he said in Patelson's. "What other sections do you like?"

Brit led him on a sheepish tour of the space and its bound music: here's where I bought my first partitas, here's where I replaced the Stravinsky that Henry spilled tomato sauce all over, here is the best edition of the Shostakovich quartets, careful not to bend the corners. She'd never led anyone on a tour of anywhere special to her before. It seemed absurd that that was true, but it was. She fumbled through the story, trying to explain how important Hindemith was in her education to someone who didn't really know what a viola was. How did people do this, construct narratives about themselves on the spot? Brit added it to her list of things to practice.

But it was what she'd first fallen for in Paul, the story of his evolution, or at least the way he told it. There were certain secrets, even for him: an alcoholic father, a disappointing gap year, a brief affair with an older, married woman. Tame confessions, but intimacies still. It would take a while to recognize it, that what she'd loved most was the way he'd let her in, more so than what she found once she was there.

And he didn't poke a finger into the story about her parents. She told him, and he let it be, didn't extrapolate it into a mythology. Didn't even ask her to connect pieces together, though over the years she doled them out, connected them for him, and he seemed content.

"What are you thinking?" he asked, flipping a massive score of a Mozart Mass beneath his nose, sniffing the scent of new stock.

"How easy this is," she said, at the same time he said, "I mean for dinner," and they laughed loudly enough that yes, the opera conductor did see them, and frowned.

It was that easy, she marveled. Someone could unzip and open up, invite you to step inside, stay awhile.

They kissed each other sloppily, moving seamlessly from choral music to opera, landing finally in contemporary Latin American chamber music, where it occurred to Brit that she wanted tapas. They held hands and walked back through the store, pushed open the door, which rang chimes that cracked through the solemn, library-like mood, and stepped out with him leading. Outside, where it was humid and noisy, she stopped short and looked around her waist. Her purse, in all the kissing and giggling, must have been set down. She patted her pockets and spun in a circle, checking the sidewalk, and when she looked up—Paul was both there and nowhere. She hadn't yet begun to recognize his walk or his stature from the back, and any number of men let loose on Fifty-sixth Street could have been him, yet none of them were. She turned in a circle again, this time looking up. The exact color of his shirt was fading, and in the dark, lamp-lit street she wouldn't have been able to discern navy from cerulean anyway. But where was he?

Well, he'd recognize her absence soon enough and come back for her.

She went back into Patelson's and caught the door to quiet it before it clanked shut behind her. She padded to the back, where they'd lingered, and scanned the bins for her purse, fighting a fluttering in her chest. Should she have stayed outside and waited for Paul to come barreling back? Or should she have come back in, looking for her money and cards and ID?

Brit was interrupted by the sight of Daniel, messy-haired with sweat rings under his arms, holding up her green leather purse in one hand and a stack of sheet music in his other. He wore his thick glasses, which were slipping down his too-large nose, warping his eyes in a way that made him look like he was a cartoon. He always wore a look like he was trying to catch up with his face. She took a step forward, looked behind her, and then back again at him. Yes, he was still there.

"I'd recognize this mess anywhere," he said, holding the purse out.

She took it. "I didn't see you in here before."

"I didn't see you, either," he said, and immediately Brit sensed he was lying, on account of how quickly he tossed off the comment, the tiny downturn of the left corner of his mouth. "Anyway, the planets," he said.

Brit looked up and saw only ceiling. "Huh?"

He shook the music in his other hand. "I was just picking up Holst. An arrangement of *The Planets*. For us."

"Movie music?"

"It's not movie music."

"It's not quartet music."

"Ah, but it could be. It's an arrangement for four."

"Not a chance. Too much percussion. Any arrangement would sound shallow without timpani."

Daniel put a fist to his chest. "You underestimate my percussive qualities."

Brit shrugged. "You underestimate how many times I had to play that in youth orchestra. Anyway, some planets are missing."

"Pluto doesn't count," Daniel said, and propped his stack of music on a shelf to root through it. He pulled out a book on the bottom and held it up. "I'm getting this, too. This can be Earth."

It was Tchaikovsky's first quartet, which, to Brit's mild surprise, they hadn't played together yet. Like everyone who's ever heard it, she was partial to the second movement, the *Andante cantabile,* which was often played apart from the other movements, sometimes as a melancholic encore. "I love that piece," she said.

"There's an arrangement for cello and orchestra, too," Daniel said. He shrugged. "But I'm just getting the quartet."

At times it was impossible for Brit to imagine having been enamored with Daniel, as when he stood in his rigidity by endlessly arguing some dry point during rehearsal, or when he shied away from any sentimental expression by making a joke or by literally shrinking back, turning sideways to a tough conversation. But instances like this brought it all back, moments in which he betrayed his underlying warmth: here was an unmitigated tenderness for something, even if it was just music.

"So," she said. "I should go. Thanks for picking this up."

"I'll see you," he said, turning back to his stack as she turned back toward the exit. There was no way for her to know if he watched her walk out, but she sensed that he did, or imagined it, which was very similar.

Once outside—it was definitely hot now, though the sun had already gone away, but it was summer in the city—she ran straight into Paul's chest and looked up, and there he was, all strawberry-colored and -flavored and grinning down at her.

"You lost me," he said.

He took her palm in his again and started off, but she turned one last time to peer through the glass into the store that seemed like a whole other world on the inside, quiet and cool and organized and lit up, stuffed with all manner of secrets. She searched for Daniel, but found him nowhere, and recognized that even if she did spot him, even if she waved at him with her other hand, he could not have seen her in the dark.

Maisie was, of course, crying. She stood saturated in the late sun, sweating in her cover-up and crying, with Clara at her feet, the child's face buried in a ball of pink-and-white cotton candy. What was it about the *Andante cantabile* that moved middle-aged women to tears? There was something in it similar to the second movement of the Dvořák "American" String Quartet from their graduation concert in San Francisco, a lilting folk-song quality that had shades of the serious and the melancholy. The tune was almost elementary, as it repeatedly came back and back, lightly ornamented with restrained, classical turns, simple in composition—led entirely by Jana with the rest of the group in supporting roles. Brit was also moved by the piece, but not so much by the sound as by watching everyone make the sounds. Because the piece was so simple (though not really, nothing was really simple), there was a certain ease they could take with it, and Brit liked to watch Jana's lids half close as she softened into a milky sound, or Henry's full-body dip when he was given the melody for half a line, or Daniel's mouth shake a little when he got to do the rich, round vibrato as bass line. She led the syncopated support beneath Jana and above Daniel, along with Henry. She was good at it, and in a piece like this, she got to do some watching. There was an art, also, to watching.

After they were done, Maisie had her arms draped around Henry's neck. Henry was still aggravatingly in his early thirties and fresh-skinned, though tired under the eyes. Clara stomped around them, sugar-spun and trilling nonsense.

"I need to piss," Daniel announced, setting his cello back in its case. "Pee, I mean. I need to pee."

"Me too!" Clara said, whipping her cotton-candy stick in the air. "Pisssssss."

"I'll take her," Brit said to Henry, whose face was now firmly in Maisie's hands.

The three of them, Daniel, Clara, and Brit, walked into the house, where the air-conditioning chilled the pool water on their skin, making them shiver. Clara grabbed Brit's hand. "I feel sick," she said.

Brit took the cotton candy from Clara's other hand. "Let's find you some water, too, then. And I'll take this."

The bathroom was down a strangely twisted hallway (money bought curved walls) and was nearly obscured by the brightness through the glass panels that lined the very tops of the walls. It was a hallmark of rich people's homes, Brit had noticed, to add features that made it seem like you were being looked in on, that fostered the notion that you were someone worth watching, being on display.

"Can you let Daniel go first?" Brit asked.

Daniel flashed a smile. "I'll be quick, Clar."

Clara sat down in the hallway and nodded. Brit joined her. The floor was cool.

"Too much cotton candy," Brit said. "But you'll feel better soon."

Clara said nothing and they listened to Daniel urinate through the door. She saw Clara grin a little, looking down at her lap. She would be devastating one day. Her pink bathing suit was already too small, her brown legs stretching out the frayed edges. Clara had seemed to grow exponentially that year, a new girl each time Brit saw her. She'd be tall and lanky like Henry, all limbs, made fun of until she was in her twenties, and then envied. Her face was all Kimiko, though, easily tanned in the summer, cherry-wood brown eyes, precise features, no mask with which to filter anything. She had long hair, hair too long for a girl her age, Brit's mother would have thought, and Brit ran her hands through the tangles in it now. Brit wanted to tell her something like *It'll be okay,* but then she'd have to explain what wouldn't be okay, and she wasn't sure she could do that. Eight was too young to think things wouldn't be okay.

"I want to make it to fireworks," Clara said.

Brit made a small braid in the back of Clara's hair. "You will. It's almost dark."

Daniel opened the door, grinning. "All done. All yours."

"I can go alone," Clara said. "But don't leave, okay?"

Of course she could go alone, Brit thought. What eight-year-old couldn't go to the bathroom alone? She had been foolish to assume the opposite. What you knew about children could be yanked out of you in two seconds, she thought.

"We'll be here," Brit said.

Daniel sat across from her. "Do you think anyone has ever sat in this hallway before? Do you think people sit on floors in this house?"

"I think people probably sit on floors after five o'clock every day," Brit said, making a drinking motion with her hand.

"Good point," Daniel said. He tugged at his borrowed shirt, which was too small in the arms. Daniel's wide chest and long arms, of course. Brit took them in, remembering with clarity the absurd span of his body.

"What?" he said. "It's Henry's shirt."

Brit looked at the way his dark hair had faded to gray at his temples and the suggestion of gray in his patchy beard. Daniel was solidly into his forties, a decade she was staring in the face. "When did you get old?"

"Easy. December, 2004. December twenty-third, to be exact. *We* got old, you mean."

Brit laughed. "What happened then?"

"Remember, we played in that Christmas concert for the department? And Kimiko brought Clara and Jack, and Jack was sick, and Jana had just started dating Finn, and Daphne was two and a disaster. We played something . . . some contemporary *Nutcracker* arrangement blah-

blah, and it was basically us playing through screaming children, and afterward Henry and Jana wanted to go do that gift exchange at Henry's place—"

"—but we made up that lie," Brit said, remembering. "What did we say?"

"That we had bad shrimp. Which was so not true. We didn't even have shrimp, and we all ate dinner together."

"Right. But they didn't notice because they couldn't notice anything but babies then."

"And then you and I went to that movie with the robots and that kid actor—"

"—oh, what was that movie? I can't remember."

"See? We're old."

"We fell asleep in the theater, anyway. So I blame the movie."

"I blame how old we were. We are."

"I thank God all the time that you'll always be older," Brit said. He smiled at her, and the light changed from orange to gray. The sun had set.

"At least we're not Paul-old. His newest hobby is building those ships in bottles. Like we're retired."

"Ugh, hobbies," Daniel said, practically spitting it. "I hope I never have a hobby. The very idea of it is offensive. Commit to something or don't do it."

"I'm sure your girlfriends say that about you all the time," Brit said.

Daniel shrugged. "So dating is my hobby."

They didn't say anything for a while. Brit pursed her lips into a smile and stared at the fading wall behind Daniel's head. When you wanted to talk to people about the past, it was never exactly the way you imagined it, Brit thought. She wanted to say something about the ocean-sized expanse of hours and years between them, how they'd once been fragile people who threw themselves at each other, and how now they were real people, more *of* the body than those twenty-somethings always on the verge of a breakdown. You aged, and even though you used your arms and hands and fingers and spine as tools to play music, your skin still sagged and your hair lost pigment, your bones ached and you were stiff in places that used to be pliable. They were just people whose physical parts were slowly failing them. They'd become adults in this strange thing they did, in the years they'd attached themselves to each other, the half a lifetime they'd orbited the quartet. They went through life as a unit, banking on the consistency of emotional expression, all the while given to the same normal tragedies and impulses and failures and passions as everybody else. Marriage, children, death, and other, more vague departures. It seemed to Brit that what they'd done was sew onto each other those moments like patches: *If you go down, I go, too.*

"Auntie?"

Clara's wet voice seeped through the door. Brit got up and helped Daniel up—"old man," she said—and inside the bathroom they found Clara on her hands and knees on the big cerulean tiles.

"I don't feel good," she said.

Brit kneeled down by the girl and Daniel filled a small glass with tap water. He sat on the edge of the tub and handed the glass to Clara, who took small sips. Her eyes were damp, and she'd taken the straps of her bathing suit off her shoulders, like she was trying to be free of it.

Brit rubbed her back. "Just breathe."

"Brit," Daniel said quietly, and jerked his thumb behind him. "Check this out."

Behind Daniel, on the rim of the oval Jacuzzi tub, was a picture frame leaning against a tile mosaic of an exotic bird. In the frame was the quartet, an old publicity picture they'd used when they first came to Stanford, before the university paid to have new pictures taken. It was the one of them standing at the corner of Van Ness and McAllister, waiting for the light to change, still students at the conservatory. They'd been impossibly young.

"Where on earth did they get that?" Brit asked.

She left Clara and stepped into the empty bathtub for a closer look. In her hands, their youth was ludicrous. Here they were, forever preserved in black-and-white, eight by ten, their faces quietly waiting and unburdened by a hundred concerts a year, muscle spasms, colicky babies, the pressure of the Kennedy Center, jet lag from another hemisphere. She touched the image of her own face like she'd be able to feel it—her face then, softer and always expecting something, wanting something, open to see what she was sure was coming. In the picture, she was looking out over the street and Daniel was next to her, holding the curves of his cello and looking down and to the side, his head cocked, his gaze on the tips of her hair in the wind. Or something in that direction. It was difficult to tell what exactly they were looking at, even Henry and Jana behind them, who had much more determined expressions, fixed on the same spot just off camera. The people standing beside them blurred. Their instruments were shiny and unreal. The picture had caught them in a *tutti tacet*, a great Grand Pause. They all had been waiting for the light to change, but their expectant faces made her sad. Their lives then had been arranged around waiting or chasing, but waiting and chasing the wrong things—success, money, recognition, a relationship, a mother, a child. It had taken them years to figure out that what they'd been after was already circulating at that stoplight.

It was like looking at another life, and Brit's whole body was filled with the kind of desperate yearning she hadn't felt in years and years. She crouched in the tub.

"It's like a time machine," Daniel said. "Isn't it?"

"I don't even know these people."

"What do you remember?"

"About what?"

"About that time?"

Brit rubbed the edge of the frame. It was cheap. When was the last time anyone had asked her what she remembered, had wanted to know, even though they had also been there? "I remember being surprised at how disappointing things were."

"And now you just expect it?"

"No," Brit said. "Now I know whatever things I was sad about weren't really disappointments."

Daniel shifted, put one leg in the tub. "And then good things happened. For us."

"Oh my God," Brit said, a realization coming over her. She turned to Daniel and held the picture up. "We're eternally taking a bath in here."

They looked at each other and smiled, recognized each other both then and now. This, she thought. This was what she meant to say: this picture, the way three words—*take a bath*—could bring reeling back an entire story, one that neither of them could really tell anymore, but one of the moments that they'd each grown around for years, that they carried inside their bodies, in their cells and molecules, what they were made of. The story spanned the distance between their past and their future, and suddenly, briefly, they were two versions of themselves. And if they were two versions of themselves, they were also all the versions in between, and their entire shared life unfolded before them. This kind of intimacy was hard to talk about or explain. This kind of clarity was hard to hold on to. But Brit and Daniel could be in it together for a few moments, in the tub. Time travelers.

And here they were, in a fancy bathroom, Brit's dirty feet muddying up a pristine tub, Daniel straddled on the edge in a too-small shirt, and the strange child on their periphery, prostrate on the floor. Here was a possible life, she thought, and for the first time she was unbothered by the thought, was instead comforted by it. Even the choices they hadn't made were contained in that space. That could be enough.

Brit leaned forward on her knees, the porcelain smashing her bones, and pulled herself up the side of the tub, to where Daniel was sitting. He was giving off warmth, his lips slightly parted, eyes still, watching her. She took her time positioning her mouth so that it matched with his, and then lightly pushed her lips against his, opened his mouth with hers, gave him her tongue, and he took it, and they passed electricity back and forth. She cupped his chin with her hands. She could feel from somewhere in the pit of her stomach an insistent urge to pull him closer to her, to finish the chemical exchange of warmth, and the recognition of its possibility expressed itself in a small whimper in her throat. This was what it was like to kiss Daniel after thirteen years, like kissing someone entirely new, a stranger who happened to be so familiar as to be cut from your own body.

And then the child vomited. A thin, pink puddle beneath her and stringing from her lips, growing larger on the expensive floor.

Brit wanted to laugh, but instead she placed the frame on the bottom of the tub and hurried to Clara, guided her to the toilet, where she retched again. Brit looked over her shoulder at Daniel, but he was already up and in the linen closet by the door, pulling out towels and spray bottles. Together, they cleaned up the floor and Clara, and Brit repositioned Clara's bathing suit straps and kissed her on the cheek. She smelled sour.

"You're okay," she said.

Clara nodded. "Okay," she said, believing her.

Outside, it had become night. The thwang of a soccer ball rang against the wall of the house and Daniel winced, but then they heard the first whinny of a rising firework, which, after half a second, they saw evidence of through the windows along the top of the wall. Brit pointed up at the billowing sparks.

"See? You didn't miss it."

Back outside, the night reasserted itself. It had grown chilly and Maisie and Richard passed out blankets, which people pulled around themselves with their necks craned upward. Everyone was mostly silent in the round boom of the fireworks, except Clara, whom Brit heard say to her father in a clear, high voice, after placing her hand firmly in his, "I was sick, but now I'm not." And then Clara leaned into her mother, whispered something into her ear. Kimiko looked at Brit, and Brit shrugged back at her. Let the girl tell, she thought, if that's what she was doing.

Brit found Paul and crouched on the grass with him. He smelled like summer: sunscreen and exhaustion with an undercurrent of something ending. He put his arm around her and she gathered into his hot shoulders. The pool hadn't gone still yet and the fireworks reflected sloppily on its surface. Next to her, Jana had Daphne on her lap, who slept upright through the whole noise of the display, her black hair across Jana's lips. That's what it should be, Brit thought, *Andante cantabile* should be something to put children to sleep to, like the Mozart tape she'd listened to as a child. Maybe that's why people were so moved when they heard it. It reminded them of their own childhoods, how easy it used to be to drift off, how even the most serious thoughts only dipped into the minor key, how every melody ended in reassurance. How hard it was to drift off peacefully as an adult.

Brit tried to fit the irregular booms into the Tchaikovsky that was running through her head, but the fireworks wouldn't fit the singing, and after a while she gave up trying, and gave in to listening to the sound that was right in front of her.

Later, after the arrangement to babysit Clara, Jack, and Daphne for an overnight was made, Paul blamed Brit, but Brit blamed Paul, and both were very sure they had not officially offered during the barbeque. Brit was very sure it had been Paul, in a moment of magnanimity that went along with whatever semi-tedious conversation topic he'd become newly obsessed with, vaccinations or school vouchers or attachment parenting. Likely he'd been lecturing Kimiko about it, whatever it was, and Brit had tried to placate Kimiko, who cared not at all about any of those things, by agreeing to whatever babysitting offer Paul had made. But there they were, three kids between the ages of five and eight, dropped off at their condo in the late afternoon, to be picked up the next morning. Kimiko and Henry were taking a night away in Monterey, and Jana, hearing this news, quickly jumped on, scheduling something for her and Finn in Tahoe, and as the children tumbled through their doorway, Brit wondered why she and Paul never went away on the weekends anymore. They used to do things like that, but the sheer number of years they'd been together made any weekend away the same as a weekend at home. They were the same wherever they were, which is why, Brit supposed, people stayed together for this long. For that sense of orderly sameness, familiarity, the reassurance that you were an immovable, consistent being.

"Thanks," Henry said, walking backward. "Call if there's a problem!"

Kimiko waved from the car. "But only a really big problem," Kimiko shouted through the open window.

Paul had set up the living room as a play area, but when Brit saw what he'd done, she wondered if he'd ever seen kids play before. He'd moved the couches back against the walls, and the carpet was a shocked white where the furniture had been. The glass coffee table had been turned upside down and pushed against another wall. He'd moved everything to the perimeter, like the children were animals who needed open space.

Immediately they all sat down on the couches, now much farther apart from each other than was comfortable.

"What should we do?" Brit asked them.

"Do you have a pool?" Jack asked.

Clara nudged him. "No, dummy. You know that already."

"We could go to a pool," Paul said, standing up.

"No," Brit said. "No, let's stay here. We can do something without a pool."

The children stared at her blankly. Brit was less afraid of the children than she'd been when they were all babies, delicate and always upset. The way babies cried instantly—whenever something was remotely uncomfortable—made her heartbroken, too heartbroken. And not because she didn't want them to be hurt (though she didn't), but because she empathized. Babies didn't know social norms, the way people constantly negotiated emotions, pushed them down, ignored them, shoved them into blacked-out corners, and crying babies reminded Brit that adults were all ignoring some deep, undulating pain, nearly every hour of every day. Babies seemed like the real people, and adults like the mediated versions, whittled away by the world. It was depressing, anxiety-producing to be around them. But children, especially ones this age, who had recently learned how people act and were excited to act similarly, this she could recognize and deal with.

Coming up with an activity for all of them to do at once was nearly impossible, however. She suggested charades (Jack and Daphne too young) and coloring (Clara too old) and tag (too boring for all of them). Not only did their ages present a unification problem, but so did their personalities. Jack, the youngest, was sweet but—and Brit would never, ever say this out loud—kind of dumb. *Uninterested* might be a better way to describe a five-year-old, she decided. Nothing she ever came up with seemed to stimulate a response, so she always resorted to hugging him. He'd be the cuddly child. Maybe he'd develop some kind of interest in the world later. Daphne was exactly the opposite of how Brit imagined Jana as a little girl: happy by default, eager to please, quick to laugh, quick to cry, a collection of emotions simmering just beneath her new skin. And Clara was a classic oldest child, and acted not only as Henry and Kimiko's oldest child, but also as the oldest child of the whole lot of them, her parents included. She often adopted an exasperated tone with her father, whom she adored, and an incredulous tone with her mother, whom she worshipped, and then acted as caretaker and leader of Daphne and Jack. She was precocious and observant and—it went mostly unremarked on, so as to not apply pressure—an extremely good violinist.

"Can I play?" Clara asked, gesturing to Brit's office, where she stored her violin and sheet music.

"Mmm, maybe later," Brit said. "Why don't we do something we can all do together?"

"Mom keeps trying to get Jack to play the piano, but he doesn't want to," Clara said.

"Piano's boring," Jack said, smiling.

"I like piano," Daphne said. "My mom puts piano on when we clean. Shoe-man."

"Schumann," Clara corrected her.

Brit looked at Paul and Paul looked back and they saw, together, the day's hours elongate like a dry, horizonless desert before them. Brit raised her eyebrows. Did he have anything to offer?

"What about a fort?" Paul said. "I moved all the furniture, so you might as well make something here."

They all seemed to get excited about that in the physical way children get excited. They squirmed off the couch, tossed their belongings (not exactly) in corners, and began tearing cushions off the chairs. Brit went to the closet to get blankets and empty boxes for propping things on and was suddenly struck by a long-latent memory: building a blanket fort with her father one Christmas Eve, a maze that led across the dining room and living room to the Christmas tree, a dark, dusty world that smelled like trees, the way everything on that island smelled like trees. Brit paused in the hallway, her arms full of blankets, and tried to remember something specific—anything—she and her father had said or done that night, but all she could conjure were the red lights breaking through the makeshift roof as she and her father crawled on their hands and knees toward the smell of pine needles and ribbon.

When she walked back into the living room, she found that the children had essentially torn it apart. Paul stood over them like a shell-shocked soldier. The furniture had been moved (how long had she been standing in the hallway?), and the picture frames taken from the mantel to mark some kind of path, which Jack kicked into place. Daphne was dragging plants to one side, for what? An entry? An exit? A garden? Clara stood on the table giving directions. Brit loved how different it all looked, and how quickly it had transformed. Paul looked at her angrily.

"Just go work in your office," she said to him. "I'll do this. You can do dinner."

She knew that Paul, Paul who harbored an aversion to anything messy, literally or otherwise, hadn't pictured a fort like this. But Brit wondered what other way there was to create a fort than to tear apart everything for materials and then rebuild. Paul tapped her back in thanks and disappeared toward the bedroom. Brit dove in.

The fort became more and more complicated, and Brit had to go digging in the garage for tent poles and stability balls. Jack devised booby traps (maybe he was interested in something, after all), which Daphne got trapped in, and Clara, the architect, designed the path through the fort with rooms and anterooms and various exits and ceiling heights and furniture. Brit's living room was transformed not just into a fort, but into an entire world, and not one of her making. She did what Clara said to do, but she rarely understood it until it was finished, and even then, the results all seemed to follow some obscure-to-her kid logic, the layout and organization patched together from pieces of adult living they'd observed or half observed. In the end, what was produced was something so messy and chaotic and full that looking at it—and the kids existing in and throughout it—made Brit's throat tighten. This was what it was like to be a kid, out of the baby world of suffering, and into the world made imperfect by your own hands.

"What's wrong?" Clara asked, seeing her face. "Do you need a kiss?"

Brit was startled by Clara's question, and Clara was clearly startled at Brit's response. Brit put a hand on Clara's head and kissed her cheek, her own face clammy.

Brit stepped through the sliding glass door to her meager backyard, where the sun had almost set and the mosquitoes were starting to emerge. She gulped some air and thought not of the transformed living room, but the transformed afternoon in the other house, the Fourth of July, only two weeks ago, when Clara must have seen her kissing Daniel (how many people in this quartet would Brit kiss?) and decided it was normal. Perhaps she'd even told Kimiko, who might have told Henry, though he'd said nothing. Brit and Daniel had also said nothing afterward, the kiss like a bubble that had grown in the bathroom and popped once they left. She didn't think about it after she left the bathroom, went back to Paul, drove home with him, went to bed, got up, read the paper, did everything all over again, and then over again. She didn't think about the kiss because she understood it to be an attempt to bridge the bizarre spread of time that had been made visible to both her and Daniel that day. The kiss was honest and complete. There was nothing else to say about it.

But that didn't mean that it didn't seep into her life somehow, a fact she'd shoved down as far as it could go these past couple of weeks. When she next kissed Paul, she felt different, as though participating in something new and separate from her, and it was a little bit exciting. It surprised her, that the kiss with Daniel was the one that felt familiar, like flipping the switch on in a part of her that had been turned off for years. But what exactly was it that was turned off? That question was what Brit thought about instead of the kiss itself, what she lay awake thinking about next to Paul's complacent, unconscious body.

Brit turned to look back through the sliding glass door, the inside of her place now lit up against the dark outside. The children were still playing in their fort, messing it up, tearing walls down, fixing them, getting lost. She'd helped build the form, but they'd inhabited it in a way she couldn't understand.

From somewhere inside the house she heard shouting, and when she slid open the door, she knew it was Paul. The two girls were standing outside the fort, looking down the hallway.

"Where's Jack?" Brit asked, and they pointed.

They found him in Paul's office, where Paul painstakingly put together his ships inside bottles. Paul stood in the center of the room and Jack cowered in the far corner. At Paul's feet was a collection of broken glass and pieces of a ship that looked, when shattered, like it was made from cheap kitchen utensils. She felt an urge to laugh, looking at the small boy, afraid in a corner, and the grown man staring and shouting at his broken toy.

"He broke it!" Paul shouted, answering a question that Brit hadn't asked. "He fucking broke all those hours of work!"

"Paul," Brit said. "Stop it. It's just a boat."

"Goddammit, it's not a boat. Don't call it a boat."

"Okay, well, you have about sixteen others over here." Brit gestured toward the shelves where, in fact, Paul had a large collection of miniature boats—ships—inside absurdly shaped bottles, a wall begging to be broken.

Paul looked up at her, looked up finally from the ruins at his feet, and narrowed his eyes, his mouth. Jack was frozen in his spot. "That's not the point. The point is that Henry doesn't teach his kids how to treat nice things."

Brit walked closer to Paul, hoping Jack and the children wouldn't hear, trying not to notice that the boy was noticing every tiny breath and utterance between the two of them.

"He's only five. You're scaring him. This is a hobby. Everyone will live," Brit said quietly.

"How would you feel if it was one of your violins? Why didn't you let Clara play your violin earlier?" Paul asked. "You know, you can't stand here and act so much nobler than me when you care about your *hobby* as much as I do. You all bank on being so collaborative and community-minded, et cetera, et cetera, but you're really more selfish than any of the rest of us blessed to grace your lives." He looked to the doorway, where Clara and Daphne were frozen. "Clara! Brit says you can play her violin. Go get it."

It's a twenty-six-thousand-dollar violin gifted to me by the foundation in Moscow, she didn't say. *It's my livelihood,* she didn't say. *I don't even own it,* she didn't say.

What she did say, slowly, evenly, coldly: "That is art. This is a toy."

Paul walked out of the room and returned with her violin. "Let her play it, Brit," he said.

She looked from the violin in Paul's smooth hands to Clara's reddened face. Clara's right hand held on to the doorway, afraid as she was to fully step inside, and her left hand clutched Daphne's. Out of Clara's mouth bubbled something so thick that it seemed at first, to Brit, like bile—except it wasn't physical. Clara said, with relief in her voice, "I saw Brit kissing Uncle Daniel."

It had been absurd to expect a child, so new to the world of logic and reason, to keep a secret like that. It would have been absurd for Brit to be shocked by Clara's admission. Paul had moved the girl into the center of their argument, a pawn, and Clara had very intelligently replaced herself with a different sort of pawn, knowledge she hadn't entirely understood except that it had been private, and that was a concept she was only just beginning to know.

Much later, Kimiko would say to Brit, "Who knows why she did that? She's a strange girl." But Brit knew. She recognized in Clara a powerful desire to please the people around her, to be liked without being the center of anyone's attention, to share the burden and the spotlight, the glory and the blame. Clara saw the connections between people, and then *became* a connection. This was what would make Clara a good chamber musician.

When the dinner had been eaten (pizza, takeout) and the baths lolled in (Brit administering, of course), the children slept in their fort. They asked, and Brit felt that she couldn't say no after what they'd had to witness. She watched them crawl in with flashlights, their small bottoms disappearing into the dark entrance, and after some rustling in various chambers and a whimper that stopped just before she was about to intervene, she turned out the light and went to bed.

Paul was already under the blanket, glasses on, book out, large glass of wine at the bedside table. Brit pulled off her jeans, tied her hair up, and climbed in on her side.

She'd been here before, on the other side, as the listener to the thing that can't be unsaid. A cheesy pub near Edmonton, a meatloaf poorly digested.

Paul put his book down, something serious with a woman in a suit on the front, claiming she could get you a better life if you followed these seven steps of good business. "I'm supposed to say I'm sorry, I guess."

"You don't have to say anything," Brit said. "You said enough."

"So did you."

Paul gave a speech—it felt like a speech. Brit could tell he'd thought about it and rehearsed it, probably when she was ordering pizza and feeding her friends' kids and bathing them and reading them stories. He was delivering a speech about how he would get over it, but. But Daniel couldn't come over anymore, and he didn't want to ever speak to him again. But how about she not kiss other men. But she can't continue to demean everything he does, whether it's manage rich people's money or build model ships (*ships*), and anyway, she took rich people's money and did something her whole life that most people would think was elite, snobby, trivial. He hadn't really meant she was selfish, but. But maybe what they did trained them to be selfish. But they all couldn't walk around expecting everyone else to understand that there was this relationship in their lives that was superior to every other relationship, and they had to understand that other people valued other things, and well, but. He seemed less upset about the kiss than about the fact that Clara knew, which meant Henry and Kimiko knew, which embarrassed him, that it was public that someone else had co-opted his *nice thing*, his boat, his girlfriend.

While he spoke, Brit heard only the word *selfish*. It had rang in her ears like a reedy note from a cheap clarinet all through dinner and bathtime. She wasn't mad, at least not anymore. She had been mad when she had to explain to Clara why what she'd said had made Paul disappear for the rest of the night. She'd seethed silently when the girl cried a little. But his accusation—that she was selfish—lodged between her ribs like shrapnel. No one had ever called her that before, though she'd thought it about many people, including, from time to time, Daniel. And Jana. And Henry, too. All of them devoted to their playing, to the career they thought they should have, to the talent they couldn't help having. But it hadn't seemed so damaging, to think them selfish. Because what they were devoted to, essentially, was her. Each other. Music.

So Paul was right. She was selfish. She had been trained that way, and she had survived because of it. She had spent so many years trying not to be alone, finding the opposite of loneliness in what the quartet did in rehearsal and on stage, and in the end, she'd made that sovereign in her life. First was the music, which was servant to nothing. Second was everything else, servant to her music.

"It's okay," Brit said, interrupting Paul. She smiled, turned on her side toward him, grabbed his hand under the blanket. All the years sweetly diffusing in front of her. "I'm not sorry, either."

PART 4

Sediment to Sky for Four
—Julia St. John

"American" String Quartet in F Major, op. 96, no. 12
—Antonín Dvořák

Octet in E-flat Major, op. 20
—Felix Mendelssohn

September 2007
The Redwoods

HENRY

Viola

There were, as Henry saw it, two kinds of pain. Short pain and long pain. Short pain wasn't just pain that lasted temporarily. It could be chronic or recurrent. It could be sharp or dull. What made short pain short was that it stopped your playing immediately, stopped you short in rehearsal. It's the kind of pain where suddenly you feel shards of glass in your elbow, and you leave rehearsal early, pop four aspirin, go to your physical therapist or doctor for some stronger pills, and come back two days later. Maybe it comes back in six months, maybe it doesn't. Short pain is like a cleaver coming down on your arm, cutting deeply, and while it's scarring and hurts like hell, it's fixable, it has the possibility of healing. Long pain, though, was the kind of pain that, while it could be acutely excruciating, specifically and precisely horrific, was deep inside the bones and tissue. Here, the cleaver has already come down with finality, you've been separated from yourself, and for the rest of your life, you are a person with reattached parts, threaded back on, a little lame, a little altered. Short pain was part of your body. Long pain was part of your life.

It was long pain that Henry was more accustomed to, though short pain was no stranger. The long pain was in the elbow and wrist of his bow arm. All his young life, playing had been easy. Playing had been the easiest thing he'd ever done. And when playing began to hurt, as it does for anyone who has played for years and years, he ignored it. Easy was the way he was used to living his life, and he would continue living that way by force of will if he had to. But when his sister was diagnosed with her heart problem, and his father, too, revealed his bad heart, Henry decided to no longer ignore the pain. When he described it to the doctor, he said that it felt like something heavy had fallen on his arm, rendering it both numb and blood-hot. He said he wanted either to ice the limb or to cut it off at the triceps. He said not playing was not an option. The doctor had looked at the X-rays, given him a brief physical test, and said, foolishly, "Can you cut back on playing?"

What the quartet knew: Henry had a particularly bad case of tendonitis in his elbow and wrist, and it was treatable if he maintained regular physical therapy and didn't participate in marathon rehearsals.

What no one but Kimiko knew: the doctors had repeatedly warned him that if he didn't cut back on playing, there would come a time very soon where there would be no playing at all. With every flare-up he was causing not only tissue damage but nerve damage, changing the very makeup between his skin and bone, grinding away bit by bit at whatever was left there to help his bow arm stay fluid or go *spiccato* at a moment's notice. His tendonitis was also musculoskeletal, and the doctors asked him to think of it as opening and reopening lesions that connected his tissue to his bone through nerves. Continuing to play at the rate the quartet played was literally destroying his right arm.

What was the worst part: he could never predict the pain's acute expression. While it always thrummed dully beneath the surface, flare-ups, as he'd experienced during the second Esterhazy and countless times since, were impossible to predict. He wished he had something like a migraine aura or some other kind of warning. Nausea, sickness, a bad mood, even.

And here it was happening at the Festival of the Redwoods, where they were teaching and performing at a chamber music festival in a grove of trees between the mythically wild Northern California ocean and the hot-gold hills of the vineyards. It was their second time at the festival, a favorite of theirs because of the location and the people and the generally relaxed attitude of all of it. They could bring their children and they slept in log cabins and rehearsals were often in the shade of a seven-hundred-year-old Sequoia, one that had been around before Haydn, before Vivaldi, before what they were doing was invented. But also here was the span of his right elbow to wrist, burning in such a way that he wanted to shake it, right before they were to go on stage for the world premiere—a soft premiere—of Julia St. John's commissioned quartet.

"Are you okay?" Jana asked, touching his arm.

"Just a—just that thing again. Can you find my aspirin? It's in the pocket of my case over there."

He was suddenly hot in the outdoor amphitheater, though the wind blew a mostly pleasant chill and Brit pulled out her cardigan to play. *Don't think about it,* he thought. *Don't think about it don't think about it don't think about it.*

Thinking about it was what got you into trouble. Because if you thought about your elbow, then you thought about that permanent knot in your neck, your lower-back spasms in bed some mornings—and the way blood flowed through the body like magic, how the magic was flawed in your sister and your father, and how your body, too, was flawed, how bodies were simply physical machines and not magic at all.

He swallowed three aspirin—okay, four—and walked a bit down

the path, asked the host to stall, tell a few jokes. He stamped his feet under some trees and visualized the pain dissipating. That's what one doctor had said to do in emergencies. Imagine it gathering together, getting all its things, and floating out of your body from a single point. Now he heard the wind, now he heard the applause. He walked back, picked up his viola, and nodded to Jana and Brit and Daniel. They went on.

The acoustics in the outdoor amphitheater were shit, and the afternoon performance wasn't open to the public, which is why they were calling this a soft premiere. The official premiere would be the following night, at the festival's penultimate concert, *indoors,* and open to the general public. But in this audience were people who mattered, professional peers, including the all-male, all-drama Sequoia Quartet, who were also teaching at the festival. Henry spotted them—well, half of them—sitting in the front row. Only two of the members of that quartet were even talking to each other, something they tried to hide from the students, which, of course, just revealed it more clearly to everyone. There was something about a few nasty interviews, someone sleeping with someone else (though Henry wasn't sure who or why that was wrong), and a theft of some kind.

The piece, *Sediment to Sky for Four,* was beautiful, deceivingly plain, a meditation on land. Julia St. John was a self-proclaimed naturalist, living on zero-carbon shared land (*not a commune,* she'd corrected someone at a talk Henry had attended once) in Mendocino County. Nothing made Henry and Kimiko squirm more than imagining communal farm living, but Julia's lifestyle didn't keep her from being recently named one of the most important living composers by *The New York Times.* She'd been Brit's friend first (Brit had been the one to spend some time with her on the commune-not-a-commune), but when Julia began sitting in on rehearsals, she was a natural fit with the group. She was wry and serious, generous without forgoing expectations. Even Daniel, with his high standards and squirrely patience, loved her.

She worked on *Sediment to Sky* quickly, and they'd gone through two rounds of back-to-the-drawing-board with her. Henry had loved participating in the process of composing, or advising to the composition, more than he'd expected, more than he'd remembered. Back in the salad days of conservatory, before children and New York, when he'd done everything to its maximum, when there'd been time and praise and women, he'd dabbled in composing. He aced composition class and started, though never finished, an opera.

The St. John collaboration came at a good time: the quartet had tired of the same old program (Haydn, Beethoven, something not too alienating from the early twentieth century), and Henry could feel everyone getting antsy and bored. They were geniuses, Beethoven and Haydn, but it was as though the quartet had agreed to read the same forty-five books over and over and over again for the rest of their lives. Henry thought (but didn't say) he was the most bored of them all, and at night he lay awake, dead tired from the day but unable to sleep, thinking about how people lived long lives, how everyone must die disappointed that they've arranged their lives so nothing ever changes too much.

The quartet sat down in the amphitheater to play, and Henry winced at the expectation of pain. It was less severe than he'd been prepared for, but he knew it would only become more intense the longer they played. The piece was told in three long movements, each movement *attacca* to the next, which is what made it exhausting in particular, but what made it exhausting in general were the emotional requirements. It put no instrument to waste, especially not the so-often-ignored viola, and took the players through the full emotional range. Henry steeled his arm, his body, his unsure heart.

The performance went well—trees were conjured, soil was wafted—but Julia still had some notes for them afterward. Don't take the second movement so fast, she told Jana, and could Daniel come out more always, she wanted a strong foundation throughout, and Henry, was everything okay? He was making faces during the performance.

"Oh, it's this," he said, holding up his right hand. "Just sometimes it's bad."

Julia looked worried. Jana put her hand on Julia's. "He'll be fine," she said. "We've been playing a lot here, those reading parties. We won't do it again until the performance."

"But the master class," Henry said. "Tomorrow we have a master class."

"Well, you're not *taking* the class. You don't have to play," Jana said.

Henry liked to demonstrate. He still remembered Fodorio sitting in with them during the master class before their final conservatory concert, how he'd taught them about energy and verve and engagement simply by playing with them instead of talking at them. Henry liked to do that when he taught. It made the students hungry.

He begged off the post-concert meal and took the long way back to his cabin, where Kimiko was reading while Jack napped and Clara did her homework on the porch. They'd taken her out of school to come to the festival, but Kimiko made sure to sit with her every afternoon and do the take-home assignments, shockingly difficult for an eight-year-old. But Clara was nothing if not precocious, which surely came from Kimiko.

Kimiko put down her book when she saw his face. "Did it not go well?"

"It was fine," he said, opening the freezer door and sticking his hand in between two bags of ice.

Kimiko put her arms around him from behind. He closed his eyes in the cold air.

"I'm sorry. Should I call in some Vicodin to the pharmacy in town?"

"I can't play with Vicodin," Henry said, annoyed she would suggest that. She knew how foggy it made him. Maybe he could play Mozart with a Vicodin, sure, but not Beethoven and definitely not the St. John.

"No need to snap."

He turned to face her and put his cold hands on her hot arms. Sometimes she was a marvel. Once this young girl he'd thought he was lucky to sleep with, someone who never wanted him to meet any of her friends, who didn't really have friends, who was too good a player for friends. She'd been a student who was intimidating in every way to him, the teacher. And now here she was his wife, his wife for many years, the person with whom he—Henry, who honestly never stopped feeling like a child himself—raised children, strange humans with their own interests and ideas. Sometimes he looked at her and saw years, and in the years he saw what religious people must see: the uncontainable presence of something impossible and divine.

But other times, like now, for instance, he saw himself from her position. How his possible self—on his own, in less pain, happier than he'd been recently—must look like a flickering, disappearing image to her. He saw himself before he'd acquired all these things and people and responsibilities, which isn't to say he didn't love the things and people and responsibilities—they were also life—but he understood he had slowly exchanged that possible self for this way of living. Kimiko's gaze always reminded Henry that he would not be both people at once, would not have both lives.

"What do you want?" he asked. "For me to go on stage tomorrow night half asleep? For them to write about the violist that doped his way through Julia's premiere?"

Kimiko stepped back, went to the day bed under the window where she'd been reading, and sat down. "I want you to feel better."

"I'll feel better if I get a new arm," Henry said, resigned. He sat down next to her. The old springs bounced them two, three times.

"If you left quartet-playing—"

He cut her off. "Not now."

"If you stepped back—listen, what I'm saying is if you retired and just took soloist gigs, taught every other semester, you could control your schedule, you could have off time when you wanted off time. When your arm wanted off time."

She was right. All those things would lessen the incessant shredding of the inside of his right arm and give him some time. That was the thing that was disappearing. Time. He lay back on the bed, shoved himself against the wall beneath the window where redwood-filtered light blasted through. It was gorgeous here. They were blindingly lucky. Kimiko lay down next to him, tucked her knees at the back of his.

"I don't want to do that," Henry said.

"So what *do* you want?"

Henry closed his eyes. He wanted Vicodin, to go to sleep, for Jack to keep napping. He wanted to go back to the moment where his arm first hurt and un-hurt it, turn a different corner, get up from rehearsal, where Jana was probably shouting at him, and Daniel was taking the solo too fast, and Brit wasn't loud enough. He wanted to go back, as far back as was required, and reconstitute his bone, restring the strings of muscle coating that bone, build thicker and more sinewy the fine tendons twitching those strings. Now he wanted to sleep, he wanted to drink.

"I don't know," Henry said to Kimiko, and meant it. He had no idea.

When he woke, it was dark, early dark, and he was alone. There was the sound of the children outside with other children, and through the window he saw Kimiko with a glass of wine and Jack shouting at the flies. Henry walked outside and the screen door slammed behind him like a memory of the countryside he'd never had. His arm ached dully now, like low-grade electricity was running through his thin ulna. It felt comfortable, that pain. Long pain.

He stood next to Kimiko and watched the children play. Clara ran after Jack, all limbs. She threw her arms about when she ran, kicked her legs so that they nearly slapped her bottom. The forest floor crunched beneath her feet, and her outline kept disappearing in the transition to night.

"I'm afraid she's going to fall," Kimiko said.

"So she falls," Henry said. "You gotta let 'em fall."

"Not her," Kimiko said, watching intently.

Henry understood what she meant was Clara's arms and hands, how good she'd become at the violin, scary good. Not prodigy good, but good enough to pay a teacher in the city $150 per lesson twice a week, good enough to start thinking about auditioning for the SF Youth, good enough that both he and Kimiko felt wary about it. Don't break your arm, they wished. Break your arm, they wished.

He sighed. "I'm gonna go check on the Sierra House."

She kissed his arm. "Don't stay out late," she said. "You need rest."

Henry walked toward the Sierra House, the common building where the students (mostly very good amateur adults from the area) and the faculty (always the Sequoia Quartet) gathered for reading parties and drinking, where they made the hot tub too hot and raided the kitchen for cheese. He had stumbled away from the concert and slept the afternoon away and felt he should make an appearance so people didn't think he was sulking.

He heard the Sierra House before he saw it: the Rimsky-Korsakov Sextet. A slight piece, Henry thought, not indicative of what the composer was capable of, or what the form could sound like. It sounded lazy when it was played, halfway toward dying. For a moment he stood outside and watched the inside scene lit up through the window. The Sequoia Quartet was playing with two more advanced students, and Henry saw it wasn't only the piece that was lazy, but the playing. Ryan, the first violinist, the handsome drunk from Alaska, was flailing all over the place. Colin, the second violinist, looked on lovingly at Sam, the violist, whom Henry actually liked. He was the most rational of the four, though he wasn't entirely sane. He was older than the rest of them and clearly bothered by it, puffing his chest during master class and sidling up to Henry partly because (and Henry knew this) of Henry's talent and status. The cellist, Jerome, was the worst of them all. He'd been the one who gave the nasty interview, the most recent one, where he'd subtly outed Colin and Sam, who were both married to other men (who were pointedly absent here in the redwoods), making an affair that was already public knowledge officially public and in print. It was semi-surprising that the quartet had ended up even coming to the festival, especially after the interview.

The worst part—what made the Sequoia truly insufferable—was that they were almost transcendently good. Almost, but not quite, the most frustrating level of talent, and Henry disliked listening to them. It was like listening to the warbling of a chord that was the tiniest of intervals away from being in tune.

Around the players, other students watched, clutching sweaty longnecks, Brit talked to Daniel at the kitchen table (something was amiss there, though it wasn't yet clear what), a golden retriever slept at Ryan's feet, and Jana sat cross-legged on the carpet, one hand on the golden and the other on her child asleep on the floor, head on Jana's lap. Jana looked tired and bored. Henry nearly turned around—surely no one had seen him yet. He felt how Jana looked. Tired and bored. Also in pain, but mostly tired from fighting the pain, and bored from the sameness of it all.

But just as he was about to turn around, Jana saw through the quartet and the windowpane and caught his eye. It was a small movement she made with her eyes, a widening and a brightening, but he knew she'd seen him, and he went in.

Henry stood in the back of the kitchen, away from Brit and Daniel, who were leaned over the table talking quietly and seriously. He saw Jana remove herself from beneath Daphne and place Daphne's head gently on the floor next to the golden's ass.

Jana opened the fridge. "Endless supply of beer," she said. The fridge was full of beer, bottles of all kinds, microbrewery upon microbrewery. A man could gain ten pounds in ale alone at this festival.

She took out two bottles and handed one to Henry.

"This isn't good," Henry said.

"The beer? Did it go bad?"

"No, this." He nodded at the group, still blindly groping their way through the Rimsky-Korsakov.

"Oh," Jana said. "Eh, they're not so bad."

He looked at her. "Really? You think they're not so bad?"

"Well, they sure put Daphne to sleep. Thank God. That child refuses to nap anymore, and today's Rebecca's night off. I think she went into Santa Rosa for a drink with friends. I told her she wouldn't have to come back till morning."

Rebecca was the nanny Jana hired to go on tour with them or to festivals like this, times when a prolonged absence wasn't quite appropriate (and anyway, who would Jana leave Daphne with?), and also Rebecca could tutor Daphne.

"Sometimes I think we should have a Rebecca," Henry said.

"Oh, a Rebecca is good. A Rebecca is the only way. I can't believe that both you and Kim go everywhere together with the kids. I mean, don't you wish we could go to Warsaw kid-free next month? Listen to me. Party in Warsaw without the kids. How did we become these people?"

"I do wish that," Henry said. "But it's nicer if Kim gets to come with the kids and travel and be with me instead of stay home alone with them."

"Sure," Jana said. "Must be nice, to have help. Finn's okay, but he's got his own thing right now, and, I mean, we can't even manage to live together. Rebecca is my Kimiko."

Henry laughed a little. "Do not ever tell Kimiko that."

"Oh, God no. She would murder me. Like separate my head from my body with a steel-core Jargar C string."

"Nah, those cost too much to murder you with. She'd use a D'Addario."

Jana didn't even laugh. Her lips hovered over the rim of the bottle. "I can't do it," she said. Her voice was low and wobbly. She looked at him with wide, serious eyes.

"Do what?"

"Daphne."

The Rimsky-Korsakov was over, finally, and sheet music was being shuffled around for the next group. The Brahms viola quintet, someone suggested, and Daniel was being pulled away from Brit to join in. The Sequoias were kicked out of their seats.

"You can't . . . what Daphne?" Henry whispered.

Jana looked at him, bumped the fridge. Some bottles shook nervously. "I don't mean I don't love her. Or that I wouldn't do it all over again. Well. I mean, there's no point in talking about that. But I guess I thought I would change. I would change like you did, just make a little hole in my life so she could fill it. But there's no hole! Where's she supposed to go?"

"I changed?"

"Yeah, but in this really steady way. You know, after Daniel punched you in Canada. Before that, you were insane about the baby coming. I thought you'd never stop waffling. But then you just . . . one day you were buying baby-sized shirts in the airports and buying a tricycle in London—remember that tricycle? Oh, it was adorable. But you were still you, you know? Just without all the crazy."

"Crazy?"

"Hen, stop acting like I'm saying something mean here, or something you didn't already know. And anyway, we're not talking about you, we're talking about me. What if I can't do this? What if—what if I'm my mother?"

Henry laughed. He put his arm around her, and his arm stung a little. He winced into his bottle. "You're not your mother. You're way more successful."

Jana leaned her head on him. "Kids don't want successful moms. They want moms who want to be moms."

Henry couldn't think of anything to say. She was right. Kids wanted who they wanted, and if you weren't that, you risked being part of the greatest disappointment of their lives. Having children was an adapt-or-die situation. That's why people did it together. It was less lonely when you whittled away a part of yourself with the person who knew you pre-whittled. He could not fathom having sex with Kimiko in a practice room. Had they really done that?

"I'm sorry, kid," he said.

The Brahms started. It was a beautiful piece, one with heart and substance. Daniel got to show off here, and he was good at showing off.

While Jana had struggled with a stiffened sound and Brit constantly switched violins to adjust to her changing left hand (and Henry's goddamn arm was falling off), Daniel's playing had actually consistently gotten better with age, more refined, more sure, more present. He was unstoppable now. Henry wanted to be playing the Brahms with them, but he also wanted to be in bed with Kimiko, to catch lizards with Jack, and to help Jack set them free.

"Watch out," said Colin of the Sequoias, who nudged Jana a bit to get in the fridge.

"Hey," Jana said.

"No, sorry, didn't mean to hit you with the door." Colin leaned in, his breath hot and malty. "I mean, watch out. Your wives and husbands could be watching."

Jana shook her head and made an exasperated sound that caused her to spit. "Jesus! Not everyone is fucking everyone else in their quartet. Well, maybe Daniel. I don't know."

"I didn't say you were sleeping together," Colin said. "You don't have to be sleeping with someone in your quartet to make your spouse jealous. Hell, I hate Jerome more than I've hated anyone I've been in a relationship with. Jerome. Fuck Jerome."

"Is Jerome leaving?" Jana leaned in, always one for gossip.

Colin wavered, belched, then whispered, "We're all leaving."

Jana gasped. "What do you mean? You're going to the Shanghai residency? I'm so jealous."

Henry imagined he could see the drink inside Colin, sloshing around his stomach, gumming up his tongue. His eyelids were half closed. How had he even been playing a moment ago?

"No, I mean we're, what's the word, disbanding. The band's breaking up. It's not worth it anymore. Fucking Ryan's on the brink of divorce, and hell, so am I. Who knows, anyway, but really, God, nothing's worse than being forced to sit day in and day out with someone who loves you *but not in that way*, you know? Sam's a blowhard, it feels good to finally say that. Don't you hate it? The way that person disgusts you, and you have to sit with them on planes, check in to the hotel, warm up, watch them sweat like a sick pig under the lights? The whole time complaining about how good we're not. But, like, he could afford to lose a few, right? And Jerome. Do not fucking get me started on Jerome. Years you spend with someone, they know all your fucking secrets, they've cried in bus stations with you, picked you up from bars in fucking Mumbai, and then a reporter flirts with them and poof! Everything you've built, the people you once were, gone. Just like that. Playing together, it's a farce now."

The first movement of the Brahms finished, and Henry was so inside Colin's recitative that he was startled by the sudden silence. The movement was already over? How had it gone by so fast, such a tough, lively movement? It was his favorite and he had missed it.

Jana was smirking, her trouble with Daphne gone. "Good God, get out, man. Sounds like a soap opera."

"It's worse than a soap opera. It's a soap quartet," Colin said, and then immediately dropped his bottle on the floor, where it shattered and spewed beer on their ankles. "Oh, sorry," he said. "My hand's been hurting today."

"I've gotta go," Henry said, backing away. "I mean, the children."

"Oh, the children!" Colin said, shouting now. The playing had stopped. "Don't forget the children!"

At the next morning's master class, Henry sat dumbly with his impotent hand while everyone looked at him with glassy, hungover eyes. He accidentally yelled at the cellist in the first group. It was frustrating; he wanted to show the cellist something, to show her the difference between a left-hand *sforzando* and a right-hand *sforzando,* and because he couldn't waste the playing on teaching, the only way he could demonstrate was to sing it and mime it, and she didn't get it. The cellist nearly cried. Henry thought she probably burst into tears the moment her group walked off stage. The director of the festival came up to Henry afterward, asked if he needed anything. *Vicodin,* Henry didn't say. "Maybe some sleep before the premiere," he did say, and the director cleared Henry's teaching schedule for the rest of the day. He slept fitfully, and only really gave in to sleep when Clara crawled in bed with him.

"Are you mad?" she'd asked.

"Mad at what? No, I'm not mad."

"You're acting mad. You kicked at the dirt outside before you came in."

"It's just dirt. It's for kicking," he said. "Shhh. Go to sleep. I'm not mad."

"Okay, but the dirt didn't do anything, Daddy. Don't be mean to it. It's just sitting there."

"It doesn't have feelings," Henry said into his pillow. "It's dirt."

"Everything has feelings," she said, and he didn't respond because maybe she was right, and they slept.

The suit jacket wasn't fitting right. The quartet was warming up in the greenroom, and Henry kept flexing his shoulders and the jacket kept pulling at the seams. He looked in the vanity mirror. Had he gained weight?

"Over here," Jana said to him.

"I know, I just . . ." Henry said, twisting to look at himself. "I can't get comfortable."

"Maybe we're good on this," Brit said, setting her violin down across her lap. "We know it. We're warm."

Jana acquiesced, and Daniel stood up and stretched. "I need some water," he said.

"I bet you do," Jana said.

"What happened?" Henry asked, checking his watch. They had half an hour until curtain.

Jana's eyes lit up. "You don't know?"

"I've been in that awful master class or asleep all day," Henry said. He walked to the mini-fridge and found some ice for his elbow. He couldn't ice his hand before a performance, but he could ice his elbow, and then right before they went on stage he would apply a heating pad. Which mostly worked.

Jana and Daniel told him the story in tandem (Brit, meanwhile, ran off to put out a fire with Paul). There'd been a meltdown in the hot tub after he left, after the reading party wound down, which escalated at the same rate that people became more drunk. Colin had been the first to get in the hot tub, and within the first ten minutes he managed to break *another* glass bottle near enough to the water to make people nervous, but not, apparently, one of the students' boyfriends, who, equally drunk, started an underwater breath-holding competition with him. Ryan, who was outside the tub, saw the two men disappear under the water and charged. Charged, Daniel said. And grabbed Colin by the hair. Everyone gasping and wet and angry. Would have been hot if it wasn't so pathetic, Jana said. And then Jerome, out of nowhere—was he even at the reading party?—showed up in swim trunks, stood there like a referee, trying to figure out what happened, and who did what to whom, and how it could possibly be resolved. And then they were screaming, everyone screaming at everyone else, even the student whose boyfriend had been underwater with Colin, and Jerome, shivering in his swim trunks, and somehow it was Jerome and Ryan who ended up wrestling on the grass. No punching, though, said Daniel with a wink.

"Who won?" Henry asked.

"Everyone lost," Jana said. "Obviously."

Henry felt depleted by the story. "That makes me so sad," he said.

Jana laughed. "Really? It's so absurd. They're just nuts, that group. We've always known it."

But it wasn't true. Henry remembered a time when the Sequoia had first made waves, maybe six or seven years after the Van Ness had come to New York. They'd been at Curtis, and were a collection of beautiful, talented men. Part of their allure was that women and men alike loved to watch and listen to them. They packed the Met Museum atrium for free shows and drank with donors until dawn. Had Henry not had a small child at home, he might have been out there with them. And they played with energy. He remembered that. The energy, like a quartet that was young and had nothing to lose, everything to prove. They played like the music had just been discovered, because it had, by them. Maybe it was true, they'd always been a little nuts. But maybe that was what you needed—to be nuts in love with what you were doing, and the people you were doing it with.

"Did I really change?" he asked.

Daniel and Jana looked at him blankly. "Huh?"

"After the babies."

"Well, you stopped making me want to hit you," Daniel said.

"No, really."

"You take this one," Jana said to Daniel. "I tried."

"I think . . . you became a little more present in your life," Daniel said.

"So was I absent before?"

The stage manager peeked her head in for the ten-minute warning, and Henry switched on his heating pad. But he didn't let Daniel off the hook. "Like, what was I before, if not present?"

"I don't know, man," Daniel said, sliding rosin up and down his bow. "I guess before . . . you were just playing around. I mean, you were so good at everything, anything you wanted to do you could do. It made sense that you played around. I guess I was kind of annoyed by it. Or jealous of it. Or something. But it meant that you could play whatever you wanted, whenever and however you wanted. And afterward, well, I guess you had to narrow your scope a little."

Daniel looked up and saw Henry's expression. "Oh, God, sorry, didn't mean to upset you. You're good, right?"

Henry nodded. "Just my arm."

"I think that's what happens when you love people more, or more people. In here gets bigger." Daniel tapped his hand on his own bullish chest. "But out here has to get a little bit smaller," he said, sweeping his hand around the room.

Julia St. John knocked and entered. She wore long layers of jewel-toned raw silk like she was a gentler Stevie Nicks, and her black hair was straight down her back. She smiled, familiar lines deepening around her face. "I thought we'd walk out together. You won't mind, sitting on stage during my introduction?"

"Not at all," Henry said.

Once they found Brit, the five of them made their way to the stage and waited to be announced—*the world premiere of Julia St. John's latest quartet by one of the world's premier ensembles*—before walking on stage. The quartet took their seats, but the spotlight shifted to Julia at a podium stage right. Her hands gripped the edge, her rings clanking in the microphone.

"I want to thank you all for coming to witness this," she began. "Those of you who missed my pre-concert talk this afternoon won't know that I've spent a lot of time getting to know the Van Ness, getting to know their rhythms both on stage and off stage, and I'm happy to report they're one of the most complex and tightly knit groups I've ever had the pleasure of composing for. This particular piece came to me after watching a performance of theirs at Carnegie Hall, many years ago, before which they were merely people, hungry, frustrated, sad, cold, and whatever host of human emotions you can imagine. But it was so striking to me because once they were on stage, they were almost inhuman. They were powerful, in control, a unified, multitoned voice. But they were also doing the most intrinsic of human feats. They were communicating to the rear mezzanine something that was emotional and extra-verbal."

Henry remembered this performance. It was when they'd received a career grant, and no one but Brit knew Julia very well. It hadn't been that many years ago, but it felt like a lifetime's distance away. He winced to think about it.

"What was remarkable in the performance, however," Julia went on, "was that these four people, they contained everything. That's what made them both human and inhuman. They encompassed everything from earth to sky, everything I could imagine. This piece, *Sediment to Sky,* speaks to some of that, some of what came from them, and also the principles that are important to me. It had long been a dream of mine to do something like this, to arrange my life around the people I love, to create a shared life with every one of them. I think probably many of you have considered this at one point or another, but thought it impossible. I think many of us strive for community and family, but often find it difficult to participate in because of, well, life gets in the way. But it is possible. It is possible to arrange your life around art, and to find, in that art, a kind of love that grows like corn, from way down here to way up here, that changes, goes away, comes back."

Henry's mouth was dry. He had done just that, had grown up like a stalk of corn in the middle of this group, in the hot center of the quad they formed on blond-wood stages across the country, the world. He felt a wave of gratitude like a distant tsunami, a large, warm swell, unstoppable. It heated his elbow down to his wrist, the fragile muscle and tendon writhing between them. It pushed to the base of his throat, where he swallowed and remembered the way his first apartment in San Francisco had been so cold that it *smelled* cold, and how it was difficult to sleep without Jana there, complaining next to him. And he remembered the one time Brit showed up at his apartment in Manhattan while Kimiko was over, so deeply upset that Daniel had gotten married, how Kimiko made her warm cider and let her cry and cry on the floor, from which she refused to get up. He remembered Daniel getting so angry at him for making him go rock climbing in the Australian bush, how Daniel had been so scared at the top about belaying down and so worried about his fingers and wrists (he had been right about that), and how Henry laughed until he cried, and apologizing only made Daniel angrier. When they came down from the mountain, Daniel made him buy all the beers, and Henry remembered Daniel's face when, over the beers, Henry told him he and Kimiko were having another child. The look: breathless, sad, reverent.

They were playing now, like they always had. It wasn't easy. It never had been. It was something like a miracle, all this music, each note a discovery you've already made, but it was also maybe the most ordinary thing in the world, to assemble and compose and perform—night after night—a life.

Then he felt his arm crumble from the very inside, from the genesis of tissue and bone. A slow, hot release like a casual spill of lava from a faraway volcano spout. Jana would tell him later, with tears in her eyes, that it felt sudden—three-quarters of the way into the piece, how his arm skidded over two notes, the low F-sharp to a D on the C string—but he felt it from the beginning, something different, a wave he wasn't going to be able to ride. What he didn't tell Jana then was that he didn't even try to ride it. He'd felt it generating from the third bar in, and once he'd completely given in, the pain lessened. He was surprised at that. Part of the torture had been the resistance. Then there were pages of music during which a very astute listener could likely hear that he lagged a millisecond behind everyone else. He was no longer anticipating, but following. When they arrived at that three-quarters spot Jana remembered, the jump and skid over an easy interval, he was no longer lagging, but not at all playing. He'd never once—not once—made a mistake during a performance, and here it was. An absence as glaring as the wrong note. In his periphery, he sensed a few faces turn and shift in the awkwardness, and six beats later he found his place. But here was the thing: when panic rose in everyone else, he felt relaxed. All the strain of the months and years leading up to this physical breakdown had been the tough part. This was the good part. He was not only playing *these* notes, *this* music. Julia's phrase lingered in his ear, and he nearly smiled through the slow disaster. *They contained everything.* So, too, did this performance, and every performance. He was not only playing now, but playing everything before now, that miracle of a concert at Esterhazy, the way they'd sung at Carnegie Hall the first time. Time rolled out through his arm in hot waves. And though he was still playing, he looked around (no longer bound by time, anyway). Jana, wide-eyed and angular, only her parted lips betraying the glass-like fragility he loved in her. Brit, round-faced, still freckled, more freckled after all these years, not looking at him, giving him his space, which he appreciated. And Daniel, glancing at him with no expression at first and then the subtlest of understanding, continuing to play his own rock-solid part, even leading a little extra, picking up whatever Henry had left behind. Henry looked for his other family, sitting in the third row stage left, and while he couldn't see her directly, he felt Kimiko knowing, clutching her armrest.

He could hardly wait to be done, to go to her and show her his arm, to ice it, to watch her hug their children, to hug them himself. And later, to watch her play, practice, perform. It would be her turn now. It seemed impossible, for this piece, a small, short piece, to contain all that, for him to see everything, to know and relax into the knowing. He'd never been here before, but now that he'd arrived, he couldn't imagine going back.

KIMIKO

Violin

While Kimiko watched Henry play on stage, her own fingertips burned. She, too, had studied the St. John piece inside and out. She knew the tricky transitions, the parts Henry had rewritten with Julia, the surprise penultimate key change. With her right hand, she held the arm of her daughter sitting next to her, who was preoccupied with Jana's daughter, Daphne, who sat beside her. Kimiko's left hand was laid on the armrest, and her curved fingers lightly tapped in time to the notes—her own fingerings, ones Henry's large, slender hands found to be, as he said, "too spidery." She was partial to left-hand position shifts. He was more into the dramatic extension. She forgot her daughter next to her and she forgot her son back in the cabin with Jana's Rebecca, and continued to silently play the armrest. She played through the whole thing, perfectly, seamlessly, and her playing continued on even when her husband's failed.

When they'd woken up that morning, mere minutes before the children, he'd turned on his side and said, with the lucidity of having been awake for hours, "Have I changed?"

She answered quickly, maybe too quickly: "No."

Kimiko wanted to ask him the same thing: *Have I changed?* But she already knew the answer. Yes, she'd changed. She'd always been the one to do the changing. Henry was the one who always wanted things and then acquired them, with no amount of change necessary on his part. That quality of his—the easy satisfaction—was what she loved about him, even when it sometimes made her sad.

In fact, their union had seemed so easy for him that there'd been two years early on in which Kimiko became convinced that she was simply a partygoer in his life who had stuck. One who was appropriately charmed by him, a prettier, more talented version of the kind of gin-breathed admirers he schmoozed with at fund-raisers. He'd insisted she wasn't, that he liked her precisely because she wasn't like that.

"Babe," he said, "no one would mistake you for someone who worshipped me." He was right about that. It wasn't in her DNA to fawn. But she also knew who she'd been in the privacy of those early lessons, in the practice rooms and the shitty apartments. She'd *felt* like that, like a girl under the spell of a boy. And when she cried that day in the park, when she told him she was pregnant, it wasn't because she was scared. It was because she had not once considered not keeping it. Because what was happening to her body—with the baby but also with him, the way he'd invaded it—was turning her into an act of self-betrayal.

What the baby had done to her body had been cruel, and it had been cruel with Jack, too, and that was something no one ever says. It wasn't the first time Kimiko had undergone pain in her body to get what she wanted, however. The pain and discomfort hadn't been the thing. It was that something else was making decisions for her. As a musician, you were trained to listen to your body, and then to ignore it, trick it, or change it. Your arm hurts, you strengthen your sacrum and relax your shoulder blades. Your left hand aches, you loosen your wrist and jaw. Visualize the interval, and your hand makes the jump. A *sforzando* comes from your solar plexus, a *forte* from your throat. In her whole life, she had never not been able to defy her body except when it was pregnant. She suddenly did not belong to herself anymore.

And if she was being honest, she never really got over the unfairness of it.

But what loving him had done to her: it had been like someone drained her of her old blood and replaced it with new blood, the same liquid that coursed through Henry. So when they touched, it was finishing a line. That love, too, had been a kind of theft.

So, yes, she'd been the one to change. Not necessarily against her will, but not fully with it, either. She reached out to touch his face in bed.

"What makes you say that?" she asked.

"I don't know," he said, sighing into her hand. "It seems like everyone else has. Jana said she didn't know if she could be a mother."

Kimiko snorted. "A little late for that."

"So maybe she didn't change," he said. "Maybe she just tried to."

"When you have kids, I guess you sort of have to change. But it doesn't mean you have to like it," Kimiko said, turning on her back. She spoke to the ceiling. "You don't have to walk around with a smile plastered on your face talking about how grateful you are for your children, the way some of these people do," she said.

Some of the people attending this conference—the older students, the concertgoers, the rich hangers-on who had enough money and time to spend a week in the redwoods with them—their mixture of self-satisfaction and fandom was nauseating. Henry was always better at socializing, even with the ridiculous ones. People were so easily taken with him, and he collected facts about them like presents to give to Kimiko later. The man with the twenty-thousand-dollar hair transplant; the beautiful woman who lived half of the year in Montana, but the wrong half; the stagehand who reminded him of Brit and Daniel mixed together, who looked like a child that would never be, a girl who was airy and sullen, slight and magnetic. It was easy for him, and easy to hit his stride at parties, even with all the shrill laughter and the clumsy segues and the close air. Even with the physical pain he was sometimes—or more often than sometimes—in. Aside from the pain, he'd always been like that.

In the bed there was a quiet, inflated moment between them. Had she said she was ungrateful for their children? Or had she said she was unhappy about it? Had Henry been frightened by that statement? Or had he agreed, so effortlessly that his own assent was what frightened him? Before either of them could open their mouths to say something, there was the sound of their children, Jack and Clara, the beginnings of a fight. It was better not to say more, Kimiko thought, not on a performance day.

"I'll go start breakfast," she said, throwing off the covers. "You stay."

After the master class and before the performance, when the forest turned blue in the falling light, Kimiko left Jack with a friend, and a napping Clara with a napping Henry, to take a walk. Alone. In moments like this, moments that had to be so carefully and precisely orchestrated so she could have her space, she wished that they had brought a nanny the way Jana had. The idea made Kimiko blush, and she hated that it made her feel bad. But for what purpose would they have a nanny? She wasn't working here herself, she wasn't playing or teaching, and there was no reason she couldn't take care of the kids.

At the entrance to an unfamiliar trailhead, she paused to read the map, and felt a firm hand on her shoulder. Jana, dressed for a champagne brunch but carrying a walking stick, smiled at her.

"Thank God," Kimiko said. "I wanted to be alone but not, like, *alone* alone."

Jana gestured to her sundress and gladiator sandals. "As you can see, I also lied about needing to get out of the house. I said I was going on a hike, but I could really just use a Bloody Mary."

The two of them ambled slowly down the path into the woods. Might as well attempt it, they decided. Kimiko was delighted that she'd run into Jana. Though things had been somewhat icy between them early on, they'd spent so much time together at this point that she was more like a sister-in-law than her husband's work friend. And when the quartet's manager had referred to Jana as Henry's "work wife" some years ago, Kimiko didn't even blink. She'd once been jealous of Jana—they'd been too alike in personality for that not to happen. But now, something else had emerged between them, a quiet understanding that allowed them to be completely stripped with each other. A kind of nakedness that she was never able to achieve with Brit or Daniel, both special tidal pools of emotions that remained obscure to Kimiko.

As they walked, she and Jana spoke about what they missed about New York (namely, how everyone wasn't completely obsessed with hiking there), and about the St. John piece, and about the upcoming string of international tour dates, and about Clara's lessons.

"Does she know how good she is yet?" Jana asked.

"No," Kimiko said, understanding. There was a turning point in young players who were good the way Clara was good. When they realized they had that leverage, a talent that earned respect from adults and could shoot them out of the world of regular children, they became haughty, demanding, and impossible. They'd all seen it happen to students, and Kimiko woke up every day hoping that Clara could somehow skip over it.

"Maybe she'll be like Henry," Jana said. "I don't think he was ever really like that."

"That's because his family never treated him like he was a god. But because of this—this world we're in, that's not going to happen. Everyone's looking for Henry's talent in her, expecting it."

"She's a good kid," Jana said. "Hell, I was probably insufferable between the ages of twelve and seventeen. And look at me. I turned out just fine."

Kimiko laughed, but she thought that if Clara turned out like Jana—queenly and willful and determined—it wouldn't be the worst thing.

Jana stopped at a clearing and swatted at a sweat bee hovering around her. She turned back to face Kimiko. "I'm sorry, we don't have to talk about the kids. I hate it when people think that's all they can talk to me about. Like, you didn't ask me where Daphne was. That's everyone's opener when I'm without her: where's Daphne? As though I couldn't possibly have a desire to do things without a child strapped to me."

Kimiko dusted off a rock and sat down on it. It would be minutes before the sweat bees came for her, but she didn't care. "I was thinking today about just that. I started to say it to Henry, but . . ."

"About what?"

"About how . . . I love my children, but that's not the same as not being able to imagine life without them. Can I imagine life without them? Yes, absolutely."

Kimiko would have never said that to anyone else out loud, maybe not even Henry. You weren't supposed to think that, let alone say it, as a mother. There were mothers here who would call Child Protective Services if they heard her say it. But with Jana, she was fine. Jana sat down across from Kimiko, planted her butt on the dirt.

"What would that life look like?" Jana asked.

"Oh," Kimiko said, looking away. She had to look away to see it. "I'd be playing a lot, recording, traveling for my own gigs, doing a lot back in Asia, seeing my family in Japan more. And Henry would be doing the same thing he's doing, traveling with you all, but because we'd be apart, the time that we'd spend together would be . . . more exciting. Special. Like the kind of marriage Daniel thought he was going to get with Lindsay. One we made up on our own."

When she imagined it, she felt her heart lift in her chest like a balloon, and then jerk against the wall of her sternum. But the weightlessness, just for a minute, that had felt nice.

She looked back at Jana, who seemed caught in her own imagination, a stricken look on her face. "Do you remember Fodorio?"

"Yes," Kimiko said. "The guy who wouldn't leave Henry alone for a while. Yeah. Sort of . . . unappealing."

Jana's mouth turned down. "He wasn't that unappealing."

Kimiko grinned. "Uh, okay."

"Well, I slept with him."

"Why?" Kimiko said, more distastefully than she meant to.

"I felt so bad about it for so long because, ostensibly, I slept with him so we could win Esterhazy the first time," Jana said. "He was a judge and I actually *said* that in bed to him—what an idiot. But then we didn't win."

"So, no harm, no foul," Kimiko said.

"Exactly," Jana said. "There was no harm, just me pretending to be rich in a fancy hotel one night, him thinking I was unique or something. And when I think about it now, I don't feel bad. I don't feel bad at all. I feel nostalgic. But I'm nostalgic for that way of thinking. Not for the actual life. I'm just saying, it's okay to long for a different life. It doesn't mean you actually want it."

It was still hot, but evening was coming in now. The blue shadows of the trees got long. Jana was absently picking bark off a tree trunk next to her, touching it with the uncurious fingers of an animal. The action reminded Kimiko of Henry—how he'd been when they met, lean and unaware of his height and stature. She was filled suddenly with jealousy. Of Jana. At first it had to do with a flash of Jana in bed with Fodorio, a man who, at the time, was much older than her, richer, more powerful. The way something like that must have felt for Jana, a flame catching oxygen inside her and burning upward, a perfect, wild cylinder. She remembered carnality like that. She'd once given not more than half a thought about a decision to sleep with a man—to whom she gave her body, and why, and how.

But in the second wave, it was jealousy that Jana, as a mother now, had resisted (Jana always resisted) that steady weight that Kimiko carried behind her. A leash tied to a sack filled with one or two or three lives unlived, or at least the possibility of them, all bound together by the promise of agility. It had to do with time. Time looked different when you were young, and whatever foolishness you engaged in was undiluted—there was always the possibility that the next promised moment would carry you somewhere else, always the possibility of more flames, more beats, more life. Time, when you were older, was something different, irregular, Kimiko thought.

Jana was still a successful musician. Jana could, if she wanted, go out tonight and have terrible, wonderful sex with a man who meant nothing.

Kimiko told her that. Jana looked at her thoughtfully. Jana said, "But you can do all that, too, if you want."

It was really beginning to get dark now, and Clara would surely be waking from her nap. Jack would need to be fetched from her friend's. How far out were they, anyway? She hadn't been keeping track. She'd just been following Jana.

"Hey," Kimiko said. "I did something like that once. I slept with my teacher at Juilliard."

"What a whore," Jana said, smiling at her.

"Best mistake I ever made," Kimiko said.

They turned around instead of finishing the loop, as they had no idea how far the loop would take them, neither of them having really studied the map at the trailhead. They walked back and didn't speak of music or of children. They barely spoke at all. Kimiko felt like she could hear the woods getting darker, the way an absence of light makes the other senses, like sound, amplified—twigs breaking underfoot, the quick rustle of birds escaping, her own labored breathing.

When the trailhead was in sight, up a short but steep hill, Kimiko stopped and said, "I just—it was never as equal as we said it would be. I mean, there's no way it could be. And you should see the way the other wives look at me here. Like I'm another long-suffering whatever like them. I hate that. But then I think they're kind of right. That I am."

"A long-suffering wife?" Jana laughed. "You? Never."

"Not like that, but. I don't know. No one looks at me like . . ."

"Like you're as good as Henry? Join the club."

"But I am as good as he is," Kimiko said, very serious now. Henry's face from years ago came clearly now to her. It had been delicate and impossibly soft and almost feminine—Jack would look like that, she thought—and his voice boyish and everything about him dirty golden. His hair, his eyes, his skin, the way he thought, what he said. He'd moved with a fluidity that made him lighter than everybody else and impossible to disappoint, but his sound remained thick and expensive and authentic. She'd fallen in love with a man for the first and only time in her life—because he'd been as she wanted to be.

"I know you are," Jana said, matching her tone. "You always were as good as him. Look. It's one thing to *be* a professional musician. It's another thing to be someone who loves one. Unfortunately, you're both."

Kimiko turned back toward the hill. "I guess we should go home."

"But here's good news, though," Jana said.

"What's that?" Kimiko asked.

"So is Henry."

At the evening's concert, as Julia St. John gave her preamble, the quartet sitting dumbly behind her, a realization came over Kimiko: how difficult it must have been for Jana to tell her she could do whatever she wanted. Because Kimiko *could* do whatever she wanted—but only if Henry left the quartet, and left Jana. She looked at Jana, sitting just left of Julia during the talk, looking down at her lap, her violin propped on her thigh. Kimiko could remember Jana's face when they first met as clearly as she could remember Henry's. Whereas Henry's face was a wide smile and young skin, Jana's was sharp and handsome. And as she aged, her face had softened. Sure, she was tired and the lines in her face betrayed that exhaustion, but now there was also a quality of—what was it?—ease.

Kimiko sat in their reserved seats with Clara and Daphne. From this angle, above and to the side, Clara looked like Henry, too. Both her children did. They bore her dark hair, round face, and almond eyes, but everything else—the jut of their chin, their dimples, the sly defiance in a simple look—was all Henry. Daphne was fidgeting in her seat, still a bit too young to sit quietly at a concert, and Clara was helping her straighten out her dress.

"No, like this," Clara whispered, patting Daphne's skirt so it was both smooth and fluffed. "That's how you look grown up."

Kimiko took Clara's hand to shush her. Julia was still talking. Henry's look, his gaze fixed somewhere between his feet and the bottom of his music stand, became more absent. "It is possible to arrange your life around art," Julia was saying, and Kimiko's entire body was flooded with the kind of urgent sadness that can only precede change. Her heartbeat quickened and her skin grew cold and limp. Clara removed her hand from Kimiko's grip.

When they played, something was off. It took her several pages of music to figure it out, but then she did, when Henry leaned down to turn a page to the right, and the bottom of the paper dragged on the edge of the music stand. She heard it, a microsecond of a skip in his note. He'd been late with the entrance after the page turn. But it wasn't that he'd turned the page too fast and disrupted the line, as is often the case with those kinds of missteps. It was that he'd turned it too slowly, as though playing on his own, not at all keyed into the time in which the rest of them were playing.

And when he stopped playing—that's what it was, a full stop where a note should have been—Kimiko felt his gaze move around the group and land, finally, on her. It happened in the space of a quarter note, but Kimiko felt the entirety of that space, three-dimensionally, so much so that she felt she could almost get up from her seat and walk around inside the moment. She'd never heard him make a mistake during a performance, even during a bad spell with his arm, and she always thought she'd be overcome by anxiety if it happened, if she had to watch him make a public mistake like that. But this wasn't anxiety. What sped the motor in her chest was something moving, not something sinking.

The urgency was this: she *had* changed, she'd felt unfairly put upon, and she had accepted it. But she was changing again. She no longer felt burdened. What had stopped her feeling this way? When Henry's own body began to really fail him. When the absence of ease sharpened him. When he needed her, when he accepted that he needed something. That had finally—physically—proven to her that he was as bound as she was, that they'd both stolen from each other.

Kimiko felt a hot wish growing inside her. The children fidgeted next to her, but she remained steely and intent, unfettered by the time and its slog. When the quartet finished, they stood as one for the applause, but Kimiko saw Henry look over to her, and Clara, and Daphne, and that was the part that would always get away from her, what he looked like then. Like a moment already disappearing into the next, and the next.

August 2009

San Francisco, CA

HENRY

Viola

There was never a good time to tell someone you were leaving them, Henry knew, but perhaps trapped on a boat was the worst place. Especially this ferry, which felt particularly old and plastic on this chilly, windy summer day, full of their children and other people's children, interminably making its way to Alcatraz on an unreasonably choppy bay. They were to play at the inaugural event of a new music festival that an old Symphony patron was trying to get off the ground on Alcatraz, but why anyone would want to go to this depressing island to listen to classical music was beyond Henry. But they'd said yes—rather, Jana had said yes to their manager, on everyone's behalf—and they showed up at the terrible tourist trap of Fisherman's Wharf, as requested, to board the ferry and ride all together to the island with a photographer who was invasively taking pictures for promotional materials. Henry, displeased at this obligation, insisted on taking Kimiko and his children in order to make it somewhat of a family day. He'd been wanting more of those lately.

Kimiko had wanted Henry with the family more, too. Her solo career had been consistent until Jack, but even then, not as buzzed about as it had once been. While she could still command a high performance fee, she wasn't as young or new as she'd been when she first appeared on the scene in New York, and the classical music industry, like most industries, loved a young, new thing.

Kimiko's desire for a different kind of life had first become clear to her after the concert at the Festival of the Redwoods—Henry's last summer there—but it was two years before she told him she wanted it.

She waited until after Henry returned home from a particularly grueling three-week stint in England and Holland, involving a residency with relentless teaching expectations. They'd put the kids to bed, and then gone to bed themselves, and Henry had been so grateful to be home again, simply because it was a place where he wasn't expected to play at a moment's notice. His arm hurt. She'd long ago stopped asking him how the pain affected his concerts; there was nothing to say in the aftermath of a performance mistake.

"You're tired," Kimiko said to him as he reached to turn out the lamp.

"Yes," he said. "Pretty obvious."

"But I'm not."

"You're not?"

"Well, I'm exhausted. I mean, I'll be tired for the rest of my life. But you seem tired in a different way."

"What are you talking about?" he asked.

"In the redwoods," she said. "Two summers ago. The St. John. You haven't been the same since then."

"I screwed up one time, two years ago, and you're still on about it," he said, defending himself, but only halfheartedly. "I don't know. Maybe you're right."

He knew she was right. She was tired, and he was tired, but in different ways, and his sometimes showed through his playing. They'd waded through the past few years as though they were something they had to get through, to survive—this period of baseline exhaustion, where they barely looked at one another, him tending to one child while she tended to the other. He knew Kimiko bore the brunt of it, though. Henry's tour schedule was full each season, and involved jumping from one country to another. It had seemed impossible, for years really, that all the schedules—his, Kimiko's, the quartet's, now Clara's and Jack's, too—could match up and allow for breathing room, a space where they could be a family. Henry saw that he and Kimiko had simply given up on the idea of it: time.

She talked for nearly an hour. She talked about how she'd been thinking how she wanted something different but denying it for almost two years, and she said she was sorry she didn't tell him sooner. She said it took time to hear the truth of it. She talked about how grateful she was to have had the chance to be the children's mother, but how she also didn't want to resent anybody or anything for a life that had almost been lived. She told him that she felt trapped—if she gave up staying at home, she'd be failing the kids, and if she didn't, if she gave up on recording and touring as much as Henry, she'd be failing a possible self. She said that she hadn't really changed, that she still wanted what she wanted when she'd entered Juilliard. A career, a life of music on stage, in practice rooms, with orchestras. She didn't want to play with a quartet, either, and certainly not the Van Ness. She wanted her own story. The idea of her existence had gotten bigger with Henry and the children, but what drove her never faded. She said she'd loved the years and how they'd arranged them, taking the kids to Brussels or Barcelona when Henry's schedule took him there. But she wanted to go there differently, she said, not only as a mother. She wanted to go as a musician, too.

"You've worked hard," Henry told Kimiko that night as she began to cry. "In every area of your life. If you change the way you spend your time, no one will think you're a failure. Least of all me."

She cried harder. Henry had seen Kimiko cry only three times before—once when she told him she was pregnant with Clara, and each time she gave birth (an angry cry, not tears of joy).

What the quartet wouldn't believe at first, he knew, was that Kimiko hadn't asked him to leave. It was entirely his idea. Because when he saw her cry in bed that night—at the unfairness of being a parent and having a career and loving a man who also was a parent and had a career—he thought of his life as a piece of music, sonata form, one that progressed through movements, in which the motif became clearer and clearer through repetition and variation, until the third movement, the menuet, when the theme distilled down to a simple, sing-able song. The song was Kimiko. He wanted to be with her more than he wanted to be in a quartet, and he wanted to be with her in a life that didn't end in her crying in bed at night. It was where they'd arrived.

The plan was that Henry would finish out the 2009–2010 season, and then stay home and take on especially promising private students from the surrounding area who needed more than their public high schools could offer. After that, he'd take the steady teaching position at the conservatory where Kimiko sometimes filled in. Kimiko's last record was only five years old, and she still had connections. It wouldn't take her long to put together a few engagements, to start to remake a career that had been swiftly dismantled like one of Jack's Lego structures.

He truly hadn't meant to tell them on the ferry, but, as with most snafus lately, it could be blamed on the children.

The ferry had just pulled away from the dock, and the quartet stood on the deck, posing against the gray sky in their concert blacks, which they'd been asked to wear. Henry could feel Jana shivering against him in her long-sleeved dress. She stood tall and erect regardless. Daniel looked a bit green. The ferry churned against the waves.

"Are you done?" Daniel asked the photographer. "This is not ideal."

"A few more," the photographer said, crouching on the dirty, wet floor to get God knows what angle. He wore a big sweater and dark jeans and he looked warm.

Kimiko and Jack were inside, shielded against the cold, and Jack was plastered against the window, waving at them. Clara stood behind the photographer, though, never wanting to miss out.

"Daddy looks too tall," she said. "You're taller than everyone!" she called over the wind.

Henry cringed. Brit laughed a little and turned to Daniel, kissed him on the cheek. Clara's outburst to Paul about the kiss she'd seen at Maisie Allbright's hadn't explicitly been the cause of Brit and Paul's breakup, but it had been the final flick up of the carpet they'd been living under. And really Brit and Daniel's kiss in the first place had been the real culprit, if you didn't blame Brit and Paul's spectacular failure to end their relationship years before. In any case, Brit and Daniel coming together had breathed new air into the quartet, a release of tension that had churned through their union since they'd first begun playing together. It hadn't been ostentatious or dramatic, them getting together, but natural and seamless, and its solidity was one of the reasons Henry felt all right about leaving the quartet.

"When Daddy leaves, you'll find someone more your height," Clara said, crossing her arms and peering into the photographer's viewfinder to check out the photos so far.

Silence like a steel door closing, and only the smacking of the waves against the hull of the ferry.

"When's Daddy leaving?" Jana finally asked.

Clara looked up, concerned at Jana's tone. She shrugged. "In time to help me to audition for show choir next year."

Henry's voice caught in his cold throat. "I was going to say something tomorrow," he said, though what was tomorrow, he didn't know.

Brit pulled on a fleece jacket and looked down at her feet, her shoulders slumped. Jana asked the photographer for a cigarette. Daniel leaned over the boat and stared at the white water below. "I am seriously going to throw up," he said.

"Oh, don't," Jana said, annoyed. "Jesus, great timing, Henry. As usual."

"Hey, I have *excellent* timing," Henry said, trying to make a joke.

"Maybe grab your instruments?" the photographer asked, oblivious to the conversation that was slowly dismantling his subjects.

"In this?" Jana waved her cigarette-clad hand around. "You want our instruments to get destroyed by the weather?"

"Just for four minutes," the photographer said.

"So you're quitting?" Brit asked in a small voice. With one hand she was rubbing Daniel's back.

"Leaving, yeah," Henry said. "It's time."

"'It's time'? What in the fuck does that mean?" Daniel asked.

"Hey," Henry said, gesturing toward Clara. "Language."

Jana struggled to light the cigarette, but couldn't get a good direction or shield against the wind. "It means," she said, with the cigarette dangling from her lips, "that he's gone as far as he could with us."

"That's not what it means," Henry said. "It means it's time for me to be with my kids and Kimiko has things she needs to do. This was fun—"

"Fun?" Brit asked. "It was fun?"

"More than fun. It's been my life."

"God, like we're dead already," Jana said.

"I'll help you find a replacement," Henry said. "I have a few ideas. I want to finish out the season. So you'll have until next summer to prepare."

The photographer ducked in: "Hey, so grab the violins?"

"It's not all violins," Daniel snapped.

They retrieved their instruments and walked back out to the deck. "Look," Henry said, desperate for the moment to dissolve. "You all knew this was going to happen eventually. Someone was always bound to leave. It happens. Groups evolve. You might even be better with someone new."

"Great, but don't look at each other, perhaps?" the photographer suggested.

They all looked at the photographer, no one smiling. Clara gave them a thumbs-up. "I just don't understand," Brit said. "Why now?"

"Because . . . it feels like the right time. Like things will be okay with you guys if I leave. And it's so hard to do this with children. Kimiko and I are going crazy. I don't want to drag my children around the world and not actually spend time with them."

"I do it," Jana said. "Take Daphne, I mean."

"But that's because you have to," Henry said, too quickly.

Jana's face became dusky.

"And you have a tutor and Rebecca travels with us, and it's only one child. That's what I meant," Henry said. "It's just different."

No one said anything. The camera snapped away.

"You've wanted to leave forever," Daniel said, practically hissing his words. "You've always thought you were better than us. How about that time I found you taking a meeting with Fodorio in Calgary? I never pushed you on that, never told Jana, because I thought it was about some personal crisis you were having about—about having a baby—but you've always been like this. One foot out the door."

Henry slowly turned to face Daniel, gripping his viola at the neck.

Only Daniel could make him this enraged. Daniel knew how to cut a person in half with words, and he wasn't afraid to do it. He was cruel and articulate, and everyone always forgave him. Hell, Brit forgave him everything enough to be with him.

"You know that's not true," he said. "You're just being mean. It's how you are. Way to go, Daniel. Way to go all lowest common denominator on us."

"I know what that means," Clara said.

"I think we're about finished here," the photographer said.

"Thank God. Interminable," Jana said. "All of this."

"Quite terminable, actually," Daniel said.

"You know, Daniel," Henry said, pointing at him with his bow, "what do you have to be so pissed about? Everything worked out for you. You always thought I had it so much easier than you, but look—look at her—she's with *you*, you of all people, after everything. Maybe you're mad because you'll no longer have me around to blame for everything bad that happens in your life."

Daniel opened his mouth to respond, but stood speechless for a moment. Brit opened her eyes wide at Henry. "Stop," she said. "Please."

"Me stop?" Henry said. "Me? See, everyone just lets you get away with this chip on your shoulder. But, like, you don't just get to walk around with a chip on your shoulder forever."

Henry was brandishing his bow at Daniel to punctuate his sentences. The ferry was rocking against the chop, and several times he had to reach out to the railing to steady himself. People around them started to stare. Daniel's face reddened as Henry continued to talk, to excoriate him, airing a list of grievances fifteen years long. They were fighting like they were kids again, when they'd been first starting out. They hadn't really fought since that night Daniel hit Henry right before Esterhazy. Henry always reasoned he had children and a wife to fight with, so it wasn't worth picking it up with Daniel. And Daniel had seemed to relax a little after the divorce, and then really after he and Brit got together, finally having freed himself from bad decisions made in haste. But here, it was as though they'd time-traveled back to a San Francisco of their youth, when they'd been eager and ambitious and hotheaded and tied to nothing and nothing could embarrass them.

Daniel had his cello in his right hand, the endpin digging into the wet floor of the ferry, and his bow in his left hand, and maybe it was a years-old grudge about being punched that made Henry tap Daniel's bow with his own, or maybe it was an accident, but the tap made Daniel reflexively lift his own bow at Henry, and there they were, in a performance but the wrong one, fighting like fencers with their bows pointed at each other. The bows were too expensive to hit each other with, they both knew that, though in the stance they silently dared each other.

"Stop it," Brit said, more seriously now.

"I'll stop," Henry said. "I'll stop when he stops."

"Stop?" Daniel said. "You're quitting. Quitting is what it's called."

At the same moment Daniel moved his bow an inch closer to Henry's face, the boat rolled, causing Henry to move his bow an inch closer, maybe more, definitely enough to loosen Daniel's grip on the frog, and the bow went flying into and with the wind, out over the bay like a bird wing fluttering, until it dropped quietly into the frothy water. Alcatraz loomed closer than Henry thought.

Daniel's mouth hung open as they watched the tender, slight bow be swallowed by the froth, and disappear under the churn of the ferry's movement. This time, the silence was whole. No one said anything for the remainder of the ride.

When the ferry docked at Alcatraz, Kimiko, who saw it all in Henry's face, said, "So I guess that didn't go very well?"

He looked at Kimiko and it occurred to him that if she simply took his place in the group, everything would be fine, or everything would be closer to fine than it was now.

Now they looked like a funeral. Kimiko and the children went to walk around the grounds while the quartet was led to a makeshift backstage area that was really an old officers' quarters adjacent to the cell house. There was supposedly a nice view of the lighthouse, but you had to go outside to see it, of course. They were left in the room with their instruments, and Henry felt bone-chilled and wet from the ride, as well as simultaneously sheepish and angry. Now he had to apologize, when it ought to have been Daniel apologizing. Daniel always made it like this.

"Feels like detention in here," Brit said, opening up her case.

"You have your spare bow in your case, right?" Jana asked Daniel.

He nodded. "Always do."

"Look, I'll buy you a new bow," Henry said.

Daniel sighed. "Don't buy me anything, please."

They were to open with Dvořák's "American" String Quartet, which had been on the program of their graduation recital all those years ago. It was a relatively unchallenging piece. The main themes in each of the movements were Dvořák's interpretations of classic American sounds, and its buoyancy made it sound almost pop-like to contemporary audiences. Even though some critics thought it was easy listening, the piece was still one of Henry's favorites. The melodies were crowd-pleasing, and the second movement was heart-wrenching. The whole thing was fun—*fun,* that word Brit had hated when he'd said it. But it was true, when they played this piece it was fun, joyful, fleetingly happy, and that was the quartet at its best. For him.

They tuned up morosely but didn't run through any parts of the "American." The stage was set up in the old cell house, which had been lit like a living room with lamps around an ornate rug. The audience was sparse and made up mostly of former students and older patrons, and every one of them had witnessed the outburst on the ferry, how Henry had sent Daniel's bow sailing into the bay. They sat down to modest claps and, after Jana adjusted her dress and Daniel pinned his endpin into the rug, they began to play.

The piece began like light glittering on water, and for a while it was Jana's show. She played more like a Russian now, Henry thought, aggressive and confident and . . . loud. He liked it, though. It sounded grown up. And he loved this jaunty theme from the first movement, striking a balance between happy and serious, like an opening to a Western. Then, of course, toward the end of the movement, Daniel had a brief, European solo, so milked and liquid that it felt elegiac, only a few measures, really, climbing the fingerboard, but he played it so beautifully that Henry felt suddenly moved. Daniel was a good player; he'd been lucky to play with him.

As the sad second movement started, Henry realized that the way they played now, compared to the way they played during their graduation concert, was different and better. They'd arrived somewhere. Playing was no longer cathartic, that strange mixture of pain and pleasure one became used to in one's twenties and thirties. It was no longer a means to an end, a way to go from stifled to expressed, from caught to free, from panicked to all right. Instead, playing was like lifting a sheet to reveal the secret, beautiful gears and pulleys at play beneath the work of living—that was it, like letting everyone in on a secret, instead of working their own way out of one. It was a different kind of relief.

When had that happened? When had they begun to play like that? Henry didn't know, and as the second movement gave way to the third, he saw definitively that things would be fine in the quartet without him. And in a backward way, it made him happy that Daniel had gotten so upset; he should have expected nothing less. They finished out the third and fourth movements and Henry was pleased that none of the strife and fighting from the previous hour had sneaked into their playing. They were steady and tight. When it was over, he heard Clara whooping in the audience like she was a grown-up at a concert, and his heart surged a little bit.

At the reception afterward, Clara explained to Daniel and Henry the history of the prison as she'd learned it. "It's a place where really bad prisoners were kept, so it's like an extra-bad prison for extra-bad people. And children lived here, too, children of the people who worked here. But they had to go to school on a boat that took them to the Van Ness Street Pier, like your guys' name. And also, there was a rule of silence. Prisoners couldn't talk except at meals."

She paused in her breathless report and they listened to the clinking of glasses and laughter echoing off the bars of the cellblock. Henry had given up trying to figure out the point of this strange venue except that it was uncharted territory, a gimmick that a rich San Franciscan had gotten the rights to. The playing had also been echo-y, despite the rug and the lamps, and the overall vibe depressing, locked in, riding against the expansive piece.

"Yes, silence would be quite a punishment," Henry said.

"Getting back on that ferry is going to be punishment," Daniel said. "It started raining outside."

Clara ran off to join Jack and some other children in a game of hide-and-seek, which, in a prison, seemed like asking for trouble, but Henry ignored it. He turned to Daniel and said, "So you want to break my bow?"

"I don't want to do anything," Daniel said. "I don't want you to leave."

"But I need to," Henry said.

"So I guess it doesn't matter what I want," Daniel said, not as though he was mad but as though he had given up being mad.

Henry crossed his arms over his chest and looked up. There were fluorescent lights above them, unlit, but for a second Henry mistook them for skylights. The era when he was ruled by the collective sum of Daniel's and Jana's and Brit's desires was soon to be over, so he said, "No, it doesn't make a difference."

May 2010
Northern California

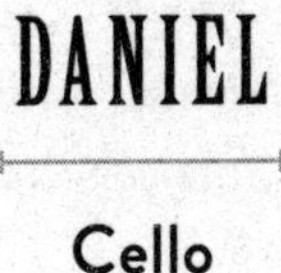

DANIEL

Cello

After one of their last rehearsals before one of their last concerts, Henry announced he was selling his records, and Brit started to cry, so Daniel thought it was an appropriate time to mention that his mother was dying. Pile it all on at once, he thought, and distribute the reaction.

"Your mother?" Brit said through tears as Jana turned from her violin case and said, "Your records?"

Daniel explained. His father, the one who'd been sickly for years now, had called Daniel on the phone, which is how Daniel first knew something was wrong. He couldn't remember the last time he and his father had spoken on the phone—perhaps once when he called his mother to say he and Brit were moving in together and his father said, *Oh hello, son,* as though reminding himself of their roles. His mother had cancer, he said, and it was pancreatic cancer, but it didn't matter now because it was everywhere, and they just named it for where it started, and that's where they think it started, in her pancreas (did his father even know what a pancreas did?), but no matter, now it was just cancer, and the doctor said maybe three months. Three months? As though there was an expiration date, a predestined time to go missing.

The news still felt unreal, but he knew it shouldn't have been so shocking. He was five years from fifty, and in the minority among his peers. No one had parents anymore. Instead they *were* parents. He'd found out that morning, and hadn't had a chance to tell anyone, not even Brit, especially when she looked so pretty and happy when she woke up. Who wanted to ruin something like that?

Daniel's father had ended the conversation with, "I hope you'll be praying for your mother."

"I will," Daniel said, which was the first time Daniel had ever committed to praying for someone or something.

When Daniel shrugged and said nothing, Henry explained. He and Kimiko were thinking of having one more (my God, Daniel thought, Henry's aging process was a stretched-out elastic band, he would never grow old, not like the rest of them), and they wanted to raise city children, so they were moving to San Francisco—"But what about the commute?" Jana asked, her voice rising—and despite the commute they thought it would be good to have the art and culture and diversity right there for Clara and Jack, and their small city was getting stuffier and whiter and richer by the startup, and anyway, there was a great deal on a place in Russian Hill, just off Van Ness, actually, wasn't that funny. So they'd bought it. Already.

"What does this have to do with your records?" Jana asked. She closed up her violin case and sat back down on her chair, her hands folded on her lap.

Henry laughed. "Oh, see, the new place doesn't have quite the space we've got here. So I can't have a record room."

Brit had stopped crying. She still had her violin propped on her knee, and she looked from Daniel to Henry and back. It always made Daniel smile a little to see how, when she was sad, the corners of her mouth actually turned down, like a cartoon of a frowning face.

"Why are you so upset?" Daniel asked across the stands.

She opened her eyes wide. "Are you kidding?"

"No, I mean about Henry."

"*I'm* not dying," Henry said. He turned to Daniel. "No offense."

"None taken. I'm not dying either."

Brit placed her bow on the stand with a clatter. "It's just, I don't know. This seems like it's real now. You're leaving."

They all looked at Henry. He was leaving. After Henry had Clara, he'd been harried, and then after Jack he'd been downright crazy, and then after the kids got old enough to walk around on their own, there'd been something different. Or maybe there'd always been something different there, and Henry had finally relaxed enough to show it to everyone. He used to be obsessed, singularly wound by music. And it wasn't his skill that faded, ever—he was still an incredible player—but something else about him faded, some way he was with them. The urgency was gone. When he played, it was hard to spot the prodigy in his eyes, the wildness that came along with diamond talent like his.

Daniel thought for so many years that Henry had just been tired. But maybe what he'd gotten tired of was the quartet.

"We're just moving an hour down the highway," Henry said, but his voice was smaller now. "It's only a few more months I'm with you all, anyway. But we're not there yet. Look, I'm just moving to the city. That's it. So I need to offload some records and before I put them online I wanted to see if there were any you guys wanted."

Brit shook her head, but didn't seem to be saying no to his question.

"Right," Jana said. "Okay. Let's not talk about this now? Let's get through the Octet performance first."

In a month, the quartet was going to merge for one night with the group that had just won the Esterhazy competition, the Seoul Quartet, a collection of young, ridiculously talented Koreans (as in barely-able-to-drink-in-America-young), all smooth-faced and shiny-haired, exceedingly nice, but pretty fierce players. The way the first violinist attacked the lower strings was somewhat alarming to Daniel. It had sounded like a cello. They were going to play the Mendelssohn Octet with the group as a sort of passing of the torch, though none of them—not Daniel, Jana, Brit, or Henry—thought they were through with the torch just yet. But it had been arranged by the Esterhazy organization, and the performance was at the War Memorial hall in San Francisco, a venue they always loved to play. And you almost never got the opportunity to play the Mendelssohn Octet.

A month after that, the quartet would play its final concert with Henry on viola, at Carnegie. The upcoming octet performance allowed all of them to ignore that looming event.

Daniel drove and Brit sat quietly in the passenger seat the whole way home. The car was a brand-new Toyota Corolla, with enough trunk space for his cello, and a soft, new-car-smelling interior. Sometimes when Daniel got in it, he felt estranged from himself. But they'd gone together to the dealership and bought the car themselves, half and half. You could purchase all the fixtures of an adult life, but Daniel wondered when you ever stopped feeling a little bit like an imposter, like a man watching yourself drive your new car around the city.

Their home was an actual house, one they owned, or at least paid a mortgage on, a one-story midcentury typical of the area, with a patch of backyard that made up for what it lacked in square footage. Daniel sat down at the dinner table and waited for Brit to come to him. He listened to her busy herself, slamming the washing machine lid shut, restacking music in their office, swooshing open the sliding glass door and then ten minutes later swooshing it again, and finally she walked into the kitchen and sat across from him at the round table.

"So," she said.

"So, we probably have to go to Houston," he said. "To say goodbye."

She nodded. "After the Octet."

Brit had only grown lovelier, he thought. More elegant. Even when she was sad, the smile lines around her lips lingered. He'd even come to see her crooked eyetooth as elegant, and she no longer tried to hide it. Her face had opened up, her freckles were darker and solid now, and her blue eyes less constantly in awe, though they had the same depth, always asking a question. And she'd grown bigger somehow. Not bigger, actually, but more present in her body. This private Brit was an utter revelation. She breathed and walked and had thoughts and made love and moved around their home in specific and wholly unexpected ways. He'd spent the last two years taking it in, and now he felt like he could spend the next however-many years memorizing it. And then it'd probably change again. He couldn't wait. He loved in a way he sometimes felt bad about, which was to say he loved her totally and completely, in the most adult, surefooted, at times ugly and at times whiplash-passionate way he had ever loved anyone ever, and he imagined Lindsay somewhere feeling cheated out of a real marriage.

Then—this was how Daniel had changed—he thought, no. Lindsay's married again, living in Brooklyn, and he saw her name pop up in his Facebook feed every once in a while, her installations featured at small gallery spaces in neighborhoods he'd never even heard of. She seems happy: I'm probably a small blip on the great big pencil drawing of her own zigzagging life.

And then, as though stemming from his own private thoughts, Brit said, "Let's get married."

He felt, and not for the first time in the last two years, grateful. Like something being gently pulled open instead of something constricting.

"But not like other people," he said, leaning over the table, touching his hands to hers, not exactly meaning not like other people, but not like the other people he'd been.

"No," she said. "Not like other people."

When Brit and Paul finally broke up (could you call it that after ten years—breaking up? *Breaking apart* seemed more appropriate; *dismantling,* even), she became unexpectedly morose. She had expected to feel sad, she said. Their relationship had, after all, been almost a third of her life so far. But the way it had happened had been a surprise, leaving neither of them time to prepare.

Some months after the party at Maisie Allbright's home, they were all eating dinner in Henry and Kimiko's backyard, the last outdoor meal of the season before November brought in the Bay Area rains. Paul had kept his promise and hadn't spoken to Daniel since Clara told him about the kiss. Daniel knew of Paul's vow, but it hadn't haunted or disturbed him. The kiss had seemed completely natural, the physical move back to each other, coming with no urgent need to do anything else. He knew where Brit was, and that she wasn't going far from him. They had time. And the fact that neither he nor Brit took precautions to make sure Clara didn't tell anyone must have meant that, on some level, they wanted to be outed. It was stranger to Daniel that Paul had stayed with Brit after he found out about the kiss, though the relationship was clearly in shambles after the summer ended. And even stranger than that was the impetus for Paul's eventual departure. At the dinner in Henry and Kimiko's backyard, Daniel bit into some undercooked corn on the cob and chipped his left incisor. Brit reached across the table and picked up the part of Daniel's tooth that had broken off, and jokingly held it up to his mouth. It must have been that, Daniel thought, her fingers in Daniel's mouth, that reminded Paul that, for the quartet, intimacy was so much more than physical touch. More than a hand in a mouth, more than laughter in the flickering light of a mosquito-repelling candle, more even than the calluses that made their fingers match. Paul stood up from the table, checked his pocket for his wallet, and walked away. Brit said that when she got home, he'd packed up almost all of his things. It was very civilized and undramatic, and it drove her crazy. She said she followed Paul around and insisted it was nothing, which made Daniel grimace when she said it, and so she stopped saying anything about the breakup at all.

But in the midst of her sadness, Daniel had come to her condo with a copy of the new music they had to learn for the next faculty recital and found her in bed, in pajamas, in the middle of the afternoon, face puffed up from crying, silent and nearly unrecognizable. He didn't jostle her out of bed, but joined her. He sat on top of the comforter and kept his shoes on. He unfolded the music and made like he was marking bowings and dynamics, but instead he wrote on the corner of the staffs funny little notes for her to find later, like *Don't be such a pansy here b/c Henry will drown you out* and *You left the burner on at home* and *Jana farted.*

When he was done, he placed it on her nightstand and waited. It occurred to him that he might have been waiting years for her.

Eventually she turned over. "I don't know why I'm so upset," she said.

"Because this isn't the first time your life has just disappeared?" He made an explosion motion with his hands.

He was a friend to her. He told her that Paul was nice, but that dating him must have been like dating the guy in the war movie who you know is going to be killed early on. He was a symbol of a man, a partner, he'd outlasted his fate. Brit nodded. Daniel watched as Brit moved through the familiar stages, like someone evolving through forms, slouching out of bed, slouching to rehearsal, given to spontaneous fits of crying while driving; and then an unsightly, prolonged state of self-hatred (*I'm too old to feel like this,* she said); and then settling into a black-and-white version of herself, until ultimately arriving, some months later, at a childlike delight at the blankness of her life. She was suddenly infused with energy, spinning from the inside, kinetic in a way Daniel hadn't remembered seeing her since their early days in San Francisco.

So in April, when Patelson's announced it was closing, the quartet exchanged wan looks, and Daniel booked plane tickets to New York for himself and Brit. He'd made arrangements to look at a cello that a patron of Juilliard was considering loaning to him, but the two-day trip was organized around a final visit to the sheet-music shop.

On the plane, Brit looked out the window the whole time, reaching her hand over to his to point things out as they traveled—the desert, the mountains, the impossible snow. As they approached JFK, Daniel's nervousness intensified, a feeling in the base of his abdomen that spread like an ink stain. The way the afternoon light changed so quickly to early evening light across her face when they were in the air made him feel—there was no other word for it—devastated. The closeness with which they sat, the way she didn't look at him before reaching her hand out to him, the small wrinkles that stretched from her eyes to her pale hairline, all of it. It had all been here this whole time. They'd been sitting next to each other this whole time. What had he been doing with that time?

With Lindsay, he thought he'd solved a problem: he'd found a way to be with someone who wanted and needed nothing from him. But when that failed, he'd given up entirely on the idea of being with anyone. And in order not to wind up in a situation like that again, he peppered his life with women in the shallowest of ways. Younger women, unserious women, women who couldn't possibly want what he'd been doing with the quartet.

But Daniel couldn't even see that he got from the quartet whatever other people got from their partners. Consistency, obligation, nonverbal understanding and misunderstanding—a deformed, ugly-pretty kind of love, knowledge that what was there wouldn't change, for better or worse.

Until he began to suspect that Henry wanted to leave, wanted to break the rules of family that he'd tacitly been living by. You *could* leave. You could choose one family over another. And it occurred to Daniel then that he did not have a second family—he had made nothing else. This was it. And the familiarity of Brit sitting next to him on the plane registered as a shock in that it was both part of his DNA and as tenuous and fragile as a hanging bow hair. It could all disappear, once they landed, in a year, in six. While the kiss in the Allbrights' bathroom had made him feel like they had all the time in the world (they knew each other in a way that required no discussion), the plane ride and her open, quivering excitement at being free from something made him feel an urgent need to make her his family, to bind her to him emotionally in the way they were already bound in music. The devastating part was that she'd been there all along, and he hadn't done it, in all those years. *That* was the time, and he'd wasted it.

That night, in his separate room in the hotel in Midtown, he barely slept. The need to have her was overwhelming, but the how was crazy-making. What if she didn't feel the same? What if she didn't want him? What if he said the wrong thing? The surety of his feelings was matched by the anxiety of, for the first time, not knowing hers.

In the morning they looked at the cello, a nervous indemnity professional hovering around Daniel while he tested it and playfully spun it on its endpin. It had a chocolaty middle register that he liked, not so buoyant and bright but settled-in and even a little scratchy. The lower register was bold and the upper register brilliant, and the varnish regal and the overall sound like breaking through a paper wall, barely separated from the inside of the instrument and the outside. In the end, it was the variety of tone that won him over, and the ferocity of its announcement. He gratefully agreed to take it, and the donor wept, hugging him and Brit at the same time.

They dropped the cello at the hotel and walked the long way to Carnegie Hall. They took a detour up Second Avenue, the East River reflecting an impossible spring sun between the buildings.

"This is the New York you can only experience after you move away," Brit said.

Where Second approached the Queensboro, they veered left and snaked back down past the spires of St. Patrick's Cathedral, the antiqued primness of Fifth Avenue that had once seduced Daniel now washed out, stuck in time, and arrived in a roundabout way at the hall. They talked their way into the performance space by counting the number of times they'd performed there and name-dropping the event services manager and the box office manager and the managing director, and an elderly ticket taker opened the door to the mezzanine, let them through, and then winked and held a finger to her lips, closing the door behind them.

"She wants us to be quiet?" Brit whispered. "There's no one here."

"Why can't we go down on stage?" Daniel said.

"What would we do on stage? What are we doing up here?"

Daniel sat in one of the red velvet chairs. The stage was all lit up in buttery lights, and in the center was a lone piano with its lid propped up and a leather seat askew. The poster outside had advertised a young

Chinese pianist whom he'd never heard of, and the recital was sold out. The whole place held the atmosphere of a rehearsal having just been abandoned.

"We'd play that piano," Daniel said.

"I don't trust pianists," Brit said, sitting down next to him. "The quality is somewhat predetermined. I feel like after a certain point, you just can't tell how good they are."

"Yeah, kind of like punching buttons or something."

"God, don't tell anyone we're saying this."

Daniel gestured at the molded ceilings. "God has ears in here, I think."

They sat in the empty hall for a while, not saying anything, listening for they didn't know what. They didn't know it then, but in two years' time, they would play their final performance with Henry on that stage, and afterward, Daniel would cry on Henry's shoulder for the second time in his life.

They weren't allowed to exit out the back, out the artists' door, so they exited the way they came in and walked around the back to get to Patelson's. The wind had picked up, and a too-warm breeze blew Brit's hair all around her face and into Daniel's face, and Daniel reached behind her and gathered it into a ponytail.

"No hairband," she said.

"No apology necessary," he said.

Patelson's was before them, but it looked as though a great *diminuendo* had slackened it. The outside of the building looked tarnished and sun-bleached and the inside was lit up like a doctor's office, fluorescent and unnatural. From outside they could clearly see that inside the selections of bound music had been picked through, and what was left was being lazily perused by uninterested people, wandering ants in a maze. Neon posters obscured the view through one large window, advertising the final liquidation sale. Daniel felt deeply sad, with a hollowed-out space in his belly. He was suddenly starving.

"Let's not go in," he said.

"Oh, but we have to," Brit said. "Maybe there are some gems left."

She started across the street holding his hand, but he stood firm. "Don't you want to remember it as it was? This, this is like a Tower Records closing-out sale."

She had one foot in the street and one foot back on the curb with him. "Don't be so tied up about it. You can still remember it like it was. This is . . . inconsequential."

Daniel doubted that, but he followed her across the street anyway, and into the shop, and straight to the chamber music section, which was nearly empty and war-torn; the place smelled sharply of mothballs in a way that made Daniel sneeze, and he buried his nose in her perfumed neck while she looked through the lesser publications of student arrangements of Mozart quartets. Brit pieced through all that was left.

In the end, they found nothing in the store, recognized no one. Their visit to the shop would not have been memorable if not for the saturated memories of the past they carried around like vintage photographs in their minds.

What made their visit memorable was later—after dinner at a no-name Italian place and an exhausted walk back to the hotel, and the too-long conversation in the hallway of the hotel, and the exact moment when Daniel asked her to come back to his room—when he, for perhaps the first time in his life, turned in the direction he was emotionally compelled, did not resist it or manipulate it or try to compel himself elsewhere.

In the way that parting from Lindsay had felt inevitable, something set in motion from the moment they'd met, this, too, felt inevitable to Daniel, and that lack of surprise didn't, as he'd feared, take away from the excitement. Instead it added an innate quality, a sure comfort, like a layer of small, plush pillows always on their periphery. What did surprise him was that, when he touched her, when they were together, the anxiety of time wasted dissipated. Their bodies were at once familiar and unfamiliar to each other, and it was thrilling to touch her, because when he touched her, he was touching two people, the Brit with the cold feet and the unsure crawl across his sheets from nearly twenty years earlier, and the Brit now, rounded and comfortable and, yes, still with poor circulation—and also all the Brits in between, and even all the Daniels in between, a whole uproar of the people they'd been or tried to be. Being with her, next to her, inside her, it was like having the power to never be erased or lost or missing, though that had happened in life, erasure, and would continue to happen. But with her, no part of his past or her past went unknown.

It was embarrassingly easy. He wondered if everyone had to wait until their forties to get it right, for the windfall.

What she said to him before he fell asleep: "Here we are again."

In the morning, in the cab on the way back to the airport, Brit leaned over the cello between them and told him what he'd said in his sleep the night before.

"You said, 'Don't go, there's something I wanted to tell you about the cake,'" Brit said. "So what do you want to tell me about the cake?"

When Daniel thought of cake, he thought of the moldings in Carnegie Hall, how they curled and flounced like frosting, how the light on the stage was like confection batter, how the seats were the consistency of sugar and flour and water. Brit's hair was like vanilla. He'd bought her a piece of cake to apologize for what he'd said after the first Esterhazy competition. He could go on. He was still very hungry.

Daniel didn't remember what he had been dreaming, but he could finish the dream anyway: "I wanted to tell you we still have time to eat it."

Everything happened so fast. Daniel's father fixed up Skype for their house, and for the first time Daniel looked at his parents through a computer screen. They sat like they were posing for a painting, and Daniel could see them staring at their own tiny image at the bottom of the screen instead of looking at the camera. His mother sat in a wheelchair in sweatpants—had he ever seen his mother in sweatpants?—and his father dressed for the occasion, and held a drink in his hand. Daniel heard the ice melt and shift throughout the conversation. His mother assured him she was feeling fine, if nauseated by the smell of eggs and dairy products, but that it was much like being pregnant, and that his brother's wife was coming in a week to help out with the housework, so he shouldn't worry. Brit joined halfway through and they mirrored his parents' postures, hands on knees or folded across the lap, upright and nervous-seeming. Brit told them that she was sorry they couldn't make it to Houston until after the Octet performance, but that the very next day they'd get on a plane and that they'd like to get married, perhaps in his parents' backyard, a small ceremony, mostly family, really (though what family? But Daniel insisted they say it this way so his mother didn't invite the entire zip code), no big deal, and would it be too hot by then? It would be too hot by then, of course, but they would do it anyway. Daniel's mother said, putting her palms together under her chin, "I'm so happy to be able to attend *this* wedding."

Daniel went around telling people they were getting married in Houston at his parents' house because it would mean so much to his mother, because that seemed the appropriate thing to say, but he wasn't so sure who exactly it was for. Walking around and waiting for someone to die, it was like being asked to live every moment as if it was your last. It was impossible. It was like being asked to never drift off, or lose focus, or forget what everything meant all the time. It was like trying to play everything *fortissimo.* Sometimes Daniel thought they were getting married at his parents' house so that they could *say* they'd been living like that, so that when they did lose themselves in meaningless preparations—flowers, dress, script—they could know it was all to perpetuate a timbre of love that they had failed to produce consistently in all the time before.

What wasn't meaningless was music, specifically what music would play during the ceremony. Daniel had played so many wedding gigs in his teenage years, all of them bad, that it seemed cruel to ask anyone, stranger or not, to do that for them. And how meaningful could Wagner's "Bridal Chorus" be at this point? Or Pachelbel's Canon? Or, God forbid, the triumphant "Wedding March" as recessional, like you'd finished a marathon or been coronated or won a prize?

Henry solved the music problem in the way Henry solved every problem, as though it wasn't a problem at all.

One bright Saturday in May, before the summer fog settled in, Daniel helped Henry move some furniture into the new place in Russian Hill, an antique couch and two unyielding dressers up two steep flights of stairs. The apartment was long and narrow and sunny, with a zigzagging hallway off which several rooms perched, one for each of the children, even the one not yet conceived, a small studio for music, and a living room with a bay window that didn't overlook the bay but rather the streetcar as it clanked by every hour.

"I didn't know this neighborhood even existed when we lived here," Daniel said, wiping sweat off his face with the bottom of his T-shirt.

Henry handed him a folded-up starched handkerchief. "I know. Now we're basically priced out. This city changed fast."

The apartment was still mostly empty, though they'd moved in mattresses and toys and some music. Enough to get Henry and Kimiko started. Half their lives was still up north, but after the weekend was over, they'd be here for good. Daniel found a couple of beers in the fridge and brought them out to the living room, where neither of them chose to sit on the ornate couch, instead leaning against the wall under the open bay window.

"Jana would have actually killed us if we injured ourselves moving this couch," Daniel said. They were only a few weeks from the Octet performance, which meant they were only a few weeks from the wedding, after which it felt like his mother would just give up and die, which was something he didn't say to anyone.

Henry smiled. "She sure would have."

"You're going to miss her giving you a hard time, aren't you?"

"You guys are talking about me like I'm already gone. I'm still here. I'll still be here," Henry said, beginning to peel the label off his bottle. "I'm sure she'll never stop giving me a hard time, no matter where I am."

"We still have to find someone to replace you."

Henry laughed. "Well, true replacement is not actually possible. But there's that girl Lauren, who just started teaching at the conservatory. A woman, I suppose, not a girl. But she'd probably be ready for a group soon."

Daniel shrugged. "Get her to agree to never have a family, and she's in."

Henry frowned, even though Daniel grinned at his half joke. "That's not entirely fair."

The streetcar rolled by, ringing its bells, and a seagull took off, squawking, and for a moment it was like Daniel had transported back to 1992, and he'd just moved to the city and was living in his first apartment by Fisherman's Wharf before he moved to the East Bay. For a moment he was that twenty-eight-year-old again, broken car, shitty cello, never satisfied, everything about him compact and tough. He had so wanted to prove his mother wrong. He had wanted to show her you could make a life outside her definition, that you could make all her wishy-washy spirituality stuff into an exact science.

"Is that why you never had kids?" Henry said. "Because of us?"

"Because of me, I think."

"But now?"

Daniel laughed. "Now? I don't even know, now. I like what I have. I have more than I deserve."

"It's sort of terrible, though, isn't it?"

"What?"

"When you get everything you wanted."

Daniel didn't say anything. But this, he thought, was the difference between him and Henry. His younger self would have been angered by Henry's sentiment, how it spoke to Henry's lucky life, how Henry had never known Daniel's constant striving. Daniel didn't think it was terrible to get everything you wanted. He thought it was terrible not to know what to want.

They finished their beers. Kimiko would be back from the park with the children soon, and they had a bedframe to put together before Daniel drove the hour back home, where Brit was waiting, where they'd make a salad and eat it on their patio in the suburban quiet.

"We were thinking you could marry us," Daniel said to Henry.

Henry held up his left hand. "I'm already spoken for."

"You sure are," Daniel said.

The door opened and Daniel heard Kimiko wrangling children. The sound of keys dropping to the floor, little feet stomping, a cry from Jack that still sounded like a girl's cry.

"Goddammit!" Kimiko said. "Did you have to put the dresser directly in front of the door?"

Henry popped up and began digging through a box behind the couch that they'd simply placed in the middle of the room on a diagonal. "Aha!" He held out a record to Daniel. "I saved this for you. I thought it could be played at the ceremony."

Daniel took it from his hands. An original pressing of a live performance (they were all live then, weren't they?) of the Budapest String Quartet performing the Tchaikovsky no. 1. It must have been from the early part of the twentieth century. Daniel hadn't known any of their recordings other than the Beethoven cycle. The record's outline had worn through the sleeve, and the whitened circle of it surrounded the picture on the front, a sepia-colored photograph of the four men in quartet formation but without the stands, leaning forward, looking at the first violinist as he said something about the sheet of music he held out in the middle of them. The music unknown, the conversation mysterious. Why a shot of them conversing and not playing? It didn't look posed at all, but entirely natural, so natural and normal that for a second Daniel couldn't tell them apart. Which one was Sasha Schneider, the only one he knew anything about? Or was it Mischa? And which incarnation was this? How many times had they turned inside out, let someone go, taken in someone new? Which Budapest was the one he'd loved, or had he loved all of their incarnations?

"The *Andante,* of course," Henry said. "I don't know if your parents have a record player or not."

When Kimiko came dragging the children into the living room, a grocery bag hanging off one wrist and Jack sobbing off the other, she found her husband and Daniel in a static embrace except for the small quakes of Daniel's chest, Daniel pressing his hand into Henry's back through an old record, his eyes screwed shut and dripping tears like a broken faucet.

Daniel had spent so much of his life not wanting children—or not wanting to want children—that it had obscured some of his own childhood memories. He thought his mother's version of his cello origin story was false, or as much willed into existence as her first vision of Jesus, but regardless, most of what he did remember from childhood was playing. In fact, he didn't remember not knowing how to play. As a child he had enjoyed the way it was like a game, getting all your limbs to work around and on the cello, the way you had to hold it up with your body and then draw from it with effort. He liked the feeling of the C string resonating in his abdomen. He liked carrying the cello on his back in the soft nylon case, how it was bigger than him and how that must have made him look special on the bus, rich with something.

And then one day he was bigger than the cello, and that was even better. He had a growth spurt at around fourteen, and found one day while practicing that he was louder than he had been before. He knew this because his older brother, Peter, pounded on the wall from the living room and told him to shut it, they were trying to watch *Green Acres*, the cloying theme song of which gave Daniel chills well into his thirties. At his next lesson, after he demonstrated the ease with which he drew his bow firmly across the strings and produced a sound so thick you could practically see it vibrate in the air, his teacher said to him in his thick Russian accent, "You are now seeing what a man can do on a cello. It is different from what a boy can do," and then he had Daniel hold his arms out so he could measure his growing wingspan.

After that, he began to notice how the instrument was shaping his body. He began to notice his body in general, as it slithered through an awkward phase of puberty and left him raw and overlarge on the other side. By the time he left for college, he had turned inward—the insides of his knees tipped toward each other and callused, the space beneath his ribs hardened and hollowed, his long arms got stronger and splayed, and his shoulders rounded, looking in toward the cello, even when there wasn't one there. He had to embrace the cello to play it, and he liked that. He didn't embrace anything else in his life like that. He carried his physical markings with pride, his body a map of his achievement.

And noticing that, the way his body shaped itself around the playing posture, was when Daniel remembered thinking he was a man and not a child, and why he held childhood in disregard for most of his life. Childhood was the vague wet-clay phase of life before the part where it was possible to achieve something great. But had he ever become great? Had he ever achieved what had been promised? Even in the peaks of the quartet's great professional success, he didn't feel the kind of tight elation he'd imagined he would. After they won the Esterhazy and before accepting the job in California, he fell into a regular kind of depression, one that felt heavier in the mornings when he counted the hours until he could reasonably go back to bed, one that made him wish the day was over and that he was unconscious, one that felt like a gentle nihilism, nonthreatening, not anything. He slept with many women then, masseuses and professors and bartenders and students, but loved none of them, and they didn't love him, either.

One afternoon at home in California, walking from the shower to his closet, he caught sight of his naked body in an alarmingly large bathroom mirror he had yet to get used to. There he was, old now. Older than he'd ever thought he'd be, at least. His muscles lay on top of his bones like they were tired, and around his waist, two small pockets of useless flesh. The indent in the center of his chest from the back of his cello was dark, and his shoulders reached over his chest toward each other like closed helmets, his spine the top curve of a dramatic *S*. He looked like something beyond a man, something that had been there for a while and gone unnoticed, had spent years sitting stonelike and waiting. He stood up straighter and turned to the side. He tried to open up his shoulders. He'd been looking inward his whole life. No wonder there wasn't room for anything else.

And then Brit. Being with her didn't feel like making room for anything because she'd always been there, as had Jana and Henry. There was no new space that needed to be carved out. But one night, early in their new, second relationship, they'd been having sex, and something shifted. It wasn't the physical, necessarily, though that was important: she'd been underneath him, legs hooked around the back of his (when he moved, she did, and when she moved, he did, and the equality of that tandem alone was intoxicating), and he'd had his face buried in her damp neck, and the whole thing had been impossibly slow—like they were taking their time just to prove how exactly they were where they wanted to be—and, like the slowest, thickest rubber-band release in the history of rubber bands, they came at the same time. That wasn't the first time it'd happened to Daniel, but with Brit it was the most annihilating. Yes, there was the physical, the two of them like insects cupped against each other, spinning a web between them, tossing the taut strands back and forth, back and forth, but there was also the way the physical caught them in the act of the unsayable. In that space—it lasted forever, it's still going on—two things were true, at least two: First, that there was room, there was a whole bunch of room, for a child, or children, or whatever. It was strange and baffling how much room there suddenly was. And second, there was the knowledge that there would never be a child. And at the confluence of the two, knowing both things were true was enough. For the first time in his life, he wanted nothing other than what was, which included the want of a child, and its impossibility.

Afterward, the room was filled with the pungent liquor-and-cake smell of excellent sex and a thin sheen of sated silence, coppery almost, as it hung in the air around them. They said nothing for a while and lay naked on top of the blankets. Brit's head was tilted down and to the side like she was looking at something on her shoulder, and she was smiling, but mostly to herself. Daniel felt his face wide-open and floating, blimp-like. Could he say it? And what could he say? Let's *want* to have a child together. They wouldn't—they were slightly too old, and if they weren't too old, they were no longer in need of it as they might have been when they were young, requiring some new, unctuous evidence sprung from their love. Brit had told him that in their first year together. She'd only ever wanted a family, and she had one, with him and with the quartet. If they never had children, if they never made the move to have children, it would be just fine, she said. This happiness is enough, she said. Too much, even.

Instead of saying something, he reached his hand across the bed to rest his palm on the part of her stomach from her belly button to her pubic bone. He felt her muscles automatically shiver back, likely from the scratchy calluses on his fingertips, but then she relaxed, and her abdomen rose to fill his hand.

"Your hand is so large," she said. "The cello never had a chance."

He smiled. When she breathed and spoke, he felt it through the walls of her stomach and muscles and skin and then through the walls of his hand and muscles and skin.

"What are you looking for in there?" she asked.

"I don't know," he said. All he could do was listen to her vibrations translated into his and then send a translation back. Everything else was a great mystery.

The Octet took only half an hour to perform in full, an amount of time that seemed not at all equal to the amount of effort that went into preparing for it. The Seoul Quartet rehearsed with the Van Ness for four solid days at their studio space near the university, and it seemed to Daniel like two of those days were spent trying to match their frequencies, not of sound but of being. The Seoul group was made up of three men and a woman violist, and they were quiet in a young way, unsure of how to enter a conversation anyone in the Van Ness started, but also energetic, which is to say they were frenzied and determined in a way Daniel recognized but could no longer join up with.

The Van Ness played all the first parts, and the Seoul played the second parts, but after the Octet opened the recital, the Van Ness would leave, and the Seoul would finish out their San Francisco debut with a Haydn quartet and a contemporary tonal Chinese piece Daniel had never played.

The eight of them could play the parts. That wasn't the problem. The problem was that it was especially important that they play the parts in the same way, because there were so many parts. Otherwise it would sound like eight people gathered around, having separate conversations. It was why the Mendelssohn Octet was so tricky and so thrilling to play. If you did it wrong, it would sound like one big, messy mistake, but if you did it right, the depth of sound was unparalleled.

The girl, Mary, was the only one who expressed worry, and she did it privately, backstage, twenty minutes before curtain, when Daniel ran into her in the hallway and she held up her hands, coated in a fresh sheen of sweat.

"I can't get them dry," she said.

Daniel rolled his eyes. "Oh yes you can," he said, and took her hand

and led her into his dressing room. He turned on the faucet so it was lukewarm. "Hold your hands under there for three minutes."

She looked at him like she'd tasted something bad, but did it anyway. She was very short but otherwise looked like Clara all grown up, black hair swept up on the top of her head and a naked, vulnerable face. She seemed, of all of them, the least assured of what they were doing. But she was a lovely violist, with a sound not all that different from Henry's, if less biting. Her sound was more tenor in mood, maybe on account of how much bigger the instrument seemed in her hands than in Henry's. Daniel saw that her career was to be a constant wobble back and forth between her talent and her insecurity.

"Are you nervous?" Daniel asked, sitting on the couch, amused.

"Aren't you?" she asked.

"Well, sure," he said. "But not like that. And I wasn't like that after winning the Esterhazy, that's for sure."

She turned back to the sink and looked at Daniel in the mirror. "So you weren't afraid?"

Daniel looked back at her in the mirror. "Oh, I'm afraid. I'm afraid, still."

Mary stood at the faucet and looked back at Daniel in a half-hopeful way he found endearing. He'd never done this water trick before. He had no idea if it would work. He was old enough to be her father. He tried to remember what he'd been afraid of at her age, but the list was overwhelming. It was easier to list what he wasn't afraid of back then: his cello, spiders, girls he'd just met (but not girls who knew him, or knew him enough to know he'd flee eventually).

"Afraid isn't the same as being nervous," he said. "I'm not nervous I'm going to play the wrong notes out there. If you got this far, you shouldn't be, either."

"So what's afraid?" She had the smallest lips, like a new bow.

Daniel stood and turned the water off. "Afraid is everything else."

"I was listening to that pre-concert lecture," she said. "And someone asked why chamber music."

"And that made you nervous?"

Mary shrugged. "I don't know if I have an answer. It's not something I remember choosing. I just do it."

Mary dried her hands on a towel and held them up in front of her face, turning them around like they were sculptures crafted apart from her. Even her hands were young, Daniel thought. Especially her hands.

"It worked," she said.

Daniel nodded and patted her on the back. "You'll be full of all my tricks sometime when you're old."

She straightened her gown, a satin magenta thing that Daniel knew she wouldn't wear again after seeing pictures of herself on stage, the fuss of the dress a blaring distraction from the playing. "You know Mendelssohn wrote this when he was fifteen? So in a way, I'm old already." And then she turned and walked out of his dressing room.

The thing about the Mendelssohn Octet was counterpoint. While playing, Daniel realized the quartet had never coached this piece, so they hadn't developed a way to talk about its organizational intelligence, but it was entirely contrapuntal. Mendelssohn was showing off, a whiz kid, look at how I can weave together not four but eight independent voices, how they all can be harmonic relatives but still adhere to separate rhythmic shapes. Chords were easy, but counterpoint added texture, that thing you didn't know you were hearing. There was Jana, furiously sawing away, eating that other violinist alive, really (poor guy), but then there were the second violins, doing their own sawing, at half a dynamic lower, and a triad apart from each other even, throwing sixteenths around but just so, to fit in the spaces between the first violins' notes so what was produced was a whole new line, made up of four voices switching allegiances and tandem partners at a dizzying pace, a guise of unpredictability glimmering out of the sure underbelly. The chords were sweet and rich, too, and Daniel admitted to loving them, milking them, as there was something almost Schubert-like about how youthful and pure they were. But it was the counterpoint, which begged reaction, that drove the piece, at once calling attention to each tiny action and allowing those actions to add up to something larger.

The movements were short, though full, and they made it to the *Scherzo,* which, if Mendelssohn wasn't showing off in the *Allegro,* he certainly was here. The movement charged forward relentlessly, nearly choking the violinists with runs that were passed through each instrument like a waterfall, the rhythms changing to give the illusion of a tempo that continuously sped up. Henry and Mary were pairing well, their disparate sounds complementing each other, until Daniel saw Mary whip one of her pages over and—nothing. There was a page missing, there must have been, Daniel reasoned, as they weren't done with the piece, but there was the black back of her stand and a barely audible gasp from her mouth.

She continued to play.

Which is what any good musician did, relied on memory, allowed the hours and years of practice to take over the muscles, addressed the sound instead of the page, the line instead of the stand. But then a funny thing happened: she took off. She just took off. She sat right next to Daniel and he saw her inch forward on her seat and dig in. It was as if she was hearing it for the first time, discovering something new and energetic about the final movement, and she began to play fast, faster than the tempo marking, and then faster. It was an accomplishment, Daniel would later admit, for the second viola part to be able to drive the other seven players into a new tempo, but she did it, short and small-lipped as she was. So that even when she rested for a bar or two and Jana attempted to recover tempo, the new speed was already established, the quality of being awake already implanted, and she couldn't.

Daniel held his breath and played faster. When he was able to, he let his left hand drop and shook it out. He saw sweat roll down Jana's temple, a grimace break across her face, and Henry, on the other side of Mary, easily keeping up and seeming calm about and even impressed by the firestorm next to him; and then Brit, who was also not breathing, was also smiling a little, amused at the way everything was falling apart. Was it falling apart? There would be a breaking point, Daniel felt sure. They couldn't keep it up for much longer.

But then it ended. It ended where it was supposed to, where it always had, at the end of the page, but they reached it so much sooner than Daniel expected, or was used to. Suddenly there were the final four flourishes, where they all met back up, their bows thrown in the air all together, like drawing with bone tips some invisible map.

Daniel was explaining the reason they had to rig up extension cords for the record player in the backyard. His mother didn't understand why they couldn't just use the boom box that didn't need all those unsightly wires.

"It's a record, Mom," he said. "It needs to sound like a record."

She was in bed, thinner already, in her bedroom, which had signs of his father's presence—a pile of boxer shorts on the floor, a cracked leather belt hung over a door handle, a swipe of construction dirt on the molding around the doorway, his father's fingerprint in the dried muck.

Perhaps they had revived a part of their love for each other now that she was dying. Daniel felt a tinge of softness for his father. He'd be the one really alone at the end of this. Brit was outside, he could hear her in the backyard with Jana and his father trying to tack lights onto the trees, but they were losing sun, and Jana's voice was getting reedy and frustrated. It was hot, too. They'd arrived two nights prior and stepped off the plane into the soup of early Houston summer. "Like walking through a warm bath," Brit said.

There really wasn't much to do except the lights and the chairs and the music, but everything felt difficult in the heat and in the face of his mother's sagging skin and sudden bouts of nausea. She carried a pink kidney-shaped bucket around with her when she moved about, which was rarely. His father refused to call in hospice care just yet. She bruised easily. She was cold to the touch, even in this heat. But she was happy, his father said. Who knew what organs were on the verge of failing her?

"What's so special about a record?" Daniel's mother asked. "I thought the point was for you not to have to carry records and tapes and CDs around anymore?"

"Okay," Daniel said, and fetched the record player from the living room and brought it up to her room.

He took his time setting it up on her dresser, as it was old and it would be just what they needed to have the needle break. He pulled the Budapest Quartet record out of the sleeve and placed it on the turntable.

"This," he said, "will change your life."

"Never too late," his mother said.

He placed the needle at the start of the second movement. "See? Hear that? That's the noise of—of the sound before the sound. The sound of people about to do something. All that white stuff. And see? It doesn't go away, not even when they're playing. You can *hear* the space around them."

"Oh, Danny," she said like she was proud of him, like she was knowing him for the first time, like it was him and not the Budapest coming out of the record player. The second movement began, gentle and sad.

"You can hear the slight attack in the bow change, the bow moving across the string, their breathing cues. You can hear how the breath is shared, how they breathe together. People in a room. They don't make stuff like this anymore, Mom."

The Budapest played devotedly through the sweet movement.

After it was over, his mother coughed lightly, but Daniel could tell she'd been saving it up. "It's so . . . imprecise," his mother said, but it wasn't an insult.

"Yes," Daniel said. "That's it."

He said he would stay with her until she fell asleep. She would sleep for only an hour or two. That was the most she got these days. Daniel let the record play out, all the way to the end, and then he flipped it over to the other side, and she fell asleep to the sound of Beethoven. He stayed and she stayed asleep, even as the record finished playing, and there was only that white sound spinning and spinning.

In 1994, it cost three dollars to cross the Golden Gate Bridge going south, so Daniel and Brit parked on the south side and walked north. They'd slept together (clumsily and silently) exactly once, hovered over each other in various states of undress a handful of times, and sat next to each other separated only by black metal music stands and a thick fog of heat for days and days and days. But now it was night, and there was fog, real fog, rolling chaotically down the hills on the north side and across the bridge. There'd been a dim sum dinner (paid for separately) and rail whiskey drinks (paid for separately at first and then generously by her) and aimless, dangerous driving (sloppily navigated by her, excitedly driven by him) and now this, a walk across the Golden Gate Bridge, something neither of them had ever done before, something so obvious and predictable that they'd never felt it was necessary to actually do. Neither of them made the decision to go. It seemed inevitable as a destination.

The cold was biting and their jackets were underperforming. The wind whipped Brit's long hair around her face, and as they walked, Daniel resisted reaching up to pull strands back so he could see her face, and then he stopped resisting. Each time he pulled her hair back, there she was, smiling. They stopped somewhere they assumed was the middle, but there was no way to know. They couldn't see the water below them or the pedestrians around them or the stars above them. Daniel thought he could hear the wind snap the cords of the bridge and looked up, but he saw nothing moving, only the burnt-red cables disappearing into black.

"Are you afraid it's going to fall?" Brit asked.

"No," Daniel said quickly, realizing too late she was teasing. Daniel couldn't see her face and he wanted to.

Brit held her arm over the railing. The chewed sleeve of her jacket shivered in the wind and Daniel's fingertips tingled in response. She held her arm farther.

"Okay," he said. "Don't."

"There's Alcatraz." She pointed, leaning out. She put one foot on the railing and then the other.

"Really, don't."

"You're not even trying to look. Find Angel Island."

He looked instead toward the lanes and the cars heading one way or the other.

She didn't move her arm, but she stepped back onto the concrete. "Why did you take me here if you're afraid of heights?"

"I didn't take you here," he said, but he said it quietly and his tone was the kind of cold that made people close up, a flower in reverse.

She looked out at her own arm like it was someone else's arm and then back to him. At the same time he stepped toward her—to embrace her, he would later say, though even later he would tell himself that wasn't what he was going to do—she pulled her arm back and moved toward him, and they crashed into each other in a way that made Daniel feel the hard, icy concrete under his stumbling feet and the incredible distance to the water.

"Just this," she said, and put her hand around his waist and drew him to the railing with her. She dangled her free hand in the abyss. He could see some of the magic of the night dropping out of her, falling down into he didn't know what. Somewhere a boat moaned, or it was the bridge moaning in the wind, or it was a whale, or it was a man in a lighthouse he couldn't see, and in any case it was a sound of warning. Daniel stood rigid and still under her arm, as if by not moving he could disappear this moment. *Don't pull me toward you,* he thought at the same time he thought, *Don't let me go.*

And eventually, she did let go. They were worn down from the cold, which was why it was empty on the bridge at night. She walked away first, back toward the car, hands hidden in pockets, hair forgotten in the weather. He clutched the railing with his hand, too afraid to release it but also petrified in the position. The time in which she walked away was a physical space that he inhabited, more than the length of an arm dangling over a bridge railing at night and less than the length of a lifetime of communal orbit—and the farther she walked, the finer the point of her image became, shimmering and darkening, merging with the black view, not breaking apart, but the opposite, until she was as exact and impossible as this question: What do you love? And another: How? She walked away, but not really.

If he thought about it too much, there was a whole lot to be angry about. For instance, his father, who never did stop drinking, and who had held Daniel at a yardstick's distance his whole life. For instance, his brother, whom he'd barely known, who'd made a new family somewhere else and left him to fend for himself. For instance, cancer, dying in general, parents dying, parents, really. But standing in the hot swelter of the backyard of his childhood home at dusk, a record player in the middle of the damp grass, waiting for Brit to appear at the end of the aisle, Jana and Henry looking on, he knew two things. First, that he could blame no one else—for who could know a man who refused to know himself?—and second, that he'd long ago forgiven himself. It was easy, as it turned out. You didn't have to ask for it.

Also, he'd made a family, too.

Brit did appear, with Jana at her side, and the women walked toward him. There weren't the thoughts he'd expected to have, though they existed somewhere in him (*she is beautiful, I am lucky, we are happy*), and instead there were pre-thoughts. No name for it. The stuff that came before you started naming things. She was a gift. He was a gift. Nothing would do.

When they reached him, Jana put Brit's hands in his and winked, and took a seat next to Daphne and his mother. Henry stood between them, but whenever Daniel tried to look at him, the setting sun behind him blackened his face. He had to look away, and so there was only Henry's voice.

Love is inexact, Henry said. It is not a science. It is barely a noun. It means one thing to one person, and one thing to another. It means one thing to one person at one point and then something else at another point. It doesn't make sense. We are gathered here today to not make sense. We are gathered here today to listen to the ineffable. I'm supposed to be explaining it, but I can't explain it. I love you, it's a mystery. Because it's a mystery, we have to take care of it. Feed it. It can go missing, but we can't tie it up. We can only tie it to someone else. Other people. Then the world is like this: full of the geometry of my rope tied to you, and to you, and yours tied to him, and to her, and hers to someone else. I love you, it's a mystery. A moment of silence.

In four months, they would all return to Houston for his mother's funeral. She'd make it longer than anyone expected, and though her organs were shutting down one by one, what took her in the end was a spill in the bathroom, a fainting spell that shattered her bones; or maybe she'd died in the faint, and the shattering came after, Daniel could never remember. It didn't seem that important. What did seem important was that at the funeral, sitting between Brit and his father, he caught himself praying—to what? But praying.

It would bring him back to this wedding, this moment where with applause growing up around them like time, he kissed Brit, she kissed him, and then they embraced, and her hair filled his mouth, filled it up and for a second he couldn't breathe. It was like kissing the space between the moment you thought something and the moment you opened your mouth to say it aloud. But then, just as quickly, he left that feeling, released it, and re-joined the clamor, the singing, the music.

CODA

Perpetual Motion

—Composer unknown

December 1992
San Francisco

We were afraid. It was like getting naked in front of someone, playing together for the first time. Though, of course, we'd already been naked in front of each other in a way. We'd all heard each other play at conservatory events or sitting in with the chamber orchestra or with another group. But not like this. Of us, Henry was the best player, a prodigy of sorts, it was rumored, but Jana the most forceful. Brit was an unknown quantity and we eyed her sideways. Daniel was charming, at least, if a little aloof. We let ourselves tune up. We noted Jana's and Henry's perfect pitch. We felt ashamed, those of us who weren't born with that, but then assured ourselves we were born with something else, a spitfire spirit that allowed us to ascend even without a scientific blessing. We had stacks of music: Haydn, Mozart, Beethoven, Brahms, Arriaga, Saint-Saëns, Schubert, Ravel, Shostakovich, Dvořák, Strauss, Sibelius, Schoenberg, Ives, and on and on.

What should we play?

Which was a different question from "What *would* we play?"

Henry said he thought it would be funny if we could play this piece from Suzuki, *Perpetual Motion*, a piece his beginner students liked to use to practice playing fast. We were alarmed to hear that he had students, as he seemed to be still a teenager.

We should play it as fast as we can, Daniel suggested. He had funny glasses he wore when he played that we got used to, over time.

It turned out we all remembered that piece. Duh-duh-duh-duh-da-da-dum-dum, Henry sang. Yep, we all said. That's the one.

We decided Jana should count us in, and Jana agreed on that, too. Three, four, she counted. Three, four? some of us thought. This piece is in 6/8! This piece is in 3/8! we didn't say. Instead, we all played our different *Perpetual Motions*, four separate pieces. We played on, and it wasn't until sometime in the middle that we recognized that we were all playing different music from memory, but we continued playing after that, and tried to make it work, tried to make the pieces fit together, and in a weird way that no one would ever want to hear—but we did, at least at the time—it did fit together. Some of us made stuff up if our piece ended too early. Some of us skipped over the parts we couldn't remember. Some of us were just playing whatever came to mind.

After, we cracked up, which was like breaking the tension after you've seen someone naked, but you really liked it.

That was awful, we said.

That was impressive, we said.

That was magic, we said.

We found one another nervous and lacking, but we found one another beautiful. We didn't say it then, but we found each other half blown apart. We found each other ugly in just the right way, though it wouldn't be right for a long time. We found each other to have good instruments around which we could organize. We found each other to have good hands that were more than just parts of bodies, and good arms and shoulders, and strong spines and stable cores, and supple necks and warm chins. We laid a pervasive claim on one another. On our hearts. Some of us more than others, some of us in different ways. We weren't yet full people, but we were required to pretend to be. We thought that together we could pretend to be until we were. We thought it might not work, but knew there was no way of really knowing. We set about infiltrating spirits. We set about aligning schedules. We set about getting better, but first we had to get known. We wanted to learn everything, but knew it might take an entire lifetime. We couldn't tell which way it would go, which we took to mean it was like falling in love, which we didn't always take to be a good thing. We found it was easier that way, to think it was like falling in love, though we didn't always stick to it. We found it was easier to obsess about recitals and bowings and the future. We found Henry to be irresponsible and Jana to be mean and Daniel to be foolish and Brit, we called to her, and sometimes she was there, and sometimes she wasn't. We found it to be more complicated than that, the people you were stuck with. We did the sticking. We found that to also be a part of the music, the sticking. We found it to be, if not pleasurable, alive. We found each other to be amenable and willing and calling, and then insistent and hungry and answering. We found each other.

Acknowledgments

This novel would not exist in your hands without the enthusiasm and wise counsel of Andrea Morrison at Writers House. I am deeply thankful for her support and wizardry. An equally boundless gratitude to Laura Perciasepe at Riverhead, whose passion for this book has made it better, sentence by sentence, than I could have imagined. I don't like to wonder what my life would look like without these two women.

So much is owed to the fellowships, residencies, and academic programs that have supported my writing over the years, including Wesleyan University and the Winchester Fellowship, everyone at the University of Virginia, the creative writing department at the University of Houston, Inprint Houston and its Alexander Prize and Barthelme Prize, the Sewanee Writers' Conference, the Oregon Literary Fellowship, the Virginia Center for the Creative Arts, Pam Houston's Writing By Writers and the Mill House Residency, and the incredible magic of the Fine Arts Work Center in Provincetown. I am so very grateful to the

National Endowment for the Arts for employing me and teaching me that art is also life.

Nothing happens without teachers. Much gratitude to those who guided me, on and off the page: Alexander Chee, Christopher Tilghman, Deborah Eisenberg, Antonya Nelson, Alexander Parsons, j. Kastely, Mat Johnson, Chitra Divakaruni, Sydney Blair, Jeb Livingood, Tom Drury, and Anne Greene.

Writing itself is a solitary act, but gathering the courage and spark to sit down and do it is a community effort. I am lucky to have found a community of artists, including those saint-status friends who read drafts of this novel, and anyone who ever let me talk about these characters over wine for too long: David Kordosh, Michelle Mariano, Jessica Wilbanks, Jacob Reimer, Nathan Graham, David Engelberg, Remi Spector, John Voekel, Kirsten Dahl, Patrick McGinty, Adam Peterson, Austin Tremblay, Danny Wallace, Ashley Wurzbacher, Dickson Lam, Thea Lim, Rebecca Wadlinger, Jesse Donaldson, Matt Sailor, Meagan Morrow, Keya Mitra, Claire Anderson, Erin Mushalla, Hannah Walsh, Katie Bellas, Joshua Rivkin, Erin Beeghly, Katie McBride, Kate Axelrod, Rebecca Calavan, Heather Ryder, Darcie Burrell, Claire Wyckoff, Maggie Shipstead, and Celeste Ng.

I am grateful to champions behind the scenes, including the inimitable Jynne Dilling Martin, as well as Becky Saletan, Geoffrey Kloske, Glory Plata, Liz Hohenadel, Drew Schnoebelen, and Geri Thoma.

Thank you to my family, especially Mom and Dad for putting a violin in my hands before I could speak full sentences, for driving me from rehearsal to rehearsal, even when I traded up to the more awkwardly sized cello, and for never letting me think that an artist's life was anything but achievable and meaningful.

Thank you to my music family, without whom my world is silent: Cassidy English, Stefon Shelton, Ivy Zenobi, Brent Kuhn, Elia Van Lith,

Linda Ghidossi-DeLuca, and Cory Antipa, and the music program at the Santa Rosa Symphony.

When I was a teenager, I played in a chamber music seminar led by the St. Lawrence String Quartet, which is where the idea for this novel first took hold. Their mastery, authenticity, and passion taught me that four serious musicians could make something bigger and bolder than themselves. I am grateful they exist and let me witness that mystery.

I'm also so thankful to every underfunded classical and chamber music series (and their student rush prices) in Santa Rosa, California, San Francisco, New York City, Washington, D.C., Houston, and Portland, Oregon.

It is a fact that I would be a lesser woman and writer without the countless e-mails from and fierce friendship of Myung Joh Wesner, Sierra Bellows, and Erin Saldin. The fortitude, lyric, and grace of these three women have propped me up over the years. This is for them.

The Ensemble Reading Group Guide

1. How did the personal dynamics of the ensemble play out through their performances?

2. How do you think the characters approach ambition and creativity?

3. Who was your favorite character and why? Who was your least favorite? All of the characters pair up at some point and have their own scene together—which was your favorite pairing?

4. Do you think this novel is a love story (echoing the opening section), and in what ways?

5. What were the strengths and weaknesses in having each character's voice present in the narrative? What does that reveal? What gets in the way? Was one character more forthcoming than the others? Was there one who you kept wishing you could stay with?

6. Did a knowledge of classical music enhance your reading experience? Or was it not necessary? (Did you look up the songs as you read?)

7. Was anything surprising to you about the life of working musicians? How was it different from what you previously thought?

8. What did you think of Kimiko having her own chapter?

9. Each of the characters creates a family in some way. Discuss.

10. How do you think the writing reflects musical qualities and structure, if at all?

11. Passion is a theme that runs throughout the novel—how do you see that manifesting?

12. Discuss the ways that parenthood is portrayed throughout the novel.